Acclaim for Mary Mackey's previous novels

"Grand adventure and a grand reading experience."
—Pat Conroy

"A complex, colorful saga . . . engrossing and realistic."
—*Publishers Weekly*

"Inventive and imaginative."
—*The New York Times*

"Deserves a place on the shelves next to the work of Jean Auel."
—*Booklist*

"Fascinating."
—Marion Zimmer Bradley

THE
Notorious Mrs. Winston

MARY MACKEY

BERKLEY BOOKS, NEW YORK

THE BERKLEY PUBLISHING GROUP
Published by the Penguin Group
Penguin Group (USA) Inc.
375 Hudson Street, New York, New York 10014, USA
Penguin Group (Canada), 90 Eglinton Avenue East, Suite 700, Toronto, Ontario M4P 2Y3, Canada
(a division of Pearson Penguin Canada Inc.)
Penguin Books Ltd., 80 Strand, London WC2R 0RL, England
Penguin Group Ireland, 25 St. Stephen's Green, Dublin 2, Ireland (a division of Penguin Books Ltd.)
Penguin Group (Australia), 250 Camberwell Road, Camberwell, Victoria 3124, Australia
(a division of Pearson Australia Group Pty. Ltd.)
Penguin Books India Pvt. Ltd., 11 Community Centre, Panchsheel Park, New Delhi—110 017, India
Penguin Group (NZ), 67 Apollo Drive, Mairangi Bay, Auckland 1311, New Zealand
(a division of Pearson New Zealand Ltd.)
Penguin Books (South Africa) (Pty.) Ltd., 24 Sturdee Avenue, Rosebank, Johannesburg 2196, South
Africa

Penguin Books Ltd., Registered Offices: 80 Strand, London WC2R 0RL, England

This is a work of fiction. Names, characters, places, and incidents either are the product of the author's imagination or are used fictitiously, and any resemblance to actual persons, living or dead, business establishments, events, or locales is entirely coincidental. The publisher does not have any control over and does not assume any responsibility for author or third-party websites or their content.

Copyright © 2007 by Mary Mackey
Cover design by Judith Murello
Cover photos: Woman in hoop skirt © Scheufler Collection/Corbis; Battle of Antietam © Captain James Hope/Edward Owen/Art Resource, NY
Book design by Tiffany Estreicher

PRINTING HISTORY
Berkley trade paperback edition / May 2007

Library of Congress Cataloging-in-Publication Data

Mackey, Mary.
    The notorious Mrs. Winston / Mary Mackey.—Berkley trade paperback ed.
        p. cm.
    ISBN-13: 978-0-425-21512-8 (trade pbk. : alk. paper)
    1. United States—History—Civil War, 1861–1865—Women—Fiction. 2. Morgan, John Hunt, 1825–1864—Fiction. 3. Confederate States of America—Fiction. 4. United States—History—Civil War, 1861–1865—Fiction. I. Title.

PS3563.A3165N68 2007
813'.54—dc22
2006049888

PRINTED IN THE UNITED STATES OF AMERICA

10 9 8 7 6 5 4 3 2 1

Chronology

NOV. 6, 1860	Lincoln elected president
DEC. 20, 1860	South Carolina secedes
MAR. 4, 1861	Lincoln inaugurated
APR. 12, 1861	Fort Sumter bombarded by Confederacy; American Civil War begins
JULY 21, 1861	Battle of Bull Run (First Manassas)
SEPT. 20, 1861	Mill owner John Hunt Morgan leads his Lexington Rifles out of Kentucky
FEB. 16, 1862	Grant captures Fort Donelson
MAR. 15, 1862	Morgan's Raiders make their first major strike, disrupting Federal supply lines
APR. 6–7, 1862	Battle of Shiloh
JULY 4–28, 1862	Morgan's First Kentucky Raid
SEPT. 17, 1862	Battle of Antietam, America's bloodiest one-day battle, with over 25,000 casualties
DEC. 22, 1862– JAN. 5, 1863	Morgan's "Christmas Raid" on Kentucky
JAN. 1, 1863	Lincoln issues Emancipation Proclamation
JULY 1–3, 1863	Battle of Gettysburg
JULY 2, 1863	Morgan's Great Raid begins
JULY 4, 1863	Battle at Green River Bridge (Tebb's Bend)
JULY 4, 1863	Vicksburg surrenders to Grant
JULY 5, 1863	Battle of Lebanon

JULY 8, 1863   Morgan crosses the Ohio River
JULY 9, 1863   Battle of Corydon
JULY 19, 1863   Battle of Buffington Island
APR. 9, 1865   Lee surrenders to Grant at Appomattox

Winston Family Tree

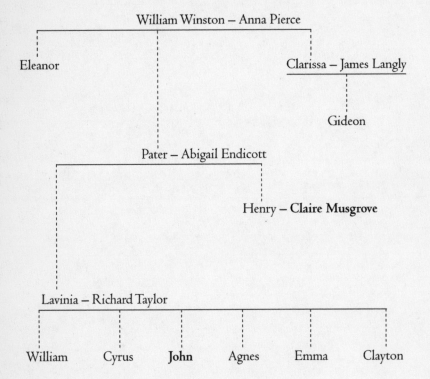

William Winston — Anna Pierce

Eleanor

Clarissa — James Langly

Gideon

Pater — Abigail Endicott

Henry — **Claire Musgrove**

Lavinia — Richard Taylor

William   Cyrus   **John**   Agnes   Emma   Clayton

Author's Note

CLAIRE Winston is a fictional character, but as many as 250 real women, disguised as men, fought in the American Civil War. The history of Morgan's thousand-mile raid into Union territory is fact, as are the details of his near-miraculous escape from the Ohio State Penitentiary. Some of the strangest details—such as the claim that the battle-weary Raiders wore women's hats and veils to keep off the dust—are confirmed by contemporary sources.

The Confederate invasion of Kentucky, Indiana, and Ohio is one of the great, rarely told stories of the Civil War, and I have presented it as accurately as possible, only occasionally taking small liberties with chronology and once or twice slightly altering events for dramatic purposes. For example, as far as I can determine, Morgan never owned a slave named Job, but he did force some of his slaves to accompany him on the raid, and in the confusion several escaped, including a valet who took Morgan's wallet with him.

One of the few purely fictional scenes is Claire's arrival at the Cincinnati city prison. There was never a person in charge named

Habakkuk Weston, but captured officers from Morgan's army were taken to the prison, and if Claire had been with them, she would certainly have been forced to reveal her secret during the intake process.

Claire

Put this on my Wanted poster: *CLAIRE WINSTON, NÉE MUSGROVE. BOSTON HOSTESS. MURDERER. ADULTERESS. HORSE THIEF. UNION SPY.* And still you will not find me, for I no longer look like the woman I was only two days ago. Indeed, I do not look like a woman at all. I have stolen the uniform of the Confederate corporal I killed and put it on. The corporal's horse is between my legs, his pistol is in my belt, and I am riding south to join John, my lover, who fights with General Morgan's Raiders. And if I am to be hanged for this, or more likely damned, let me say now—clearly and without reservation— that I would happily lose my life a hundred times over to see John again. . . .

Part One

FEBRUARY 1861

Two months before the start of the Civil War

Chapter One

SHE sees him for the first time in a place where nothing can be heard, said, or even seen clearly thanks to the clatter of the looms and the cotton dust that fills the air. He stands at the far end of the main hall talking to her husband, surrounded by a halo of small particles of lint that twist and revolve around his head like smoke. Although Claire can guess who he is, she cannot be sure; so for a few minutes longer he is a complete stranger, this lean, broad-shouldered young man in high boots and black wool trousers.

The jacket he carries casually slung over one shoulder suggests he comes from the western territories, but it is his hair that stops her in her tracks. In the harsh light that floods through the tall windows, it appears to be a deep, red-tinged yellow that glows like ripe wheat. For a moment she is paralyzed by its beauty. *He looks like an angel,* she thinks.

She instantly tries to correct this impression, but it is stamped on her mind so firmly she can't shake it. A winter spent in Italy listening to her husband rhapsodize over pale, boyish Virgins has obviously infected her with a tendency to view people as works of art. Whoever this stranger is, he is certainly no angel. He could as easily be a thief, scoundrel, or, worse yet, a slaver who wants to rip the Union apart so he can go on trading in human flesh.

She takes a deep breath, coughs on the cotton dust, and struggles to see the stranger as nothing more than a man who has come to discuss business with Henry, but it is already too late. As she stands in the doorway, one foot resting on the threshold, her stays suddenly seem too tight. She touches her skirt with the palms of her hands as if stroking her thighs, shakes her head as if clearing water from her ears. The thrum of the machines makes her head ache; her mouth feels dry and bright as if it has been lined with a scrap of the cloth that is pouring out of the looms. She has to fight an impulse to walk over to him, touch his hair, and see if it feels like silk or finely spun gold wire.

She should recognize this moment for what it is—the beginning of an obsession—but she doesn't. Later, she will put her finger on the date in her journal and say: *It all began here on the twelfth of February, at this place and this time, just as the War to Preserve the Union began nearly two months later to the day.* But she is cursed—or perhaps blessed—with the blindness of all the young women of her generation who cannot see the full fury of the storm that is approaching.

Instead, she is ashamed. So it has come to this: her honeymoon is not over, and already she is attracted to other men. Thank God her parents will never suspect she has such desires. She will never act on them, no matter how much they torment her, and perhaps if she prays hard enough and long enough, they will go away and she will be able to be happy in her marriage; or if not happy, at least not so wretched.

The moment she thinks the word "wretched," all the dreary misery of her honeymoon rises up to choke her. Too proud to let the women tending the looms see her cry, she turns her back to them and stares out the nearest window. In the distance, just beyond a ragged gully, she can see the remains of the forest: a few barren maples and leafless sycamores.

If only Henry would be a real husband to me, she thinks. There is no one she can talk to about the way he treats her: not her parents, not her minister, certainly not her childhood friends. The secrets of her marriage bed are not something she can discuss in a town as small as Charlesport. Yet keeping them makes her feel a vast, aching loneliness, as if her heart had been removed and replaced with a block of marble.

She hardly knows herself these days. She has never been so sad, so constantly upset. If she could have a child to love and spoil, perhaps this corrosive loneliness might go away, but under the circumstances there seems to be little chance of that. Many of her friends are already mothers. She tries not to envy them, but she has always dreamed of having a baby to hold in her arms. That was what she expected when she married Henry: happiness, love, an equal partnership of two souls perfectly matched, children to fill their house with laughter, grandchildren in their old age. But so far she has nothing except a hope that grows fainter with every passing day.

Wiping away her tears with an impatient gesture, she forces herself to calm down. She is not hysterical by nature—before she married Henry she rarely cried—and she hates these unexpected fits of despair almost as much as she hates the thoughts that provoke them. She reminds herself that her marriage is still new, and that in the months to come, her relationship with Henry may improve. Yet at the same time, she can't help thinking what an utter fool she has been.

She can't chalk all her troubles up to naivete. She bears responsibility for her own misery. True, she did not marry Henry for his money, but she knew she was sealing a financial bargain with him when she walked down the aisle. They never mentioned it openly, yet it colored every moment of their courtship. If she agreed to be his wife, Henry implied, he would save her parents from financial ruin. Well, he had been as good as his word, she has to grant him that. This mill—or rather, giving her father the contract to design it—had been Henry's wedding gift to her. It had been a gift easy to accept because at the time she thought she loved Henry and he loved her.

My parents urged me to wait, she thinks, *but I refused to listen. They told me they would rather lose the farm and the stables than see me unhappily wed, but I assured them I was not marrying Henry for their sake. I knew that this was not the whole truth, but I stubbornly refused to admit it. I knew I could never console them for Ned's death, but I believed that by following my own inclinations and marrying a man I loved, I could give them security in their old age. Why should I wait to accept Henry's proposal when it would expose the two people I loved most to the risk of bankruptcy? I was convinced that by becoming Mrs. Henry Winston without delay I could make everyone happy: Mama, Papa, Henry, myself. And now, foolishly and in reckless haste, I have bound myself forever to a man I thought I loved, only to discover that I have no idea who he really is.*

She wonders if Henry also regrets marrying her. Did he get full value for his money or does he wish he had spent it elsewhere? Possibly he wishes he had chosen a wife of his own social class—but she thinks not. He seems completely content with her. For example, he constantly assures her that her face and body are so perfect they make him swoon. "Swoon" is a word Claire has always associated with ladies calling for smelling salts, but there is nothing ladylike about Henry. Quite the contrary.

How can he see her so differently from the way she sees herself? She knows she is far from ugly, but she has never been one of those plump little quails men are supposed to be attracted to. She's tall, lanky, coltish, and small-breasted, with narrow hips, full lips, a straight nose, and a firm chin. There's something permanently boyish about her no matter how many petticoats and silk dresses and yards of lace she wears. Her waist-length, chestnut-colored hair can be braided into coils on either side of her head, but never quite controlled. Like her mind, it keeps escaping to places it isn't supposed to go. Blue eyes are in fashion, but hers are gray and solemn.

Worse yet, she is strong-willed, outspoken, stubborn, impulsive, and rebellious. Or at least she used to be before she married, before her will was broken by surprise and grief, before rebellion started to seem futile, before that strange, shameful wedding night she can't bear to speak about even to her own mother.

Again, she catches herself on the verge of tears. This must stop. She cannot let her parents suspect how unhappy she is. It would break their hearts. Henry is another matter. She would be grateful if he bothered to notice but instead he treats her like a piece of Chinese porcelain. When she cries with anger and frustration, he dismisses her tears as charming and unimportant. He resists any attempt to discuss the state of their marriage; he is polite but firm; he determines how she wears her hair, how she speaks, walks, sits. He dresses her in expensive clothing she would never choose for herself, making her the envy of every woman she meets.

Today, for example, she is wearing a frock of pale blue silk that matches the milky blue of the February sky so perfectly that if she could rise above her troubles like one of those hot air balloons she saw in Paris, she would disappear without a trace. The square neck is edged in antique Belgian lace, the long sleeves cuffed with more lace, like the gauntlets of those seventeenth-century musketeers who haunt the portrait galleries of Europe. Her waist, tightly laced in a cage of whalebone stays, is encircled by a belt of black satin held in place by a small gold clasp set with an aquamarine as clear as water. Beneath her skirt is a cascade of ruffled hoops, taffeta petticoats, lace pantalets, silk stockings, garters; and peeking out just beneath the hem, a pair of pale blue, low-heeled leather shoes with butter-soft tops and soles as thin as eggshells.

Henry has already photographed her in this outfit a dozen times. He has dressed her in other costumes, equally expensive. At his insistence, they spent the first two months of their honeymoon in Paris so she could be fitted out in the latest fashions by the best Parisian couturiers. Henry personally supervised every detail: chose her bonnets, her parasols, her shawls, even her gloves. He took his mother's rubies and hung them around her neck, decided they looked all wrong, and had them reset at great expense. He bought her sapphires and emeralds, had cameos carved for her. Good God, what sane woman could complain of such a husband and if she did, who would listen?

There are ten albums bound in black leather that contain photographs of her wearing these costumes, and wearing others too, for Henry delights in dressing her as the heroines and goddesses of antiquity. She has been Helen of Troy; Athena; Penthesileia, Queen of the Amazons. Once he even dressed her as a Vestal Virgin. These photographic portraits of her have already been displayed in Boston in a public exhibition that won Henry great acclaim, for he is remarkably skilled in capturing the most minute variations of light and shadow, the angles of her face, the peculiar grace of her fingers. She is, as he never ceases to tell her, the most perfect of models.

She knew about his enthusiasm for photography when she married him. She even knew that he had taken up the art to please his late mother, whom he adored nearly as much as he hated his father. His mother had wanted him to be a portrait painter, but even after years of instruction, Henry had lacked the ability to draw anything remotely resembling a human face. Abigail Winston had not been the kind of woman to give up easily. It was she who, shortly before her death, had bought Henry his first camera; she who had been her son's first model. Henry always claimed photography had been his salvation. He had a knack for the mechanics of it, just like his knack for making business deals.

Claire had first met him when he knocked on their door and asked her father and mother if he could photograph her, so from the earliest days of their courtship, she expected to appear in the black albums. But what she did not know was that there would be other albums, bound in green leather, that he would keep locked in a special bookcase. In them are photographs of her no one else is ever supposed to see, photographs that make her burn with shame and humiliation and fill her with despair.

She realizes she can't go on thinking about the state of her marriage or she will go mad. Clenching her fists, she shakes herself back into the present and turns away from the window. Her thoughts from start to finish have taken only a few minutes, but when she follows the line of the looms to the end of the hall, she sees her husband and the blond stranger disappearing through an open doorway. For a moment she stares at the spot where they stood as if it has some message to give her. Then she presses her skirt and hoops against her legs so they will not catch in the machinery and hurries after them.

Her hoops make it necessary for her to take mincing steps and clutch at banisters as she descends the stairs, so by the time she reaches the ground floor, retrieves her cape from the attendant, and goes outside, Henry is already setting up his camera. The stranger and her father stand next to him, examining the apparatus.

The camera, with its brass lens and highly polished mahogany casing, is a thing of beauty. The tripod it stands on has the grace of a long-legged heron stalking the river shallows, and its glass photographic plates are as exotic as ritual objects used in pagan rites, but Claire hates it. No, hate is too weak a word: detests. She has come to think of the lens as the barrel of a gun. Even now, when it is pointed in another direction, she feels as if she is standing in the crosshairs.

Dry-eyed now and fully in control of herself, she approaches the men briskly through a world where every blade of grass is encased in frozen water. Her husband, her father, and the stranger have their backs to her, but the cold, dry air amplifies their voices.

"Forty-nine days now," she hears Henry say. She pauses to listen and realizes he is talking about the plight of the Federal troops besieged in Fort Sumter, South Carolina, since the day after Christmas. "And what has President Buchanan done to end the crisis? Nothing, gentlemen. He is as lame a duck as ever occupied the White House, and Lincoln is powerless for three more weeks."

"Meanwhile," says the stranger, "the South continues to fear a Northern invasion."

"Fear an invasion?" Henry pauses in his attempt to level the tripod. "Say rather the Confederate States would welcome an attack. Why else have they drawn up a constitution and elected a president?"

"Let us pray cool heads prevail," says Claire's father, always the peacemaker.

"Cool heads are few in number," Henry says. "War is coming, Ephraim, and I fear there's little we can do to avert it."

Henry has been talking of nothing but the coming war since he and Claire returned from Europe. He inherited his money and his mills from his father, a rough, violent man whom he never speaks of except with contempt. Yet like the father he loathed, Henry is a shrewd businessman. He has multiplied the three original mills into a dozen. All of them, he insists, will become gold mines if the Federal government invades the South.

True, his supply of Southern cotton will be cut off, but as usual he has anticipated this. Two years ago when cotton was cheap and war seemed unlikely, he signed contracts with suppliers in Brazil and Egypt. Recently he installed machines in his mills which also allow him to produce woolen fabric. Wars, he never tires of telling Claire, mean soldiers and soldiers mean uniforms.

"If it comes to a war between the states," the stranger says, "I intend to throw in my lot with the South."

"Surely, sir," Claire's father says, "you will not fight for the right of men of one color to own men of another."

"I do not own slaves, Mr. Musgrove, nor do I support the institution of slavery, which I hold to be evil; but I have a mother who believes Jefferson Davis is God, two sisters who are already knitting socks for the Confederate army, two older brothers who will fight for the South, and an eleven-year-old brother whom I fear they will take with them for a drummer boy. I cannot take up arms against them, nor can I face at the other end of a gun my old comrades from the Marion Military Institute, who will die to the last man to defend the sacred soil of Kentucky if the state secedes."

"Sacred soil?" The men wheel around at the sound of Claire's voice. In three rapid steps she is upon them. Her father gives her a warning look, but she chooses to ignore it. Recently she has been having moments when she can't govern her tongue. She doesn't know why except that it has something to do with the misery of her marriage and all this endless talk of war. She plants herself in front of the stranger and suddenly, as quickly as it came, the impulse to lash out at him passes, taking her anger with it. "No soil is more sacred than a human soul," she says in a moderate tone, as if she were a reasonable woman instead of one given to sudden rushes across gravel driveways to confront men to whom she has not yet been introduced.

"On this, ma'am, we agree," says the stranger, clearly taken by surprise. She examines his face, trying to catch the emotion beneath his words. Given that he speaks with a Southern accent, she expects to see the tight lips and bright eyes of a secessionist fanatic. She has encountered many since she and Henry arrived in Charlesport, where one can look across the Ohio River to Kentucky, where slavery is legal and, unless war comes, likely to remain so. But the stranger has a handsome, open countenance that suggests honesty, goodwill, and—much to her surprise—regret.

There is something in his face that reminds her of Ned. She was only eight when Ned drowned in the river while trying to save a friend. She had adored him with the kind of worshipful love a little girl gives to an older brother, and when the search party brought him home and laid him out on the kitchen table, the wail of her mother's grief had ushered in what she later came to think of as the end of her childhood.

The stranger's face contains something of Ned's kindness, dignity, and intelligence, some hint around the mouth that, like Ned, what he is about to say is sure to be interesting; but otherwise the two could not be more different. Ned was only thirteen when he died, and this stranger is a grown man: blond and clean-shaven except for a mustache, fully six feet tall with a long, slender nose, closely cropped hair, and eyes that appear to be neither brown nor green but a color that combines the two. There is something about the way he stands that suggests military training, but there is nothing fierce about him. *If he is a warrior,* Claire thinks, *he is a reluctant one.* Already she has forgotten that moment in the mill when she saw him as an angel.

"Do not waste your breath trying to reason with my nephew," Henry says. "I am afraid he is a romantic young fool who is quite willing to throw his life away for a cause he does not believe in, but his foolishness is no news to anyone in the family." Henry pauses and turns to her with a gaze that makes Claire feel as if someone has raked fingernails across a slate. It is a look of complete, happy possession, as if he has just unpacked a crate containing yet another marble statue.

"Claire, allow me to present John Taylor, my sister's third son, twenty-four years old and already a patron of lost causes. John, this your beautiful aunt Claire. Had you attended our wedding, you would have met her sooner, but Mexico called, did it not?"

"Actually, Uncle Henry, I ended up in Colorado. That's the name they're planning to give the new territory."

"No doubt you went looking for gold," Henry says.

"No, I rode for the Pony Express."

Claire's father looks at John with renewed interest. Ephraim Musgrove is an architect by profession, but he has dedicated his life to breeding the fastest racehorses on the Indiana-Kentucky border. Henry, in contrast, appears to disapprove of his nephew dashing across the western territories on horseback to deliver mail, although why, Claire cannot imagine. Uncle and nephew exchange a look she can't read. There's something strange in Henry's face she can't connect to anything she knows about him.

"You may kiss your aunt on the cheek," Henry says. "I believe, under the circumstances, that is appropriate."

John flushes with embarrassment, and Claire perversely discovers she enjoys his discomfort. She inclines toward him and presents her cheek. He hesitates, then darts forward and gives it a respectful peck. Later, she will look back and ask herself if she felt anything out of the ordinary at that moment, but she will be able to remember nothing. It was the kind of kiss a man could give a child or his own mother.

"Aunt Claire," he says, "it is a pleasure to meet you." It's odd to hear him call her "aunt." He's only two years older than she is. When she thinks of aunts, she thinks of old ladies in black crepe who come to dinner and fall asleep in front of the fire. But Henry is twelve years her senior, so it makes sense that his eldest sister, Lavinia, has grown children.

"The pleasure is mine," Claire says. She feels she has made her point about souls and sacred soils. That is not something she often manages to do these days. It's a small victory, but sweet nevertheless. "I have heard so many good things about you." This is perilously close to a lie. She has heard nothing about Henry's nephew except his name and the fact that, after two years in the West, he has returned because of the impending war. Since he is passing through Indiana on his way to Kentucky, he will no doubt be at his mother's house when she and Henry travel to Lenoir to visit her. Still, having won the first skirmish, she can afford to be generous. She doesn't want to make an enemy out of any of Henry's relatives, and she certainly doesn't want to continue their argument about slavery.

No, that is not true. She does wish to continue it. She has a passionate interest in the subject, but her family harbors a secret that forbids them to discuss certain things in public except in the most general terms. Somehow, by the grace of God, she never confided that family secret to Henry even during the first months of their courtship when she believed—mistakenly, it now seems—that he loved her.

She links her arm in her father's, afraid she has already upset him by talking so openly. Then she remembers with relief that she has not actually said anything specific. Perhaps her meaning has been obscure. Her father gives her an affectionate smile. He is a tall, lanky, awkward man who looks rather like the new president, only more handsome. Claire loves him dearly. Since Ned's death, she is his only child, and in many ways he has raised her as if she were the son he lost. *But now,* she thinks, *he is worried that I have gone too far.* "Shall we go home, Papa?" she asks. "Mother will need help with the pies."

Henry gives her a startled look. He has never gotten used to the idea that Claire helps her mother in the kitchen. When they finally settle into their home in Cambridge, she will be directing a large staff of servants. The prospect fills her with a mixture of dread and excitement, for as much as the idea of being served by others makes her uncomfortable, she suspects it will be rather thrilling to stand behind the scenes of a well-run household like a puppeteer of domesticity. But Indiana is only a few decades away from the frontier, and here customs are different. A woman who doesn't bake her own pies is hardly considered worth marrying.

But she is mistaken. Henry is not worrying about her coarsening her hands as she scrubs the pastry board. Abruptly he reaches out and places two fingers on her arm. "I have not yet taken your photograph," he says, drawing her toward him like a man reeling in a hooked fish.

Claire feels a chill come over her. There is a pause. Then, as if on cue, a breeze springs up and the ice-covered twigs of the trees begin to clack together. Slowly, she wheels around. She has forgotten the camera. She turned her back on it, and once again it has taken her by ambush.

She longs to tell Henry she will not allow him to point the lens at her, but there is no decent way to go about this without risking a scene when they are alone together, so she gives in. "Where would you like me to stand?" she asks. Has she managed to keep the reluctance out of her voice? She hopes so. If not, Henry will make her pay for it later.

"Over there, my dear," he says. "In front of the mill."

She wonders if there is any hope of talking him out of this. "I thought you intended to send this photo to an illustrator in Cambridge, so he could make a sketch for the newspapers to publish. Surely any image of me will be in the way." Again, she tries to keep the anger out of her voice. She cannot let her father suspect there is anything seriously wrong between her and her husband.

Henry does not reply. Twining his arm through hers, he leads her to a spot in front of the mill precisely between two tall towers that rise a hundred feet or more into the air. The moment she turns to face the camera, Claire feels diminished. She can sense the mill behind her, crouching and predatory: a huge, five-story block of gray limestone with banks of tall windows that glare out at the ruins of the forest. Although her father designed and built it, she has never been able to shake the sense that it is haunted by something unpleasant. Perhaps this is because she remembers the forest that formerly stood on the site, or perhaps she dislikes the mill because, if it had never existed, she might never have married Henry.

If Henry notices her discomfort, he ignores it. He turns her to the right, reconsiders, and turns her to the left. He tilts her face up slightly to catch the light, and then, to her surprise, whips off her cape. As the wind cuts through the silk of her dress, she shudders.

"I am afraid you may have to suffer a bit for art, my dear," Henry says, "but it will only be for a moment." He examines her dress and a look of pleasure suffuses his face. Claire follows his gaze and sees she is covered with lint. She starts to pick it off, but Henry puts his hand on her wrist to restrain her, positions her arms, and does something to her skirt that she doesn't dare look at. She knows that if she moves, he will spend the next five minutes repositioning her.

Returning to the camera, he removes the photographic plate from its lightproof holder, inserts it, and racks the lens in and out. Claire stares back at it the way she might stare at an enemy who is in the process of attacking.

"Now," Henry commands. Claire obediently takes in a breath

and holds it as he removes the lens cap and begins to count off the seconds. As he photographs her, she takes a mental portrait of him. Over the last year, there have been many different Henrys, all looking roughly the same but not to be confused with each other. There was the handsome Henry of their courtship: he of the coal-black hair, heavy brows, soft brown beard, and dark eyes; the man of wit, polished elegance, and European manners who made a good impression on people, particularly on women, particularly on her. This was the Henry she had believed she loved enough to marry.

Next came the Henry of the early weeks of their marriage: beard trimmed to a neat goatee that elongated his face and exposed a surprisingly full lower lip. This was a Henry she still found attractive; one she believed she might be happy with if she exercised enough patience, gave enough understanding and love.

Finally, there is this stranger who examines her from behind the camera with a polite smile that has been put on for public consumption. This is not the expression her husband assumes when they are alone together. Then he gazes at her in a way that makes her blush with shame, and although she knows he must still be handsome, she can no longer see him that way.

Henry finishes counting and puts the cap back on the lens. "Do not move, my dear," he says. "I want to take another photograph of you while the light is right." Claire stands like a statue as he changes the plate.

How long can I go on living like this? she thinks. *Am I doomed to spend my whole life posing for his camera?* She tastes something salty and realizes she has clenched her teeth so hard she has bitten her tongue.

Chapter Two

HENRY has converted a covered wagon into a mobile dark-room, complete with a black leather canopy and bottles of chemicals packed in wood shavings to avoid breakage. The dark-room, which to Claire's eyes resembles nothing so much as a hearse, is so cumbersome that every time they travel, their luggage occupies the better part of a railcar, but when it comes to his photography, Henry spares no expense. As a result, he is able to develop the photographs that very afternoon.

At dinner, as they sit around the remains of her mother's apple pie, he produces the best of the lot and offers it up for universal admiration. Much as Claire hates to admit it, the photograph is brilliant, but then Henry's work always is. The mill, with its two great turrets, looks like a castle. In front stands a slender figure whom she barely recognizes as herself. The bits of lint Henry prevented her from brushing from her dress have caught the light. Some chemical process has turned them into shards of silver, so that hundreds of small stars appear to shine from her skirts and hair. She looks ghostly and unreal, as if a breath of wind will blow her away.

John leans over, takes the photograph out of Henry's hand, and stares at it for a moment. Then he looks up and his eyes meet Claire's. "You are very beautiful," he says. There is such intensity in his voice that everyone, including Claire, is slightly shocked. This is not the voice of a nephew admiring his aunt; it's the voice of a man admiring a woman. Claire feels a thrill pass through her, followed instantly by guilt. She finds Henry's nephew attractive, and apparently he feels the same way about her. Henry takes the photograph from John without a word and arranges it on the table where Claire's mother and father can see it more clearly. His face is blank, but Claire can feel him seething.

"Thank you," Claire says to John. She makes her voice as neutral as possible, and is dismayed to realize she has gone too far. She sounds priggish and slightly offended, whereas she only meant to sound indifferent. John nods. He doesn't seem to realize he has said anything unusual, nor that Claire has greeted his compliment with the barest courtesy.

Determined to save the situation, she continues more warmly: "My husband is a very talented photographer." She hears herself emphasize the words "my husband." She doesn't know why she has chosen to defend Henry. Does he care? Is he jealous? She believes he is, for at her words his face darkens even more, as if she were intentionally flirting with his nephew instead of showing him a loyalty he hardly deserves. *How foolish I am,* she thinks, *to play these sad, silly games.* She lowers her eyes and pretends to be interested in what remains of her pie. She wants to rise to her feet, throw down her napkin, and leave the room, but for her parents' sake she must pretend to be unaware that, through no fault of her own, John is attracted to her and Henry is furious about it.

Henry puts down his fork, leans forward, and points to the photograph. His index finger lingers on the fragments of cotton that cling to Claire's dress. "The mill workers call this 'fly,' " he says. "It is worse on the spinning floors. Sometimes one can hardly see for it."

"Do the workers breathe in the lint?" Claire's father asks.

"I suppose so." Henry turns to Claire, although there is no reason for him to do so because he continues to speak to her father. "It is all part of the process. It cannot be helped."

At this, something snaps inside her. She has been so patient, so well-meaning, so determined to do what is right, yet at the same time, she has been struggling to make a decision. Now Henry, with his jealousy, his infernal camera, and his indifference to the health of his workers, has made it for her.

After dinner, she manages to be alone with her father. "If you are going to the river tonight, Papa," she says, "I want to go with you." Her father is clearly surprised. She is supposed to be on her honeymoon. He frowns and examines her dress: another of Henry's selections: thirteen yards of dark blue velvet held out by a stiff hoop.

"Not in that, I hope," he says.

"No, of course not." Claire is relieved that he does not ask her why she does not wish to spend this cold February night in bed next to her husband. Yet, at the same time she knows that by uttering this abrupt request, she has risked letting him suspect her marriage is not happy. "I know I should tell Henry," she continues, "but I cannot bear to. He worries constantly about my welfare. He loves me so much, you see." She smiles brightly and soldiers on. "I will let him know our family secret by and by, but not yet." Impulsively, she throws her arms around her father's neck. "Oh, Papa," she says, "I love you so very much. And I am happy with Henry. Very happy."

Although her father returns her embrace, perhaps she does not completely deceive him, for he asks: "Truly happy, Claire? Truly sure you've made the right choice?"

"Truly happy, Papa. Truly sure." She steps back and quickly changes the subject. "I will put on trousers so I can ride astride and hang on to the children if there are any."

"Reverend Burke tells me there will be one, perhaps two."

Walking over to the window, Claire's father presses his fingers against the frost on the glass. "Poor souls," he says. "What a cold trip they must be having."

"I will row," Claire says. "Will that do?"

Her father turns and touches her affectionately on the arm. "That will do very well, Clairey," he says. "I can always rely on you."

<hr />

During more than a quarter century of marriage, Claire's parents have developed a mysterious system of communication. Claire is not sure how it works, but, although she is positive her father has had no opportunity to speak to her mother in private before they retire, by the time Claire mounts the stairs, candle in hand, to join Henry, her mother is waiting for her on the second-floor landing.

At the approach of middle age, Amanda Musgrove is still beautiful, with a wide brow, serene brown eyes, and dark hair as yet untouched by gray. A former schoolteacher and sweet-tempered by nature, she has always encouraged Claire not only to be independent, but to follow her conscience no matter how unpleasant the consequences. Tonight as proof of this, she holds in her arms a pair of men's trousers; sturdy, thick-soled boots; and a heavy black sweater that seems to absorb light rather than reflect it. These are the clothes Claire always wears when she accompanies her father on that family mission that must never be spoken of in front of strangers. There have been three sets of such clothing over the years, growing in size as Claire grew. The first pair of trousers were small enough for a tall girl of fourteen who wished to pass in the darkness for a boy. There were not many mothers who would have allowed a daughter of that age to ride out with her father in the dead of night, but Amanda Musgrove is not ordinary in any sense of the word. In fact, she would be riding to the river with Ephraim and Claire tonight if she were not prevented by physical disability from sitting firmly in the saddle. Born with a slightly clubbed foot and weak ankles, she cannot be sure of the stirrups. So Claire rides for both her mother and herself.

"I will leave these in the kitchen for you," Amanda says, shifting the clothing from her right arm to her left. "The moon should be up by then, so if you open the shutters, you won't need a light."

"Thank you, Mama."

"Does Henry know?"

"No."

"And you have seen no reason to tell him?"

"No."

"Claire, there isn't anything wrong between you and Henry, is there?"

"No, Mama. We couldn't be happier." The lie almost chokes her, and she finds herself on the verge of confessing everything. "Henry loves me so much," she says quickly, not meeting her mother's eyes. "He would insist on coming along to protect me, but he can't swim."

The ghost of Ned suddenly hovers over the conversation. Claire's mother turns slightly pale and grips Claire's hand. "Then you must not tell him," she says. "The river is running very high." Claire feels so guilty about using Ned's memory to deceive her mother that she cannot reply.

"You must slip out after Henry falls asleep," her mother continues. "Both you and your father will need to move with particular quiet. The floorboards in the hallway still creak." She makes no attempt to persuade Claire to stay home. Amanda Musgrove believes that there are some things more important than family or even life itself. Human freedom is one of them.

"Henry is a sound sleeper, Mama," Claire says. "I do not think he is likely to wake."

"Good." Suddenly Amanda reaches out, twines her arm around Claire's waist, and draws her close. Her hoop touches Claire's and the full skirts of the women, one of blue velvet, one of mauve taffeta, bound gently away from each other like soft bells. "My dear," she says, "you will be careful, won't you? The bounty hunters are coming across the river armed like hunters in pursuit of deer. The closer war approaches, the bolder they become."

"I will be careful," Claire says, but her pulse begins to race, and she feels the first twitch of the bone-chilling fear that always accompanies her when she rides to the river with her father. She had not realized the situation was so dire. So the slave hunters are crossing boldly into Indiana these days, heavily armed, as if the pursuit of runaway slaves was a blood sport instead of a matter of human lives? Do they cross from Kentucky to Indiana because the hunt amuses them, or do they come for the reward money? Claire hopes they only come for the money. Greed is something she can understand.

Amanda kisses Claire on the forehead and releases her. "You had better go up to Henry now," she says. "He will be wondering what is keeping you."

In the upstairs bedroom Claire occupied as a child and now temporarily shares with her husband, she finds Henry sitting on the edge of the bed in his dressing gown, examining the rest of the photographs he developed this afternoon. He looks up when she enters and smiles pleasantly. Henry is so unfailingly courteous that she often longs to throw something at him.

Laying the photographs down on the embroidered counterpane, he examines her. "Turn for me," he orders. Not wishing to provoke him into questions or delay him from retiring for the night, she centers herself where her full skirt will not knock bric-a-brac to the floor, and spins in a slow circle. Her taffeta petticoats make a faint rustling sound like rain washing against sand. On the wall, a series of shadow-Claires turns with her, multiplied by the candle flames.

Henry regards the shadows as intensely as he regards the flesh-and-blood woman who turns before him. She can see he is making notes in his head, calculating how many seconds he might need to count off to expose the plate properly and capture the effect. For a moment she is afraid he will insist on setting up his camera, but then she realizes that, even if he lights a magnesium ribbon, he will never be able to photograph the shadows. Since these seem to be his main object of interest, she is probably safe.

"You may stop," he says. Claire completes a revolution and comes to a halt facing him.

"Dark blue is your color; velvet your texture," he observes. "As are emerald green and burnt umber; silk and muslin." Four generations of mill owners have produced in Henry an almost encyclopedic knowledge of cloth. He cannot tolerate Claire in velveteen but finds silk velvet charming. The idea of her wearing nankeen or drabbet makes him bilious, whereas cashmere wins his enthusiastic approval. Claire is certain he would rather see her dead than clothed in the trousers and sweater that await her in the kitchen.

"I dream of a future when the camera will be perfected," he says. This is no news to Claire, who waits impatiently for him to continue. "Someday photographers will be able to record color. What vistas of beauty will then be opened! Imagine capturing the golden penumbra of a daffodil, or"—he points to the wall—"the colors of those shadows. Can you see them? Purple, violet, red, gray?"

"I see only shadows," Claire says. "And they all appear to be the same color to me, Henry."

He sighs. "You do not have the eye of an artist."

"No," she admits. "I do not." At moments like this she is sure she is as much of a disappointment to Henry as he is to her.

"I do not want you to become too friendly with John," Henry says. Claire is taken by surprise by the sudden shift in the conversation. Her confusion must show in her face, for Henry adds impatiently, "My nephew. I do not want you to befriend him."

"Why not? He seems pleasant enough."

"There are some things you do not need to know, my dear."

"Does John have an evil reputation, Henry, or are you angry with him for saying that he will fight with the Confederacy? Do explain, I beg you. Drunkard, cad, traitor? Which word shall we pick to consign your nephew to a place where his own aunt cannot be civil to him? They all sound very exciting."

"Come to bed," Henry says. "I will help you out of your stays." He rises to his feet and starts toward her. So the conversation about John, brief as it was, is now at an end. Claire is annoyed that Henry will not elaborate on his warning. *He is definitely jealous,* she thinks. For a moment she wishes he had cause. Then she does her best to dismiss John from her mind.

Her good intentions last until she slips into her nightgown and crawls in beside Henry, who immediately scuttles to the far side of the bed and turns his back on her.

"Try not to touch me," he says. "I cannot sleep if you go hanging on me all night."

"I'll do my best," Claire says, "but the bed is very narrow." For some reason Henry's words wound her more than anything else he has done—or, rather, not done—since their wedding night. All day she has been on the verge of tears. Now she finds herself crying in earnest. If only Henry would turn over, take her in his arms, and comfort her. But he never touches her if he can help it. He does not even want to be in this bed with her.

He does not ask her what is wrong, and by the time she has stopped crying, he is asleep. For a long time she lies beside him listening to him breathe and wondering how it is possible to feel so alone when you are lying next to a man you call your husband. Finally, when she is sure he is not likely to wake up, she carefully pulls back the covers on her side, slips out, throws on a robe, and tiptoes downstairs to the kitchen, where her father is already waiting. Papa has not lit a candle, for which she is grateful. She would not like him to see her face right now. It would tell him far too much about the state of her marriage.

Chapter Three

THE Ohio is broad and calm tonight, curled by deep currents and silvered with moonlight. As Claire rows toward the Kentucky shore, streams of water drip off the tips of the oars and fall back into the river like ribbons of liquid mercury. *How beautiful the moonlight is,* she thinks. *And yet, how deadly.*

She clutches the oars more tightly, and her mouth grows dry with fear. She wishes she could tell her father she is afraid they are being watched, but she and Papa have done this dozens of times and he is undoubtedly as worried as she is. Besides, even though he sits so close she could lean forward and touch him, she can't risk a single unnecessary word. Sound carries remarkably well over water. Papa taught her that the first night he took her out. *Whisper, Claire,* he said. *And don't even do that unless you must.*

Twelve years ago, he underwent a religious conversion. This is why they are rowing across the river tonight and why bounty hunters concealed in the brush on the Kentucky shore may already have lifted their rifles and taken aim at them. Although the war between the North and South has not yet officially begun, a small, deadly war has been going on around Charlesport for almost as long as Claire can remember. On one side are the people who row from Indiana to Kentucky. On the other are the bounty hunters who shoot at them whenever they think they can do so without getting caught.

Beside the boat, the water churns in small whirlpools. At the center of each is a black spot the size of an eye. Claire closes her own eyes and imagines the bottom of the river, conjuring up the bones that lie there under the mud: bones of those who were shot, those who drowned, those who died rather than be captured and dragged back to their masters.

Every time she thinks of the slaves who failed to swim to freedom, she remembers a trip her father took to Memphis to buy a stallion called China Doll. She recalls the name of the horse because at the time she had thought he was going to bring back a real doll with blue glass eyes. Instead, he had come home with nothing: not the stallion, not the purchase price, his pockets empty like Jack-and-the-Beanstalk. She had been bitterly disappointed not to get the doll and had sulked for days. Her mother had been strangely understanding. *There was no help for it,* she told Claire a few years later. *At ten you would not have understood the real reason your father came back from Memphis empty-handed even if we had been willing to risk telling you.*

Shortly after he returned without the stallion, Papa started leaving abruptly in the middle of the night on some sort of mysterious business Claire was never to mention to her friends. She kept the family secret without knowing what it was, earned her parents' trust, and on her thirteenth birthday, they told her the truth: In Memphis, for the first time in his life, her father had seen human beings sold like animals. As he watched the slaves climb up onto the auction block, he was filled with shame and horror. *Their faces still haunt me,* he told Claire. *I gave the money I was to have spent for the stallion to a group of Quakers who bought slaves to free them. You will hear some argue that the Bible condones slavery, but I do not believe it. Slavery is a great moral evil, perhaps the greatest.*

Did God speak directly to her father as he stood watching that slave auction? Claire doubts it, but the truth is, she has no idea what happened. Papa never speaks about the details of his conversion. He remains a member of the Charlesport Methodist Church, although the church has been divided on the issue of slavery for decades; and he does not criticize slavery in public except in the most general terms. But secretly, he gives more than he can afford to antislavery causes; and on nights like tonight—despite the fact that his only son drowned in this river—he risks his life and the life of his daughter to row across it.

The current suddenly slackens. Claire pulls hard on the right oar and turns the boat so it can enter the back current that runs upriver below the point. Since the moment they stepped off dry land, they have been in Kentucky, but now the state becomes a tangible presence. A tangled mass of brush and trees sweeps by. Claire sees a barren cornfield, a stand of tall reeds, a grove of chestnuts. Her father nods and reaches under his seat for the dark lantern. As he stands and prepares to open the shade, she holds her breath and prays that the crack of a rifle will not shatter the silence.

Her father opens and shuts the shade three times. Light spills out onto the water. He waits, then repeats the process as Claire sculls the oars to keep the boat in place. Up on land, the chestnuts look like gaunt giants. She strains to see if anything stands at the base of their trunks, but the shadows are too deep. *They aren't there,* she thinks. And then she thinks, *They must be, or we have risked our lives for nothing.*

Immediately she feels ashamed. How can she worry about risking her life when faced by the silence of those shadows? Have the bounty hunters been successful tonight? Perhaps not. For now as her father signals a third time, light answers from the chestnut grove. *Pull!* he mouths. Claire pulls on the oars with all her strength. The boat speeds toward the light and shudders to a stop as the bow strikes the mud, cracking a thin plate of ice. Before they can climb out, three shapes dash toward them. No, she realizes: four.

The woman holds a child in her arms. The little boy is two, per-haps three: limp as a half-filled bag of flour, eyes closed, head wobbling on a thin neck. Beside the woman is an old man, quite toothless. Claire has never seen a man this old try to make it to freedom.

"The man is her father and the boy's grandfather," the Under-ground Railroad conductor whispers to Claire's father. "We had almost given up hope that thee would come tonight." By his speech, Claire knows he is a Quaker. She helps the woman and child into the boat as her father assists the old man.

"Lie down in the bottom," her father whispers to the adults, "and we will cover you." The old man and the woman stretch out in the bottom of the boat. Pulling the child closer, the woman curls around him protectively. The child does not make a sound.

"I have given the boy laudanum so he will not cry out," the Quaker tells Claire's father. "Pray it is not too much." Claire's fa-ther nods grimly. Sometimes the children never wake up, yet this has to be done. The price of a sound made at the wrong time is too terrible to contemplate. *What must the mother be feeling?* Claire thinks. *What was it like for her to watch a stranger spoon liquid opium into the mouth of her child?* She considers the terrible choice this woman has made and is awed by her courage.

Claire's father picks up several warm blankets and throws them over the people huddled in the bottom of the boat. Over the blan-kets, he tosses a square of canvas. The slaves look like cargo now: bales of tobacco or perhaps barrels of whiskey being smuggled across the river at night to avoid federal taxes.

"God speed them to freedom," says the Quaker. He takes Claire's father's hand and shakes it. "And God be with thee and thy son."

"Until we meet again," Claire's father replies. But this, Claire knows, is unlikely.

The Quaker helps push the boat into the river, then turns and hurries back into the shadows. Claire's father sits at the oars, using all the strength he saved by letting her row earlier. They head for the Indiana shore so rapidly that it seems no time at all before she can make out their horses picketed beside the landing. Just before they reach the northern bank, a small, callused hand slips out from beneath the canvas and grasps Claire's. Claire gives it a reassuring squeeze. "Almost there," she whispers. She wonders if the woman knows that reaching Indiana does not mean she and her family are safe. They will have to make it to Canada to be truly free.

The journey from the river to the church is unremarkable. Her father rides with the old man sitting behind him, clinging to his waist. Claire rides with the woman balanced on the saddle in front of her. The woman holds the boy. The horses are two of the swiftest in Papa's stable, but since there is no sign of pursuit, they ride slowly.

Gradually, Claire's fear dissipates, and she begins to relax. Since they left for Kentucky, the weather has changed. It is warmer, and there is a hint of thaw in the air. For a long time the only sound is the clopping of the horses' hooves and the creak of the saddles. Once when they pause for a moment, she hears the hoot of an owl.

In the kitchen of the rectory, Reverend Burke and his wife are waiting with hot soup, corn bread, fresh buttermilk, and coffee laced with chicory. The old man and the woman fall ravenously on the food. To Claire's relief, the child wakes and eats too, sucking on bits of corn bread that his mother dips into the buttermilk. The little boy seems dazed but not frightened. *Sometimes,* Claire thinks, *it's a blessing to be too young to know what's going on.*

She wonders what their names are, what their story is, what happened that made them willing to risk everything. Did they have a cruel master? Was the family about to be broken up? Perhaps they simply longed to be free. In any case, Canada will be a good place for the boy to grow up. He can have a decent life there.

Suddenly, she is overwhelmed by such an intense wish to have a child of her own that she has to put down her cup to keep from spilling coffee in her lap. What good is Henry's money or his house in Cambridge or all those trunks filled with clothes so beautiful they could adorn a museum? She has nothing that really matters, and she is more lonely and unhappy than she has been since the year Ned died.

Again she is forced to confront the secret of her marriage, and again the pain of it drives her to the edge of tears. Picking up her cup with trembling hands, she forces herself to take a sip of coffee. She cannot break down in front of Papa and the Burkes, nor in front of the runaway slaves, whose troubles are so much greater than her own, but she cannot go on living this way either. She must find some way to make Henry listen to her. She is not his doll or his photographic model. She is a woman with a woman's needs, none of which are unreasonable.

The meal continues. Gradually the pain subsides and Claire grows calmer. She never learns the mother's name or her story. Nor does she learn anything about the boy or the old man. As usual, everyone eats without speaking a word more than is necessary. This is always the case. The less you know, the less chance there is that the links will be broken. The runaway slaves are given into your care. You feed them, clothe them, hide them, and pass them on to the next stage. Claire always does her best to forget their faces.

Tonight, however, despite her best efforts, two scenes imprint themselves on her memory. The first is the mother feeding her little boy corn bread. The second is less obvious. It begins when Reverend Burke rises from the table and invites them to walk with him to the church to join in a prayer of thanksgiving. Claire dutifully stands up and follows the others out the door, across the lawn, and into the sanctuary. She is not a particularly religious person, certainly much less religious than her father, but she has no objection to thanking God, although she has never been convinced that He listens.

Since this is a Methodist church, there is only a simple altar, hard pews, a brass lantern, and a floor of well-scrubbed pine planks. Claire kneels with the others in front of the altar as Revered Burke offers up a prayer, which, since the church is drafty and unheated, is mercifully short. Later she does not remember a word of it. When he finishes, there is a brief pause and then the woman places the sleeping boy tenderly in one of the pews, and she and the old man rise to their feet, clasp hands, and begin to sing a camp meeting hymn called "O Brothers, Will You Meet Us on Canaan's Happy Shore?" Claire knows the words, so she stands up, takes their hands, and joins in. For several minutes, everyone stands before the altar singing and holding hands, and something close to joy fills the room.

It is a moment Claire never forgets, not just because it is one of the few happy intervals in an otherwise painful night, but because of what follows: Five months later, not long after the start of what then will still be called "the War to Preserve the Union," men from the Twelfth Massachusetts Infantry will march to the defense of Washington, singing the same hymn with new lyrics. The following December, a forty-two-year-old poet whose husband does not approve of her speaking in public will hear their version and change the lyrics once again. In February 1862, the poet's version will be published in *The Atlantic Monthly*. The editors will pay her five dollars and, after searching around for a suitable title, decide to call it "The Battle Hymn of the Republic."

Chapter Four

As Claire stands inside the church singing, John stands outside watching her. Earlier in the evening, awakened by the sound of horses' hooves, he had gone to his bedroom window and recognized her riding down the gravel driveway that led to the front gate. She was wearing black trousers and a wool cap, and her father, also dressed in black, rode beside her. For a moment he had simply stood there, unable to believe he wasn't dreaming. He kept thinking of the way she had looked at dinner: laced into a blue velvet dress cut low in the bosom; pearl pendants dangling from her ears; long arms, pale and smooth in the candlelight; a pleasant smile; quiet gray eyes; her face as unreadable as the desert after a dust storm. So what the hell was his uncle's wife doing riding around in pants and a boy's cap? And where were she and her father going this time of night? Clearly they were up to something, but what?

Well, whatever it is, he had told himself, *it's none of my business.* But on the way back to bed, he changed his mind. He'd bet a twenty-dollar gold piece his uncle had no idea Claire had gone out. Should he wake him and tell him his wife had ridden off with no one but her father to protect her? No, if his aunt didn't want her husband to know she was sneaking out dressed as a boy, John wasn't going to be the one to tell him.

Returning to the window, he stared at the empty road. Only yesterday, the *Evansville Courier* had warned that the borderlands on either side of the Ohio were more dangerous than they'd been in decades. Claire and her father might need help. On the other hand, the last time John had tried to help a woman, it had ended badly. For nearly a year he had lived in an atmosphere of suspicion and scandal, caught up in one of those insane blood feuds that plague small Southern communities. On two memorable occasions he had been shot at. After Lucretia's brothers had ambushed him a second time, he had disarmed them, thrown their guns in a creek, and gone west to make a new life for himself. He had intended to live on the frontier forever, moving on just ahead of the settlements, but rumors of war had brought him back.

Rubbing the hem of the curtain between his fingers, he watched his breath condense on the glass. He still couldn't decide what to do. It was cold out, but not so cold that the ground would be frozen solid. If he wanted to follow Claire and her father, it would be easy. He had ridden off to the Mexican war a drummer boy and come back a scout, trained by Claude Duvivier, the half French, half Jicarilla Apache who was probably as responsible as anyone for the American victory at Buena Vista, although of course being half Indian, he never made it into the history books. Thanks to Claude, John could track anything that didn't fly, but given the scandal that was still attached to his name, all hell would break loose if anyone learned he had chased after his uncle's wife in the middle of the night.

For a moment, he had a grimly comic vision of his Boston-bred uncle challenging him to a duel. Then his thoughts took a more sober turn. He remembered an afternoon he had spent sifting through the ashes of a settler's shack looking for enough of the man's wife and four children to bury, and the daughter of a Mexican trader who had ridden off by herself one evening to admire the sunset and was never seen again.

Damn it, he thought, *I won't be able to sleep if I go back to bed while they are out there wandering around like chickens waiting to be set on by polecats.* For a moment he imagined Claire as she had appeared in the photograph: floating, ghostlike, and fragile. Later he would laugh at his own ignorance. Claire Winston was about as fragile as a cougar; but he did not yet know her strength.

In the end, gallantry, his uncle's camera, and sexual desire had sent him after her. For he wanted her, of course. He had wanted her from the first moment he caught sight of her.

Turning away from the window, he got dressed, shoved his pistols into his belt, went to the stable, saddled Cruz, and took off after them. The tough little mustang was as fast as a racehorse, and for the last eleven months the Central Overland California and Pikes Peak Express Company had been paying him one hundred dollars a month to average ten miles an hour, so it did not take him long to catch up. He tracked them to the river, watched them row across to Kentucky and return with the runaway slaves.

As he waited, he noted two additional sets of hoofprints in the mud, a half-burned curl of paper that someone had used to light a pipe, and a scrap of discarded gun wadding. At the sight of the wadding, the spit went out of his mouth and he felt the way he always felt before a battle: calm, alert, and wound up like a spring. He forced himself to stop thinking and simply waited. When Claire and her father rode off with the slaves, he followed, keeping to the shadows and staying on the leaf litter so they wouldn't hear the sound of Cruz's hooves.

After a while, he halted and tethered the mare in a place where no one was likely to stumble upon her. By the time the moon had begun to slip toward the horizon, he was moving on foot through the forest. When he reached the churchyard, he stopped and looked for places where men with guns might take cover. In one of the lighted windows of the church, he recognized Claire's profile.

He had intended to check to see if she was safe and then move on, but he has been unable to muster the will to turn away from the sight of her. He can see her lips forming words, but he does not understand a syllable of the hymn she is singing because her face is filling his mind, leaving no room for anything else.

The light from the lanterns picks out the copper highlights in her hair. She seems to float against the white wall, shadows clustered around her like the pale wings of moths; but it is not simply her beauty that has him frozen on the other side of the glass. Something is drawing him to her like iron filings to a magnet, and he has a pretty good idea what that something is. She is not happy in her marriage, he is sure of it; perhaps not even in love with her husband. John has seen enough of the world to know that unsatisfied wives radiate a desire that draws men to them. Some women do this intentionally, but even when they have no idea what they are up to, they can't help it.

He has always been immune to the lure of unhappy wives, so why now and why Claire Winston: the one woman he should not under any circumstances get involved with? She has not flirted with him or given any sign she is attracted to him, so when in blazes did all this begin? In the dining room when her arm brushed his by accident? On the road back from the river? One thing is certain: her husband never should have passed that photograph of her around the dinner table. It was that image of her, silvered with light and floating like a woman treading between life and death, that first made him look at her the way no nephew should look at an aunt.

He knows he needs to get on with his search for the bounty hunters who are lurking somewhere in the shadows, but still he does not move. He can feel Claire's face being permanently engraved in his memory, and he knows that unless he can somehow manage to turn his back on her, this moment will return to haunt him. *She is a married woman,* he thinks. *She is my aunt. I have no business imagining how she would look naked, how smooth her skin would be, what it would be like to bury my face in her hair.* Yet even as he thinks this, his lips go dry, something shakes loose inside his chest, and he knows he would rather be shot down in his tracks than accept that his feelings for her are wrong. This is the moment when he first suspects that he has fallen in love with her.

John Garwood Taylor, he thinks, *y'all are a bigger fool than a moose in rut. This is not the kind of trouble you need.* This brief sermon must work because almost at once he is again able to see her as a vulnerable target, which was why he stopped to look at her in the first place. Turning away from the window, he tries to put her out of his mind, but her face continues to linger just under the edge of his awareness as he moves around the church, alert for the sounds and scents of trouble.

After a while, he stops beside a grave topped with a stone angel and concentrates on a faint scuffle of something in the bushes and a clink of metal that might be bullets rolled in a hand or coins jingling in a pocket. Continuing to circle the church, he sniffs the air and picks up the scents of tobacco, soap, and gunpowder. How long would these men have lasted if the Apache scouts had been on their trail? Half an hour? He doubts it.

He finds the bounty hunters just where he thought they would be, heavily armed, muffled in wool coats, lurking in the shadows of a pecan tree with their rifles pointed toward the church door. John checks to see if there are others with them, but they are alone. Their arrogance borders on idiocy. In fact, if it wasn't so likely to be fatal, it would be amusing. They rode down the center of the road as if they were about to drop into the rectory and ask the preacher's wife for a cup of coffee. Then, having given away their position so thoroughly that even a child could track them, they were foolish enough to picket their horses out of earshot. Those horses are long gone by now, running wild with a handful of cockleburs jammed under each saddle.

Y'all are going to have a long walk back to the river, John thinks. Silently he draws his pistols, approaches the men, and pauses. He is so close, he can hear them breathing, but they still don't suspect he's behind them. Taking three quick steps forward, he jams the barrels of his pistols against their skulls and feels them jump like rabbits.

"Gentlemen," he whispers, "y'all yell and you're dead." He steps back swiftly so they can't kick his legs out from under him, but he's made his point. The bounty hunters have felt the cold metal of the gun barrels. They freeze, and the younger one makes a choking sound as if he's swallowed a wad of tobacco.

"Drop your guns nice and slow," John orders. They hesitate, then drop their rifles to the ground, pull the pistols out of their belts, and drop them also. "Now your knives." Their knives appear and fall to the ground beside the guns. There is a slight clink of metal blades against stone, but no one in the church hears. They are too busy singing hymns about the promised land they are headed for when they die. John can't help thinking that Claire and the others might have gotten to "Canaan's happy shore" about a quarter of an hour from now if he hadn't come along.

"Move," he commands. He turns the men in a half circle, pistols still aimed at their heads, and marches them away from the church. They have not seen his face, and he intends to keep it that way in case he ever meets up with them on the other side of the river. When they are well into the forest, he forces them to lie face-down in the mud with their hands behind their heads, searches them, and comes up with a small pistol and a leather sapper filled with buckshot. In the older man's pocket he finds a Wanted poster: *200 DOLLARS REWARD! Ran away from the subscriber on the 27th of January my black slaves: man answering to the name MARCELLUS, woman answering to the name SUSIE, plus male child of same.* Ages, color of skins, name of owner. *Above reward paid if said slaves taken near the Ohio River on the Kentucky side or 400 DOLLARS if taken in Indiana and delivered to the subscriber near Knottsville in Daviess County, Kentucky.*

John sticks the poster in his pocket, checks the small pistol, and determines it is loaded. "Y'all are sporting quite an arsenal for men who were about to attack old folks, women, and babes-in-arms," he says.

"Some of them abolitionist sons-of-bitches shoots first and asks questions later," says the younger of the two men, encouraged perhaps by John's Southern accent. "We got a legal right to defend ourselves."

"Also," says the older man, "we got a legal right to be here. There's three runaway slaves in that there church back there, and the law says——"

John interrupts him. "The law may say y'all can sneak over from Kentucky to haul back runaway slaves, but I'm personally opposed to acknowledging the legal rights of varmints."

"What makes you think we're from Kaintuck?" says the younger man.

"Well, gentlemen," John says, "if y'all aren't citizens of that great commonwealth, then I untied the wrong boat." He can't see their faces, but he hears their sharp intake of breath.

"You untied our damn boat!" says the older man. "How the hell we gonna get home?"

"Swim," John says. "The runaway slaves do it all the time. Some of them even make it to Indiana in the dead of winter. Actually, for all I care, y'all can walk on water if you can manage it. The one thing you can't do is stay in Indiana. If I see you again, I won't personally kill you, but I guarantee you'll end up in jail for lying in wait to gun down innocent civilians, one of whom—in case y'all haven't noticed—is a preacher. Now in ordinary times, the Charlesport jail might not be so bad, but what with the war rumors, feelings are running high."

"Are you saying we'd be drugged out of the jail and lynched?" cries the younger man. There is mortal terror in his voice.

"Mysterious are the ways of God," John says. "And even more mysterious the ways of mobs. I'm not saying some pack of slave-hunter-hating, abolitionist Yankees are going to rip you out of the sheriff's custody and hang you, and I'm not saying they aren't. But y'all have to ask yourselves if the extra reward money you can get by slipping across the state line without deputizing a posse is worth the risk. Now take off your boots."

"Our boots!" cries the younger one. "It's February!"

"Shut up, Lem," snarls the older man. "He knows damn well what month it is, and in case you ain't noticed, he's pointing his pistols at our butts." Faces still flat in the mud, the men reach out and awkwardly tug off their boots.

John gathers up their boots and stands for a moment looking down at them. As he knows it will, his silence makes them nervous. After a few minutes, he leaves as he came, drifting silently back into the forest. Taking cover in a thicket, he stands and observes them. First, they try to talk to him, but since he is no longer there, he does not answer. After a while, they roll over, look around, and cautiously get to their feet. They peer into the shadows and see nothing, but they are smart enough to know he is still watching. With exaggerated innocence, they blow on their hands and beat their arms against their coats to warm their numbed bodies. They search for their boots but only in a half hearted way.

At last, they turn and limp off into the forest, arguing and cursing every step of the way. John returns to the pecan tree, gathers up their weapons, retrieves Cruz, and follows them to the river, where, as he promised, they find their boat missing. He has not really expected them to try to swim the Ohio in mid-February. Instead, after another bout of snarling and cursing, they limp off toward the ferry. *If they're lucky,* he thinks, *they'll be back on the Kentucky side before the grits on the breakfast table get cold.*

By the time Claire and her father return to the farm, John has Cruz stabled and is back upstairs in his nightshirt trying to warm his feet on the brick Mrs. Musgrove tucked under the covers at the foot of his bed. He is just poking at the lukewarm dish towel that enfolds it when he hears them tiptoe into the kitchen. Father and daughter converse in low voices. After a while, Mr. Musgrove climbs the stairs, pausing outside John's door as if reassuring himself that John is asleep. At last, with a creak of old floorboards, he walks down the hall to his bedroom and shuts the door.

Claire stays in the kitchen for about as long as it would take for her to change back into her nightgown. Then she comes up the stairs, her bare footsteps as soft as dust against the carpet. John listens to her walk down the hall, pause, and blow out her candle. Entering the room where her husband lies sleeping, she closes the door behind her with a muffled thud.

Suddenly, John dislikes Henry so much he can hardly breathe. It's not fair, but there it is. The thought of Claire married to a man who cares so little about her that he hasn't even noticed she has been absent is intolerable. He longs to grab his uncle by the lapels and shake him until his teeth rattle. *Do you have any idea of the danger your wife was in tonight?* he wants to yell; but he can never admit he watched over Claire and kept her from harm; nor can he tell his uncle where she went.

Put her out of your mind, he tells himself, but he can't; and when he shuts his eyes and tries to sleep, he keeps seeing her standing in the church with her head slightly bowed. He rolls onto his left side, then onto his right trying to make the image disappear. It does, but what follows is worse, because now he sees her as she appeared in the photograph. Opening his eyes, he stares at the shadows on the wall and imagines reaching in, brushing the lint off her dress, kissing the edge of her mouth, and making her smile.

You fool! he thinks. *You're thinking about your uncle's wife in a way that could get you called out and shot. So you love her and want to make her happy, do you? Well, what makes you think she isn't happy already? Maybe you're wrong about her. Maybe she adores her husband. Maybe being Mrs. Henry Winston is her idea of bliss.*

At last he falls asleep, only to wake the next morning feeling as if he has trekked across the Jornada del Muerto Desert. Stumbling down to breakfast, he finds the elder Musgroves already seated at the table. He is just pouring molasses on his pancakes when Claire and Henry appear. Claire wears a white wool dress; her hair is braided in an intricate coil, her neck pale and delicate. She sits down across from John, takes a single pancake from the platter, cuts it into small pieces, and stabs each one with the tip of her fork. There are dark smudges under her eyes, and she seems weary and distracted. Her hands flutter from syrup pitcher to butter dish.

Restless hands, John thinks. Suddenly he feels as if he would risk everything, even his life, to lean over and kiss her hands and lips and . . .

"You are unusually quiet this morning, Mr. Taylor," Mr. Musgrove says. "Are you unwell?"

John starts and nearly drops his fork. "No, sir," he says. "I am fine, thank you."

"Did you sleep well?" asks Mrs. Musgrove.

"Very well, ma'am," he says and feels the blood rush to his face. He lies poorly. Always has. Probably always will.

"I am sorry you must leave us so soon," says Mrs. Musgrove, to whom he has already made his apologies.

Henry picks up the coffeepot, fills his cup, and stares at John over the rim. "I thought you said you planned to leave the day after tomorrow," he says. John braces himself for an interrogation, but the truth is, his uncle has very little interest in whether he stays or goes. "I am taking the train to Evansville this afternoon to do some business," Henry continues. "Shall I stop off at the telegraph office and send a message to your mother telling her to expect you on Friday?"

"Yes," John says. "Thank you. I would like her to know."

Claire says nothing. She too seems to have no interest in whether John goes or stays; but then, why should she?

After breakfast, he goes back upstairs and packs his bags. Well before midmorning, he is riding down the road that leads toward the river. Just before he gets to the ferry dock, he remembers that the bounty hunters will also be waiting to cross the Ohio this morning. Turning Cruz into the woods, he hitches her to a poplar and takes a book out of his saddlebag. For nearly two hours, he sits on a log reading. Twice he takes out his pocket watch and consults it. The watch, which once belonged to his father, has a lid crafted from a Quarter Eagle gold piece. When his father was fatally wounded in the Battle of Buena Vista, John carried the watch back to his mother. Even though by rights it should have gone to his elder brother, William, she gave it to John. He was only ten at the time, but William never objected.

At eleven thirty, John pockets the watch, puts away the book, and rides to the dock. Half an hour later, he is in the middle of the river, steaming toward Kentucky. Traveling with him are half a dozen men, most of whom stand at the rail, chewing tobacco, spitting, and talking about the possibility of war. Lincoln is damned and defended. War isn't coming, but if it does, Kentucky will fight for the Union. No, Kentucky will fight for the South. No, you damn pack of fools, Governor Magoffin will see that the state remains neutral.

Blast it, sir, are you a fence straddler?

I sure as hell am, mister.

That seems like a kinda yeller-bellied point of view, if yuh ask me.

Hold on there. Are y'all calling my brother a coward?

The man in the top hat and the man in the coal dust–smeared trousers back off and hastily apologize to a rough-looking giant in a blue wool jacket.

No, mister. Ah weren't saying nothing of the kind.

I regret my hasty words, sir. I meant to give no offense to your brother.

The giant in the jacket accepts the apology with a grim nod and turns away. Hands that had been fumbling for weapons go back on the rail, leaving John with the feeling that he has almost witnessed bloodshed. *What hope is there for peace,* he thinks, *if men can't make a simple voyage across a river without threatening to do each other mortal harm?*

The wind rises and small clouds scud overhead, blown north like a flock of gray birds. Again John thinks of Claire, and how if war comes, he may not see her for years. The prospect of such a long separation makes him half wild with desire. *I must be out of my mind to want her so much,* he thinks. And then he thinks how easy it would be to take the next ferry back to Indiana as soon as this one arrives in Kentucky.

Chapter Five

Two weeks later on a chilly March afternoon, Henry and Claire stand in the stern of a steamboat called the *Western Star* watching its wake spread out in a lacy V. They are finally on their way to pay Henry's sister Lavinia a visit, and today Claire is feeling hopeful, even happy. Although she cannot put her finger on the exact source of her optimism, the time she has spent in Charlesport has definitely lifted her spirits. As always, Mama and Papa enfolded her in their love. This, combined with helping the runaway slaves escape, has made her feel like her old self again; and now as she stands at the rail, looking at sunlight gather in the ripples like handfuls of copper coins, she experiences a rare sense of being in exactly the right place at the right time.

"A beautiful view, is it not, my dear?" Henry says.

She turns to find him looking at her with an expression that proves beyond a doubt he is not a mind reader. Her face is flushed; her eyes bright. There is something about the set of her jaw and the tilt of her lips that would tell him much about his wife if he were good at looking beyond the surface of things.

"Beautiful indeed," she says. It is a relief to be able to agree with him about something.

They stand for a while longer admiring the river, then turn and stroll down the deck to their cabin. As they enter, Claire's newly found confidence recedes, and again she feels the weight of her ill-considered marriage pressing down on her. The cabin is small but luxurious. Red velvet drapes have been drawn across the windows, leaving the interior in shadows. A white china teapot rests on a tray next to a bottle of sherry, two crystal glasses, a plate of sliced cake, and a silver kettle perched over a small spirit lamp. On the table next to the glasses sits a photograph album bound in green leather.

Claire flinches at the sight of the album.

"Are you cold?" Henry asks.

"No," she says. She notices that some of his photographic equipment has been stowed in the corner near the window. Turning her back on it, she walks to the table, tosses her shawl over the back of a chair, pours herself a glass of sherry, tilts back her head, and drinks it off as if it were a shot of whiskey. This is a very unladylike thing to do, but Henry, who is bending over to inspect his equipment, does not notice this small act of rebellion.

Claire studies the green album with growing hostility. Suddenly she is distracted by a sharp pain. Looking down, she realizes that she has gripped the sherry glass so hard, she has snapped the stem. Henry straightens up and turns toward her.

"Did you say something?"

"No." She conceals the broken glass in her palm, and as soon as he bends back over his photographic equipment, she transfers the pieces to a potted plant. The cut, which is almost unnoticeable, is the only sign that she has come to a decision: whatever the cost, she will have no more of Henry's camera. The part of their marriage that involved photography is over.

She knows she must tell him this immediately, but she does not know where to begin. Returning to the table, she pours out two cups of tea, sits down, and turns over one of the serving plates.

The bottom is stamped with the image of a stern-wheeler and the words "Western Star."

"Whatever are you doing?" Henry asks.

"Reading the china." He gives her a puzzled look. Claire returns the plate to a more serviceable position and places a slice of cake on it.

"That is far too much," he objects.

"You need not eat all of it, Henry."

"It forms an unpleasant impression," he says, and then adds: "Visually, I mean. As you know, I am sensitive to volumes and spaces."

"I am not," she says, but she removes the cake from Henry's plate, replaces it with a smaller slice, and hands the plate to him without further discussion. This is not the right moment to fight over something petty.

"Henry," she says, "I am no longer going to allow you to photograph me."

"I am not particularly fond of white cake," he says.

She is confused. She spoke clearly, but apparently he did not hear her. "Did you understand what I just said? I am no longer going to let you photograph me."

"Drink your tea before it gets cold," he says. "We will discuss this when you are in a more reasonable frame of mind."

"I wish to discuss it now."

"You are being ridiculous, Claire."

"Ridiculous!" She feels a tight sensation in the pit of her stomach and then blinding anger. Rising to her feet, she sweeps the plates and teacups aside, grabs the green album, flings it open, and slaps it down in front of him.

"Look what you have made of me!" she cries. "If I am ridiculous, then who is to blame?" She points at the photos. "Here you have photographed me as Julia, the depraved wife of the emperor Tiberius, draped in a piece of transparent silk that reveals my entire body. In the black albums, among those portraits which you recently displayed to such acclaim, you photographed me as the virgin goddess Athena, but here you have me as a bare-breasted whore."

"Claire! Control yourself. Such words are . . ."

"Not fitting for a lady? Is that what you were going to say? I agree. Nor are the words I might use to describe this." She turns the page and jabs her finger at a photograph of herself standing beside a horse. "Here you have me as Catherine the Great. I thought this was an innocent portrait, until a certain countess in Paris who shall remain nameless told me about Catherine's—what shall I call it?—Catherine's 'strange proclivity' for horses. Are you shocked that I know about such things, Henry? I admit that I barely under-stand. But about this next one, I have no doubt."

She points to a photograph of herself sitting on a low marble pedestal examining her bare foot as if extracting a thorn. "Here, once again, you have photographed me without clothing, and you have done something else, something I am at pains to understand. During the developing process, you erased my breasts. How did you accomplish this, Henry, and why would a man choose to make his wife look like an adolescent boy?"

"That is a copy of a famous Greek bronze."

"I do not care if it is a reproduction of a piece of classical sculpture. Nor do I care if this one"—she turns a page and points—"is meant to imitate Ingres's *Grande Odalisque*. I am nude or partially nude in all of them."

"These are works of art, Claire."

"No, they are not. They are . . . I do not know the word, but I am sure one exists."

Henry takes a sip of tea, puts his cup down, and looks at her the way one might regard a child who has chosen to make a scene. "My dear, you are in a nervous state and hardly know what you are saying. I suspect you are about to get one of your headaches. Would you like me to ring for a cloth soaked in vinegar?"

"No!" Claire says so sharply that he flinches. "I am not ill. I am trying to explain why I have decided not to let you take any more photographs of me. I might have been able to accept the nudity and the odd subject matter. I might even have been willing to go on posing for you in these ridiculous costumes if you had ever offered me the kind of tenderness and affection a husband should offer a wife, but I have come to the end of my ability to tolerate the state of our marriage. I am unhappy, Henry. I grieve for you and for me and for all we could have been and are not. You never touch me except to arrange me for your camera. When we wed, I thought you loved me. You said you did, and you were very convincing. But over the past five months I have learned to my sorrow that I am nothing more than your doll. I do not want to be your doll, nor do I want to be your photographic model. I want to be your wife. To put it plainly: I want us to have a normal marriage. At the very least, I want a child. I was raised on a farm. I have seen mares and stallions mating, and I know—at least I think I know— what a man and woman need to do if they are to get children. We do not do any of those things."

Henry's face goes white. "I forbid you to speak of such things," he says.

"Very well." Claire shuts the album and stares at him defiantly. "We shall not speak of them; but until you make me your wife in fact as well as in name, I will not allow you to photograph me in private or in public. Do you understand?"

"I thought only to spare you," he says.

"My God, Henry, I do not wish to be spared my husband's affection!"

"You do not know what you are asking for. You are too innocent to understand how beastly the desires of men are."

"Henry, listen, please. You are wrong. It is true that I am inexperienced, but I am not without desires of my own. I would not be repelled to receive physical attentions from you. There is nothing sinful about a husband and wife wanting each other."

"I would be," Henry says.

"You would be what?"

"Repelled. If you no longer wish me to photograph you, I will refrain from doing so, but I cannot accept your terms. I find the human body repugnant except when transfigured by art. The body of a pregnant woman is particularly grotesque." This is so much worse than Claire has anticipated that words fail her. She gasps as if she has been struck and tears fill her eyes. Henry gives her a disapproving look and closes the green album.

"I am going for a stroll on deck," he says. "The light strikes the water at a lovely angle in the late afternoons. I shall return around six thirty, and we can dine at seven if that is agreeable."

"I cannot tolerate this," she says. "You must change, Henry. You must try to love me as a husband. If you do not, I will be forced to make some kind of life for myself without you."

"Do not threaten, my dear. It does not become you. When you wrinkle your brow and bite your lips, you look a full five years older than your actual age. Let us put this conversation behind us and forget it took place. I am sure, when you have the leisure to think over what you have said, you will regret your hasty words and see there is absolutely no reason for us not to go on living together in perfect harmony."

"There is every reason!" Claire cries, but the door is already closing behind him.

For several minutes, she paces around the cabin. Finally she sits down and pours herself another glass of sherry. She spends the next hour or so sipping it, staring at the river, and sifting through her life trying to make sense of it. She is angry, shocked, and bitterly disappointed. Despite the fact that she has wrung a promise from Henry not to photograph her, she is still not convinced he understands what she said and why she said it. She will never be able to forgive him for saying that he finds the body of a woman carrying a child "grotesque," and she cannot imagine how she made such a terrible mistake in choosing a husband or what she is going to do about it.

Chapter Six

"AND now, ladies and gentlemen," Henry says to the guests assembled in his sister's parlor, "on the count of three..." There is the sound of a match being struck followed by a flare of light so intense Claire feels as if she has been thrown onto the surface of the sun. After a few seconds, the magnesium ribbon burns out, and she is left staring at a pair of blue stripes that appear to be branded on her eyeballs.

On Henry's photographic plate, an image of Lavinia's parlor has been etched for posterity: the heavy velvet drapes tied back with gold-tasseled cords; the Persian carpet; the waxed walnut sideboard groaning under salt-cured hams, pan-fried quails, candied yams, and a magnificent silver epergne laden with Lavinia's famous chicken salad sandwiches. In front of the buffet stand the guests Lavinia has invited to meet Claire and Henry: the men in black woolen suits, the older women in dark silks that will look black in the photograph, the young girls in gay colors that will appear as dull as a midwinter sky.

Claire stands in the center, between Lavinia and Lavinia's eldest daughter, Agnes. Although only twenty-one, Agnes is already considered unmarriageable by the bachelors of Lenoir, who prefer pretty, docile women who do not stoop and squint. Agnes has turned away from the camera and appears to be frowning enviously at Claire, the new bride who is the focus of this photograph. Well might Agnes frown. Claire is clad in a tea gown of pale blue Chinese silk embroidered with small yellow birds and pink peach blossoms that makes Agnes and all the other women look like a flock of crows.

Henry has triumphed again. He has succeeded in dressing Claire up like a doll and photographing her, knowing that she cannot refuse him in the presence of his sister's guests. The promise he made on the boat has not lasted two days. Claire lets go of Lavinia's hand, stares at the fading blue bars, and feels the bitterness of her defeat as all about her people gather around the camera uttering exclamations of delight.

The problem is not that Henry has once again photographed her in public. This she can tolerate. The real issue is that, as far as he is concerned, their conversation on the *Western Star* never took place. She looks at him, trying to see the world as he must see it. He is explaining the photographic process to Mrs. Lewis, a middle-aged widow who dominates the Baptist Ladies' Bible Study Society, the Lenoir Ladies' Book Club, and another newly formed organization, as yet unnamed, whose members are frantically sewing gray uniforms. His cravat is tied to perfection, not a hair on his head is out of place, not a word he utters is less than exquisitely polite. What is he thinking? What, if anything, is he feeling? He appears content, but there is no way she can tell if this is true or merely another superbly crafted illusion.

This is more than simply a question of her will against his. There is something wrong with him. Not some small flaw, but something so fundamental that she lacks words to describe it even to herself. Suddenly she is struck by a thought so obvious that she knows instantly it must be true: this is who Henry really is and always will be. No matter how long she waits or how hard she tries, he is not going to change back into the man who courted her. There is nothing she can do to make this marriage work. Unless she leaves him, she will live her whole life more alone than any spinster, die childless, and never know anything about love except what she reads in books.

"Mrs. Winston," a voice calls. Claire looks up to see Mrs. Lewis's eldest daughter, Ophelia, floating across the room toward her like a large, gaily colored balloon. Ophelia, the reigning belle of Lenoir, favors diaphanous spring gowns that make her resemble a charming child of fourteen, although Claire estimates her real age to be closer to twenty. Hanging on to the crook of her arm like a grim afterthought is Agnes—the last person Claire wishes to speak to in her present state, since Agnes is sharp-eyed, intelligent, and overtly hostile.

"Mrs. Winston," Ophelia repeats in honeyed tones as she draws nearer, "Agnes and I were just talking about Mr. Leonardo da Vinci's painting of *The Last Supper.*"

"Fresco," Agnes says. "It is a fresco, Ophelia, composed, as I have repeatedly told you, of oil and tempura on plaster."

"Well, whatever it is, honey," Ophelia says, giving Agnes's arm a playful squeeze, "I imagine Mrs. Winston has seen the thing with her own eyes, since she and that handsome husband of hers just spent the winter gallivantin' around Italy."

"Excuse me," Claire says, "I need to step outside for some fresh air. I am feeling unwell." She knows she needs a better lie to cover her exit, but she is not in an inventive mood. To her surprise, Ophelia gives her a delighted smile, and Agnes's eyebrows shoot up.

"Oh, my stars," Ophelia says breathlessly, "is this an announcement? How excitin'. Mama would be absolutely rabid if she knew you were tellin' me, because I'm not supposed to know about such things and neither is Agnes, but we've got eyes in our heads and a girl doesn't see kittens come into the world and still believe in storks."

For a moment, Claire has no idea what Ophelia is talking about. Then she remembers that when a bride of five months declares herself "unwell," it is likely to mean only one thing. She knows Ophelia has not meant to be cruel, but the irony of her comment is too much to bear. "You are mistaken," she says sharply. "I am not with child."

Ophelia's and Agnes's mouths drop open. Ladies do not speak such words to young unmarried girls, nor do they speak them at afternoon teas in the presence of gentlemen.

"Oh, my stars," Ophelia says and sits down abruptly on Lavinia's horsehair sofa, while Agnes glares at Claire as if storing up this breach of etiquette for future use. Unable to trust herself to speak, Claire wheels around and makes her way quickly through the guests who are still too enthralled with Henry's camera to notice she is leaving. Striding down the hallway, she barges into the kitchen and nearly collides with Bridget, Lavinia's stout Irish cook.

"Would you be requirin' anything, ma'am?" Bridget asks as she dodges Claire.

"No, thank you," Claire says. "I am just going into the garden for a breath of fresh air." Bridget gives Claire a puzzled look. When Lavinia's female guests take fresh air, they do so on the front veranda. Only gentlemen go to the back of the house to smoke or, in some instances, chew tobacco.

"Going out, are ye?" she says kindly. "Ah, well then, ma'am, ye'd better be takin' this." Licking the flour off her fingers, she reaches out, plucks her shawl from the back of a kitchen chair, and offers it to Claire.

Claire thanks her, throws the shawl around her shoulders, and walks out into the kitchen garden. There on a wooden bench, among a ruin of crooked tomato stakes and dry corn stalks, she closes her eyes, puts her hands over her face, and tries to think things through. Obviously she must end this sham of a marriage as soon as possible, but a divorce, provided she can get one, will be both scandalous and horribly expensive, and she is sure Henry will never let her go without a fight. What grounds does she have for divorcing him against his will? He is not a drunkard; he has not struck her nor abandoned her, nor been unfaithful. Perhaps, given that their marriage has not been consummated, she can get an annulment, but who will believe her?

Then there is the problem of her parents. She suspects that besides giving her father the contract to build the mill, Henry loaned him a great deal of money. If her marriage is annulled, will her mother and father lose the farm and stables? And even if her separation from Henry has no financial repercussions, she will have to admit to Mama and Papa that she made a terrible mistake when she married him. No matter how she frames this confession, they will blame themselves. They suffered so terribly when Ned died; how can she cause them more suffering? And what will it be like to return to Charlesport as a once-married woman and live in their house like a child: sleeping in her old room, hearing the whispers when she goes to church on Sundays, seeing pity and disapproval in the faces of old friends?

What about children? If she leaves Henry, chances are she will never receive a second proposal of marriage. She will not be an unmarried girl nor even a respectable widow; she will be damaged goods—not quite as damaged as a woman who has been caught in adultery or run away from her husband, but the scandal of divorce will follow her for the rest of her life.

Perhaps she should do what so many woman do: stay with her husband, paste a smile on her face, and carry on as if nothing has happened. Although she will still be miserable, her misery will remain a secret. She is too proud to become an object of pity. She cannot bear to have people whispering *Poor Mrs. Winston* behind her back; but if she stays with Henry, she will never be loved for anything but the way her face looks in his photographs, and what kind of life is that?

For a moment she allows herself to feel the full agony of her defeat. After months of struggle, she has come to a dead end.

There is nothing she can do that will bring her happiness. She has made a fatally bad decision, and now she is condemned to suffer the consequences.

She must make some sound of grief as she faces this painful truth, because suddenly she feels someone take her hands and gently pull them away from her face. Startled, she opens her eyes to find John Taylor sitting on the bench next to her.

"Claire," he says. "What's wrong? Are you ill?" She stares at him in confusion. What is he doing here? He is supposed to be thirty miles away rallying to the Confederate cause. "Are you in pain?" he says. "Is there anything I can do to help you?"

For an instant, she is seized by an impulse to tell him the truth about her marriage, but she stops herself just in time. And that is when it happens: the sun settles on John's face so that it seems illuminated from within, a flock of garden sparrows rises into the air with a rush of wings, the earth seems to turn beneath her feet, and something closer to pain than pleasure moves through her. She shudders, removes her hands from his, and tries to right herself, but there is no going back. John's face has been etched on her mind as permanently as Lavinia's parlor has been etched on Henry's photographic plates.

She stares down at her hands, which seem to belong to some other woman. She suspects she is feeling something that will change her life, yet all John has done is inquire after her health. It is a thing a nephew can reasonably do—a little unusual perhaps, but not greatly so. Nothing appears to have happened, and yet . . .

"Thank you," she says. "But I am not in need of help." She rises to her feet, and John rises with her.

"I'm sorry to have intruded on your private thoughts," he says. "I didn't intend to startle you, but you appeared distressed. I only wished to offer you . . ." His voice trails off.

"Thank you. That was kind, but entirely unnecessary. I am, as you can see, quite well." The lie is so transparent she almost expects him to protest. She brushes the palms of her hands over her skirts to settle the folds in place and discovers she is trembling. "Please excuse me. I must return to your mother's party. I am the guest of honor." She turns and begins to walk back to the house.

"Claire." At the sound of his voice, she stops and faces him again. John stands silently for a moment, then he walks up to her and takes her hands in his. Lifting them to his lips, he covers them with kisses. "I am in love with you," he says. "Hopelessly in love with you."

Claire is too shocked to reply. As his lips move from her hands to her wrists, she gasps. She knows she should pull away, but instead she throws back her head and closes her eyes. For the second time that afternoon, she is caught in an explosion of light. She has never experienced anything so intense.

"Claire," he murmurs. She feels him bending toward her. Suddenly, there is a burst of laughter from the house. Startled, she opens her eyes to find him preparing to kiss her.

"No!" she cries, pulling away.

"Claire, I mean you no harm. I only want—"

"I am married. People will see us!"

"I don't care."

"I do. A woman has to. I can't ..." She can barely speak. She knows she must reject him at once, but there is a terrible, guilty joy in hearing a man who is not her husband say that he loves her. This is what she has been longing for, but it is coming at the wrong time from the wrong person. Her life is already difficult enough. If anyone should see them ... if Lavinia or Mrs. Lewis or, worse yet, Henry should start wondering why she left the party and come out to find her ...

"You must leave," she says. She speaks in an angry tone, because she *is* angry: not at him but at herself for having been such a fool as to marry a man who will never kiss any part of her with so much passion if she lives to be a hundred.

"You're my husband's nephew. You must never touch me again, and you—you must stop looking at me like that or you will ..."

"Will what?" he says gently.

She starts to say "break my heart," but again she catches herself in time. "Please! Just go away before someone sees us."

"Claire, I will do anything for you, even leave if that's what you want; but . . . I can't stop loving you. If you're ever in trouble or need a friend—" He does not complete the sentence. Turning abruptly, he walks out the back gate, slamming it behind him.

⁓

"Are you feeling better?" Lavinia asks as Claire reenters the front hall and takes up her place in the receiving line. "Agnes and Ophelia told me you nearly fainted dead away on the parlor rug."

"I am fine." The words stick in Claire's throat, but somehow she gets them out. She feels shaken and at the same time elated. John Taylor loves her! She cannot accept his love, if that is what it really is. She cannot even allow herself to think too much about it, but even if she spends the rest of her life married to Henry, John's words and the kisses that accompanied them will be something to hold to her heart on lonely winter nights.

Lavinia looks down and her eyes widen. "My dear child, whatever have you been doing? You have mud all over your shoes and the hem of your dress." Before Claire can fabricate a convincing lie, a new guest arrives. Lavinia wheels around like a soldier on drill and adopts the expression she habitually uses to receive newcomers. It doesn't quite do, because Southern women are evidently trained from birth to meet every arriving guest with the bright-eyed enthusiasm of a cocker spaniel; but, considering she is a New England–born Yankee, her smile is impressively hospitable.

"Claire," says Lavinia, "allow me to present Mr. John Hunt Morgan. Mr. Morgan, my sister-in-law, Mrs. Winston."

Claire looks up and finds herself gazing into the face of a tall, handsome, bearded man whose gray eyes give only the faintest glimmer of acknowledgment. Later she will learn Morgan has no eyes for women, not even for a pretty young bride with flushed cheeks, because his own young wife, Rebecca, whom he calls "the delicate spring flower of his life" is dying, and beneath his courtly manners, he is nearly frantic with grief.

"Mr. Morgan," Lavinia continues, "comes from Lexington, where he owns a woolen mill, so I imagine he and your husband will have a great deal to talk about. He is an old friend of the family. He fought with my late husband at the Battle of Buena Vista and was at Richard's side when Richard was fatally wounded. He is presently in the process of outfitting a company of men to defend the commonwealth against foreign aggression."

Claire is in such an agitated state that she does not register the fact that by "foreign aggression" Lavinia means Federal troops. Morgan is arming a troop of secessionist sympathizers who intend to shoot any Federal soldiers who venture into Kentucky. Automatically she extends her hand. "How do you do, Mr. Morgan," she says. Morgan accepts her hand and bows over it.

"A pleasure, ma'am," he says. "I wish you every happiness on the occasion of your marriage."

Claire is tempted to treat him to a display of hysterical laughter, but she bites it back. "Thank you," she says.

Morgan releases her hand and walks away to join the men as Claire turns to greet the next guests. She does not look after Morgan; indeed she is so preoccupied with what happened in the garden, she forgets him the instant he moves on. The front door opens again to admit two more guests, closes, and then opens once more to admit John.

"John!" Agnes cries, and rushes forward to embrace her brother. Claire stands next to Lavinia and tries not to meet John's eyes. Behind her, she can hear a group of men talking politics.

I hear Lincoln skulked into Washington to be inaugurated like a thief in the night.

Jeff Davis is worth ten of Lincoln.

Kentucky will go out of the Union now, or I vow my boys and I will go out of Kentucky.

Seizing John by the arm, Agnes brings him over to Lavinia and Claire. Lavinia kisses her son on the cheek and tells him how pleased she is he could make the reception. As John approaches, Claire discovers that she can hardly breathe. It would be ironic if, after all this, she really did faint, but she is not the fainting type. She regains her wits and manages to say something polite, but she does not offer him her hand.

When he leaves to join the conversation about Lincoln and the coming war, Agnes leans down and puts her mouth to Claire's ear. "I saw you and my brother in the garden just now," she hisses. "And if I were not too much of a lady to let such indelicate words cross my lips, I would tell Uncle Henry what a shameless hussy he has married."

Chapter Seven

SUNSHINE pours through the French windows, slides along the coils of the rag rug, and settles on Lavinia's silver epergne. The parlor is unusually silent this morning because most of the humans who frequent it are elsewhere. Bridget has been given half a day off to visit a widowed friend who suffers from rheumatism. Twelve-year-old Emma and eleven-year-old Clayton returned late yesterday evening, but even so, Lavinia woke them at dawn, scrubbed them mercilessly with lye-based soap, and packed them off to church with everyone else.

Only John remains behind, asleep in the four-posted cherry bed in the second-best guest bedroom. Lavinia has given her favorite son a dispensation from attending church this morning because he is suffering from one of his periodic attacks of malaria, which is known in Lenoir as "the trembles" or "Roman fever." Malaria is common in the Ohio and Mississippi river valleys, and earlier in the century, thousands of settlers died from it. About half the inhabitants of Lenoir either have the disease or have had it at some time or another. John came down with his case during the Mexican campaign and ever since he has had days when he burns and shakes and sometimes dreams strange, slightly disturbed dreams that leave him giddy the next morning.

Popular opinion has it that the fever is contracted by exposure to bad air. This means that in summer, the citizens of Lenoir shut their windows on even the hottest nights and sleep fitfully from June through early September; but now in March, only six days after the inauguration of President Lincoln, the bedroom is pleasantly cool and John, who has been dosed with quinine and nursed all night by his mother, is sleeping soundly.

Outside, the weather is changing rapidly. To the west, an ominous black cloud is advancing on Lenoir, and the wind is stripping the buds off the willows and making the cottonwoods tremble. John sleeps on until the first crash of thunder. Startled, he sits bolt upright as rain strikes the windowpanes with so much force the glass shudders. The bedroom is so dark that for a moment he thinks he has slept through the day and on into the night. Striking a match, he lights a lamp. Then he gets up, goes to the window, and flings aside the drapes. He is a little weak, but his fever has broken, and he feels hungry and ready to face the day.

The storm is raging full force. He stands for a moment enjoying the spectacle. The rain is blowing sideways, coming down so fast the gutters on the porch roof have started to overflow. His mother's wildflower garden is a disaster, and the oaks that line the driveway are flailing about wildly. He is just wondering if the rain will be followed by hail when he hears a rhythmical thump that brings him back to more practical matters. Somewhere a shutter has come loose.

Pulling on a pair of pants, he pads down the hall in his bare feet, checks his mother's room, and finds her windows tightly closed. Agnes too has secured her windows, as has Emma, but Clayton's are wide open, and there is a wet spot on the floor that will likely earn him a whipping, for although Lavinia is a loving mother, she is strict.

John mops up the evidence, closes Clayton's windows, and locks them against the storm. Then he moves on, pursuing the thumping sound, which he soon realizes is coming from the one room he does not want to enter. For a moment he hesitates outside the door. Then he shrugs and goes in.

The room contains a large double bed, twin walnut dressers, a pink-skirted vanity with an intricately carved mirror, a writing desk, and a rosewood commode. On the walls, imprisoned in gold frames, Godey prints of ladies in old-fashioned high-waisted frocks simper at gentlemen hunters in green coats. In the corner farthest from the windows, some of Henry's photographic equipment is stacked in a neat pile. At the foot of the bed rest two leather steamer trunks, one open. The open one, which spills dresses, petticoats, and stockings, is obviously Claire's.

Spotting the loose shutter, John strides across the room, secures it, and closes the window. As he wrestles down the sash, the full force of the rain hits him in the face. He wipes the water out of his eyes, turns, and approaches the open trunk. Crouching down, he inspects the contents for damage. Except for a stocking that has been blown into a puddle near the window, the rain has left Claire's clothing untouched.

He puts his hand on the lid of the trunk to close it, then stops. For the space of four or five breaths he does nothing. Then impulsively, he reaches out and runs his fingers over one of Claire's dresses. The silk is cool and soft, gray and calm as her eyes. Giving in to temptation, he lifts the dress and buries his face in it. The silk smells like Claire: a complex blend of French perfume, rose-scented soap, and some scent uniquely hers that he has no words for.

A flash of lightning and a crash of thunder bring him back to his senses. He shuts the lid and rises to his feet. As the woman whose clothing he has just touched recently reminded him, she is his uncle's wife. He has no right to be in their bedroom for a moment longer than it takes him to secure the contents from the storm. *This is folly,* he thinks. *What has come over me?* He is lucky she hasn't told her husband what happened in the garden. He has been acting like a lovesick boy.

This must stop. He must stop thinking about her, stop dreaming about her, stop wanting her. He has seen men seized by similar passions destroy themselves and take innocent people down with them: railroad clerks falling in love with bankers' wives; lieutenants sending billets-doux to generals' ladies; not to mention cowboys, the most romantic fools who ever sat on horses, getting shot for some preacher's daughter who wouldn't look twice at them.

And yet ... to fall in love with a woman, even the wrong woman, is no small thing. John has only been in love once before—not with the woman whose brothers tried to kill him—but with a girl named Carrie. It was the summer of 1846, a few months before he left with his father and brothers for the Mexican war. Carrie was eight; he was nine. She was from New York, a cousin of one of Agnes's friends, the first Yankee girl John had ever met. Her family had come to Lenoir for the summer to visit relatives and she had no friends, so he had befriended her, which was an unusual thing for a nine-year-old boy to do; but he had loved her immediately, perhaps from the first moment he saw her, not because she was beautiful—Carrie was gangly, skinny, and freckled from head to toe—but because she was brave, smart, adventurous, and not afraid to speak her mind. All summer, the two of them were inseparable. In early September, Carrie's family left to go back east. He never saw her again or knew what became of her, but he thought of her almost every night when he was in Mexico, and he never forgot her.

The love of a boy and the love of a man are different, but not as different as most people imagine. Now, as he stands in front of Claire's trunk while the storm rages outside, John thinks of how similar Claire and Carrie are in spirit and how inevitable it was that once he followed Claire to the river and understood the depth of her courage, he would love her. And then he thinks again what dangerous ground he is trespassing on and that, unlike a boy, a grown man can govern his passions by reason.

There is a simple solution to the problem of being in love with his uncle's wife. In fact it is more or less the same solution he tried a few weeks ago when he abruptly left Charlesport. Tomorrow, he will saddle Cruz, kiss his mother and sisters good-bye, chuck Clayton under the chin, and do what Claire herself commanded him to do: he will leave and ride south to join his two older brothers and his classmates from the Marion Military Institute who are already camped near Roxboro, drilling with a newly formed group called the Blackford Rifles. In theory, the Blackford Rifles is a social organization whose members plan to entertain themselves and their friends by parading down the streets of Lenoir on fine cavalry horses and staging target shooting competitions; but that pretense is not likely to last a day longer than it takes for the governor and legislature to decide once and for all if Kentucky is going to maintain its policy of neutrality or throw in its lot with the Confederacy.

Less than a week ago, Lincoln used his inauguration speech to plead for a reconciliation between the Northern and Southern states. He spoke of "bonds of affection," "mystic cords of memory," and the "better angels of our nature," but John doesn't see angels appearing on the political horizon any time in the near future. In the same speech, the new president warned that no state has a right to leave the Union, which means that soon, whether Kentucky secedes or not, there will be a war to fight. Almost everyone, including John's mother and sisters—and even his older brothers, who should know better—believe the war will be short, but from what he saw during the Mexican campaign, John figures it is more likely to be long and bloody. The moment hostilities begin, Uncle Henry will return to Boston, taking Claire with him.

Once he has decided to leave, John feels calmer. Rising to his feet, he picks Claire's wet stocking out of the puddle by the window and drapes it over the lid of the trunk. The carpet is damp but the dye is holding fast, and no doubt it will dry quickly. On the writing desk, a brass vase containing crocheted tulips has been knocked over. John rights the vase and rearranges the tulips, which he recognizes as Agnes's handiwork. The wind has scattered some papers on the floor. He picks them up and stacks them back on the desk. He does not read what is written on them. He is a gentleman and gentlemen do not snoop.

Or do they? He is just about to leave when he spots a photograph album balanced on top of the leather case that houses Henry's camera. *That album,* he thinks, *undoubtedly contains photographs of Claire.* He knows he has no business opening it, but nevertheless a few moments later, he finds himself seated at the writing desk staring at its glossy green cover. It is still not too late to put the thing back. No one will be the wiser. Yet, no one will be the wiser if he opens it, either; and since he has decided to leave tomorrow, what harm can it do?

I would like to know what Claire looks like when she lives that part of her life I can never share, he thinks. *I would especially like to take another look at the photograph my uncle took of her in front of his mill, because I am in that scene, out of sight, true, and well behind the camera, yet it is the closest I am ever likely to come to her except for those few moments in the garden when I held her hands.*

He runs his index finger down the side of the album, takes a deep breath, and opens it. In the precise center of the first page, an oblong of heavy white photographic paper is anchored by small black paper triangles set at each corner like feathers on a lady's hat. John looks at the image. It's Claire, alright, but much more of her than he expected to see. To his astonishment, the photograph shows her emerging naked from a forest pool.

He turns the page. The next photograph is of Claire dressed as a boy. She is sitting on a low marble pedestal and appears to be taking a thorn out of her foot. Although she wears nothing but a loincloth, her naked chest is as flat as Clayton's. John realizes this is some kind of photographic trick, but nevertheless he finds the absence of her breasts disturbing. He turns more pages and sees her sprawled on a divan wearing a transparent gown that reveals more than it conceals. He sees her mounted on a horse as nude as Lady Godiva; sees her in her bath with her eyes closed, her head thrown back, her breasts floating on the water like two white globes.

John stares at the photos with growing disbelief. He is not

shocked by the sight of Claire's nudity. He is awestruck by her loveliness, aroused, and not the least ashamed of his desire. A man would have to be made of stone not to want her. Yet, what kind of man takes photographs like this of his own wife? This question becomes even more urgent when he comes to the final section of the album and discovers that the last images are of young boys and girls, also naked, posed as fairies or miniature Greek gods and goddesses. This all could be innocent. Artists who use paint or sculpture in stone often depict nudes, so why shouldn't those who use cameras do the same? But John has a bad feeling as he looks at the children.

Although he has no reason to believe they are anything but willing, he is assailed with the disturbing suspicion that both they and Claire have been stripped against their will and held up for inspection. The camera—and more ominously, the man behind it—seems to be spying on them. John has no way to confirm this, but one thing is clear: he has trespassed on the intimacy of Claire and Henry's marriage and uncovered secrets he was never meant to know. If he needed more reasons to leave immediately, these photographs would suffice.

Closing the album, he rises to his feet, but the photographs will not leave him in peace. As he picks up the album to put it back where he found it, one comes loose, flutters to the floor, and lands facedown. John retrieves it and starts to stuff it back in the album without looking at it, but the temptation is too great. Flipping the paper image side up, he again sees Claire emerging from the forest pool: flesh glowing, hair curled in wet tangles, arms lifted, breasts high and lovely, hips circled by ripples, the dark V between her legs sewn with tiny drops of water that glitter like sequins. The sight of her takes his breath away. He has never stolen anything in his life, but now that he is leaving her forever, he cannot bear to part with this photograph. Putting it on the writing desk, he walks across the room and replaces the album on Henry's camera case.

An hour later, Henry and Claire return from church and

immediately go up to their room to exchange their wet shoes for dry ones. As she passes her trunk, Claire plucks her stocking off the lid. Ever since the storm began, she has been fretting about having left the bedroom windows open. She is so relieved to see someone has closed them it never occurs to her to wonder who it was.

Henry, on the other hand, possesses a memory nearly as accurate as a photograph. The first thing he notices as he enters is the green album, which he had left, as is his custom, at right angles to the camera case. Now it lies athwart the case like a drunken sailor. In theory, the maid could have moved it, but nothing else has been dusted this morning; and according to Lavinia, the pale, anemic upstairs maid belongs to some kind of peculiarly Southern form of Protestantism that keeps her occupied from dawn to dusk on Sundays, praying, singing, and participating in a barbaric rite called "speaking in tongues," the nature of which Henry shudders to contemplate.

As Claire settles down at the vanity to brush out her wet hair, Henry walks quietly across the room and opens the album. On the first page, four paper triangles enclose a blank. Henry is not a man to jump to conclusions. Methodically, he pages through the album looking for the lost photograph. By the time he reaches the back cover and concludes that it is not to be found, his face has changed so much that if Claire were to look in the mirror and see it, she probably would cry out in alarm.

Henry knows who stole that photograph. He had a disturbing tête-à-tête with Agnes this morning that ended with him reprimanding his niece for fabricating salacious gossip. Now, it seems, he owes Agnes an apology. He puts the album back on the camera case, lining up the bottom edge with the edge of the case. His face is slightly pale; but his hands are steady. If Claire looks in the mirror now, she will not see murderous jealousy in his face. She will only see a Boston gentleman whose expression is, as usual, unreadable.

Henry walks quietly out of the bedroom and down the front stairs. Greeting Lavinia, who stands in the hallway arranging a vase of forsythia blossoms, he plucks his walking stick from the umbrella stand. Gripping the brass knob, he lifts the stick at a forty-five–degree angle and pauses for a moment to relish the heft of it. "I think I shall go for a stroll," he says.

Lavinia is surprised since it is still pouring rain, but she makes no objection. There is something in Henry's eyes she recognizes, something no one else—not even Claire—would notice. As his older sister, she recalls many things about Henry that perhaps he himself no longer remembers, including that, from the age of two until shortly before his fourth birthday, he sometimes banged his head against walls in a blind rage while their mother wept and pleaded with him to stop. Henry outgrew these fits of temper. In the past twenty-five years, Lavinia has not heard him so much as raise his voice to a servant, and if he still falls into rages, she has not been present to witness them; but she knows better than to cross him when his eyes go blank.

"Enjoy your stroll," she says.

Henry plants the brass tip of the walking stick on the carpet beside his right foot. "I have no doubt that the exercise I am about to take will be most gratifying," he says. He speaks in a reasonable, even pleasant, tone, which is a bad sign. The more angry Henry is, the more polite he becomes. Approaching the umbrella stand again, he selects an umbrella.

"Will you return in time for dinner?" Lavinia asks. "Or shall I tell Bridget to keep a plate warm for you?"

"I shall be back soon," he says. And then he adds as if as an afterthought: "Have you seen John this afternoon?"

"Yes." Lavinia immediately regrets her honesty. She does not want to direct her brother to her son at the moment, but it is too late to claim she has no idea where John is. "He is out."

"Out where, pray tell?"

"I believe he is in the stable tending to his horse. He just informed me that he intends to leave tomorrow. I have asked him why he must depart so suddenly, but his answer has been most unsatisfactory." Lavinia adjusts the forsythia blossoms and gives Henry a nervous, placating smile. "You know how young men are these days—always off on some mysterious business connected with the preparations they are making to defend the state should we be plunged into war. It is rather noble, really, do you not agree, Henry, this attempt of my son not to alarm his poor mother?"

"Most noble indeed," Henry says. "Now if you will excuse me, sister." Tucking his stick under his arm, he opens the umbrella and walks out into the rain. A few moments later, he is standing in front of the open door of the stable watching John, who is at the tack rack inspecting the cinch on a western saddle. Henry does not approve of western saddles, which are large, crude, rocking chair–like contraptions with leather horns. This particular one is tooled with Mexican designs and excessively adorned with silver.

How vulgar, Henry thinks. And then he thinks how perfectly that odious saddle fits the man who owns it. He caresses the knob of the walking stick with the tips of his fingers. He need only take a few steps forward and shatter John's skull to rid himself permanently of this nephew who threatens to make him a laughingstock. Henry has no doubt what people will say if they learn his much younger wife has entwined herself in adulterous embraces with a man her own age. The word "cuckold" is ugly, and the very thought of becoming the object of such a coarse insult is intolerable.

Yet satisfying as it might be to smash John's skull, murder is not a viable alternative. If he had actually caught his nephew and wife in flagrante delicto, that would be another matter; but no jury—particularly no Southern jury—is likely to acquit a husband who creeps up on his rival from behind and murders him on mere hearsay. The *code duello* demands that Henry challenge John to a duel if he wants satisfaction; but only a few days ago, Henry watched his nephew shoot a hole through the center of a silver dollar at a hundred paces. It would be ridiculous and possibly fatal to duel with him.

Could he accuse him of thievery? Henry adjusts the umbrella

so the rain runs off more efficiently and ticks off the pluses and minuses of this approach. First, stealing a photograph is probably only a misdemeanor at worst. Second, in the process of lodging such a complaint, he would be forced to reveal the contents of the green album. Such a display is out of the question, particularly since he has no desire to regain his stolen property. John's touch has forever sullied this radiant vision of Claire's innocence, which Henry took without her knowledge when they were as yet unmarried and which he has treasured above all his other photographs. He never wants to see it again.

John finishes inspecting the cinch, picks up the saddle, and approaches his horse—an odd animal with spotted hindquarters, a small head, and thin legs—which, in Henry's opinion, should be ground into glue instead of being allowed to survive and corrupt the bloodline. Gently, John reaches over the top of the stall and runs his hand down the horse's neck.

The similarity between the bestial desire of this man for Claire and the tenderness with which he touches his horse makes Henry sick with repulsion. He gags as if vomiting out the evil of his nephew's lust, and his mind—that lovely, logical organ that always moves with the cool precision of a mechanical loom—stops suddenly, leaving nothing behind but the rage of a wounded animal. Rushing forward, he raises the walking stick and deals John a blow on the back. "Stay away from my wife!" he cries.

He has struck with all his might, but John does not go over. Instead, to Henry's horror, he catches himself on the edge of the stall, whirls around, grabs the stick, rips it out of Henry's hand, and gives his uncle a hard thwack. Henry drops the umbrella with a yelp and clutches at his chest.

"What the hell are you doing?" John yells.

Henry gasps for breath. The pain is excruciating. This barbarian has no doubt broken one of his ribs, perhaps punctured one of his lungs. He is on the verge of calling for help when he remembers he wants no witnesses.

"Horrible, cursing, vulgar boy!" he cries. "I will not have the two of you making a fool of me!" He is trembling now, partly from rage and partly from fear. John is ten years younger than he is and taller by a good five inches. Henry takes a few judicious steps backward and repeats his demand. "Stay away from my wife!"

"Claire—" John says.

"Be silent! You are not to speak her name. I will not have it defiled by your lips. She has broken two vows by giving you that photograph: one of fidelity and one of obedience—but that is my concern, not yours."

"Listen to me, you damn bullheaded Yankee," John says. "Claire is innocent. She hasn't betrayed you, although I wish to God she had. She doesn't want to have anything to do with me, and she didn't give me that photograph. I took it."

"Then you are a thief as well as a scoundrel."

"Call me anything you like," John says, "but leave her out of this."

"You are lying," Henry says. "You have been entwined with her in adulterous embraces. I thought she was pure, but she has depraved desires. She told me so herself."

John's face darkens. Stepping forward, he slaps the shaft of the walking stick against Henry's throat and pins him against the side of the horse stall.

"If you were any other man," he says, "I would call you out for saying such foul things about her, but you couldn't hit a squirrel if it was doped up, caged, and asleep in the sun. You're a fool, Uncle. Claire is a good and faithful wife to you. Far more faithful than you deserve."

Henry claws at the stick and his lips move in silent curses.

"I think you mean her harm, Uncle. I think you abuse her. That may wash up north, but down south we don't hold with men abusing ladies, so I'm going to stick around and keep an eye on you; and if I see any sign that you've hurt her—if, for example, she comes down to breakfast with a bruise on her chin and claims she's bumped up against a door—I swear by almighty God I'll track you down Apache style and cut off your fine Boston balls. Y'all have anything to say?" John eases up and gives Henry a breath of air.

"Bastard!" Henry says.

John removes the walking stick from Henry's throat, breaks it over one knee, throws the pieces on the ground, and gives Henry a bow. "At your service, sir," he says. "And the next time you come at a man with a pretty stick, don't do it from behind like a damned coward."

Chapter Eight

ALTHOUGH Claire cannot see John, she can feel him sitting behind her two rows back and one seat to the left. For an entire week, ever since their encounter in the garden, she has known exactly where he is without needing to look. When he enters a room, she knows it without lifting her head; when he leaves, she can feel the faint stirring he creates as he passes. Ever since he kissed her hands, this mysterious ability to locate him has come over her gradually like the onset of a fever. Yet unlike a fever, it brings her happiness instead of misery.

This happiness both delights and confuses her. She refuses to think about what it implies and tries not to notice when John comes and goes; but despite this, she always knows. Tonight, to quell the strange tingling sensation that has taken over the top of her spine, she concentrates on the floor of the showboat heaving gently beneath her feet as waves from a passing ferry slap the hull against the side of the wharf. Other than this soft rocking motion, she could be on dry land. The theater, which does not look in the least nautical, is a pretty little jewel box–like affair with racked seats and a few private boxes, which they arrived too late to occupy.

Decorated with gilded carvings, it is illuminated by lamps filled with kerosene, a new fuel distilled from coal, which Henry claims will soon replace whale oil.

Opening her program, she begins to read about the upcoming performance, which is to feature "musical numbers, short skits, amusing comic interludes, living history tableaux, and selected dramatic scenes from Mr. William Shakespeare's *Julius Caesar.*" Although she finds this combination strange, she is eager for the curtain to rise. She could use something to distract her and allow her to forget the world outside the theater for a few hours—and not just because John is sitting behind her. Yesterday brought more disturbing news: the Confederate states are on the verge of declaring Richmond, Virginia, their new capital, which means the country is drawing ever closer to civil war.

As she closes her program, that powerful sense of John's presence returns with renewed force. She glances over at Henry, who sits beside her, upright as a statue, staring fixedly at the painted curtain. Does he suspect anything? she wonders. He has been in a strange mood ever since last Sunday when he slipped on a muddy stone and cracked one of his ribs. When they are alone, he hardly speaks to her. Instead of dressing her in lace and jewels, he has been selecting frocks that are plain, dark, high-necked, and long-sleeved, and he has not attempted to point his camera at her for over a week.

Lavinia suddenly leans over and gives Claire a playful tap with her fan. "How pleasant it is to have the entire family together this evening," she says.

Startled, Claire jumps and her own fan clatters to the floor. "Yes, it is," she agrees. She wonders if she should fish around for the fan and decides not to bother until after the performance. Hoop skirts are not made for bending over in.

"So thoughtful of my boys to come all this way to attend the theater with us," Lavinia continues, "but I have always reared my children with a love of Shakespeare, and *Julius Caesar* is so rarely performed in these parts. Generally, when the showboats dock, we are treated to bowdlerized versions of *Hamlet*. Once I took the boys to see *King Lear* and was dismayed to discover some hack had given it a happy ending. The boys were so irate, they threatened to tar and feather the director." She lowers her voice to a whisper. "Cyrus threw rotten tomatoes at the actors and William hurled a dead cat. Although I deplored their means of protest, I had to agree that this was not the *Lear* we had paid for."

Cyrus and William are Lavinia's two eldest sons, and Claire can easily imagine them pelting actors with rotten tomatoes and dead cats. For weeks the "boys," as Lavinia calls them, have been camped near Roxboro, drilling with a group of Confederate sympathizers. John was scheduled to join them a week ago, but to everyone's surprise—except Claire's—he has not left Lenoir. Yesterday, Cyrus and William appeared unannounced and threatened to take him to Roxboro "hog-tied to his horse if necessary."

When the rest of the family decided to drive down the river to take in the show, the "boys" proclaimed that they wouldn't miss it for anything. At the moment, they are sitting two rows closer to the stage, surrounded by their wives and children. Claire finds it hard to think of them as family men, but from the little she has seen of their domestic life, both are exemplary husbands and fathers. Cyrus is in his late twenties, and William, Claire calculates, must be at least thirty. Stocky and dark, with long mustaches, loud voices, full red lips, and ready smiles, they look nothing like John except around the eyes. They ride like demons, drink like mule skinners, fill every room, dominate every conversation, and are fanatical supporters of the Confederate cause. Henry loathes them, but against her better judgment, Claire likes them, even though she disagrees with virtually every word that comes out of their mouths.

"I think—" Lavinia begins, but Claire never learns what Lavinia thinks, because at that moment the orchestra strikes up "Turkey in the Straw," and the curtain rises. The tingling sensation

at the back of Claire's neck subsides, and for the moment she ac-
complishes her goal of forgetting where John sits. Settling back in
her seat, she makes peace with her stays and prepares to enjoy the
show.

The performance begins with a brisk march that features all
the members of the troupe. Julius Caesar strides across the stage in
a toga accompanied by a large man costumed as a bear who must
belong to another skit. A formidable woman in black bombazine
drags a thin man in a clerical collar along behind her like a pet dog.
A ballerina, exposing a rather shocking expanse of leg, pirouettes
around two small children dressed as a miniature bride and groom.
Then, without warning, something so unexpected happens that
for a moment Claire is frozen to her seat in disbelief.

The music stops. The actors form a line and take several steps
back, and two men walk out on stage. One carries a banjo, the
other a fiddle. The men are dressed identically in gray, stiff-billed
caps, gray wool pants, and short gray wool jackets with rows of
shiny brass buttons down the fronts.

The audience goes wild at the sight of them, clapping, cheering, yelling, and stamping their feet; and Claire realizes that, for
the first time, she is seeing the uniform of the new Confederate
States Army. *Stop!* she wants to cry. *We are not yet at war!* But even if
she yells, no one will hear her over the din; and, with the possible
exception of Henry, who sits beside her unmoving and expression-
less, she appears to be the only person in the audience not longing
for the hostilities to begin.

The soldier with the banjo raises his hand, and the audience
gradually falls silent. "Howdy, folks," he says. "I'm Pat O'Donnell,
impresario of this troupe, and this boy here with the fiddle is my son
Danny. We're cousins to Harry McCarthy, a first-rate Irish come-
dian from Mississippi. Last January when Mississippi's Ordinance
of Secession was signed, the folks down there raised a blue flag over
the State Capitol Building. Cousin Harry was in the crowd, and he
was so inspired by the sight that he wrote a song to commemorate

the occasion. I don't know if he's sung it in public yet. He told me he's fixin' to debut it in Jackson this spring, and to tell the truth, he's not much of a letter writer; but he gave Danny and me the go-ahead to sing it for y'all tonight, so that's what we're gonna do."

O'Donnell nods to his son and the two men lift their instruments and launch into a rousing Irish melody that Claire finds vaguely familiar. As the melody begins to repeat, the orchestra joins in and the entire troupe begins to sing a song that in only a few months will become, with "Dixie," the unofficial anthem of the Confederacy:

> *We are a band of brothers*
> *And native to the soil*
> *Fighting for the property*
> *We gained by honest toil*
> *And when our rights were threatened*
> *The cry rose near and far*
> *Hurrah for the Bonnie Blue Flag*
> *That bears a single star!*
>
> *Hurrah!*
> *Hurrah!*
> *For Southern rights, hurrah!*
> *Hurrah for the Bonnie Blue Flag*
> *That bears a single star.*

Within seconds, the audience learns the words to the chorus and joins in. Lavinia sings lustily, beating out the time with her fan. Cyrus and William rise to their feet, and their wives and children rise to sing with them. Yet as Claire looks around the theater, she can see a number of people who, like herself, are not swept away on a wave of Confederate patriotism: a man in a frock coat sits in one of the private boxes looking on grimly; an entire family gets up and walks out; half a dozen others—undoubtedly Union sympathizers—are clearly not enjoying this display. Kentucky is bitterly divided, and no song, no matter how rousing, is going to bring its citizens together.

More verses follow, but Claire's mind has stopped on the word "property" and refuses to move on. In theory, "property" could mean land, houses, and livestock, but she knows with absolute certainty that in this song it means slaves. As the audience cries out for Southern rights, she finds herself remembering the old man, woman, and little boy she and her father helped to escape. Perhaps states do have a legal right to leave the Union as Jefferson Davis claims; perhaps, as President Lincoln insists, they do not; but no one has the right to own grandfathers with gray hair, small children who eat corn bread dipped in buttermilk, and weary women in faded calico dresses who hope their families will have a better life if they can only make it to Canada without being captured and sent back south in chains.

> *Hurrah!*
> *Hurrah!*
> *For Southern rights, hurrah!*

Rising to her feet, Claire pushes past Lavinia with a mumbled apology and heads for the exit. She cannot stay and hear the song out. She cannot watch the faces of the audience as they sing.

Outside, a low mist rises from the river and swirls around the wharf. Walking to the rail, she stares at the dim outline of the Illinois bank. *I want to go back to Europe,* she thinks, *live in Florence or Paris, not witness the bloodshed.* Instantly, she is ashamed of herself. These are cowardly thoughts. She loves her country. To abandon it in its time of trial is unthinkable.

Back in the theater, the singing is getting steadily louder. The actors have produced blue flags with a single star, plus several of the new Confederate flags, and are waving them to the delight of the audience.

"Hurrah for the Stars and Bars!" yells Cyrus Taylor, and then he gives a peculiar, ear-splitting cry that William and several of the other younger men in the audience take up with gusto. Henry winces and he leans across Claire's empty seat.

"What is the significance of this barbaric ruction?" he asks Lavinia.

"Pardon?" Lavinia says, giving him a blank stare.

"This infernal noise my eldest nephews are making: what does it signify?"

"I have no idea."

A beardless young man leans forward and taps Henry on the shoulder. "That's a Rebel yell, sir," he shouts over the piercing shrieks that again have risen from all corners of the theater. "It's the war cry of the Confederacy. Splendid, ain't it?"

"You need not shout, sir," Henry says. "I am not deaf, although if this screeching goes on much longer, I am like to be." Being in an irritable mood, he might have said more, except at that moment he notices John making his way toward the exit.

Abruptly, Henry stops speaking. He turns to face the stage but sees nothing. For a few seconds, he remains blind and deaf. Gradually, as if receiving an incoming tide, his brain is flooded with jealous rage. Claire has not gone to the ladies' cloakroom as he supposed. She has gone to meet her paramour. He imagines his present and future combined like two superimposed photographic plates: in the present, Claire and John stand on the deck of the boat entwined in an adulterous embrace; in the future, men point at him and women laugh behind his back. *That is Henry Winston,* he hears his tormentors say, *the photographer whose career was ruined when his young wife developed an unnatural fondness for his nephew.*

Rising to his feet, Henry grips the back of the seat in front of him. By now, Lavinia is also standing, singing at the top of her lungs. "Excuse me," he says.

Mildly annoyed to be interrupted, Lavinia draws back so he can pass across her. The touch of her skirts makes his flesh crawl. He moves by her as quickly as possible, reaches the aisle, and walks toward the exit. Deep beneath the surface of his rage, he can feel a terrible heaving, as if the cords that anchor him to sanity are being stretched to their limits.

~~~

"It's a lovely night," John says.

Startled, Claire turns away from the rail and faces him. "Yes," she agrees cautiously, "it is."

"Some hold that a full moon is best," John continues, "but I've always been partial to the sight of the Milky Way." He looks at the sky and river as if searching for the right words to capture their beauty, but when he speaks, it is not of scenery.

"I imagine it is pretty upsetting for y'all to hear the boys in there yelling for Southern rights, but you don't need to worry. There's not one of them who would lay a hand on a lady."

"I am not afraid of Southerners no matter how loudly they cry for war," Claire says. She knows she should not be talking to him without someone else present, yet she can't bring herself to tell him to go away. Her heart speeds up and her breath grows quick and shallow. *This conversation is both unwise and foolish,* she thinks. And then she thinks that she has not felt so alive since the afternoon of Lavinia's party.

"I am glad to hear you don't fear Southerners," John continues, "for I am one, and I'd hate to think I scared you."

"I can take care of myself." It's a reckless comment. She should be telling him to leave instead of saying something intriguing guaranteed to make him stay. "For example, I can ride and shoot as well as most men. After my brother died, Papa taught me to do a lot of things only men do." She points to the far end of the wharf. "You see that barrel over there? I am not saying I could hit it in the dark, but by daylight I could probably put a bullet through the top two staves." She finds it thrilling to tell him this. No one, not even Henry, suspects how well she can shoot a gun or ride a horse or row a boat. There are so many things about herself she has to keep hidden.

John studies the barrel for a moment, and then looks back at Claire. "I'm impressed," he says. "You're an unusual woman, and that's a fact. Still, as I said a few days ago, if you ever need help, just let me know."

This reference to their encounter in the garden is not lost on Claire. Struggling to govern her emotions, she turns away and stares at the river. In the main channel, a flatboat is drifting downstream. As she watches it float by, she is filled with a poignant sense of loss. Again she thinks of the coming war and how it will split the country in half. John will be on one side, she on the other; and this river, already a border between free and slave states, will become a battleground.

"I understand you and your brothers are leaving us tomorrow morning," she says.

"No, Cyrus and William are riding off at first light, but I have decided to linger."

"Your mother will be glad to have you at home a while longer."

"Yes, but you know it's not for Mother that I am staying."

Claire inhales sharply. This time there is no mistaking his meaning. "You must not keep saying such things!" she says. "They only torment me!" She did not mean to speak so bluntly, but once the words are out of her mouth, she finds she has no desire to call them back.

"Do you really wish me to remain silent?" John reaches out, takes her by the shoulders, and turns her around so she faces him. "You're crying," he says. "Why are you crying, Claire?"

"War is coming, and . . ."

"And what? Will you miss me? No, you don't have to answer that question. I can see in your face that you will." Again he takes her hands in his. Stripping off her gloves, he lets them fall to the deck. As he kisses her palms and fingers, Claire's sorrow is replaced with a sweet delight so intense she feels like thanking him.

"Claire," he says softly, "I know I promised to go away, but I can't leave until I know what's in your heart. Are you happy? I see so much loneliness in you, so much pain. You're strong and brave, but even so, sometimes you remind me of a songbird in a cage. I don't think Henry treats you the way he should. I think he's a danger to you. Maybe I'm mistaken. If he's good to you, if you truly love him, tell me, and I'll never trouble you again."

She is too moved to speak. Letting go of her hands, John wipes the tears off her cheeks, bends toward her, takes her face in his hands, and kisses her on the lips. For an instant she resists. Then she gives in and flows with the kiss as if it were a great river sweeping her away from the loneliness and pain of her marriage, from all those nights when she cried and Henry never comforted her, from the burden of keeping secrets from her parents and pretending to be a happy bride.

"John," she murmurs, "I—"

Suddenly she feels a hand grip her arm. With a cry of alarm, she pulls back, turns, and finds herself confronting Henry.

"It is time for us to go home, my dear," Henry says pleasantly. He nods to John. "Good evening, nephew."

"Good evening, Uncle," John says. "If you don't take your hand off Claire in three seconds, I will knock y'all over the rail and we'll see how well you can swim."

Henry smiles and releases Claire's arm. "My, my," he says, "what brought that on?" He turns to Claire. "It seems you have an admirer, my dear, but he is rather fierce, is he not? 'He's a good dog and a fair dog: can there be more said?' That's a line from *The Merry Wives of Windsor*, although I suppose that under the circumstances something from *The Comedy of Errors* would be more appropriate."

Taking Claire's arm again, Henry tucks it into his. "My dear, let's go home. The show is a bore, Brutus keeps forgetting his lines, and it is late." He speaks so pleasantly and matter-of-factly that

Claire doesn't know what to say. Is he angry? He doesn't appear to be. She considers pulling free and telling him that she will not return to Lavinia's with him, but she can hardly desert him for a man she hardly knows on the strength of one kiss.

Reluctantly, she says good night to John and allows Henry to lead her to the waiting carriage. It is an awkward parting: at least awkward for her and John. Henry seems perfectly at ease.

Chapter Nine

THE road that leads from the river to Lenoir is a twisting, rutted channel filled with damp red clay that clings to the wheels of the carriage and muffles the sound of the horses' hooves. It takes Claire and Henry the better part of a cold, uncomfortable hour to return to Lavinia's house, during which time Henry does not utter a word of rebuke. In fact, he does not speak at all.

Claire finds his silence unsettling. Surely he must have seen John kissing her, yet he does not seem upset or even curious. His face is composed; his hands lie quietly in his lap; he is the portrait of a perfect gentleman. As they bump past pastures and unplowed fields, she wonders if he is capable of anger. *Perhaps he is cold all the way through,* she thinks, *or perhaps he only cares about photography.* Maybe he has lost interest in her since she told him she would no longer pose for his camera. Might he divorce her? If he did, what would she do with her life? Would she offer herself to John if she were no longer married to Henry, and if she did, would John want her? She is almost sure he would, but she is too inexperienced to be certain.

Again she feels a rush of desire that warms her from head to toe. *If John makes love to me*, she wonders, *will I enjoy his caresses?* She has heard her mother's friends speaking of the duties of matrimony. Apparently, it is a well-known fact that no decent woman takes pleasure in the act necessary to produce children; but how can anything that promises such sweetness be unpleasant?

Perhaps I am different from other women, she thinks. *I wanted Henry to touch me even after I realized he had no interest in such things, and now I want John.* She closes her eyes and sits lost in thought, trying to sort out her feelings. Gradually, as the carriage rolls toward Lenoir, she forgets that Henry sits beside her. Despite John's warning, she does not fear him, nor does she feel particularly guilty. She begged him to treat her as a wife, and he refused. If he upbraids her when they reach Lavinia's, she will remind him of that.

Her belief that she can handle Henry proves to be a serious miscalculation. When they reach Lavinia's, he hands her out of the carriage, politely bids the maid good evening, sees Claire up to their room, and then, to her horror, he goes quite mad.

He begins by closing the bedroom door and locking it. It is unusual for him to lock a door in his sister's home, but he constantly worries about the theft of his photographic equipment, so such caution is not entirely uncharacteristic. Still, the gesture makes Claire uneasy; and when he transfers the key to his vest pocket instead of leaving it in the keyhole, she becomes uneasier still. Removing her shawl, she throws it on the bed, sits down beside it, and waits. She expects him to say something to her, but still he does not speak. Stirring up the fire, he pours himself a glass of whiskey, which he drinks off in one gulp instead of taking his customary well-measured sips. "I am going to ravish you," he says. "That's what you want, isn't it?"

This is so unexpected that for an instant, Claire cannot believe she has heard him correctly. Then she panics. Leaping to her feet, she dashes toward the door, but before she can reach it, he grabs her arm, spins her around, and throws her up against the wall so hard it knocks the breath out of her.

"How many times have you committed adultery with my nephew?" he demands.

"Never!"

"Liar!" Without warning, he strikes her across the face so hard the stone in his ring cuts her lip. Inhaling a mouthful of air and blood, she screams in surprise. Henry grabs both her arms, pulls her toward him, and throws her back, causing her to hit her head on a framed print. As she fights to break his grip, the print tumbles to the floor, scattering broken wood and glass in all directions. "How many times?" he repeats.

"Let go of me!" she cries. She is frightened, in pain, and furious. She tries to kick him, but the toe of her shoe tangles in her hoop, and she pitches forward into his arms. Grabbing her by the shoulders, he shakes her so hard she bites her tongue.

"Liar! You have had carnal knowledge of my nephew! Do you think I am blind? Am I your fool? Your cuckold? Tell me the truth." Again he strikes her. "Have you lain with him twice? Three times? A dozen?"

"Never! Let go of me, or I swear I will—"

"Will what? Divorce me and marry my nephew? Put that hope aside. You are going to be my wife for the rest of your life and you are going to do exactly what I tell you to do, or else I will chastise you every night until you remember your vow of obedience." Slamming her up against the wall a second time, he shoves his face so close she can smell the whiskey on his breath. His eyes are rolled back in his head; he looks like a man who is having a fit.

"Scream all you want. No one will come between a husband and wife. Have you forgotten I am your husband? Well then, let me refresh your memory." Again he hits her. This time the blow lands on her throat. Claire gags and with a cry of rage, lowers her head, butts him in the chest, and sends him reeling back. Instantly, he is on her again. Doubling up her fists, she begins to punch him in an attempt to keep him at arm's length. As her blows connect with his body, her rational mind dissolves, and she aims for the precise spot where his cracked rib lies. She does not even remember the injury until he gives a bellow of pain.

"You whore!" he cries. "You traitorous little whore!" For an instant, he loses his grip on her, and it seems as if she may be able to escape or at least make him stop hitting her. She is younger than he is and nearly as strong, but her corset cuts off her breath, her skirts make her clumsy, and Henry seems to be possessed by demons.

With another curse, he knocks her legs out from under her and sends her tumbling to the floor. Before she can get up, he throws himself on top of her, seizes her by the shoulders, and slams her against the carpet. Jerking her skirt and hoop over her head, he sits on them, trapping her inside and nearly smothering her. As she fights to escape, he rips off her pantalets with so much force he breaks the drawstring.

He's going to rape me! she thinks. The thought makes her angrier than she has ever been in her life. She thrashes ferociously, claws at the inside of her skirts, and screams at the top of her lungs. When he grabs her legs, she tries to lock them together; but he sticks a boot between them and pries them apart. For a few unbearable seconds she feels his thighs press against hers as he tries to force himself into her; and then, abruptly, he stops. For a moment, she cannot understand why. Then she realizes he has not changed his mind about raping her. He can't.

"Damn you!" he yells. "Damn you for humiliating me, you evil little slut!" Grabbing Claire's shoulders through her skirts, he pounds her against the carpet, and tries a second time; but again he is not sufficiently aroused.

At some point, she loses track of time. Perhaps he writhes fruitlessly on top of her for a minute, perhaps for as long as five. At last, he gives up and rolls off. Beneath the darkness of her skirts, she can hear the sound of him crying. Cautiously, she frees herself and sits up. Her hands are trembling, but except for a cut lip, bruised shins, and some tender spots, she appears not to be seriously injured. The room is in shambles. Chairs have been over-turned, one of the drapes has been ripped off the rod; the coal scuttle has been upset and chunks of coal are scattered from the hearth to the bed. Beside her, Henry lies facedown on the carpet with his trousers around his ankles.

"Forgive me," he sobs.

Claire is so angry, she cannot trust herself to speak. Rising to her feet, she seizes the china pitcher from the commode and pre-pares to smash it over his head. "You son of a bitch!" she yells. "If you ever hit me again, I'll kill you!" It's a fine curse, which, like head butting, she learned from her father's stable hands. She has never heard a woman utter it, but the expression fits Henry so beautifully that it partially satisfies her rage and at the last second, she veers off and instead of splitting open his skull, she slams the pitcher down on the stone hearth and watches with satisfaction as it smashes into a dozen pieces.

"You are pathetic!" she yells. "Pathetic!"

Henry says nothing. He continues to sob. Turning her back on him, Claire waits until the urge to harm him subsides. When she feels calm enough to think coherently, she restores her clothing to some semblance of order, picks her hairpins out of the carpet, and sticks them back into her chignon.

What should she do next? Leave, certainly. She can no longer go on living with Henry. But where should she go? The most obvi-ous choice is her parents' home. This is not an attractive option, but she can see no alternative. She can hardly expect to survive do-ing the few jobs women are allowed to do.

Stepping over Henry, who still has not risen from the floor, and who continues to beg her to forgive him, she walks to the cor-ner where he keeps his photographic equipment. Pausing in front of the green album, she stares at it and imagines herself in the pho-tographs: exposed and vulnerable, raped by Henry's lens if not by his body.

She is tempted to make those secrets public. The citizens of

Boston are not as freethinking as those who dwell in Rome and Paris. Any one of these images would wreck Henry's artistic reputation beyond repair; but in hurting him, she would only injure herself, so instead she carries the album to the fire, throws it in, and stands over it with a poker until the flames have reduced it to ashes.

She is just stirring the coals, when a powerful blow sends her crashing into the mantel. Instinctively, she turns and lashes out with the poker. There is an ugly cracking sound as the poker connects with Henry's head. Reeling back like a bird that has collided with a windowpane, he looks at her in disbelief and tumbles to the floor with a thud that shakes the boards under her feet.

She stands over him, horrified, as the blood from a ragged gash in his forehead seeps into the carpet. *My God, is he dead?* She was only defending herself; she never meant to kill him. Dropping the poker, she bends down and presses her fingers to his neck. He has a pulse. She has only knocked him out. Straightening up, she grabs on to the corner of the mantelpiece to steady herself. For a moment she feels dizzy with relief and then her anger returns. He is a coward, a liar, a would-be rapist. After begging her to forgive him, he hit her when her back was turned, and if she is foolish enough to stay with him, he will hit her again.

She abandons her plan to return to her parents' home. If she does, Henry will follow her and drag her back to Cambridge. He may physically threaten her mother and father or even strike them. She has an aunt in Portsmouth, New Hampshire. Could she take a train to Portsmouth? No. As her husband, Henry has a legal right to board it and force her back into his bed. . . .

Her mind suddenly goes blank. Letting go of the mantel, she takes a few steps toward the door; but halfway there, her legs begin to tremble so violently she is forced to sit on her trunk to keep from falling over. Her head aches and everything in the room seems too bright: the lamp, the flames in the fireplace, the blood-streaked half oval of Henry's face. She remembers her wedding day, the smell of chrysanthemums and candle wax, Henry standing by the altar waiting for her. Marrying him was the worst mistake she ever made.

No sooner has she thought this than she hears a strange sound. Opening her eyes, she looks around the room. For a few seconds all she can hear is the crackling of the fire. Then the sound is repeated: a moan, long and low like wind passing over the rim of a crystal goblet. Henry's eyelids flicker. "Whore," he whispers. "Whore."

John's horse is the swiftest in the county, which means he usually gets home well before the rest of the family. Claire knows this, and when he rides up to the house a half hour later, she is waiting for him on the front lawn with a carpet bag at her feet.

"I thought I'd killed him," she says, "but I didn't. You said you'd help me. You must get me out of here now."

John does not have to ask her whom she thought she had killed. Her torn dress, bruised neck, and cut lip tell him all he needs to know. His first impulse is to go into the house and horsewhip Henry, but instead he says something comforting that in the years to come neither of them can remember. Perhaps he promises to protect her from Henry or perhaps he simply tells her he is willing to take her wherever she wants to go. In any event, she hands him her bag and he throws it over his saddle horn. Reaching down, he offers her his hand. Claire takes it and he pulls her up behind him. Long before Lavinia and the others return, aunt and nephew have disappeared so completely that, the next morning, no one in Lenoir remembers seeing them ride off.

Part Two

MARCH 1861

Three weeks before the start of the Civil War

Chapter Ten

THEY become lovers that first night in the dim coolness of a steamboat cabin, which they occupy under the names Mr. and Mrs. Ezekiel Crane, and as they embrace each other in that narrow bed, the bitter winter of Claire's marriage ends, her heart opens, and she allows herself to feel joy again.

John's face darkens when he sees her bruised face in the lamplight. Gently, he takes the pins out of her hair, lets it fall, buries his face in it, and again breathes in the sweet scent that is uniquely hers. Then, carefully, so as not to hurt her, he kisses her poor, cut lip and caresses her bare arms with a touch so light it feels like silk. Together, they take off her clothing: undoing her buttons and laces, tossing her dress and corset, petticoats, stockings, and pantalets aside. As they lead each other to the bed, Claire is surprised to discover she is not shy with him. She has never seen a naked, aroused man before, but the whole of John is so beautiful and curious that she feels no fear.

Taking her in his arms, he pulls her to him and whispers that she is beautiful and lovely, and that he wants her the way a drowning man wants air; that he has wanted her since he saw her but will do nothing unless she wants it, nothing unless she consents. When she says "yes" with a gasp and a nod, he pulls her even closer, and for the first time she feels the indescribable pleasure of her body touching his and smells that odor of sex and excitement that no perfume can ever reproduce.

"I never dreamed that touching a naked man could feel so wonderful," she whispers. To her surprise, he suddenly stops caressing her. "Did I say something wrong? Are we not supposed to talk?"

"Claire . . ." He hesitates. "Are you . . . could you possibly be . . . did you and Henry never . . . ?"

"No, we never did. Do you mind?"

"Mind? Great god in heaven, no, I don't mind! I'm just astonished that a woman as beautiful and sweet as you could have been married all this time and—" He breaks off in midsentence and draws her to him again. "Come here, darlin', we're going to do this the right way."

For a long time all he does is kiss her. Gradually, he begins to stroke her body—stopping and starting, arousing her bit by bit. Closing her eyes, she relaxes and lets the pleasure build. Finally, when she is ready, he enters her slowly, kissing her and continuing to stroke her. When at last he climaxes, she grits her teeth so as not to cry out, but the pain is over quickly and the pleasure that follows is long and sweet. They make love a second time and a third, and each time her pleasure grows. She discovers she was right when she suspected she would enjoy lovemaking, but she is surprised how intensely she enjoys it.

Afterward, she feels happy and oddly light, as if only the weight of his arms is anchoring her to the bed; but she has promised herself she will live life on her own terms from now on, and she does not intend to let anything turn her into what she became on the day she so foolishly married Henry.

"You must never try to own me," she says. "I am done with being treated like a piece of property. I will never promise to be obedient to you. I will not exchange one master for another."

John smiles, and then, seeing how earnest she is, he grows grave. "Darlin'," he says, "you will always be free to do as you please. I give you my word of honor." Claire believes him. Her suspicions disappear, and that night as they lie in each other's arms, they pour out their hearts in a long conversation so intimate that by the time it is over, Claire is convinced that she has finally found a man who can love her the way she wants to be loved.

John begins by telling her about his father. "Half a dozen times a day, I look at his watch," he says, "and every time I do, I miss him. Sometimes, when there is no one else around, I even talk to him. I tell him I love him and ask him if he's proud of the man I've become. Every once in a while, I have a dream where I learn that it was all a mistake; he isn't dead after all. I see him coming down the driveway whistling an old Welsh harp tune my mother always loved, and I run out to meet him and tell him how glad I am he's back, but I always wake up before I can get to him."

"I have the same kind of dreams about Ned," Claire says. "But I'm luckier than you are. Usually, I get to talk to him. Ned was five years older than I was, and he died when I was eight, so whenever I dream about him, I'm always a child. Sometimes he tosses me up on his shoulders and lets me pretend he's my horse, but mostly he just laughs and tells me not to grieve for him. I wish I could take his advice, but half the time when I dream about him, I wake up in tears. I've never understood why the people we love have to be taken from us. . . ."

She stops speaking and buries her face in John's shoulder. For a long time they lie there quietly, comforting each other. After a while, they fall asleep. Later, when the sky has started to lighten, they wake and share a cup of cold coffee, and Claire tells John about the misery of her marriage and Henry's coldness, about her love for her parents and their love for her, about the joy she feels when she rides bareback, and her plan to learn to play the piano well instead of merely competently. She does not tell him about her longing to have children—it is far too soon to speak about such things—yet once, when he lets his fingers drift slowly across her belly, she wonders if he too is thinking of their future.

They spend most of the next week in their cabin, only venturing out to eat or take brief strolls on the deck. During those seven days, Claire learns every inch of John's body, and for the rest of her life she only has to close her eyes to conjure up the leanness of his hips, the width of his shoulders, the birthmark on his back that looks like a spot of ink, the long scar on his left shin, the odd bend of the little finger on his right hand, the way the color of his eyes shifts from green to brown depending on the light.

Between bouts of lovemaking, they continue talking, and often, to Claire's dismay, they argue. "When we get to New Orleans," he tells her, "I will see you safely aboard a ship headed for your aunt's home in Portsmouth, but then I must return to Kentucky. God knows I don't want to be away from you for even an hour, but the war could start any time; and if Kentucky does not secede, my brothers and classmates will be going to Tennessee with Morgan to enlist in the Confederate army. The C.S.A. has already set up recruiting camps just over the border, and everyone knows Morgan will take his men out of the state the minute something definitive happens."

"Are you telling me you intend to put me on a boat, then go off to risk your life for a system that enslaves human beings?" Claire glares at him, wondering if she has been a fool to trust him. "You've been telling me you love me. What kind of love is this? When you speak this way, I feel as if I hardly know you. I hate slavery, John—hate it with every bone in my body."

"I hate it too, darlin'. Slavery is evil. The institution is abominable and should be abolished. But I have to be realistic. Kentucky is going to remain a slave state whether or not it secedes. At present, it is about to be invaded by Federal troops. Only the Confederacy is preparing to resist them. What should I do? Join the men who have sworn to defend Kentucky, or enlist in the U.S. Army and help the Yankee invaders kill my friends and relatives?"

"Neither. You should refuse to fight, as the Amish do."

"I am not the kind of man who can run from a fight, and I'm not just protecting my home state. I owe Morgan a debt I can never repay. At the Battle of Buena Vista my leg was broken by a Mexican bullet. The surgeons wanted to take it off. Morgan kept them from amputating it and made sure I was tended day and night to keep the green rot from setting in. I was only ten. I had just seen my father shot and killed. If Morgan had not intervened, I'd be dead or a cripple. I'd follow the man to hell and back."

"You talk about Morgan as if he were Christ!"

"I know the man has flaws, but he and his Lexington Rifles are Kentucky's best defense against a Federal invasion."

"Kentucky be damned, John!" And on they go, making love and arguing, until, little by little, Claire begins to prevail. Perhaps it is not entirely fair of her to pit John's love for her against his sense of honor, but one thing is certain: she cannot let him return to Kentucky once they reach New Orleans. So seeing she cannot persuade him that fighting with Morgan's men is wrong, she stops talking about politics and tells him a more intimate truth: that she loves him, does not want to be separated from him, and cannot bear the prospect of losing him.

"In every war ever fought, soldiers are killed by the thousands. You may not be afraid of death, but I am afraid for you. Suppose you die? Your mother would never get over it, nor would your sisters. As for me, I still wake up crying when I dream about Ned. How do you think I'd feel if I got a letter telling me you were dead? I'd mourn you the rest of my life. Is that what you want?"

At last, through love and persistence, she gets her way. One evening, as they stand on the upper deck watching the sun set, John tells her he has decided not to go back. Instead, he says, when they arrive in New Orleans, he will buy passage on a ship bound for South America, and if Claire is willing, she can come with him and they will make a new life together.

Taking a gold chain out of his vest pocket, he offers it to her. "I want to marry you," he says. "If you can get a divorce from Henry, will you be my wife? I'll buy you a proper wedding ring as soon as I have money enough, but meanwhile I want you to have this. It belonged to my father."

Claire accepts the chain and slips it over her head. "I'll marry you if I can," she says, "and if I can't, I'll live with you and not care what people say." She knows Henry is unlikely to give her a divorce no matter how far she runs; but if she is ever free, it would be a fine thing to become John's wife. Tears of joy fill her eyes. She smiles, wipes them away, and they seal their engagement with a kiss. John slips his arm around her waist, and for a long time, they stand side by side at the rail.

Several days pass. As they travel deeper into the South, large plantations begin to appear, interrupted by stretches of forest and swampland. Occasionally, neatly trimmed green lawns run down to private wharves or a weather-beaten cabin totters on stilts in the mud. The air becomes so moist that breathing is like inhaling honey. Although Claire does not find the weather particularly hot, the other female passengers begin to scurry back to their cabins after the midday meal to lie prostrate on their beds.

Appropriating a patch of shade beneath a canopy, she continues to stand at the rail. She is fascinated by the sight of tree limbs swathed in grayish green moss; drowned forests that seem to float on ebony mirrors in the dark backwaters; exotic scents that drift toward her like expensive French perfumes. At times, their boat navigates narrow passages between islands, known as chutes. When this happens, the trees come so close that later she finds her shoulders and hair dusted with pollen.

This passage through the heart of the cotton states would be idyllic except for the sight of the slaves who labor in the fields or load cargo at the wharves. Sometimes as the boat drifts past, Claire hears them singing mournful hymns. Powerless to help them, she stands at the rail and forces herself to witness their misery and remember it.

When their boat docks at Vicksburg, she and John go ashore to stretch their legs. The city, built on a high bluff, has fine brick houses, graceful churches, a grand, pillared courthouse, and a busy port that brings wealth to its inhabitants. In only two years, the people who throng its streets will be living in caves and eating mules, and Vicksburg will have been reduced to rubble by Union Navy batteries, but in the spring of 1861, Claire finds herself wishing she and John could stop here and live quietly in a house with a view of the river.

John buys a copy of the *Daily Citizen*, and they sit down on a park bench to read it. The Territory of Arizona has declared itself out of the Union. Lincoln has decided to hold Fort Sumter and has ordered an expedition to be ready to sail by April 6. The South Carolinians have surrounded Charleston Harbor with heavy cannons and are still preventing any supplies from reaching the Federal troops at the besieged fort. War can only be a few weeks away at most.

Turning to the back page, Claire begins to scan the notices, and bad news turns to worse. Tucked between two advertisements is a request for information from an unnamed gentleman who is "seeking a lady who recently left Lenoir, Kentucky, in the company of a young man not her husband." The "unnamed gentleman," who is offering a three-hundred-dollar reward for any information about her, can be no one but Henry. She reads the notice twice to make sure she has not made a mistake. Then she shows it to John.

They return to the boat immediately and stay in their cabin until it casts off. They appear to have attracted no notice in Vicksburg, but they cannot be sure someone has not read Henry's offer, seen them together, and realized who they are. That night, as she lies in bed unable to fall asleep, Claire is torn between her growing love for John and an impulse to flee to some place where not even he can find her. She even rises and begins to pack her bag, but the thought of never seeing John again causes her such pain that she never finishes; and a few hours later, when the boat pulls up to a dock to unload some casks, she does not have the heart to walk down the gangplank.

As they move closer to the mouth of the river, the reeds in the sugarcane fields are replaced with cattails and the air begins to smell of salt and delta mud. One morning, Claire sees a row of chinaberry trees running across the top of the embankment like a palisade. At the sight of them, something cold slides through her. She shudders, then laughs.

"What's so amusing?" John asks.

"I was just thinking that I do not believe in premonitions."

"And yet you have them?"

"No, you can't have something that doesn't exist. The future is a closed book. I cannot read it. I believe you and I will be happy together, but I cannot see our happiness the way I can see those trees over there. Tell me, what do they look like to you?"

"Like a row of trees," John says, and then he too laughs. "I am afraid you are going to discover that I am a very practical man."

As they near New Orleans, they find themselves floating near the top of the levees that protect the city. Below, the land is so flat, Claire can look down on the roofs of houses. John tells her the captain has said it is customary for steamers bound upriver to leave the wharves together between four and five in the afternoon. They are scheduled to arrive too late to see this spectacle, but their boat makes unusually good time, and they arrive at three thirty, just as the first of the outward-bound boats are preparing to depart. For two or three miles, they pass steamers spouting long columns of black smoke. Bells clang, passengers rush on board, gangplanks are drawn up, and cannons boom as one by one the boats pull away from the docks and form a long procession that moves slowly upriver.

Claire never forgets the parade of departing steamers, but later she discovers she has only a blurred recollection of the city itself. She does not see the slave market, reputedly the largest in the South, nor the poorer sections of the town. All she recalls are brick warehouses, a long expanse of wooden wharves, boats of all sorts, crowds of people trying to leave the city, and planters scrambling to ship their cotton to England before the war begins.

The streets are dusty and crowded, clogged with wagons and carriages of every description. In the French Quarter the buildings are packed closely together, walled with plaster and decorated with wrought-iron balconies. They take a room in a small hotel with windows that open onto a walled garden. The room is twice as expensive as it should be, but they only plan to stay a day or two at most.

After John helps Claire settle in, he leaves to buy their tickets. Claire is amused to discover she misses him as soon as he is out the door. Closing the shutters against the late afternoon glare, she pours herself a glass of water, pulls the pins out of her hair, and shakes it down around her shoulders. Then, deciding that it is still too hot, she pins her hair up again and begins to unpack the few items of clothing they possess. At dusk, John returns with disappointing news. So many people are trying to get out of New Orleans that there are no places to be had on any boat scheduled to sail to South America this week or next.

For the next two days he tries without success to find a captain willing to take them to Europe, Mexico, or any port north of Washington, D.C., but there is nothing available even at triple the usual fare. While he is at the docks, Claire does not leave the hotel. Although she longs to see something of the city, the risk of appearing in public is too great.

By the morning of the third day, she has begun to worry in earnest. South Carolina is warning that if Lincoln resupplies Fort Sumter, it will mean war. New Orleans is the South's largest city and major port. Sooner or later, the Union fleet will try to take it. At the very least, there will be a Federal blockade that will make it impossible to get out. She and John could be trapped here for the duration of the war.

At breakfast they reconsider their options. "Let's go back up the river," Claire suggests. "There must be people who were planning to travel north who have changed their minds. Perhaps spaces are still available. With luck, we could be in Saint Louis before hostilities begin. From there, we could travel west to Colorado."

They talk the situation over for another quarter of an hour and agree to try to book passage upriver. Kissing Claire good-bye, John again goes out to try to buy them tickets. Claire remembers that kiss for a long time. Often, in the years to come, she calls up that moment: empty coffee cups, crusts of toast, lilacs in a blue vase, pale spring sunlight streaming through the jalousies; John's face bent lovingly over hers, the easy way she takes his affection for granted and believes it will continue forever.

After he leaves, she goes back up to their room and splashes cold water on her face and wrists. Already, it is hot. *If New Orleans is like this in April,* she thinks, *what is it like in August?* Retrieving a copy of Balzac's *Eugénie Grandet* from the top of the dresser, she settles down in an armchair to try to puzzle out the French.

John has been gone for several hours when she hears a knock at the door. Expecting the maid with fresh linens, she tosses the novel aside, walks to the door, flings it open, and finds herself face-to-face with Henry.

Chapter Eleven

HE stands in a pool of sunshine like a nightmare cut out of black paper: hair dark as the bottom of a well, eyes black as coal, beard so neatly trimmed it seems to have been clipped one strand at a time. At his elbow stands a short man with sandy hair, a small chin, and unnaturally pale skin. At the sight of them, Claire feels a rush of fear that makes her throat go dry, then anger at being hunted down and cornered by this husband who has never really been a husband to her.

"Go away!" she cries. She tries to slam the door in their faces, but Henry prevents this with an easy motion that reminds her how strong he is. For a moment they wrestle with the frame: she pushing, he pulling.

"My dear Claire," he says, "let me come in. You have nothing to fear from me. I swear it. I have not come to do you harm. I have come to apologize." If he had told her he had come to raise the dead, she could not have been more surprised. She loses her grip on the door, Henry pushes it open, and he and his companion enter with smiles on their faces that make her want to slap them. No, more than slap them. Fight them. If Henry and this man, whoever he is, try to drag her off against her will, she will . . . Taking a few steps backward, she looks around for a weapon, but there is not so much as a poker or a cut-glass perfume bottle in sight.

"How did you find me?" she demands.

"The world is always smaller than we imagine," Henry says. He and the sandy-haired man remove their hats as if paying a formal call. Claire decides if they try to lay hands on her, she will kick, punch, and scream her head off.

"I demand to know how you knew I was here." She points at the stranger. "Who is he? A bounty hunter who is claiming the three-hundred-dollar reward you offered for me as if I were a common criminal? A private detective? The bailiff, perhaps?"

"Goodness no," the stranger says. "I am merely Mr. Winston's attorney."

"Allow me to present Mr. Beech," Henry says. "Mr. Beech, my wife, Mrs. Winston."

"Pleased to make your acquaintance, madam," Beech says.

Claire stares at him grimly. She is relieved to discover he doesn't have handcuffs in his pockets, but he has the damp-handed, cowardly look of a born toady. No doubt he will do whatever Henry orders him to do. Still, he is small. He does not present much of a physical threat.

"A lawyer," she says. "How convenient. Mr. Beech, let me begin our acquaintance by saying that I intend to divorce my husband. I say it plainly so neither you nor Henry can mistake my meaning: I no longer consider myself married to Mr. Winston. I wish to regain my freedom. I do not know what legal steps I need to take to do this, but undoubtedly you do."

"Whatever Beech knows or doesn't know is irrelevant," Henry says. "I cannot allow you to divorce me, Claire. Such a separation would cause me unutterable pain. I love you still. I want to cherish and protect you. None of this is your fault. My nephew is a known seducer of women, something you are far too innocent to understand."

Claire turns on him, her lips pale with anger. "You hypocrite," she cries, "to slander John and then speak of 'cherishing and protecting' me!" She is so furious she can hardly speak. "Mr. Beech, did Mr. Winston tell you what he did to me the night I left him?"

Beech clears his throat and looks at Henry as if seeking permission to speak. "I understand that you and Mr. Winston had a difference of opinion, Mrs. Winston, although I am not privy to the details."

"A difference of opinion!" The look on her face must alarm Henry, for he flinches. "Is that what you told your lawyer it was, Henry? Merely a 'difference of opinion'? How mild that sounds." She turns back to Beech. "For your information, sir, my husband brutally beat me and attempted to ravish me, after which, fearing for my safety, I fled."

Beech clears his throat. "An interesting story, Mrs. Winston. Do you have proof such an attack occurred?"

"Proof! What proof do you need other than my word? I will be happy to testify to this under oath in any court in the land!"

Beech clears his throat again. "Ah," he says.

"What does 'ah' mean, sir?"

"It means, I am afraid, that what you propose to do will not be possible, Mrs. Winston. You see, under the legal doctrine of coverture, a married woman cannot testify in court on her own behalf."

"The legal doctrine of *what?*"

"Coverture. Essentially it states that upon marriage, a woman's identity is assumed—that is, 'covered'—by her husband. Thus she cannot sue or be sued, testify in court, make contracts, or even earn wages in her own right. Legally, once a woman marries, she ceases to exist as an individual. Were you a single lady, Mrs. Winston, this would not be so."

"Are you telling me that I cannot obtain a divorce by testifying that Henry assaulted me unless I am already divorced from him?"

"That, indeed, is the case, Mrs. Winston. I should add that ravishment, or, to speak plainly, rape, cannot legally exist in a conjugal relationship. Should you be able to locate a witness—say, a male servant—who is qualified to testify that Mr. Winston caused you physical harm as you allege, you need to be aware that the court often looks favorably on the chastisement of a wife by her husband. You are bound by your marriage vows to obey Mr. Winston, a biblical injunction that has been incorporated into the common law."

Feeling more and more like a trapped animal, Claire tries to put more space between herself and Henry, but the room is small and there is nowhere to go. "If the law says Henry can rape me and beat me, then the law is wicked. As for God, the God I worship is a God of mercy. Do you think He smiles when men strangle their wives and split their lips? Do you think Christ, who forgave the woman taken in adultery, would have wanted her to go meekly back to a husband who had brutalized her?"

"Pray compose yourself, Mrs. Winston. I fear that you are becoming overly excited. There is no credible evidence that Mr. Winston—"

"Enough," Henry interrupts. "Claire is telling the truth. I did attack her on the night she left, an act I bitterly regret." Beech's eyebrows rise in warning. He appears to be about to speak, but Henry silences him with a gesture and turns to Claire with a look so close to real repentance that she is dumbfounded.

"Claire," he says, "nothing I have ever done has made me more ashamed than the way I treated you that night. I am not the same man who assaulted you. I do not know even now what came over me. Since then, I have wrestled with my conscience and come to understand that I wronged you terribly. Can you find it in your heart to forgive me?"

Despite everything he has done, this apology touches her. She loved Henry once—or at least she thought she did—and although she does not love him now, it is not in her to hate him if he is truly sorry. *Perhaps there is good in Henry after all*, she thinks. *A core of decency buried in him like a small child trapped in a deep well. What a pity it comes out so rarely.*

"If you really regret what you did and are ashamed of the way you treated me, I will try to forgive you," she says. "But it will not be easy."

"I have burned the photographs in the remaining green albums," Henry continues. "Photographs," he quickly adds, "that Mr. Beech knows nothing about. I will never ask you to pose for me again; I swear it on my honor. So you see, you can have everything you want, if only you return to me."

Claire's sympathy dissolves. They are back to where they started: she telling him she wants a divorce; he refusing to hear her. Suddenly she feels very tired and far older than she actually is. "I am glad to hear you have changed for the better," she says, "but this all comes too late. I cannot be your wife any longer. I am in love with your nephew. Again, I speak plainly so there can be no mistake. I love John, so if you truly care about me, let me divorce you."

"I will," Henry says.

For a moment, she cannot believe he has consented. "Mr. Beech," she says, "you are a witness to the fact that my husband has just agreed to let me divorce him."

"I only require one thing of you," Henry says. Something inside Claire freezes. She can tell from the way he utters each word separately and precisely that he is about to impose impossible conditions. Never, not even for an instant, should she have allowed herself to hope he would set her free. She imagines a strongbox with the word *Wife* written on it and Henry locking her inside as if she were a stack of gold coins.

"At present, only Mr. Beech and my sister know you eloped with my nephew," Henry continues. "No one saw you ride off together. Lavinia has told her friends that her son went to Roxboro to join his brothers. You are believed to have returned to Charlesport to visit your parents. In other words, your reputation is spotless, and I intend, for both our sakes, to keep it that way. You must return to Cambridge with me and live as my wife for a full eighteen months. I have my reasons for selecting that particular amount of time, but they need not concern you. Suffice to say that at the end of a little over a year and a half, we will have avoided any hint of scandal. I will then allow you to sue me for divorce. We will part as amicably as possible, and I will see that you are well provided for."

"No," Claire says. "Not on those terms. I cannot. I will not. I tell you frankly, Henry, I would rather live in sin with John for the rest of my life than pretend to be your wife for so much as an hour. I will not go back to Cambridge with you. As for scandal, it does not alarm me. I do not care what they think of me in Massachusetts, or anywhere else, for that matter. John and I are planning to go abroad. He has asked me to marry him, and I have accepted his proposal. I shall send you our address when we are settled. Perhaps in time, you will relent, give me my freedom, make it possible for me to become his wife. If not—"

"My poor Claire," Henry says, "you do not know what you are saying. You have been deceived. My nephew can never marry you. His proposal was not sincere."

This accusation makes Claire so angry that she cannot reply. Turning her back on Henry, she walks to the dresser and stares at him in the mirror. The imperfections in the glass make his face waver as if it were under water. For the first time she wishes he would disappear, drown, die in a train wreck, suffer an attack of apoplexy. She knows it is wicked to wish him dead, but she cannot help herself. He cannot be trusted. He manipulates her, lies to her, raises her hopes, then dashes them. "You do not know John as I do," she says. "He loves me as I love him. I do not doubt the sincerity of his proposal. I think you know very little about love, Henry. I think you have never loved anything except your own reflection."

Mr. Beech clears his throat. "Mr. Winston," he says, "I hate to impose on such an intimate conversation, but I am afraid the time has come to tell Mrs. Winston some unpleasant facts."

"Yes," Henry says, "I am afraid it has, although I devoutly wish we could avoid doing so."

Claire spins around and confronts Beech. "What facts?" she says. "What are the two of you concealing from me?" Instead of replying, Beech opens a leather portfolio and extracts several documents.

"Shall I?" he asks Henry.

"Yes," Henry says. "I suppose there is no longer help for it. Please tell my wife what I had hoped she would never need to know."

Beech removes his pocket handkerchief, takes off his spectacles, and polishes the lenses. Then he puts his spectacles back on and looks at Claire so calmly that he might be about to read her the footnotes in one of the religious tomes that occupy the bookcases in the hotel parlor.

"First, Mrs. Winston," he says, "I need to advise you that if you do not return to Mr. Winston and live as his wife for eighteen months, he will not allow you to divorce him. Since you already know this, perhaps it is superfluous to state it, but I wish there to be no misunderstanding. Am I to take it that you understand the conditions your husband is imposing on this divorce?"

"I understand what Henry wants all too well, Mr. Beech," Claire says, "and I have given him my reply. Pray continue."

Again Beech looks at Henry. Henry nods as if to say *Get on with it.* "Second," Beech says, "you need to know that whether or not Mr. Winston allows you to divorce him, John Taylor cannot legally marry you now or in the foreseeable future. Mr. Taylor's proposal of marriage was, as Mr. Winston noted, insincere. You see, he has a living wife."

"Liar!" Claire cries.

"No," Henry says. "It is true. My nephew has a wife. Surely he told you."

"You are both lying. I do not believe you."

Henry gives Claire a look of pity. "My poor dear, so you did not know? Beech, be so kind as to show Mrs. Winston the marriage certificate."

Beech reaches into his portfolio, draws out a heavy sheet of paper stamped with a gold seal, and hands it to Claire. The document is a copy of a marriage license issued by the Commonwealth of Kentucky certifying that on the twenty-second of February, 1856, one John Garwood Taylor, bachelor, and one Lucretia Ann Conway, spinster, were united in holy matrimony.

Claire reads the certificate and throws it aside. Again, she feels a rush of anger that makes her light-headed. "This is obviously a forgery," she says. "What kind of fool do you take me for? Horse traders used to come to my father's stables all the time with certificates linking their sorry nags to the great Arabian bloodlines. We laughed in their faces and used their forged documents to light our lamps."

"I assure you that this is a valid certificate of marriage, Mrs. Winston," Beech says. "Note, please, that it is a certified copy of the original."

"If it is valid—which I do not for a moment believe—then this Lucretia Conway must be dead. John would never have asked me to marry him if he had a living wife. He would have told me about her. Unlike Henry, he tells me everything. I trust John completely, and I trust Henry not at all. You insult my intelligence, Mr. Beech. What did you expect me to do when you showed me this worthless piece of paper: throw myself on Henry's mercy and go meekly back to Cambridge? If my husband wants a wife without backbone, he should divorce me and marry another woman. Then we will both be happy."

"I know this must come as unwelcome news, Mrs. Winston," Beech says. "Indeed, it must be most painful for you to accept that you have been deceived. I do not wish to distress you further, but you also need to know that John Taylor has a child, born, as you will see when you examine her birth certificate, in April of 1856, two months after her parents wed. The child's name is Marie Louise. At present she is five years old." He offers Claire the birth certificate, but Claire does not take it.

"Spare me your forgeries," she says. "There is no child, or if there ever were, she too must be dead. You say John has abandoned his five-year-old daughter? Preposterous. Why not tell me he has six starving children, is a drunkard, and is wanted for murder? Clearly you are not a man of much imagination."

"My dear Claire," Henry says gently, "you have been betrayed."

Claire takes a step toward him. Holding up his hands, Henry makes a gesture as if to pacify her. She takes another step, and he retreats to the relative safety of the doorway. "Slander John one more time," she says in a voice hardly above a whisper, "and I will walk out of this room. Should you and your attorney attempt to stop me, I will create such an uproar that you will regret ever having come to New Orleans to try to lure me back to Cambridge with these improbable lies. If you want to accuse John of seducing and betraying me, do it to his face instead of sneaking around behind his back. If he is married—which, I repeat, I do not believe for a moment—let him confess this to me in person. Let him say: 'Claire, I have a wife and child.' But John will never say such words and you know it, because he is not married and has no child and—"

"Less than an hour ago," Beech says, "Mr. Taylor himself confirmed that what we are telling you is true."

Ignoring him, Claire advances on Henry with such fury that he backs out of the room entirely. "Lies, lies, and more lies! I will hear no more of this. Go back to Cambridge, and take your trained puppy with you."

"Mr. Beech is only speaking the truth," Henry says. "Before we came here, we spoke to my nephew."

"You followed him? You spied on him?" Claire looks at Henry with contempt. "How like you: nothing ever done openly, always an attack from behind."

Henry continues to stare at her with a pity that is doubly infuriating since it is undoubtedly insincere. "Yes," he says. "Mr. Beech and I waited until my nephew left this hotel, followed him to the docks, and watched him attempt to buy two tickets on any steamboat headed upriver. He had no success, of course. There is no passage to be had. As he started back, we revealed ourselves and confronted him with the fact that we were about to tell you that he had a wife and daughter. Naturally he was furious, but his fury diminished considerably when I offered to send money to his family and secure him passage on a steamer bound for Kentucky if he would agree to return to them. I have connections in New Orleans. Many of the boats that ply the Mississippi bring cotton to my mills.

"At the moment, he is bound for home. He promised to write to you once he reached Lenoir, but I am afraid you cannot depend on him to do so. To give him credit, he was very ashamed to have deceived you."

"Indeed? How touching. I am devastated. I may even faint. John is on his way to Kentucky, is he? You are lying, Henry. Oh, you lie well. You always have. But perhaps you forget I had the pleasure of watching you bend the truth to your own convenience for the better part of half a year.

"You never spoke to John. He is still down at the docks, and you are hoping to persuade me to leave before he comes back. Well, give up that hope. When he left this morning, he told me he would return for luncheon. We can either wait here until he does or we can go to the docks and find him. Personally, I would prefer a trip to the docks. If you have told the truth, you have nothing to lose by coming with me to inquire if a man fitting his description has boarded one of the departing steamships."

"With all due respect, Mrs. Winston," Beech interrupts, "we do not have time to wait. Our train leaves in less than an hour and a half. If we miss it, we may not get out of New Orleans for months. Perhaps you have not heard the latest news. A boat has departed from New York with provisions for Fort Sumter. Tomorrow another supply ship leaves from Virginia. War is upon us. If we are to leave the South, we dare not delay."

Claire opens her mouth to say that this proves beyond any doubt that they are both liars, but Henry speaks before she does. "There is no need to hurry Mrs. Winston, Beech. If we miss one train, I will see that we get on another." He turns to Claire. "I have a carriage waiting outside. I will be happy to drive you to the docks to make inquiries, but I am afraid you will be disappointed, because you see, my dear, we are not lying to you. My nephew has left New Orleans."

Claire has not expected Henry to give in. She is sure he is bluffing but the only way to find out is to take him at his word. "Fine," she says. "Let us go now." She starts for the door and then stops. "I want to leave John a note," she says. "If he returns before we do, I do not want him to worry about me."

"Of course," Henry says. "Beech, be so good as to supply Mrs. Winston with paper and a pencil."

It only takes a few moments for Claire to compose the note. She tells John that Henry has appeared and made ridiculous accusations, which she does not believe. *I have gone down to the docks to find you,* she writes. *Wait here, my darling, until I return.* As she signs it *Love, Claire,* she finds herself hoping that Henry is reading over her shoulder, but when she looks up, he is standing several paces away with his back to her. Propping the note up in front of the dresser mirror where John is sure to notice it, she puts on her bonnet and draws on her gloves.

"Would you like to confess you have lied to me, Henry?" she says. "It would save us all an unnecessary trip." But Henry merely looks at her solemnly and puts on his top hat.

The docks are close enough to walk to, but Claire enjoys the ride. She is sure she will soon see John, so for one last perfect quarter of an hour, she revels in the golden light of New Orleans, the graceful palm trees, the brightly colored flowers, the grand sweep of the river. When they arrive, she insists on getting out of the carriage and searching for John unaccompanied.

"I will not have you or Mr. Beech directing me to someone you have paid to lie," she says. She does not wait for Henry to object that he is innocent of any plan to deceive her. She has heard enough of his lies to last a lifetime.

The cobbles of the landing are covered with mud, driftwood, and other debris. Lifting the hem of her skirt, she begins to thread her way through the crowd toward the wooden wharves where the steamers are anchored. John is nowhere in sight, but that does not discourage her. He is probably aboard one of the boats negotiating with the captain.

When she reaches the steamers, she walks up each gangplank and makes inquiries. "Have you seen a tall man with blond hair and a mustache? His name is John Taylor. He is trying to buy passage for two upriver." She gets blank looks and sometimes looks of pity, but no useful information until she comes to a boat named the *Lula Belle.*

"I saw him an hour or so ago," says the captain. "He tried to buy tickets, and I told him there were none to be had."

Encouraged, Claire moves on to the next steamer, where again she learns John has tried to buy tickets. So it goes, for half a dozen steamers in a row, but although some of the captains remember John, their answers grow increasingly disturbing.

"He was here an hour and a half ago, I reckon," says one.

"Maybe two hours ago," says another.

"Earlier this morning, if I recollect rightly," says a third.

Realizing that she is following John's route backward, Claire returns to the first boat. "Did you see where he went after he left here?" she asks the captain.

"No, ma'am," he says. "Perhaps he boarded one of the steamers that left around ten." This is not what Claire wants to hear. She feels an odd sensation in her chest, as if someone were winding a metal band around her rib cage. For the first time, she begins to fear Henry might be telling the truth.

"Did you actually see him leave on another boat?" she asks.

"No, ma'am," says the captain. "I'm only a-speculatin'."

Claire thanks him and walks back down the gangplank. In the distance she can see Henry and Mr. Beech waiting for her. Only a-speculatin', she thinks. Well, of course the captain did not see John board another boat. John is here somewhere. She stands for a moment looking in both directions, trying to decide where to go next. Perhaps she will catch sight of him if she stays in one place. Perhaps he has returned to the hotel. Perhaps... A hand tugs at her skirt. Looking down, she sees a small, dirty-faced boy dressed in torn knee britches and an oversized brown hat.

"Pardon, miss," says the boy, "but I seen him git on the boat."

"Who?" she asks.

"The gentl'mun y'all wuz askin' fer. The one with the yallar mustache. He got on the *Spirit o' Kay Row* not more'n an hour past. They'd jest drawed up the gangplank and the boat was pullin' away, when a gust o' wind come up and blewed his hat off, and I catched it. The gentl'mun waves and calls out fine as you please, 'Sonny, it's yers.'" The boy removes the hat and offers it to Claire. "She's a right nice hat, miss, but I reckon if y'all wants her, y'all should have her."

Claire takes the hat from him and stares at it, willing it to be the hat of some other man, but there is no mistaking who it belongs to. John's hat has an unusual band made of two pieces of leather twisted together and so does this one. Too sick with surprise and grief to speak, she hands John's hat back to the boy, turns away, and walks aimlessly along the docks, allowing the hem of her skirt to drag in the mud. When she comes to one of the wooden mooring posts, she sits down, covers her face with her hands, and stays frozen in that position, unable to cry for the pain of it all. If John left New Orleans less than an hour ago, then everything Henry has said about him must be true.

How could he not have told me he had a wife and daughter? she thinks. *How could he have asked me to marry him when he was already married? The man I thought I loved never could have done this to me. How can this be?* The shock of his betrayal is so great that for a long time she cannot think beyond it. Finally, she manages to gather her wits. Removing her hands from her face, she looks toward the place where Henry's carriage stands waiting. Slowly, she rises to her feet, picks up the hem of her skirt, and returns the way she came.

"You told the truth," she tells Henry. "John is gone. Let's leave for the train station immediately. I never want to see New Orleans again." Henry, to his credit, does not look triumphant.

"My poor Claire," he says gently, "you have been wickedly betrayed. Perhaps you would like me to have my nephew arrested when he reaches Kentucky. I can easily do so if you wish. When you left Lenoir, you took your jewels with you. Mr. Beech has advised me a strong case could be made that John's motive for persuading you to flee with him was to steal them."

"No," Claire says. "I do not want John arrested. Let him go back to his wife and child." She looks at Henry, who seems to sit far away like a man at the end of a long tunnel. "Let's go back to the hotel and gather up my things. I will return to Cambridge with you and pretend to be your wife for eighteen months, but then you must let me divorce you."

"I will not do so willingly," Henry says, "but if that is what you wish after our time together has elapsed, I will do it."

"Do you promise me this divorce, Henry?"

"I promise, Claire, on my honor as a gentleman. When we reach Cambridge, I will give you a sworn statement to that effect. Mr. Beech can draw it up." Henry gets out of the carriage and helps Claire in. When he sits down beside her and puts his arm around her, she flinches. "I shall always look out for your welfare," he says, and his words fall into her heart one by one as if they were drops of poison.

At the hotel, Claire packs everything into her carpetbag except two dresses she bought when their boat docked in Memphis. She had worn them when she believed John loved her. Now—like New Orleans—she never wants to see them again. Plucking her note off the dresser, she crumples it into a ball, slips the gold chain John gave her over her head, and leaves it where the note had lain. She will not write him a second note. She has nothing to say, and in any event, he is gone.

They set out for the station, but there is one further delay. Just as they are walking out the front gate, Mr. Beech remembers he left his spectacles behind. Claire and Henry wait while he scurries back to retrieve them. When he returns with them safely perched on his nose, they hurry to the station and catch their train with five minutes to spare.

<hr />

The first-class carriage is crowded with families fleeing north before the war begins. For hours, Claire rides in silence, numbly staring out the window. After a while, her grief breaks into a flood of tears that flows down her cheeks and falls on her hands. She cries silently, proudly, with her face turned away from the other passengers. She loved John more than anyone: more than Ned, even more than her mother and father. Now she can never have him back or put the pieces of their love together again. It's as if he has died.

I am leaving everything I love behind, she thinks. The phrase becomes a chorus that repeats itself over and over in time to the clacking of the wheels. Gradually her grief and despair turn to anger. She gave herself to John without reservation, and what did he give her in return? Physical pleasure, a proposal of marriage that had no meaning, a story of his life that left out everything that made it understandable. For a brief period she had thought she could live happily with him on her own terms. *And now,* she thinks, *what does the future hold for me? What will I do once I am divorced from Henry, and how will I ever be able to trust another man enough to love him?*

It is a long, terrible trip with a terrible ending. As they approach New York, their train makes an unexpected stop at a suburban station. On the platform people are running up and down, yelling. In the distance, Claire can hear church bells ringing, firecrackers being set off, cannons booming. Most of the passengers, including Henry and Mr. Beech, get out to see what is going on, but Claire does not need to. She knows with sickening certainty what has happened. A few moments later, a hatless, excited Mr. Beech returns clutching a newspaper.

"Mrs. Winston," he says, "early this morning Confederate forces fired on the Federal post at Fort Sumter!" He places the newspaper in her lap and points to the headline. "We are at war!"

Claire looks at the date: April 12, 1861. *I am leaving everything I love behind,* she thinks. And then she thinks, with all the irrationality of a love she is still powerless to put aside, that John will now be fighting on the Rebel side, and that if he is wounded or falls in battle no one will tell her.

Chapter Twelve

HALF a dozen Boston society matrons clad in white aprons are arranging tin plates, cups, and soup kettles on shelves under Claire's supervision when Claire discovers she has not left everything behind after all. It is a hot day in early June some two months after the Rebels fired on Fort Sumter, and the new kitchen for Union soldiers in transit is so stifling that the women setting it up are all gasping for breath and longing to take off their corsets. They are working slowly since it is easier to stay cool that way. Besides, there is no rush. The war has gotten off to a slow start; despite a few skirmishes, nothing about it seems quite real yet.

Claire, who is standing beside the freshly blackened stove, wipes the sweat off her forehead and points to a line of hooks. "I think we are meant to hang the ladles there," she says, and then without warning, she crumples to the floor.

"It was the strangest thing," she tells her friend Dorothea Wolcott that afternoon as they sit in Dorothea's parlor going over plans to obtain special allotments of sugar and tea for the kitchen. "I woke up with three women fanning me and a lump on my head the size of a quail egg."

"Have you ever fainted before?" Dorothea asks.

"No, never. That's what makes it so odd. One minute I was showing them where to hang the ladles, and the next I was on the floor."

Dorothea sits back in her chair and gives Claire an oddly conspiratorial look. "Are your breasts by any chance tender?" she asks. "Do you feel sick to your stomach in the mornings? Have you missed your monthly courses?"

"Why, yes. What's wrong? Do you think I'm seriously ill?"

Dorothea smiles. "No, my dear," she says, "I think you are with child."

John's child! For an instant, Claire is filled with joy. Then she remembers that John already has a wife and daughter. She will never be able to tell him about this baby. Overcome with the bleak loneliness that has haunted her ever since she left New Orleans, she throws down her pencil and gives Dorothea a look of utter misery.

"Claire, dear, whatever is the matter?" Dorothea asks. "Would you like me to ring for the smelling salts? I thought I was giving you good news, but you look as if you have seen a ghost."

Claire begs her not to mention the possibility that she is pregnant to anyone; and Dorothea, who is alarmed by Claire's reaction, swears she will remain silent, although she cannot resist giving Claire the name of the doctor who attended when she gave birth to her youngest, adding that labor pains are not bad, really, and that in any event, you quickly forget them.

Over the course of the next week, Claire's morning sickness becomes more pronounced, and she becomes increasingly certain that Dorothea was right. At first, the idea that she cannot share this news with John torments her; but as her body continues to change, she turns away from the past and starts to concentrate on the future. She has always wanted to be a mother, and she begins to eagerly anticipate the baby's birth, which, if her calculations are correct, will occur some time after the first of the year.

By late June, her corset strings are stretched taut and the constant loneliness she has felt since she left New Orleans has been re-placed by a sense of being accompanied at all times by a small, loving presence. She knows she cannot keep her condition secret forever. She and Henry do not occupy the same wing of the house and he never sees her undressed, but by mid-September he—and anyone else who takes the trouble to look—will be able to tell she is with child. Sometime well before then, she will have to tell him what is going on, and this will change her life in ways she cannot predict. He may disown this child; she may be forced to go live with her parents; no decent woman, including Dorothea, may ever speak to her again. Or worse yet, Henry may claim the baby as his, refuse to divorce her, and for the child's sake, she will be forced to spend the rest of her life pretending he is the father.

But for the time being, while her condition is still invisible, she chooses to make no decisions. Instead, she revels in the miraculous gift she has been given and holds it to her heart. Often, as she lies in bed waiting to fall asleep, she entertains herself by imagining what her baby will look like and what lullabies she will sing beside its cradle. On summer evenings, when she sits alone in the front parlor with nothing to occupy her because everything is being done by servants, she thinks not of the many duties she has under-taken to help the Federal troops rushing to defend Washington, but of names: Judith and Sarah, Gideon and Christopher; Mabel and William. One thing is certain: if her baby is a boy she will not call him Henry, but there are many other names and each one is a potential gift she can give this child who will be hers to love and care for.

By the beginning of July, her baby has become so real that one afternoon while Henry is off inspecting one of his mills, she walks to a store in Harvard Square and buys two small nightgowns, one trimmed with pink ribbons and one with blue. She takes the baby clothes home in a brown paper parcel and, feeling as if she is hid-ing a Christmas present, she conceals them in a dresser drawer where she can take them out and look at them when she is alone.

Then on the tenth of July, around two in the morning, she wakes up racked by cramps. Concerned, she lights a candle and finds a small spot of blood on the sheets. The cramps quickly subside, but for the rest of the night she lies awake, terrified she may be losing the baby. *Dear God*, she prays, *let me keep this child! I will be a faithful wife to Henry for the rest of my life. Let my baby be born strong and healthy. Please, please, do not take it from me!*

At dawn, she gets up and gets dressed. It is far too early to call for the carriage and go consult the doctor whose name Dorothea gave her, but she has had no more cramps and is not bleeding, so, feeling somewhat reassured, she sits at her dressing table with her hand over her belly talking to the child and telling it to wait. At eight she goes down to breakfast as usual.

"You look haggard," Henry observes as she unfolds her napkin and prepares to pour herself a cup of tea. "I would really rather you did not come downstairs when you are not looking your best."

Resisting an urge to tell him he is being cruel and insensitive, Claire somehow manages to get through the meal. The smell of the food makes her ill and she has never disliked Henry so intensely, but she chokes down a slice of dried toast, drinks two cups of tea, and utters the usual polite, meaningless phrases that have become the staple of their married life together.

"I am going to need the carriage this morning," she says as the servants carry away the plates. Henry is pleased. He disapproves of Claire walking, which he considers beneath a lady of her social position. He does not ask why she needs the carriage—he never shows any interest in how she spends her days.

While the carriage is being readied, Claire starts up the stairs to get her bonnet and gloves. She has just reached the second landing when another wave of cramps sweeps through her, so intense that she has to stuff her kerchief into her mouth to keep from crying out and alerting the servants. When the cramps subside, she manages to finish climbing the stairs. In the privacy of her bedroom, she inspects herself and discovers fresh spots of blood on her pantalets. With a cry of dismay, she pulls them off and puts on one of the cloths she uses when she has her courses. *Please!* she prays as she puts on fresh pantalets. *Please. Not now. Not yet!*

Somehow she makes it back down the stairs, but as she climbs into the carriage, another bout of cramps seizes her. Biting her lips, she waits until it passes, then gives the driver the doctor's address. His name is Dougherty and according to Dorothea, he is the best obstetrician in Boston. If she can get to him in time, maybe he can save her baby.

"Hurry," she urges. The carriage lurches forward and begins to roll over the cobblestones. With every bump, Claire's cramps grow worse. By the time they reach Dr. Dougherty's, they are so bad, she is on the verge of panic.

She does not have an appointment, but the receptionist takes one look at her and immediately ushers her into the doctor's office. Dr. Dougherty is an elderly man with a kind face. When Claire enters, he moves toward her, takes her by the arm, and helps her to a chair.

"My dear madam," he says, bending down so their faces are level, "you are clearly in great distress. Who are you and what is wrong?"

"I am Mrs. . . . Mrs. Musgrove," Claire says between cramps, biting off each word with a gasp, "and I think . . . I think, that I am . . . miscarrying." As soon as she stops speaking, wave after wave of cramps passes through her body. The pain is so bad she can hardly breathe. "Please help me!" she pleads. "Please save my baby!"

"I do not know if I can do anything for you, Mrs. Musgrove, but I will try. It is good you came to me when you did." Dr. Dougherty quickly summons a female assistant, who helps Claire disrobe behind a screen. Sponging the blood off her legs and thighs, the assistant drapes Claire in a clean cotton shift and helps her stretch out on the leather obstetrical couch that occupies a corner of the doctor's office.

As soon as Claire is settled on the couch with her legs slightly elevated and covered by a blanket, Dr. Dougherty reappears and offers her a cup of something that gives off an unpleasant aroma. "This may stop the cramps and bleeding," he says. Claire takes the cup and drains it. The medicine is so bitter it makes her gag, but somehow she manages to keep it down.

The doctor sits beside her on a low stool, takes her hand in his, and feels for her pulse. Except for asking her how she is feeling, he does not speak, for which Claire is grateful. There is nothing more to be said. All they can do now is wait and hope the medicine works. When the cramps come, Claire cries out. When they stop, she prays. Finally the cramping grows so bad and so constant she can no longer think.

Dr. Dougherty keeps holding her hand while his female assistant puts a piece of knotted linen between her teeth and tells Claire to bite down on it. There is a moment of blinding pain when her whole body seems to rise up off the couch in a single agonizing spasm, and she feels a warm rush of blood flowing out of her, taking her baby with it. Then it is over.

For a moment she lies on the doctor's couch, shaking and drained, too weak to utter a sound or even fully understand what has happened. "Have I lost my child?" she whispers.

"Yes, Mrs. Musgrove. I regret to say you have."

Turning her face away from him, Claire begins to cry. Gradually, she begins to feel a great emptiness.

"You are a young, healthy woman," the doctor says gently. "You have not lost a great amount of blood. You will recover quickly, and you can have other children."

"Other children will never replace this one," Claire says. She feels guilty, as if the loss of the baby were her fault. She knows this is not true, yet she cannot stop sobbing.

Worried by the intensity of her grief, the doctor gives her another drink, which is sweet instead of bitter. It must be a painkiller and a stimulant because by the time the female assistant has helped

Claire clean up and put her clothes back on, the after-bleeding has slowed and she is no longer crying. Instead, she has begun to feel as if she were floating a few inches off the ground. Thanking Dr. Dougherty, she pays his fee and writes a false address on the form his receptionist hands her. She is amazed to discover she is strong enough to walk to her carriage.

The drugged, floating sensation lasts until she is back in her own room sitting at her dressing table, studying her reflection in the mirror. Her face is white, her lips are gray, and there is a haunted look in her eyes she has never seen before. She is just picking up the rouge pot to try to put some color back into her cheeks when the terrible truth of the morning hits her again. Tossing the rouge aside, she puts her hands over her face and begins to sob uncontrollably. *I have lost my baby,* she thinks. The word "lost" multiplies in her mind until it deafens her. *Why did you leave me?* she asks the child who was never born. *Why, darling, why?*

For over a month, she is so lost in grief that she can hardly eat or sleep. At last, she begins to face the fact that for her own health and sanity, she must give up mourning for this nameless little spirit she loved so fiercely. It is not easy to let go, but bit by bit she begins to.

One morning when Henry is out, she takes the two small nightgowns out of her dresser drawer and cries over them one last time. Wrapping them up, she sends them to a charity that provides clothing for poor children. Then, because she is too strong to die of grief and because, frankly, she has no alternative, she goes on living as best she can.

Part Three

JUNE 1863

Chapter Thirteen

On a mild morning in the summer of 1863, Claire dons her gloves and bonnet and travels across the Charles River to consult a lawyer and finally get the divorce Henry promised her. The Boston she passes through is not the Boston she came to as a reluctant bride. In the past two years, everything has been transformed by the war. In February of '62, Grant took Fort Donelson, and in April of the same year New Orleans fell to the Federal fleet. Places that had hardly been on the map now haunt her dreams: Shiloh, Fredericksburg, Stones River, Chancellorsville, and Antietam—terrible Antietam, where Dorothea Wolcott's eldest son perished, and where it was said that if the dead, both Union and Rebel, had been stretched out end to end, they would have lined the road for twenty-five miles.

In the midst of so much death and suffering, Claire has finally come to terms with her own grief. Sometimes she still allows herself to imagine what her baby might have looked like, but she no longer grows sick with longing when she sees mothers with young children. Yet what she cannot seem to do, no matter how hard she tries, is to forget John. As she busies herself supervising the transit kitchen and nursing the wounded, who now number in the thousands, Morgan's Raiders rampage through Kentucky and Tennessee: burning bridges, tearing up railroad tracks, attacking supply depots, and spreading panic. Federal troops are hard-pressed to find them, much less stop them.

Although she cannot admit it to anyone, not even Dorothea, every time Claire reads that Morgan's men have eluded their pursuers, she secretly weeps with relief. She wants the Union to win the war, but she is so worried that John will be wounded or killed, she can hardly open the mail for fear of finding a black-bordered funeral card from Lavinia. The truth is, she still loves him. She would rather not, but it seems that once she gives her heart, she cannot take it back. She knows the baby has a lot to do with this, and she often finds herself thinking that once you have carried a man's child in your body, you are bound to him in ways impossible to describe.

But this morning, as she walks past the Boston Common where soldiers in blue uniforms sit on benches saying hurried farewells to wives and sweethearts, she is not thinking about John; she is thinking about Henry and how best to finally rid herself of him. Thus the lawyer, a Mr. Gabriel Hood, whom Dorothea has recommended as a man of honesty, intelligence, and discretion. As Claire mounts the steps to Hood's office, she is not sure she will like him. The only lawyer she has ever been acquainted with is Mr. Beech, who in her opinion is enough to turn any woman in her right mind against the whole profession.

But Hood lives up to Dorothea's praise. Claire trusts him instinctively the moment she lays eyes on him, so for the first quarter of an hour, as she sits in his office describing her situation, she feels optimistic. Here, she thinks, is a man who can help her. Or so she believes until Hood sits back in his chair and begins to ask questions.

"You say your husband promised to allow you to divorce him if you lived with him for eighteen months?"

"Yes. That's correct. But when the eighteen months elapsed, Henry informed me that we would now need to separate, and that I would have to wait a full year before I could claim abandonment and institute divorce proceedings."

"He is presently residing in London?"

"Yes. Henry has developed an interest in Etruscan bronzes, and there is an importer there he frequents."

"Etruscan bronzes are expensive, I presume?"

"Yes, very." Claire shifts uncomfortably in her chair. She can't see where these questions are leading.

"Are you wealthy in your own right, Mrs. Winston?"

"Only in the love of my parents, Mr. Hood. My father was deeply in debt when Henry began to court me."

Hood frowns. "Curious," he says. "Very curious. And now, you say, you have had a letter from your husband's aunt?"

"Yes, a very alarming letter. Aunt Eleanor has written to say Henry will be leaving London by the end of the month. Apparently he has promised to arrive in Cambridge in time to help her celebrate her sixty-fifth birthday. But he can't do that, Mr. Hood! He promised me he would stay away a full year so I could claim abandonment, and he has not been gone six months."

"Have you brought the agreement that you say you and your husband signed in April of 1861?"

"Yes." Claire opens her reticule and takes out a piece of paper. "It is only one paragraph, but there is no room for misinterpretation. In it, Henry promises not to contest my suit of divorce or do anything to impede it." She surrenders the document to Hood and sits back to wait while he reads it. This should not take long, since, as she has said, it is brief, but Hood ponders it for some time before he looks up at her with an expression that makes her breath catch in her throat. Something is terribly wrong; she can see it in his eyes.

"Mrs. Winston," he says, "I fear your husband has misled you in a number of ways, but unfortunately none of them is illegal.

You have no grounds to sue him for divorce. What you are proposing to do is impossible."

"Impossible?" Claire grips the arms of the chair and leans toward Hood. "You must be mistaken. Surely that cannot be true."

"I am afraid it is. The fact that Mr. Winston is returning from London before a year has elapsed is irrelevant. You see, under Massachusetts law, there are two kinds of divorces. The first, divorce *a menso et thoro*, is a legal separation under the terms of which your husband would be obliged to support you in a separate establishment. Neither of you would be free to remarry. The second, which I gather is the sort of divorce you are seeking, is divorce *a vinculo*, which totally severs the marriage tie, returning you to the status of a single woman and permitting either of you to remarry. As I said, you have no grounds for either action."

"What about this?" Claire points at the document on Hood's desk. "Surely it gives me the right to file a petition for divorce a— what was the term?"

"*A vinculo*," says Hood and gives Claire a sympathetic smile. "No, I am afraid it does not. In fact, this agreement between the two of you is worse than useless. In the first place, it is not properly witnessed and notarized, which means it has no legal force. And if it were witnessed and notarized, that would be worse by far, for it would stand in evidence against you should you petition the court for a legal separation."

Hood returns the document to her. "This is evidence of collusion, Mrs. Winston. A petition for divorce is based on the premise that one spouse has injured the other; that one party is guilty, the other innocent. A married couple cannot amicably agree to divorce each other. The law does not allow it. Does your husband have a copy of this? If he does not, I suggest you destroy it at your earliest possible convenience."

Claire is too stunned to reply. Henry must have known his promise was invalid from the moment he offered to put it in writing; or if he did not know, Beech certainly did. Hood waits patiently.

Undoubtedly he is used to his clients being struck dumb when they realize they have been victims of fraud and deception.

"My husband has a copy of our agreement," she says at last, "as does Mr. Beech, his lawyer. Mr. Beech drew up the document. Are you absolutely sure it has no force?"

"None whatsoever."

"Our marriage was never consummated. Perhaps that is grounds for annulment."

"Under such circumstances an annulment is possible," Hood says, "but you would be forced to submit to a court-ordered medical examination to prove you are still a virgin."

"I would not pass the medical examination." Claire looks Hood straight in the eye, daring him to judge her. "As you may have surmised, I am not a virgin; but that is no thanks to my husband. I am not ashamed of this."

"Nor should you be," Hood says.

"But I am angry."

"That is quite understandable, Mrs. Winston."

"Can I sue Henry for fraud?"

"I regret to say that any such suit would not only fail, it would lead to every door in Boston being permanently closed to you. You would become a social pariah."

Claire pauses and tries to gather her wits. What a fool she was to trust Henry! She wonders if there is any chance his ship will sink, taking him down with it. What weapons does she have to fight him? She has no money to buy him off. That leaves only one course of action open to her.

"Shame," she says aloud.

Hood gives her a blank look. "Excuse me, Mrs. Winston?"

"I have committed adultery," she says. "I could threaten to tell everyone that I have had an affair with my husband's nephew. Henry hates scandal. I could compel him to divorce me or become an object of ridicule. In other words, blackmail."

"Again," says Hood, "I am compelled to be the bearer of bad

tidings. Your husband condoned your adultery when he took you back under his roof. Not only do you not have grounds to divorce him, he has no grounds to divorce you unless you two are near-blood relations . . ."

"We are not, thank God. The only thing worse than being Henry's wife would be being his sister."

"Insane?"

"Possibly, but not in the legal sense. Mr. Hood, is there *nothing* I can do? The power the law gives my husband over me is intolerable! Henry has collected me as if I were one of his bronzes, and if I cannot get a divorce, he will keep me on display in his parlor for the rest of my life. My marriage is a prison, and I want out. You have to help me escape!"

"Let me think." Hood stares at a spot just over Claire's left shoulder. At last he speaks. "What I am about to say is delicate in the extreme. I am going to ask you a question that may shock you. If it does, I apologize in advance. I can think of only one ground on which you might be able to successfully petition the court to grant you a divorce. Even it is not certain. Many wives before you have tried and failed. They reaped only scandal and ended up many times more miserable than they were before. Are you a courageous woman, Mrs. Winston?"

"Yes," Claire says. "More to the point, I am determined to stop at nothing to win my freedom."

"Good. For if you choose this route, you will need the courage of a soldier." He pauses. "Do you have—have you ever had—reason to believe your husband has committed unnatural acts?"

Claire puzzles over the meaning of this question and comes up blank. "I am not sure I understand."

Hood sighs. "I was afraid you would not. So few women do. Let me speak more plainly: is your husband a sodomite?"

"I still have no idea what you are asking me."

"You have not even heard the term?"

"No, except in the biblical sense, of course. The Sodomites

were great sinners. I seem to recollect that Jehovah destroyed their city with fire and brimstone."

"And the nature of their sin, Mrs. Winston?"

"I have no idea," Claire says, feeling as foolish as if she were a schoolgirl who had not done her lessons. "It never occurred to me to inquire."

"Very well, I now must be blunt to the point of obscenity but I see no other alternative. Does your husband have intimate relations with men? Does he, in a word, have male concubines?"

"Are you asking me if Henry is committing adultery with men?"

"I am."

"Is that possible, Mr. Hood?"

"I assure you that it is."

"I had no idea such a thing could be done. I have seen dogs, of course. Dogs will . . ." Suddenly she understands. How amazing! Men embracing one another the way they embrace women. She wonders if it is pleasant, if they enjoy it. They must; otherwise they would never take such a risk. She tries to imagine Henry lying naked in bed with a man and fails utterly.

"My husband," she says, "has never shown the slightest interest in having intimate physical relations with anyone, male or female. He regards all such acts, even when sanctified by marriage, as bestial. He told me once that he finds the human body repugnant except when transformed by art."

As Claire says the word "art" another idea occurs to her. "But perhaps I do not know him as well as I thought I did. He has photographed a number of young children nude. Small girls and boys, mostly between the ages of four and eight. Might the courts construe that as evidence of unnatural interests?"

"Frankly, I doubt it," Hood says. "Young children are thought to be so innocent that no shame is attached to seeing them unclothed in works of art. Do you presently have these photographs in your possession?"

"No, I burned some, and Henry burned the rest."

"No matter. As I said, I doubt we could make much of a case for divorce even if we had them. However, in my personal opinion they imply possibilities that are well worth pursuing." He leans forward and looks at Claire with great earnestness. "Mrs. Winston, where is your husband at present?"

"To the best of my knowledge, he is still in London."

"Then you have time to act. When you leave this office, go home and immediately search his effects. Read his letters, pry open his journal if he locks it, pay particular attention to any photographs he may have taken. Look for evidence of an unnatural interest in children or sodomy. You may discover nothing. However, if you are fortunate enough—or perhaps I should say unfortunate enough—to find evidence that your husband has had clandestine physical relations with men or with children of any age, male or female, I will take you on as a client, file a petition for divorce *a vinculo*, and do my best to win you your freedom."

<hr>

There are sixteen rooms in Winston House, not counting the kitchen, attic, woodshed, and cellar, and over the course of the next two days, Claire searches all of them; but in some thirty hours of turning out drawers and burrowing into closets, she does not discover a single photograph, journal entry, or letter that proves Henry has ever done anything more daring than buy dozens of pairs of expensive waistcoats and spend outrageous sums on Etruscan bronzes.

Finally, having run out of alternatives, she enters the bedroom of the late Mrs. Winston. Since his mother's death, Henry has maintained the room exactly as it was on the day she died. Abigail's silver-handled brushes still lie on the walnut dressing table, and her high-necked flannel nightgown hangs over the back of a chair as if Henry expects her to rise from the grave and put it on. Claire has always found this shrine to filial piety unsettling, so it is with reluctance that she begins to rifle through the dead woman's possessions.

. As usual, she finds nothing. Abigail's bureau contains half a
dozen black-bordered handkerchiefs, two weeping veils, and an assortment of unbleached muslin undergarments. Her closet is equally
unpromising: four horsehair petticoats, four black crepe dresses
with plain collars and broad weepers cuffs, and a bombazine
mantle—all stinking of camphor. In addition, Claire comes upon
assorted boots and shoes—all exceptionally ugly—and several
crepe-trimmed bonnets that resemble coal scuttles.

The pièce de résistance of Abigail's widowhood is a broach woven of human hair taken from the head of Henry's late father. This
macabre trophy rests in the dead woman's jewel box on top of a
coil of jet mourning necklaces. When Claire shoves it aside to
make sure the box contains no photographs or letters, she finds
herself wincing. She is not ordinarily superstitious, but she has
never seen a room so devoted to death. Even the portrait of Abigail that hangs above the fireplace depicts a sharp-faced gorgon
in widow's weeds who seems to glare out at the world with vitriolic disapproval as if lamenting the demise of gibbets and witch
burnings.

The only pretty thing in the room is a Florentine writing desk,
and it has been exiled to a dark corner as if serving a prison sentence for frivolity. When Claire opens the drawers, she finds them
empty except for one whose contents she cannot determine since it
is locked. Unless she wishes to break the latch, her search is now at
an end. She has explored the house from top to bottom and found
nothing that will help her win a divorce from Henry.

She contemplates the locked drawer, thinking what a pity it
would be to force it open and possibly destroy the desk beyond repair. Then, descending to the kitchen, she selects a long-bladed
fish-boning knife, and—feeling a bit like Bluebeard's wife—
reenters Abigail's room. For several minutes, she tries without success to force the lock. Finally the catch springs back with a click,

and she is able to open the drawer. Inside she finds a black silk scarf, which gives off a faint scent of tuberoses, and a pair of false teeth, which must have once belonged to Abigail.

Claire is trying to imagine why Henry chose to bury his mother without her teeth, when she notices that the sides of the drawer are only half as long as they should be. Jerking the drawer out of the desk, she puts it aside, then reaches in and fumbles around, and her fingers encounter another handle. Grasping it, she gives a tug and out comes a second drawer.

Eagerly, she examines the contents. There are several bundles of letters and documents bound in twine, more receipts for Etruscan bronzes, and a small leather pouch that contains something heavy. The letters in one of the bundles are in John's handwriting; and they are addressed to her, which must mean Henry intercepted them.

John wrote to her! Did he confess, apologize, say he loved her? What is in these letters that made Henry so eager to keep them from her? The sight of John's handwriting brings back a flood of memories almost too painful to bear. She remembers the bed where they first embraced, the sound of his voice, and the weight of his body. For over two years she has fought off such thoughts as if they were the entire Rebel army, yet sooner or later she has always found him somewhere: in the faces of strangers, in a piece of glass the color of his eyes, in the scent of a rose that reminds her of the roses that grew in the courtyard of their hotel in New Orleans. More than once he has come to her in dreams, filling her with a longing so intense she has awakened feverish with desire.

After she lost the baby, a little at a time, and with great difficulty, she managed to erect barriers between her heart and her head. In the past few months, she has dreamed of him less often. Recently, she even allowed herself to believe her love for him was like a disease that could be cured by rest and time. But now, as she stares at her own name, it seems as if no time at all has passed since she kissed him good-bye and sent him off to the docks to buy them tickets.

She reaches for the letters with trembling hands, but before she can pick them up, she notices something in another bundle that makes her draw back with a sharp intake of breath. The top envelope is bordered in black and the handwriting is familiar. A chill of foreboding spreads through her. Carrying the drawer to a chair near the fireplace, she sits down and stares at the contents. Half a dozen letters from John. A death notice from Lavinia. She can only think of one reason Henry hid them together.

If John is dead, she would rather not know it for as long as possible. Upending the drawer, she dumps everything into her lap, puts aside the letters and receipts, unlaces the drawstrings of the pouch, and turns it upside down. There is a glint of gold, and something heavy falls into the folds of her skirts. Reaching down, she fishes out John's watch. She stares from the watch to the black-bordered envelope and suddenly feels such an overpowering sense of grief she can hardly breathe. When people die, you send their possessions to their relatives.

She stares at the Quarter Eagle gold piece that forms the lid. The Army must have sent John's watch to Lavinia, who sent it to Henry, who ... She is too upset to figure out how the watch got into Abigail's desk. Slipping it back into the leather bag, she puts it aside. She knows she must now read the death notice, but she still cannot bring herself to do so.

Picking up John's letters, she unties the string and arranges them by postmark. There are seven, the first mailed the day she left New Orleans, the last dating from November of last year. Bracing herself for the worst, she opens the first envelope: *My dearest Claire,* John writes, *I returned to our hotel to find you gone and a letter from Henry's lawyer insisting that you have returned to your husband of your own free will. Is this true, my darling? If so, I ...*

Claire stops reading abruptly. John found a note from Mr. Beech in their hotel room? How can that be? Suddenly she remembers that as they were leaving, Beech ran back to get his spectacles.

He must have left John a letter, which means he *knew* John was coming back! Henry must have known too.

She gives a little cry of joy. They lied! John did not abandon her! Eagerly she reads on. There is no mention of a wife or a child in this letter or the next or in the ones that follow. There is only love, concern, hope, and plea after plea for her to write to him and let him know she is well and happy. John does not tell her what he is doing, although presumably he is still fighting with Morgan's Raiders, for the ink becomes pencil and the final envelope is splattered with mud.

I love you, he writes. *I will always love you. You are my life, Claire. I think about you when I wake in the morning and before I go to sleep at night. I dream of you. Could you not send me a line, a word, even if it is to tell me to stop writing to you? If I knew you did not wish to receive my letters, I would fall silent; but not knowing is so difficult. We face death in battle every day, but your silence is like a second death, deeper, more profound. I worry that my uncle is holding you against your will. I worry that he abuses you and that you are helpless to resist him. I hope you are laughing when you read these words. I hope you are thinking "John is a fool to think Henry would hurt me"; for if he has harmed a hair on your head, I swear by almighty God, I will hunt him down and kill him. Please write to me and tell me I am worrying without cause.*

Claire puts John's final letter back in the envelope and stares at the postmark: November 2, 1862. Did John live to see the third of November? If he is dead, then he died believing she did not care enough to write to him. She will never forgive Henry for keeping these letters from her. Never.

She takes up the packet that contains the death notice and attempts to untie the string, but her hands are shaking so hard she cannot get a grip on the knot. Seizing the knife, she severs the twine and three envelopes fall into her lap. She can see now that all three are bordered in black.

Three letters from Lavinia, all on mourning stationery, all mailed on the same date? She stares at the black-bordered envelopes trying to make sense of them. Finally she opens the one on top. Inside is an engraved funeral card announcing the death of

John's oldest brother, William. Quickly, she rips open the remaining envelopes and finds cards announcing the deaths of Cyrus and Clayton. All three died on April 7, 1862.

Shiloh, she thinks. *They died at Shiloh. My God, what unbearable grief Lavinia must have felt when she got the news! Clayton was only twelve. How did she get up the morning after the telegrams arrived? How did she go on living?*

She sits with the funeral cards spread out in her lap, torn between grief for the unspeakable tragedy of William, Cyrus, and Clayton's deaths and the growing hope that John may still be alive. None of the cards bears his name, but he appears not to have written to her for over seven months.

Picking up the card that announces Clayton's death, she thinks again about the unbearable pain of losing a child. She is about to put the card back in its envelope when she sees something she has been too distracted to notice earlier: it is not addressed to "Mr. Henry Winston, 121 Brattle Street"; it is addressed to "Mr. Henry Winston, c/o General Delivery."

⁓

Two hours later, a young widow approaches a clerk at the main branch of the Cambridge Post Office. The lady wears a black crepe dress with wide muslin weepers cuffs, black gloves, a bonnet shaped like a coal scuttle, and a long veil that conceals her features. Sharper eyes might notice the skirt of her dress has been let down some two and a half inches and that everything she has on reeks of camphor, but the clerk is not in the habit of stepping out from behind the counter to inspect the hems of ladies' garments.

"I have come to collect my late husband's mail," the lady says.

"What is the deceased gentleman's name, madam?" asks the clerk.

"Henry Winston." Pulling out a black-bordered handkerchief, the widow dabs at her eyes, revealing for a moment a very pretty face and a mourning broach.

Ten minutes later, Claire is in possession of three more letters,

all addressed to Henry, and all, if the handwriting on the envelopes is any indication, from Lavinia. Retreating to a park
bench, she begins to read:

December 28, 1862

Dear Brother,

   Thank you for sending me the funds to pay for Emma's
tuition at the Female Seminary in Ann Arbor. You know on
which side of this war my sympathies lie, and how I must hate
the prospect of sending my youngest daughter to a Yankee
school in Michigan, but Kentucky is no place for a fourteen-
year-old girl these days, particularly one as pretty as Emma.

   Agnes and I are well and in good spirits, but the cook and
the rest of the household staff decamped for parts unknown
shortly after the outbreak of hostilities. . . .

Claire skims the rest of the letter, looking for news of John,
but finds none. Opening the second envelope, she finds Lavinia
continuing her catalog of disasters:

March 14, 1863

Dear Brother,

   Since I last wrote to you, Lenoir has changed beyond
recognition. Three weeks ago, Union troops burned the
courthouse to the ground, destroying all records. The fire
spread to most of the shops on Main Street. Those that were
not reduced to ashes were looted by either Yankee soldiers or
common thieves pretending to be part of the invading army.
Some of the scoundrels even entered private homes and stole
silver and other valuables at gunpoint, although fortunately
none appeared at my door. . . .

Again Claire searches for news of John and finds nothing. Although Lavinia strongly implies she and Agnes need money, she does not ask Henry outright to send her any. Impatiently, Claire tosses the letter aside and opens the third envelope, only to discover that it contains not, as she has supposed from the address, a letter from Lavinia to Henry, but a letter from Lavinia to her. It was written on the sixth of May.

Dear Claire,

I am asking Henry to pass this letter along to you if he believes it is appropriate to do so; hence I do not know if you will ever read it. I am writing to tell you that John has been wounded. Two days ago, his comrades brought him back to Lenoir so I could nurse him. The truth is, I believe they brought him home to die, for although the wound itself is not serious, it has become infected. He is running a high fever and Dr. Bolander has prepared us for the worst.

In his delirium, John calls for you constantly. He has begged me to bring you to him, which of course I cannot do; but if you can find it in your heart to come to him, I think it might ease his mind. As you know, I have lost three of my beloved sons. John is the only one of my boys who survived Shiloh, and now the shadow of death is on his brow, and he too is preparing to leave his poor mother and sisters.

I do not know what passed between the two of you, but if my son has sinned against you in any way, I beg you to forgive him. I am sure John himself would ask your forgiveness, but last night he took a turn for the worse, and this morning he is incapable of speech. If you are coming, make haste or I fear you will only arrive in time to help us bury him. . . .

Chapter Fourteen

Despite Lavinia's letters, Claire is shocked by the devastation and filth that greet her as she enters Lenoir. The courthouse is a pile of rubble and most of the shops on Main Street are boarded up and abandoned. Almost every woman she sees is wearing mourning, and the men are either elderly or invalids.

"Let me off here, please," she tells the driver who brought her up from the river.

"Yes, ma'am." The driver pulls back on the reins and the mules halt, their lanky bodies wet with sweat. Beneath the wagon, the cobblestones are strewn with manure and a gritty layer of cinders. Claire pays him twenty-five cents, thanks him, and climbs out. As he drives off, flies rise up around her in a pestering cloud. Waving them away, she lifts the hem of Abigail Winston's black crepe dress and begins to walk toward Lavinia's house so rapidly that she draws stares of disapproval.

Even after sunset, heat enfolds everything like a wet rag, and soon she is perspiring. On she goes: to the end of town and up the gravel driveway, past the tall oaks and Lavinia's stone birdbath with its three simpering cupids. In the gathering dusk, the house looks cool and aloof. Somewhere out of sight is the kitchen garden where John first declared his love. Now in this place where it all began, the memory of him seizes her with such intensity that she almost expects him to come walking toward her.

But that is not an illusion that lasts long. The truth is, she is terrified. It has been over six weeks since Lavinia wrote to say he lay near death. If she has come too late, if he has died . . . She cannot bear to finish the thought. In the past few days she has come to understand that living without him will be like living without oxygen. She no longer cares if he has a wife or if loving him is a sin. All she wants, for better or worse, married or unmarried, is years of waking every morning to find him beside her, his children to love, a life spent together in a home of their own.

Approaching the front door, she knocks, waits, and knocks again. At last, she hears the soft shuffle of footsteps. A crack of light appears beneath the shade.

"Who is there?" a familiar voice inquires.

"It's Claire, Lavinia."

"Claire?" The door is thrown open, and Lavinia stands on the threshold. "Claire!" she cries. "How wonderful to see you! We had no idea you were coming."

"I tried to send word before I left Cambridge, but the telegraph lines were down." She searches Lavinia's face anxiously, but it betrays nothing.

"The lines are almost always down," Lavinia says. "If the Union boys don't cut them, our boys do." The expression "our boys" removes any lingering doubts Claire may have as to which side of the war her sister-in-law is on. She wonders if Lavinia will remember she is an abolitionist Yankee and send her packing; but Lavinia puts down the lamp she is holding, kisses her on the cheek, takes her hands, and draws her into the house.

"Come in, my dear," she says with real warmth. "How tired you must be. You are in luck. Agnes and I did the washing today and we have clean sheets—mended, but clean."

Claire steps into the entrance hall. The carpet is more worn than it was two years ago, but the brass umbrella stand still occupies its customary place beside the marble-top table where visitors leave their calling cards. The only major change is a set of three photographs displayed in elaborately carved walnut frames and draped with black ribbons. The photographs depict William and Cyrus in Confederate uniforms, and Clayton, dressed in a little jacket with brass buttons, proudly holding a drum. Three photographs, not four. Claire feels almost sick with relief. But this may mean nothing. Perhaps John never had his portrait taken, or perhaps . . . Suddenly she notices Agnes glaring at her with undisguised hostility.

"Hello, Agnes," she says.

"'Lo," Agnes mumbles with the barest hint of civility. No doubt the girl has been sitting beside John's sickbed, hearing things that would have been better for her not to have heard, but for the moment Claire does not care what Agnes thinks of her. Clutching Lavinia's hands, she draws her closer.

"Is John alive?" she says. "Please tell me at once."

"Alive? My dear, he's completely recovered! You cannot imagine how relieved we were when his fever finally broke. Dr. Bolander had given up on him, but Agnes and I never gave up, did we, Agnes?"

"No, Mama," Agnes says.

"Dear God!" Claire cries. "I have never had better news! Thank you, Lavinia! Thank you!" Lavinia seems bewildered by her enthusiasm, but Claire cannot contain her joy. She feels like a reprieved prisoner. She wants to laugh and cry and demand the details, but most of all she wants to see John. "Where is he? Has he gone out, or is he—?"

"My brother is not here," Agnes says, biting off each word as if it were a piece of wire.

"Where is he then?"

Instead of replying, Agnes looks Claire up and down, and then gives a gasp. "Whom do you wear mourning for?" she exclaims. "Is my uncle dead?"

Claire is tempted to tell her the truth, but she decides this is not the right time to brag about the cleverness of traveling through war-torn Kentucky disguised as the widow of a Union—or when necessary, Confederate—soldier. The photographs suggest a simpler solution.

"Your uncle is alive and well, Agnes. I am wearing mourning for your brothers." She does not like to start her visit with a lie, but she had not anticipated Agnes's question. The fact is she would gladly have put on mourning for Clayton, William, and Cyrus before she left Cambridge if she had thought of it. The sight of the three dead boys staring out at the world with such brave smiles makes her heartsick. But for the grace of God, John's photograph would be hanging there with them.

Agnes's face softens; then her eyes harden again. "If Uncle Henry is alive, why has he not accompanied you?"

"Agnes," Lavinia murmurs. She motions for Agnes to stop interrogating Claire. "Come into the parlor, my dear," she says to Claire. "I will fix you a cup of tea. You must be exhausted. How brave you are to have come all this way unescorted."

"I'd love a cup of tea," Claire says, "but . . ."

"But you have questions," Lavinia says with a bright smile. "Of course you have, and I shall answer them all presently; but first you must let me give you something to eat and drink." Ushering Claire into the parlor, Lavinia tells her to make herself at home and goes off to put the kettle on. Claire sinks into the sofa, removes her gloves, and throws back her veil. Agnes approaches and settles herself on the edge of the loveseat.

"It is quite hot," Agnes says, as if reciting a passage from a book entitled *How to Make Polite Conversation with Unwelcome Guests*.

"Yes," Claire agrees. Where is John? It is obviously useless to ask Agnes. An awkward silence ensues. Claire wiggles her toes in her boots, looks impatiently around the parlor, and notices that Lavinia's silver epergne is no longer on display.

"Mama has given everything to the Cause," Agnes says.

"Ah," Claire says with what she hopes comes across as enthusiasm, "how admirable of her."

Agnes purses her lips. She seems to be on the verge of asking inconvenient questions, but before she can speak, Lavinia reappears bearing a tea tray. Before the war, she would have welcomed an unexpected guest with at least two kinds of cake, but tonight all she has to offer is a plate of dried peaches and a small pitcher of something black and gummy that resembles tar.

"That's sorghum," she explains as she settles the tray on a nearby table. "I would love to give you sugar, but we have not been able to buy any for months." Pouring out three cups of tea, she hands one to Claire and one to Agnes and sits down.

"So, my dear," she says, "tell me all about Boston. What are the ladies wearing this season?"

"I have never had much interest in ladies' fashions," Claire says. Putting down her cup, she leans forward and plunges to the heart of the matter. "I am very relieved to hear that John has recovered from his wounds." Lavinia's smile remains as fixed as the smile on a china figurine. Somewhat disconcerted, Claire continues. "But I am sorry to learn that he is not at home. Where is he?"

"Why should Mama tell you?" Agnes says.

Claire turns to face her. "Because I want to see him, Agnes. Surely that does not surprise you. Surely you know that is why I came to Lenoir."

"You cannot see him," Agnes says.

"Cannot? What do you mean, 'cannot'? I most certainly can."

"My dear Claire," Lavinia says gently, "Agnes speaks the truth. You are welcome to stay with us as long as you wish, but you cannot see John. He is not here, and neither Agnes nor I will tell you where he is. Please do not ask again."

Claire has imagined Lavinia saying many things, but this is not one of them. She feels betrayed, not to mention confused. "I don't understand," she says, fighting to keep the anger and disappointment out of her voice. "You yourself wrote to me, Lavinia. You begged me to come."

Lavinia takes one sip of tea, then another. "Well, yes," she admits, "that is true, my dear, but I realize now that I was wrong to summon you. At the time, I thought John was dying. He was calling for you in a most piteous way. How could I not grant my dear boy his dying wish? I did not suppose Henry would be happy about it, but I thought he would understand even if he did not approve. I even thought he might accompany you. But now John has recovered, and that makes your presence here quite a different thing, as I am sure you can see."

"I do not see. Please, Lavinia. I need to know where John is." Is John living nearby with his wife and child? she wonders. Is this why Lavinia is refusing to tell her his whereabouts? *One thing is certain,* Claire thinks, *I am not going to travel hundreds of miles only to return to Cambridge without speaking to him.* "John wants to see me. He wrote me more than half a dozen letters, all of which Henry intercepted. I only found them a few days ago."

"Even so, I cannot help you commit adultery. God has forbidden it. Love does not justify it. I will pray for you, but I will not be your accomplice."

"Adultery?" Claire leans forward and places her hand on Lavinia's arm. "Dear Lavinia, you mistake the situation. I was Henry's wife in name only. I—"

Lavinia jerks her arm out of Claire's grasp. "Please, Claire! I cannot sit here and listen to you say such things about my brother. Whatever problems you and Henry have are between man and wife. I cannot interfere, nor can I help you deceive him. Those whom God has joined together, let no man put asunder."

Claire represses an urge to slap her. Obviously she has not read that part of the Bible where Christ warns his followers not to judge others. Picking up her cup, she forces herself to take a sip of tea.

"I know John rides with General Morgan's men," she says, thinking that if prizes were being handed out for self-control, she should be getting one. "They should not be hard to locate. Why not spare me the trouble and tell me where Morgan is presently camped?"

"John no longer rides with General Morgan. He fights on another front in another division." Lavinia seizes Claire's hands and gives them an affectionate squeeze. "I am very fond of you, but you must remember you are married to my brother."

"Please, Lavinia . . ."

Lavinia drops Claire's hands, picks up the pot, and gestures toward Claire's cup. "More tea?" she asks brightly. The conversation is clearly at an end.

Claire is tempted to leave at once even if it means sleeping in a field, but common sense and fatigue prevail. She drinks a second cup of tea, eats two dried peaches, makes conversation, accepts the mended sheets, helps the women make up the bed in the guest room, and somehow manages not to say anything to make the situation worse.

The next morning, she wakes to a sky that looks like curdled buttermilk. For a full quarter of an hour, she lies there trying to think of a way to force Lavinia and Agnes to tell her where John is, but nothing comes to mind. Breakfast is served and eaten, and still she cannot think of a plan to make them reveal his whereabouts.

After helping them wash the dishes, she dons a broad-brimmed straw hat, appropriates a pair of work gloves, and flees to the kitchen garden to try to figure out what to do next. The morning is hot and strangely silent. No wagons roll down the road, and if it were not for the smell of charred wood and Lavinia's empty stable, it might be possible to forget there was a war going on.

As she passes the garden bench, she pauses. *Here,* she thinks, *I sat and wept because my marriage was miserable and I thought I was trapped in it forever. Here John kissed my hands and I fell in love with him, although I did not know it at the time.*

Only two years ago she had been so unhappy; then she and John had been briefly happy together; and then everything had fallen apart. A horsefly lands on her arm and prepares to bite. Flicking it away with a sigh of exasperation, she draws on the gloves, walks to a patch of turnips, and begins to tug up burdock and ragweed. Twice she pulls up large bunches of Queen Anne's lace. In the center of each lacy blossom is a small purple velvet star, which, her mother once told her, is the "Queen." It seems a shame to throw something so pretty on the refuse pile, but the weed has a deep, carrotlike root that will crowd out the turnips.

Later she will remember Queen Anne's lace for a more sinister reason. On the day Morgan starts his great raid, it will be growing from southern Kentucky to northern Ohio, and she will never again be able to look at it without seeing its white blossoms splashed with blood. But this morning she has no premonition of what lies ahead of her, and she works methodically down the row, thinking of nothing more dire than the growing heat and a dull ache in her right shoulder. After a while, she goes to the shed and gets a shovel. She has another small task to accomplish; and after she finishes digging and burying what needs to be buried, the weeding goes more swiftly.

She is almost to the end of the last row when Agnes appears. She has left the house without a bonnet, which is not like her. Her face is flushed and her eyes are bright.

Claire straightens up and wipes the sweat off her brow. "Hello," she says.

"Hello," Agnes replies. The girl is no beauty but sometimes when she smiles, her face softens. Unfortunately, she smiles rarely. This morning she is not smiling at all. She has an unfortunate habit of gnawing on loose locks of hair. Now, as she does so, she squints at Claire, as if trying to bring her into focus.

"I imagine next spring if the war continues, I will have to hitch myself to the plow. Mama is not strong enough to turn the soil, and thanks to the Yankees, there is hardly a horse or mule left in the county except for the team that hauls passengers up from the river and the stage that carries people to Paducah."

Claire is astounded. This is, without a doubt, the most friendly series of sentences Agnes has ever directed toward her. "Let us pray the war will soon end," Claire says.

"With a Southern victory," Agnes says and gives Claire a sharp look.

"With a Southern victory," Claire agrees. She smiles at Agnes, but her smile is not returned.

"You do not fool me any more than you fooled Mama," Agnes says. "You are a Yankee sympathizer, and I have never liked you. Nevertheless, I have decided to tell you where John is."

Claire cannot believe her luck. Cautiously, she leans the hoe against the bench and waits for Agnes to continue, afraid if she utters a word, the girl will change her mind.

"Ha!" Agnes gives Claire a triumphant smile. "Took you by surprise, didn't I?"

"Yes," Claire admits, "you did. I thought you disliked me."

"Oh, I do; but John told me to send you to him if you showed up here. I know you are stupidly in love with him, so I do not think you will betray him either on purpose or by accident, although Mama must, for she just gave me another lecture about keeping my mouth shut around you. Mama is famous for her tongue-lashings. You would never know it by looking at her, would you?"

"No," Claire says cautiously, "you wouldn't."

Agnes shrugs. "When I said you were stupidly in love with my brother, I did not mean you were stupid to love him. I love him myself, but you look like a moonstruck calf when you mention his name. I do not understand why loving men turns women's brains to mush. I am an affectionate person, yet my brains are perfectly solid. Is it love that drove you to commit adultery?"

"No," Claire says, "although it was a contributing factor."

"What a pity you will not have time to tell me about your affair from beginning to end." Obviously in no hurry to get to the point, Agnes plucks a rosebud from the bush beside the bench and begins to shred it.

"I should like to know all about adultery. Mama has kept me so ignorant that I know almost nothing about what goes on between men and women. I am an old maid, you see, which means everyone speaks in my presence as if I were a baby. They believe I will never catch a husband, so they treat me as if I were an idiot." She tosses the remains of the rosebud down and plucks another. "Is adultery enjoyable?"

"Yes," Claire says. "Very. And you are still young, Agnes. You may still marry."

"Oh, I doubt that. I am not even sure I want to. Men are so loud and coarse. Also, all the young ones are dying, so I doubt there will be anyone left for me. Even belles like Ophelia Lewis may end up old maids if the war keeps on much longer. I adore children and would like to have half a dozen, but I know that to get babies one must have a husband." She tosses the mutilated rosebud at Claire's feet. "Tell me, do you think you are a sinner?"

"No," Claire says. "Not really."

"Nor do I," Agnes says. "I do not believe in sin or in God. What do you have to say to that?"

"Again, I admit I am surprised."

Pulling down another of her curls, Agnes puts it in her mouth and begins to nibble. "When my brothers died, I gave up on God. What kind of God would kill three boys in the same family? Clayton was only twelve. A God who slaughters twelve-year-old boys is no better than the Devil, in my book. Mama would be scandalized if she knew I had lost my religion. She is very pious. That is why she will never tell you that John is with General Morgan in Alexandria, Tennessee."

"Alexandria!" Claire cries. Realizing she has yelled like a mule skinner, she lowers her voice. "But your mother said he was fighting in another regiment."

"Mama lied. John is still in the Second Kentucky Cavalry, and the Second Kentucky is in Alexandria. My brother worships General Morgan. You could not part him from the general at gunpoint."

Claire represses another shout of triumph. "Thank you, Agnes," she says. "If there is ever any way I can repay you, all you have to do is ask."

Agnes removes the curl from her mouth and spits out a strand of hair. "Do not thank me," she says. "I have no love for you. I just hate God and want my brother to be happy."

"You are very bitter for a young woman," Claire says. "I think you should not give up on God, who always loves us even when we do not love Him."

"You might as well say that hoe loves me or those turnips. If I am bitter, these are bitter times." Agnes shrugs. "Do not try to console me or attempt to drag me back into mealymouthed piety."

She pauses. "You can take the stage to Paducah and catch a train headed for the Tennessee border. I do not know how far you will get. Our boys are always tearing up the tracks to prevent Yankee troop transports. Alexandria is about thirty or forty miles east of Nashville. I imagine you will have to hire a wagon to get there. Tell Mama you are going to Charlesport. If she suspects I've told you John is in Alexandria, she will skin me alive. And by the way, you wasted your time weeding those turnips. John hates them."

Chapter Fifteen

BEFORE the war, Paducah was a quiet river town with dusty streets, wooden sidewalks, and a wharf littered with barrel staves and driftwood. Now it is a Federal garrison teeming with sutlers' wagons, caissons, mule teams, horses, soldiers, gunboats, and armaments of every kind. Here a woman in widow's weeds can move through the streets unnoticed and buy a paper that offers news less than a day old. Sometimes if the wires have not been cut by Rebel raiding parties, she can learn of events that happened only hours ago, and if she is very lucky and there are not too many troop transports, she can even buy a ticket south.

So it is that on a warm Sunday morning, Claire finds herself comfortably ensconced in the only passenger car attached to a train carrying ammunition. On her lap lies a newspaper informing her that the home of Confederate president Jefferson Davis was recently burned by Federal troops, Union gunboats are still bombing Vicksburg, and the Fifty-fourth Massachusetts Volunteer Infantry Regiment—the first all-black regiment in the Union army—has fought a battle somewhere in Georgia. As to Morgan's Raiders, the paper is silent. Are they—and by extension John—still in Alexandria as Agnes claimed, or have they moved on? Claire has no way of knowing, but she is about to travel south as fast as a civilian can these days, and with luck she will find Morgan's camp right where Agnes said it would be.

Her hopes are soon dashed. The engine starts up with a burst of steam; they chug slowly along for the better part of an hour, and then—just when it seems all is going well—the train comes to a halt, throwing Claire forward so hard she bites her lip. Recovering her balance, she pushes aside the curtains, sticks her head out, and sees the engineer and fireman standing beside the tracks staring at something up ahead. Readjusting her veil, she turns to the passenger next to her.

"Do you know why we have stopped?" she asks.

"No, ma'am," he says. "But I can guess: the Rebs must of ripped up the rails again." He takes off his hat, tips it to her, and puts it back on. "Beggin' your pardon," he says, "but I reckon we ain't gonna be goin' nowheres for quite a while."

Claire sees that he is not a man, but a boy of perhaps twelve or thirteen. He is quite tall for his age, but his cheeks are smooth, and he is so bashful he is unable to look at her. Puckering up his lips, he begins to whistle nervously. The tune he chooses is "The Battle Cry of Freedom," which marks him as a boy from a Union family.

"I am glad the engineer saw the gape in the tracks in time to stop," Claire says.

"Yes, ma'am," says the boy. "And good thing the Rebs didn't set the ties on fire, neither, or elst we'd be blown to kingdom come." He tips his hat again. "Not meanin' to alarm you, ma'am, but we are carryin' explosives back on them flatcars."

"I am not afraid," Claire says. Which oddly enough is true. Ever since she left Lenoir, she has experienced an intoxicating sense of freedom and well-being. On the other hand, she cannot help wondering what would be left of her after the explosion. The boy gives her a quick look out of the corner of one eye as if trying to pierce the mystery of her veil.

"Yer husband die?" he asks.

"He is dead to me," Claire says.

The boy does not hear the subtle difference between what he asked and what she replied. Claire knows she should lie and say Henry is dead, but as she draws closer to John, she finds herself becoming superstitious. She and the boy sit in silence for a while. At last he unfolds himself and rises to his feet.

"I reckon I am gonna get off here," he says. "All we are gonna do is back up all the way to Paducah, and I hate being on a backing train. Kind of sickens a fellah."

"Are you sure they will not be able to repair the tracks so we can proceed?" Claire asks.

"No, ma'am. I don't reckon they'll be able to fix the line inside of a couple of days. When the Rebs tear up the ties, they run off with the rails to melt 'em down for bullets."

Claire rises and gathers up her cape and reticule. "I shall also disembark," she says. "I too have no desire to return to Paducah." The boy gives her a surprised look and then informs her she has to stay on the train because there is nowhere for a lady to lodge within five miles. Quite soberly, he warns her she will expose herself to unspeakable dangers if she attempts to spend the night beside the tracks. As he speaks, he becomes increasingly protective, almost as if he were Claire's older brother instead of a tall, gangly child.

"The woods is full of Rebs," he says.

"Then why are you getting off, Mr. . . . ." Claire pauses for the boy to fill in his name, which he does with great pride, perhaps because no one has ever taken him seriously enough to call him "Mister" before.

"Payne," he says, taking off his broad-brimmed hat and twisting it in a nervous circle. "Rubin Brashear Cahaba Payne, ma'am. Please to make yer acquaintance. And you would be . . . ?"

Claire laughs at his eager sincerity and the absurd length of his name. "Mrs. Henry Winston," she says. "How do you do,

Mr. Payne." She offers him her hand. The boy takes it, holds it uncertainly for a moment, then jerks it up and down like a pump handle.

"Well," he says, "don't this beat all. Here I am on my way to bring my pa back and yer on yer way to bring your husband back, and don't the two of us just fall in together like the hand of Destiny done touched us." Despite his bad grammar and thick backwoods accent, the boy has such a cheerful way of speaking that it takes Claire a moment to realize what he has just said.

"Has your father recently passed away?" she asks.

"Yes, ma'am, of the quinsy. He enlisted and would have fought for the Union but he didn't have time before he succumbed. You reckon Ma will still get his pension?"

"Yes," Claire says. "I'm sure of it." She has an urge to console him with a motherly hug. He must be no older than Clayton was when he fell at Shiloh. She thinks sadly of all the boys who are being forced to grow into men before their time.

"I was gonna bring Pa back in style," the boy continues. "I got his coffin stowed back there on a flatcar. Made it myself. Fifth one I done made. Two brothers, two babies, and now Pa. The babies' boxes was small, of course. Hardly took no time at all. Pa's took a whole week, but now, since this train ain't goin' nowheres but back to Paducah, I reckon I'll just go get the wagon and haul Pa back to Ma by mule. It's gonna be real slow, though. Not likely to be much left of him by the time I get him home."

Claire flinches at the thought of a decaying corpse being transported through the summer heat, but the boy does not seem perturbed. Perhaps he is so stunned by grief he cannot imagine what lies before him. He puts his hat back on and quickly removes it again as if remembering that he should wait until he is outside to wear it.

"If you will be excusin' me now, Miz Winston, I got to leave. I got a ways to walk. Home ain't but two miles from here, but I got to find the mules Ma and I hid from the Rebs. Then I got to catch 'em, and that ain't never easy."

"Mr. Payne," Claire says, giving him her sweetest smile, "I wonder if you might consider . . . ?"

The smile works. Four hours later, Claire is sitting beside Rubin Payne on the front seat of a wagon. In the back, sliding back and forth and making a drumming sound, is the coffin, which they have just retrieved from the spot where Rubin unloaded it from the train and dumped it into the bushes to, as he put it: "keep it from becomin' some Reb's campfire."

The mules taking them south are big, long-eared, intelligent animals, so well-fed and hardy that Claire can see why the Paynes hid them. Rubin's mother has sent them off with a pan of corn bread and a lump of cheese. Although Rubin seems slightly shocked by Claire's brazenness, she has pushed aside Abigail's weeping veil and is eating a piece of the corn bread and drinking cider from a stone jar. From time to time, she glances over at Rubin, who drives the mules skillfully but never looks in her direction if he can help it.

"How far is it to the Tennessee border?" she asks.

The boy ducks his head and colors slightly. "Two or three days, more or less. We gotta take the side roads and such. Don't want to run into no Rebs."

"Days!" Claire had no idea they would be on the road so long. Dismayed, she puts down the cider jug and glances over her shoulder at the bouncing coffin. They should have brought blankets, more food, and a lantern. Rubin follows her glance.

"You can sleep in the back of the wagon, ma'am. I reckon the ground's good enough for me."

"Thank you." His kindness touches her. She wishes she could do something for him in return, but so far he has refused her offers of money with a courtly nonchalance that would sit better on a much older man.

"If you will look around by your feet," he continues, "you will find something down there I reckon you might need."

Claire looks down and sees a pile of rags. One is folded as if it contained something. Hoping for more cheese, she opens the package and finds herself staring at a small, pearl-handled pistol.

"That's Ma's," the boy says. "She used to work on the riverboats. Pa was a gambler until he lost all his money; then he was a cook. Ma tole me she got herself that little derringer in case one of the gentlemen passengers got too friendly. It's loaded. Ma said to tell you it's a ladies' insurance policy."

"Thank you." Claire inspects the pistol and tucks it into her waistband. The boy's mother is right. She is riding in a broken-down wagon through a war zone with only a twelve-year-old boy to protect her. Anything could happen.

But nothing does. They drive until dusk. When it gets too dark to see the road, Rubin pulls off under a tree, unhitches the mules, curls up on the ground, and falls asleep so fast he is snoring before Claire has managed to make herself a nest between the coffin and the side of the wagon. In the morning, she gets up, dirty and stiff, to see him already leading the mules back from a nearby stream.

"Found some berries," he says. He offers Claire his hat, filled to the brim with blackberries the size of marbles. They sit on the seat of the wagon, sharing them as delicately as if they were at a tea party in Cambridge. After they finish, Rubin hitches up the mules and once again they jolt down the road, which by this time is hardly more than a track.

He still does not talk much, either from shyness or because he is not a boy to waste words, so for the next few hours, as the temperature climbs and the sun beats mercilessly down on them, Claire is left to sit sweating in her black dress in a silence punctuated only by the creaking of the wagon and the clopping of the mules' hooves.

After a while, she falls into a state halfway between sleep and waking. The wagon moans like a windmill; the mules plod along kicking up clouds of dust; Queen Anne's lace is blooming in the ditches mingled with some tall, purple flowers she does not recognize; and the day is so windless she can watch bees hovering above patches of clover. Up ahead there is a shallow stream that they must ford, and just before the stream, a stand of dense brush and a grove of cottonwoods.

They seem to approach the stream very slowly, as if, Claire later thinks, she were looking at it through the wrong end of a spyglass. The sun is so bright it blinds her. She shuts her eyes and wonders when this interminable trip will be over. All at once there is a sharp crack and something whizzes past her left ear. She screams and opens her eyes just in time to see Rubin fall into the back of the wagon. His body hits the coffin so hard the impact flips him out onto the ground. Suddenly there is blood everywhere: on his hair; on the back of his shirt; running down one thin, white, boyish arm. For an instant Claire does not understand what has happened. Then she realizes he has been shot. Horrified, she grabs for the reins, jerks the mules to a halt, jumps out, runs back to him, and tries to stop the bleeding by pressing her fingers to his neck.

"Don't die, Rubin!" she pleads. "Don't die, sweetheart! You're too young! You're just a little boy!" Ripping off her veil, she tries to fold it into a compress, but instead drops it. As she bends over to pick it up, rough hands seize her by the shoulders, pull her to her feet, and spin her around, and she finds herself looking into the face of a stranger who is smiling so broadly she might have just told him a joke, except there is a dying boy lying on the ground behind them.

"What a pretty little widow you are," he says. His eyes are small, green, and closely set; he is missing one front tooth; his breath smells of chewing tobacco; and he wears the uniform of a Confederate corporal.

The corporal grins, tears off her bonnet, and throws it on the ground. Then before she even fully understands what he is doing, he stuffs his bandanna into her mouth and pins her arms to her sides. Claire struggles to wrench loose, but fighting him is nothing like fighting Henry. The man is a trained soldier and his grip is so tight he is easily able to immobilize her.

"You are gonna be one tasty little piece," he says. "I'm gonna fuck you, sweetheart, until you scream for more; and then I'm gonna kill you and take your mules, 'cause mule stealin' is my job and killin' Yankees is my pleasure, even randy little Yankee widows."

Claire thrashes about in helpless horror. She tries to scream, but the gag prevents her. Dropping her arms, the corporal grabs her shoulders again and begins to wrestle her back down to the ground.

"You're a live one, ain't you?" he cries. "Come on, sweetheart, fight me some more. I like it!" He pulls the bandanna out of her mouth. "What's your name, little widow?"

"Claire Winston!" Claire yells; and, jerking the derringer out of her waistband, she slaps the barrel against his neck and pulls the trigger.

Part Four

JULY 1863

Claire

The campfires of Morgan's men are burning down to a dull glow, draping a necklace of garnets across the blackness of the valley, and I have arrived at my goal at last. How I got here, wrapped in the dead corporal's cape with General Morgan's blessing and an ancient muzzle-loading rifle for company, is a story of stealth, poor planning, outright lying, and incredible luck, combined, I suppose, with courage—although I hate to give my reaction to having a rifle barrel jammed in my back such an exalted name. Still, after what I have been through tonight, I can never again doubt that I am, at the very least, a stubborn woman.

I am writing this in a small leather-bound journal I found in the pocket of the dead corporal's jacket. The first page bore an inscription, but I tore it out without reading it because I do not want to know his name. The rest of the pages are blank. I intend to fill them as time and circumstances permit.

Where should I begin? After I killed him, I rode for almost two weeks, making slow progress since I was often forced to take detours to avoid Union and Confederate patrols. I hid in caves, slept under bushes, starved, was pelted by rain and burned by the sun, and through it all I longed for John's touch the way a person dying of thirst longs for a glass of water.

From the start, I decided it was too dangerous to travel in the dead corporal's uniform, so I packed it away in a saddlebag, cut off my hair, ripped my chemise into strips, and bound my breasts to my chest. Then to the corporal's stolen horse I added some stolen boy's clothing that had been draped over a fence to dry. Disguised as a civilian, I was able to move freely and even call at farmhouses without exciting suspicion. Early on, I heard rumors that Morgan was proposing to invade Kentucky again, so I abandoned my original plan of riding to Alexandria and set out to try to meet up with him. I had no way to know what his route would be, but I calculated he would probably move in more or less the same direction he took last Christmas. Luck was with me. Last Thursday I stopped to beg a meal from a farmer's wife who told me Morgan's army had crossed the river that divides Tennessee from Kentucky.

"The Rebs came out of the waters of the Cumberland nekkid as God made 'em and yellin' like banshees," she said. "Our boys was so taken aback, they threw down their guns and skedaddled like rabbits."

"Were any of the Rebels killed?" I asked.

"Reckon so," she said, "but we ain't got the lists yet."

I rode on, caught between fear and joy. John might have been killed or wounded during the crossing, but if he had survived, I was drawing ever closer to him.

The roads were clogged with refugees fleeing from the invasion. I questioned them whenever I could, and this afternoon an old man told me Morgan had fought another battle and been soundly defeated. It seemed that during last winter's raid he burned the Green River bridge at Tebb's Bend. The bridge was rebuilt. This morning he tried to destroy it a second time and failed.

The old man said the fighting was fierce. Apparently the commanding Union officer, a colonel from Michigan named Moore, dug a trench on top of a steep bluff, protected it with felled trees and sharpened sticks, and stationed riflemen in it. Morgan's artillery shelled this fortification repeatedly, but the Union boys held them off, although they were outnumbered at least twenty to one.

"Bravest fellas you ever see'd," the old man said, "and stubborn as mules. When the Great Horse Thief—that's what folks in these parts call that devil Morgan—when he demanded that Colonel Moore surrender, Moore fired back a polite note sayin' that since this was the Fourth of July, it was a damned bad day for a surrender. Then his sharpshooters picked off Morgan's gunners like they was squirrels."

"How many Rebels were killed?" I asked.

"I hear'd about forty," the old man said, "and more yet wounded. Moore only lost six, but that's six brave boys in blue who will never go home to their mothers, wives, and sweethearts. And I hear'd another thing too, though you ain't gonna believe it: one of the wounded Union boys turned out to be a girl by the name of Lizzie Compton. A girl soldier? Can you imagine that?"

The news that forty of Morgan's men had died at Tebb's Bend made me so sick with worry that I had no time to think about Lizzie Compton. Later, I wondered if she too had loved some soldier and found no other way to be with him.

This evening, after questioning more refugees, I finally located Morgan's camp. The Boston newspapers had described the Raiders as a band of mounted guerillas, so I thought Morgan only commanded a few hundred men. Imagine my astonishment when I saw their campfires strung out along the base of the hills and realized that this "Thunderbolt of the Confederacy" had marshaled an invasion force of thousands.

I imagined John sitting by one of those fires, and I wondered if he could sense my presence. I was so close I could have walked down and asked for him by name, but something stopped me. I was suddenly uncertain if it would be wise to make myself known. He might have changed his mind since he wrote me those letters. We had only had a month together, and we had been separated for more than two years. During that time he had been wounded and nearly died. That sort of experience changes a man. He could have reconciled with his wife and decided to forget me. Or worse yet . . .

For a split second I had a vision of his body lying in a trampled cornfield. The scene was so real, I could smell the freshly turned earth, but then I remembered I did not believe in premonitions. Taking the dead corporal's uniform out of my saddlebag, I put it on. It did not fit, but I doubt there is a noncommissioned officer in the Confederate army who wears a coat of the correct size. The officers of higher rank have their uniforms made by the same tailors who make their suits in civilian life, but since I was disguising myself as a lowly corporal, sleeves that were too long were quite in style. As for the corporal's boots, I had not taken them off since I first put them on. During my rambles, I had discovered they were much more comfortable than women's shoes, and if I kept them stuffed with rags, they fit nicely. He had little feet.

For days I had managed to impersonate a boy with great success, so tonight as

I stood watching Morgan's campfires, I calculated that given my height, leanness, and the havoc the sun had wreaked with my complexion, I could easily pass for an unbearded Confederate soldier, albeit one young for his rank. Although I had lost both the derringer and the corporal's pistol while attempting to ford a stream, I had come up with an ingenious plan for getting past the sentries so I could roam quietly among the campfires until I found John; but I might as well have tramped down the hill singing "The Bonnie Blue Flag," because in less than five minutes, I was captured by a tall, raw-boned fellow who could not have been more than seventeen.

He must have been walking on the balls of his feet like a panther, for I did not hear him until he poked the barrel of his rifle in my back and suggested in a slow, easy drawl that I halt and identify myself unless I wanted to be "splattered from Lebanon to kingdom come." Lebanon was the town the Raiders were headed for next, so I imagine he thought this was a fine joke, although I was in no mood to laugh.

Being captured so quickly taught me never to underestimate Kentuckians. They are the best trackers, the best hunters, and the best sharpshooters east of the Mississippi. If the Confederate government in Richmond had been able to supply them with food, shoes, horses, and ammunition, they would have been unstoppable; but they were living on bacon grease and cornmeal, and getting their bullets off dead Federal soldiers. They ran mostly on raw courage, and they did it day after day with few complaints.

I raised my hands over my head and informed the sentry that I was a Confederate corporal who had escaped from the Union prison compound in Indianapolis. Fortunately, the time I spent in my father's stables taught me a number of words ladies rarely hear, so I was able to revile the conditions at the camp with a string of convincingly masculine curses. On hearing me describe the filthy, vermin-infested, pestilence-ridden hellhole that the Yankees had confined me to, the sentry lowered his rifle and started nodding in sympathy and cursing along with me.

All of this was quite unfair, since my mother had told me Camp Morton was one of the best Union prison camps, with excellent sanitation and a very low death rate, but the sentry did not know this, and by the end of my diatribe, he was slapping me on the back and telling me that, by God, I had come to the right place to get even. I cannot remember all the lies I told him except I believe I said my comrades and I subsisted primarily on rats. I managed to speak in a very convincing Southern accent. Charlesport is separated from Kentucky only by the Ohio River, and I've always had a good ear.

Since I was unarmed and obviously a danger to no one, he led me down to the camp where I spent an anxious quarter of an hour being interrogated by a sharp-eyed lieutenant who did not appear to believe my story. The most difficult question he asked me was what unit I had been attached to before the Yankees took me prisoner. I had been thinking about this for days and believed I had come up with a satisfactory reply. I knew I could not say I belonged to the Second Kentucky Cavalry, since my lie would soon be found out; but I had not counted on so many other regiments being part of Morgan's force. Was the Seventh Kentucky also here? The Ninth? Which absent regiment could I safely mention? As I stood there stuttering, I was seized by an idea.

"Sir," I said, "I have a confession to make: I lied to y'all. I have never been in the Confederate army, although I deeply wish with all my heart to enlist in General Morgan's Raiders and kill me some Yankees." This was not true. I had no intention of fighting—much less killing—anyone, Yankee or Rebel. I only wanted to be with John. But to be with him, I needed to find him, and unless I posed as an enthusiastic recruit, I was likely to be turned back before I could go any further. "I got this uniform off a dead man," I continued. Well, that was true enough. "I came across his body beside the road where some cursed Yankee had left him to bleed to death." Also more true than I cared to consider.

There was a flurry of excitement at this. The lieutenant turned to another officer, and they conversed in whispers. I prayed that I had mixed enough truth in my lie to make it credible, but when the lieutenant turned back to me, my heart sank.

"Did you kill that corporal?" he demanded.

"No, sir," I said.

"Then why did you defile his corpse by stripping him naked and putting on his uniform? Have you no respect for the Confederate dead?" His face was so stony it took my breath away.

"I wrapped him in my own clothes," I said, neglecting to add that the wrapper was a black crepe dress that had once belonged to a wealthy Boston matron. "And I dug him a grave. I put on his uniform because I wanted to avenge him, *and I was afraid y'all wouldn't let me enlist if I showed up in my own clothes. I am young for a soldier."*

"How young?"

"Seventeen next month."

"Don't lie to me, boy. You're not a day over fifteen, are you?"

"No, sir." I lowered my head and tried to look abashed, but inside I was jubilant. He did not suspect I was a woman!

"What is your real name?"

"Crane, sir, Ezekiel Crane." Mr. and Mrs. Ezekiel Crane were the aliases John and I had adopted when we ran away together. I immediately regretted choosing it, but it was the first name that came to mind, and it was too late to take it back.

"Well, Zeke," the lieutenant said, "give me one good reason why I shouldn't shoot you as a Yankee spy."

His threat came as a shock. I had promised myself I would never do anything to endanger John; but I had also promised myself that if I had a chance to help the Union, I would. Could the lieutenant read this on my face? If so, I was as good as dead unless I revealed I was a woman, and if I did, he would send me away. "I am just . . . a boy," I stuttered.

The lieutenant's answer when it came was not comforting. "You're plenty old enough to die as a man," he said. "Give me another reason."

"I am John Taylor's cousin. Take me to John and he'll vouch for me." This was the centerpiece of my lie, but it did not have the effect I anticipated. Once again the lieutenant and the other officer conferred in whispers.

"Taylor's not here," said the lieutenant. "I reckon you knew that."

"No, sir," I said. I was very alarmed by this news. "He isn't wounded, is he, or"—the word stuck in my throat so tightly I could hardly utter it—"dead?"

"For God's sake, boy, Taylor's not dead; he's just not in camp right now." The lieutenant gave me a disgusted look, but I think my distress finally convinced him I was harmless. "You are his cousin, you say?"

"Yes, sir. His papa's mama was my mama's . . ."

The lieutenant did not wait to hear out the tangled ties of Southern kinship that supposedly bound me to John. He turned to the sentry who had captured me, and this time there was no whispering.

"Take the boy to General Morgan," he said. "If he really is Taylor's cousin, the general is going to want to talk to him. If he isn't, we can always shoot him later."

And so it came to pass that on a warm summer evening, when whip-poorwills called from the ash grove and fireflies drifted through the air like tiny Chinese lanterns, I was led at gunpoint through a camp of sleeping Rebels to meet John Hunt Morgan for the second time.

Chapter Sixteen

Up ahead is a handsome two-story brick house, its windows ablaze with light as if a summer cotillion is in progress. A group of men is sitting on the lawn around a campfire, singing sentimental ballads, and someone is playing a fiddle so sadly the tune sends chills down Claire's spine. As she approaches, she is worried that her lie will not be believed and that Morgan—whom she met two years ago at Lavinia's—will recognize her; yet as the sentry nudges her into the firelight with his rifle barrel and the singing stops, her first thought is that she has not interrupted a party of Confederate soldiers, but a band of cavaliers who by some inexplicable accident have wandered into the wrong century.

Although she is almost certain that all the men staring at her are officers, they are not wearing uniforms or insignias of rank. Instead they are dressed in tight black or fawn-colored riding pants; long flowing linen coats; knee-high leather boots with outsized spurs; and broad-brimmed felt hats, pinned up on the right-hand side with glittering stars, silver crescents, and assorted Masonic symbols. They range in age from a boy who cannot be much more than eighteen to a man in his midthirties, and they are, with few exceptions, extraordinarily handsome.

One has dark brows and a square, brushlike beard that gives him a stubborn air. Claire will later learn he is Basil Duke, Morgan's brother-in-law. On either side of Duke sit two men with sandy hair and drooping mustaches, both clear-eyed and intense and so alike that if they had not been a decade or more apart, she might have taken them for twins. The oldest sports a mustache that has been waxed and twirled up jauntily at the ends. As he catches sight of Claire, he reaches out, gives it another twirl, and looks quizzically at a darkly handsome young man who sits to his left. These are Morgan's three brothers: Calvin, Richard, and Charlton.

The smooth-faced boy with wavy brown hair and an angelic smile is Tom, another brother; for Morgan never likes to be separated from those he loves, and this raid, like all the others he leads, is a family affair. Tom holds a fiddle in one hand and a bow in the other. To his left sits a wiry, balding, sad-eyed man dressed in a plain black coat and a rumpled shirt. Claire's eyes pass over him without registering much more than the fact that he appears as out of place as a crow in a flock of peacocks, but his looks are deceptive. He is the infamous George "Lightning" Ellsworth, Morgan's personal telegrapher, a technical genius who climbs the poles, splices into the lines, and confuses Federal troops by spreading rumors and misinformation.

The centerpiece of the group, the man to whom all eyes turn by instinct, is Morgan himself. Having met him before, Claire recognizes him at once. The general is at least six feet tall and powerfully built, with gray eyes, slightly curly hair, and a sandy-colored beard. He is by far the most handsome man in the group. Even his hat seems to sit more dashingly on his head than the hats of his officers. In brief, he is—and at the same time is not—the same man Claire saw in Lavinia's parlor two years ago. That Morgan was consumed with sorrow; this one is fit, lean, and happy. No, he is more than happy. When he stares at Claire, his eyes burn with an inner fire that makes it impossible for her to look away. It is the gaze of a saint or a fanatic, the look of a man who is living out the best days of his life and knows it.

Unlike his officers, who perch on logs around the fire, Morgan sits in a chair that has been carried out of the house and placed on the lawn. Upholstered in pale golden brocade, it gives him the appearance of a king lounging on a throne. The others are drinking something—presumably whiskey—out of tin cups, but not, Claire notes, Morgan. A cut-glass decanter filled with bourbon rests on a small table to his left. In his hand, he holds a crystal goblet that sends small rainbows of light scudding across his immaculate white shirtfront.

Morgan has never seen why he should cease to live the life of a Southern gentleman just because he has gone to war. During the weeks to come, Claire will never see him sleep on the ground or take shelter in a tent. He will stay in private homes like this one, or in inns, or—whenever possible—in the best room in the finest hotel in whatever town they have just captured. During the great raid—the longest of the war—his men will ride for thirty-six hours at a time, cross three states, travel for over a thousand miles, and wear out a half dozen horses apiece while their commander travels in his personal carriage with Glencoe, his warhorse, tied behind. When the carriage is captured by Federal troops, Morgan will order his boys to steal him another. Not until the very end will he climb into the saddle, but when he finally does, he will ride like a demon and outsmart his pursuers at every turn.

"Your name, boy?" Morgan asks.

"Crane, sir," Claire says. "Ezekiel Crane." As Morgan looks her up and down, she remembers how he once bowed over her hand and wished her happiness in her marriage. No doubt he would bow to her again if he realized she was female, but tonight she stands before him disguised as a boy, so he does nothing gallant, which bodes well for her chances of passing unrecognized.

Claire knows a great deal about Morgan, since she has devoured every account of him she can get her hands on, and as he continues to stare at her without speaking, she nervously tries to put some of the pieces together: Born and raised in Kentucky and educated at Transylvania College, from which he was expelled for a serious incident no one is willing to talk about. Fought in the Mexican war and commissioned a lieutenant at the age of twenty-one. Mason, captain of Lexington Volunteer Fire Department, member of the city council. Before the war a prosperous business-man who owned woolen mills and a hemp factory. Slave trader and thus, not surprisingly, ardent, early supporter of the Confederacy. Tragic personal life. Restless, moody, given to bursts of elation and black fits of despair. Brilliant military tactician but undisciplined enough to win reprimands from superior officers. Hard drinker. Legendary for his bravery and sense of honor. Hated and feared by the North; loved to the point of idolatry by his men. What does all this tell her? Nothing. Because when all is said and done, Morgan is most famous for being unpredictable.

"Your reputation precedes you," he says at last. "I have already received a message from Lieutenant Drake informing me that you claim to be John Taylor's cousin. Is this true?"

"Yes, sir, General," Claire says, looking him straight in those remarkable eyes.

"Lay out the Begats for me, son."

"Excuse me, General, I do not take your meaning."

Morgan chuckles. "I thought a lad with the name Ezekiel would be more of a Bible reader. I am ordering you to tell me exactly how you claim kin to one of my best scouts."

If she hesitates, Morgan will know she is lying. Squaring her shoulders, Claire takes a deep breath and quickly gives him the false bloodline she has concocted, and in the course of her lie discovers she has an unexpected talent for fiction. It is a complicated story by necessity, for Morgan is an old friend of the Taylors' so it will not do to pretend to be a cousin once or even twice removed.

But she has thought out her supposed family tree carefully, and by the time she has finished spreading its branches for Morgan to inspect, she is relieved to see that he appears to be convinced. But not, it appears, completely.

"How are Mrs. Taylor and Miss Agnes?" he asks.

Claire manages to keep her face impassive. "Cousin Lavinia is well," she says, "and bearing up as bravely as any woman I have seen, although her loss was grievous. As for Cousin Agnes, the Yankees will be sorry if they ever tangle with her. She told me to tell y'all to come drive them out of western Kentucky before she has to do it herself. When they stole the horses, they trampled her flower bed, and she says she will never forgive them for the destruction of her daylilies."

Morgan relaxes and takes a sip of whiskey. "And Chad," he says, "how is he doing?"

Claire cannot believe her luck. "Chad is dead, sir, I am sorry to say. He did not survive Cousin Clayton's death. Cousin Agnes told me he set to howling on the eve of Shiloh and did not stop until the telegram arrived with the terrible news. He died soon thereafter." This is eighty percent fabrication, since all Claire knows is that the dog is dead, but Morgan's face softens. Fierce in battle, implacable in his hatred of Yankees, he has a soft spot in his heart for women, small children, and dogs.

"Ah," he says, "no doubt the poor beast's noble heart broke. Dogs are better than men, Zeke." He gestures at Claire, inviting her to draw closer. "Sit down, son. You are going to have a long wait for your cousin. I sent him off to Indiana to look around."

Claire must look dismayed because all the officers laugh.

"Don't fret," says Duke, "when Taylor and the other boys come back and tell us where the damn Yankees are, we're gonna go up there and show those Hoosiers what raisin' hell is all about. Then maybe we'll take a little ride through Ohio jest to admire the scenery."

"And cook our slosh over railroad ties," says Richard Morgan, taking a slug of whiskey and grinning at Claire.

"Hell no," Calvin objects. "Those ties are no damn good for cooking. They make the slosh taste like tar."

Claire looks around the circle of laughing men. The Raiders look fierce and jolly, as if war were like deer hunting, only with smarter game. *They have just said they are going to invade Indiana and Ohio,* she thinks. She is just wondering if she has misinterpreted their remarks, when Morgan addresses her directly.

"Zeke," he says, "any cousin of John Taylor's is fit to fight Yankees. I hereby appoint you a corporal in the Second Kentucky Cavalry. I am putting you under Brother Tom's command—that's Lieutenant Morgan to you. I expect you to water your horse before you drink and feed him before you eat, ride until you drop, fight until you fall, be as courageous as Richard the Lionhearted and as fierce as Attila the Hun, and behave like a Southern gentleman whenever you encounter ladies. We're gonna carry the War of Northern Aggression onto Northern soil. Now give me a Rebel yell."

Claire has only heard a Rebel yell once, but she has not forgotten what it sounds like. Taking a deep breath, she emits an ear-splitting, yipping scream that makes Morgan smile.

For the next hour or so as the campfire dies down to a heap of glowing coals, she sits on a log next to Ellsworth, sips whiskey from a tin cup, and listens to Tom Morgan play his fiddle. The men sing "Home Sweet Home," "Lorena," "Just Before the Battle, Mother," "God Save the South," "Dixie," "The Rebel Soldier," and other familiar songs, but Claire does not join in because she is afraid the timbre of her voice will betray her. Fortunately, no one appears to notice, or if they do, they are too full of whiskey to care.

Tom's music drifts through the orchard, wrapping the sleeping army in a mist of nostalgia and longing. In the firelight, his face is radiant. After a while, his companions begin to grow tired of singing. Sensing this, he lowers his fiddle, and a chorus of crickets rushes in to fill the silence.

The Raiders talk and drink for a while longer. A plug of tobacco is passed around. Claire takes the smallest bite possible and nearly chokes on it. At last, Morgan yawns, drains his glass, and rises to his feet. "Y'all should get some sleep," he says. "In the morning we have a date with the Louisville and Nashville Railroad Depot in Lebanon." Bidding everyone good night, he goes into the house to follow his own advice.

"Last time I seen that depot, a baby could take it while sucking its mama's titty," Charlton Morgan says.

"Don't let the general hear you say that," Duke warns. "He does not tolerate crude jokes about motherhood, particularly these days." Claire later learns that Morgan has remarried and that his wife is pregnant.

Finishing off their whiskey, the men rise and stagger into the house, leaving Claire alone by the fire. She is just trying to figure out whether she should follow them, when Tom Morgan reappears and sits down beside her. He is holding an ancient muzzle-loading rifle that has a hook embedded in the stock as if it had been hung above someone's mantel for decoration.

"I reckon y'all can shoot and ride," he says.

"Yes, sir." Claire wonders if she should stand up and salute him since he is her superior officer, but he does not seem to expect this formality. It's odd to be taking orders from a boy who is probably a good five years younger than she is. If he knew he was commanding a married woman who had run off to join her lover, he would probably have to brace himself with more whiskey before he could speak to her.

Tom hands her the gun. "This weapon is not really suitable for combat, so your first job tomorrow will be to get yourself a better one."

"Yes, sir." Holding the gun makes Claire feel uncomfortable. Despite its antiquity, it appears to be in working order, and Tom Morgan expects her to shoot Union soldiers with it. Could she actually pull the trigger and kill some man who had never harmed her? She remembers Dorothea Wolcott's agonizing grief when she learned her son James had fallen at Antietam. *I will shoot over their heads*, she decides. *I will not kill some mother's boy. There is nothing worse than losing a child.*

Tom picks up an abandoned cup, shakes it, tips back his head, and drains the contents. "Where did y'all hide your horse?" he asks.

Claire is so startled, she momentarily forgets he outranks her. "How did you know I came on horseback?"

Tom puts the cup aside and grins at her. "You smell like a horse, Zeke. So where is he?"

Claire tells him and he nods. "You can go get him in the morning before we move out. So now that we've made a Rebel soldier out of you, what do y'all know about the army?"

"Not much," she admits.

"Y'all know a first lieutenant outranks a corporal?"

"Yes, sir."

"Can you recite the other military ranks and tell me the chain of command?"

"No, sir. A private is on the bottom. I know that. And a general is on the top. But in between . . ." She shrugs.

"Y'all know what a battalion is?"

"Big?" Claire guesses.

"How about a brigade?"

"Isn't the Second Kentucky one?"

"Y'all don't know anything," Tom says, "and there isn't time to teach you. That may not amount to a hill of beans since I think the general is fixin' to make a pet of you. He feels terrible about what happened to Mrs. Taylor's boys at Shiloh, especially little Clayton. He just told me he doesn't intend to lose another member of the family, no matter how distant a cousin. So remember this: tomorrow when the shooting begins, keep your head down and stick close to me.

"As a corporal you are empowered to issue orders to privates, but—no offense meant, son—I wouldn't trust you to tell my boys how to tie their shoes. As for your superior officers, you are supposed to be under the immediate command of Sergeant Gray, who jumps when I tell him to, but I don't want to have to face my brother across your grave, so I reckon I will personally run you through the streets of Lebanon like an unbroken colt. Of course, when I mention your grave, I am speaking metaphorically. If you take a bullet, we won't have time to stop and bury you. We'll have to leave you to the Yankees and the buzzards."

Having issued this cheerful warning, Tom Morgan rises to his feet and goes back into the house. As soon as he is out of sight, Claire spits out the wad of tobacco and rinses her mouth with water from her canteen. Pulling the dead corporal's cloak around her shoulders, she writes in her journal for a while and then settles down in front of the fire.

Despite the whiskey, sleep comes hard. When she first mounted the corporal's horse and began to ride south, she knew she was putting herself in grave danger, but she believed she would gladly sacrifice her life to see John again. During the past two weeks, she has repeated this to herself as if defying someone to contradict her. But now death takes on a new reality.

Tomorrow I may be killed by a Union bullet, she thinks, and her mouth grows so dry with fear that she can hardly swallow. *Ever since I can remember, I have been told Christ will be there to greet me when I pass over, but what if there is nothing on the other side of the grave but cold, empty blackness?*

She stares into the fire trying to imagine what it would be like not to exist. Is seeing John again worth the risk? The answer, when it comes, does not emerge from her mind but her heart.

Yes, she thinks. *Yes, it is.*

Chapter Seventeen

WHEN the history of the Battle of Lebanon is written, the story will have logic and coherence. Historians will observe that the town was strategically located in central Kentucky at the terminus of the Louisville and Nashville Railroad and thus was a major site for storing supplies for Federal forces. On July 5, 1863, the chroniclers will note, Confederate general John Hunt Morgan attacked with a force of three thousand men. Defending the town was a Union garrison of four hundred men under the command of Union colonel Charles Hanson. When Hanson refused to surrender, Morgan warned women and children to evacuate, then shelled the town. About one thirty in the afternoon, Hanson, who was running out of ammunition, surrendered, and he and his men were taken prisoner.

This is the Battle of Lebanon as history will record it, but it is not the battle Claire sees. The Raiders may ride into combat like cavalry, but they fight like infantry, so within minutes of crossing the small creek that marks the city limits, she finds herself on foot with a limited line of sight. As she runs through the streets with Tom's troop, the noise is deafening. The Confederate artillery thunders so ceaselessly that the concussion drives the air out of her lungs, and as Rebel yells echo off the buildings, nothing seems to make sense. Where is she? Is her troop following orders or have they taken off on their own? Only Tom Morgan knows, and he is not about to stop and tell her.

Oddly enough, she is not afraid. Or rather she is afraid, but her fear is so well sealed off it seems to belong to someone else. She worried she might panic at the first sound of gunfire and end up getting shot for desertion, but now, as she dashes past rows of red-brick storefronts, the minutes seem to expand into hours and she finds herself filled with a strange, drunken elation that a more experienced veteran would immediately recognize as potentially fatal.

Strangers are trying to kill me, she tells herself, but the words have no meaning. The bullets, which are sending chips of brick flying up around her like hail, seem no more than a minor annoyance; the very idea that she could die seems ludicrous.

As they approach the center of the town, she hears pounding hooves. Looking up, she sees two horses come careening around a corner dragging a driverless wagon.

"Go get 'em," Tom commands.

He is speaking to a bandy-legged man with a tobacco-stained beard, but in the heat of battle, Claire hears the order as directed at her. Glad to be of use, she tosses down her rifle, runs forward, leaps into the wagon, throws herself onto the horses, and rides the terrified animals to a standstill with one foot planted in the back of each. *Look at me!* she feels like yelling. *See what I've done!* She is half crazy with pride and at the same time amazed. Whom should she thank? Her father, who taught her to ride almost before she could walk, or some distant warrior ancestor, who has willed her a streak of insanity that, when not examined too closely, resembles courage.

"Well done, Zeke!" Tom cries. Claire hands off the horses and wagon to a grinning, gap-toothed Raider, and the troop moves on. Some of the men slap her on the back, and one offers her a plug of tobacco. She bites off a hunk and spits it out when his back is turned. Her hands are shaking, her mouth is dry, her heart racing, but still she cannot feel her own fear.

On the railroad tracks that run down to the depot, a bloated donkey lies gathering flies. She suddenly realizes she has left her rifle behind. She is a terrible soldier, or perhaps lucky. The gun was so old it probably would have exploded and blown her head off if she had fired it.

Turning a corner, they suddenly come upon a troop of Raiders holding lighted torches. The air is acrid with the smell of pitch.

"What are they going to burn?" Claire yells to the man nearest her.

"Clerk's offices," he yells back and gives an earsplitting Rebel yell.

"Why?"

The raider looks at Claire as if she is a simpleton. "Because they got treason indictments in there against men who support the Cause."

The Raiders run down the street yelling like demons, but no one opposes them. They throw their torches on the roofs of the offices, and within seconds the shingles catch and fire streams out of the windows. Claire stands so near Tom she can feel the heat radiating off the arms of his coat. Yet even as she takes shelter in his shadow, she is still incapable of feeling anything except drunken elation.

"Duck!" Tom cries, striking her on the back and knocking her to the ground. A bullet whizzes by, and behind her a man screams. Claire rises to her feet but sees no one. Did someone take a bullet meant for her?

Tom is firing at a second-story window. Suddenly a man tumbles over the sill and falls, turning in the air and landing facedown in the gutter.

"Go get it!" Tom commands. Confused, Claire hesitates. "Take his damn gun, boy!" Tom yells. "What are y'all waiting for?"

Running to the man, Claire kneels and starts to unfold his fingers from the stock, but they are still warm. Grabbing the barrel, she jerks the rifle out of his hand.

"Now y'all got yourself a real weapon," Tom yells. "Keep a good grip on it, y'hear? I can't go kill a Yankee for you every time you drop your rifle."

Claire stares at the man who lies at her feet. She knows he will never get up again, but she cannot believe this the way she believes in concrete things like the taste of soup and the sound rain makes on windowpanes. There continues to be something theatrical about the battle, as if they are putting on a performance for an invisible audience.

Leaving the center of town, Tom's troopers circle behind the railroad depot, perhaps with the intention of taking the defenders by surprise, but when they fire, they shoot at unseen targets. Several more buildings are burning by now, and the smoke is suffocating. What lies behind that smoke? Wagons? More dead donkeys?

No, the enemy is out there, firing unseen into their midst. Two Raiders fall and another is wounded; but Claire is not near either of them. Whenever she sees a Union soldier looming out of the smoke, she shoots over his head. When her companions fire, she fires too; and when they reload, she reloads. But she only kills weathercocks and shears off roof shingles, and no one notices Zeke Crane is fighting a separate war.

Around noon, it begins to rain. As they turn down a side street, fine white houses with graceful porches loom out of the mist like slices of a misplaced birthday cake. The man beside Claire suddenly curses. She looks over and sees that his arm is bleeding. Sitting down on the steps of a nearby house, he puts his head between his knees. Claire knows she should be shocked by the sight of blood, but she simply moves on with the troop, past a Presbyterian church with its steeple blown off, past a woman with a bonnet dangling from her neck, who dashes out of the smoke clutching a small girl by the hand.

At the corner of two residential streets near the depot, Calvin Morgan, the brother with the jaunty mustache, intercepts Tom.

"Brother," he says, "the general orders you to withdraw behind our lines and take your men with you."

"Withdraw?" Tom says. "Why, there are Yankee sharpshooters all over this town like rats in the corn, and me and my boys can kill 'em as good as anyone. You can tell our brother from me, Cally, that I am no baby to be coddled."

"No one doubts your courage," says Calvin, "nor the courage of your men, but you have orders which you must obey."

Tom looks as if he may make more objections, but apparently he reconsiders because he shrugs. "If I must, then I must." He turns to his troop. "Retreat, boys," he says, or rather he begins to say this, for he hardly gets the word "retreat" out of his mouth before a Union bullet takes him square in the chest.

Claire remembers that moment forever: the sheen of smoke clouding the gray sky above Lebanon, the cool spray of rain on her forehead, the smell of burned wood, the sound of gunfire coming from the depot, and Tom Morgan with a look of disbelief on his boyish face, staggering back as if struck by an invisible blow and crumpling into his brother's arms.

"Brother Cally," Tom says, "they have killed me!" And then a great red rose of blood blossoms through his shirt.

Claire wails in horror, but no one hears her because the rest of the men are wailing too. As Calvin weeps over Tom and pleads with him to hang on, Tom leans back and closes his eyes. The light goes out of his face, and all at once, the war becomes terrifyingly real.

Claire

After Tom Morgan died, I ran. I had not been capable of fear until that moment, but when I saw his life snuffed out as carelessly as you might swat a mosquito, I was suddenly more afraid than I had ever been in my life. Throwing down the rifle I had taken from the Union sharpshooter, I took off without a backward glance. I was done with soldiering forever. If John loved me, let him find me after the war was over. I was a woman, made for home and children. If men wanted to kill each other, they could do it without my help.

As I passed through the streets of Lebanon on my way to the creek that marked the edge of town, the news of Tom's death followed behind me in a long wail that seemed to interrogate the very heavens. It was a cry of fury, rage, and disbelief. No one hearing it could have doubted that the Raiders would now burn the town and slaughter the Union prisoners, and I did not intend to be present to witness the massacre.

My horse was still picketed where I had left him, tended by two boys who could not have been older than thirteen. They were drummer boys, by the looks of them, a guess made more probable by two battered drums that lay on the ground nearby. The gelding was saddled, so all I had to do was mount him and take the reins. If the boys wondered where I was going in such a hurry, they did not bother to inquire. No doubt they thought I was being sent to bear a message, perhaps by

Morgan himself, for news had spread quickly through the army that I was John Taylor's cousin and a friend of the Morgan family. The boys did not yet know Tom Morgan was dead, and I did not have the heart to tell them.

For some time—I have no idea how long—I galloped through the rain. Since Morgan was planning to ride north, I headed south, which was foolish since we had left an angry, unsecured populace in our wake, but I was more lucky than I deserved to be and met no one. Finally, I turned off the road and made my way up a hill to a small clearing. Perhaps I would have had a view of the burning of Lebanon if the weather had been clear, but all I could see from my post was the gray sheet of the storm.

Dismounting, I threw myself down on the wet grass and wept. You must not imagine my tears were the romantic tears of those heroines who appear in senti-mental novels. They were great, gasping, choking sobs, childlike and unpleasant, and I gagged on them as I repeatedly attempted to vomit out the memory of the danger, suffering, and death that I had been unable to feel for so many hours. No longer numb to the horrors of war, I felt abandoned and distraught, and I bitterly regretted every decision I had made, starting with the moment when I first laid eyes on Henry. I think at one point, I even called for my mother.

Gradually, the storm of emotions subsided, leaving me weak and shaken. I sat up and realized for the first time that I was wet through to the skin and uncom-fortably cold. I had no food, having come away with empty saddlebags, little money, and not much of a future in front of me unless I wanted to go crawling back to my husband.

It was then I saw John. He came to me on that hill, not as a memory but as a living presence. For a moment, I even smelled the scent of his hair. I know this sounds insane, but at the time I was not completely in my right mind, and all I can report is that John was as substantial as the wet grass and the rain on my face. I still cannot explain how I came to have such an intense vision of him. Even now, I suspect there was something almost sacrilegious in the experience. I knew he was not real in the ordinary sense of the word; I was never that deluded. But he came to me just the same. Call it a hallucination, if you like, or a message sent without telegraph wires. Since I have never believed in premonitions, I do not know what to call it, but it changed me.

He only stood before me briefly, but in that instant I was filled by an overwhelming sense that he was in grave danger and needed my help. I waited, hoping he would reappear. When he did not, I rose to my feet and remounted my horse, who had stood contemplating me with puzzlement as I wept. Slowly, I made my way back down to the road. When I came to the muddy track, I halted. To the south lay escape; to the north lay General Morgan and John. There was really no decision to be made. I knew this was a love I could not run from.

I took a shortcut, so it cost me no more than half an hour to return to Lebanon. There I found the depot a smoldering ruin. The whole town was in flames, which was no surprise. Shortly after Tom died, Colonel Hanson had surrendered and now the Raiders were busy looting everything of value: guns, flour, meat, bullets, clothing. As I selected my third rifle of the day from a stack that had been taken from Hanson's troops, I saw one of Richard Morgan's boys ride past with a dozen pairs of shoes tied to his saddle horn; but what I did not see was a massacre, which was surprising. I knew most of the Raiders came from Kentucky and Tennessee, states whose people have a long tradition of blood feuds and vengeance. I had expected them to act as their Scotch-Irish ancestors would have, taking an eye for an eye in the old tribal fashion, but General Morgan had forbidden his men to revenge his brother's death.

I have no doubt that he was shaken to the depths by the loss. Indeed, I do not believe he will ever get over it. The next time I saw his face, he looked years older. But Morgan believed war should be a fair fight and that men who surrendered should be treated with respect. When his brother Charlton grabbed Colonel Hanson by the beard and threatened to slaughter him on the spot, the general stepped between them, drew his pistol, and said he would shoot the first man who harmed a prisoner.

You must not imagine by this that Morgan was softhearted. He enjoyed killing Yankees, and he hated in equal measure spies, traitors, and abolitionists. He marched Hanson and the prisoners he had spared at saber point double time to Springfield before he paroled them, and some died on the way. Indeed, if it had not been for the cooling effects of the rain, more Union boys would surely have perished from heat stroke on what can only be described as a death march. But shooting prisoners in cold blood was not in Morgan's nature. Despite Tom's death and the horrors of the raid, he always clung to a romantic view of battle that was more in tune with the fourteenth century than the nineteenth.

As for my absence, in all the confusion no one had noticed. I returned and took my place in the cavalry as seamlessly as if I had never deserted. From Lebanon we rode past fields of tobacco up to Bardstown, burning a trestle, capturing a train, and relieving the passengers of their valuables while Ellsworth spread rumors via the telegraph lines. By morning, newspapers throughout the state were carrying banner headlines that screamed contradictory warnings: Morgan was going to attack Cincinnati. His real target was Louisville. He was marching on Frankfort. He had four thousand men; eight thousand; eleven thousand.

I have to hand it to Ellsworth: he was a genius at promoting panic. He could hide an army of three thousand men in plain sight just by climbing a telegraph pole. I never liked the man, but I probably owe my life to him.

In Bardstown, we slept in the home of a longtime friend of the general's. I say "we" because after Lebanon, Morgan took me under his wing just as Tom had predicted. Although he never said so, I believe the general viewed me as a substitute for his youngest brother. At the very least, it was clear that he wanted to keep me alive until my "cousin" John showed up.

Some ten years before, while staying in the same house, Stephen Foster had composed "My Old Kentucky Home." We all sang the song that night in honor of Tom; and his brothers and the other officers wept together, for even bone-tired and stained with blood and battle, they were a sentimental lot, and the cords of affection that bound them together were real enough. I am not ashamed to admit that I wept with them. When a young soldier dies, it is a tragedy no matter which side he fights on, and I could not help thinking that if John and I ever had a son, he might someday end up like Tom Morgan.

The general himself handed me a blanket and ordered me to stretch out on the carpet by the fire. I was grateful to lie there instead of on the wet ground, but although the officers were friendly and several praised me for my supposed "courage under fire," they watched me all the time as if, in poor Tom's words, I were the new "baby to be coddled."

Still, I was perfectly placed to learn more about Morgan's invasion plans, and as the night passed and whiskey loosened their tongues, I came to understand for the first time the logic behind our mad dash through Kentucky. From the conversation, which came in fits and starts, I gathered that General Bragg and the Army of Tennessee were under considerable pressure. It seemed Bragg wanted to fall back behind the Tennessee River at Chattanooga, but he could not do so without exposing his men to a Union attack; so a few weeks ago Morgan had gone to him and volunteered to create a diversion by invading Kentucky.

The problem was—and only the inner circle knew this—Bragg had specifically ordered Morgan not to cross the Ohio River, but it appeared from what I overheard that Morgan was going to do it anyway. He had already sent a scouting party over to Indiana disguised as Union soldiers to see what support he might expect from Hoosier Copperheads and other Confederate sympathizers. The scouts were under the command of a captain named either Hans or Hines—my companions' accents made it hard to determine which—who had not yet reported back, either from "cussed laziness" or because "the damn Yankees had captured him."

I considered asking if John was one of the scouts in the missing party or if he had been sent into Indiana separately, but Morgan and his officers had forgotten I was there, and I did not dare risk drawing attention to myself. So I lay there propped up on one elbow, sipping our host's fine Kentucky bourbon, and listened to the officers say things they never should have said in my presence, and I worried.

I had plenty to worry about. John might be dead or rotting in some Yankee prison camp. Meanwhile, I was part of an army of three thousand men who were being led by a renegade general. Once we got into Indiana, Federal troops would outnumber us many times over and could pick us off at their leisure. As for the Copperheads, as the Confederate sympathizers were called, they were common around Charlesport, and I knew them well enough to know that Morgan was making a grave mistake if he was depending on them for support.

That night, I could not sleep. For hours, I lay awake trying to convince myself that the vision I had had of John was meaningless; that although the scouting party had not returned and no one had heard a word from them, he was not in danger and I was not on a suicide mission with a band of fanatics who would rather die gallantly than live to tell war stories to their grandchildren. And I wondered, as I have often wondered since, what strange wine God pours out to intoxicate ordinary men with visions of glory.

The next morning we rode to Garnettsville, camped for the night, and then moved on to Brandenburg, a little unfortified town on the banks of the Ohio. When we arrived, the general was pleased to find two boats already waiting to transport us across the river. The John T. McCombs *was a big packet that ran between Louisville and points south, and the* Alice Dean *was a side-wheeler. Both had been stolen by some boys from the Tenth Kentucky Cavalry, who let the Yankee passengers disembark and politely returned the ten thousand dollars they had left with the pursers for safekeeping.*

The town of Brandenburg was not so fortunate. Elated by the sight of the river, the Raiders looted a hotel, rolled several barrels of whiskey out into the street, and commenced to drink toasts to their impending victory over a hostile territory that stretched from southern Indiana to the Canadian border.

While the sheriff and other Unionists made themselves scarce, the local Rebs greeted Morgan as a liberator and cordially invited him to stay in the Buckner House. Located at the top of the bluffs, the place commanded a clear view of the river plus a spectacular panorama of the blue hills of my home state.

Sitting in the parlor with a cigar in one hand and a glass of bourbon in the other, the general proceeded to supervise preparations for ferrying his entire army across the river. We were going to invade Indiana, and there was nothing I could do about it, so I sat down out of range of his cigar smoke, pulled a handful of goober peas out of my pocket, and shelled and ate them as I stared at the land I had grown up in.

I thought of all the people I loved in Indiana: my parents, my friends and neighbors, Reverend Burke and his wife, and the men in my father's stable who had been so kind to me when I was a little girl. No doubt many of those same stable hands were now serving in the Union army. I might meet some of them in the days to come. What would they think of little Claire Musgrove if they saw her decked out like a Rebel raider? They would never recognize me, of course; but I might recognize them. I cannot shoot at people I know, I thought.

For the better part of an hour, I sat there weighing my love for John against my loyalty to the Union. When at last I looked up, one of Morgan's servants was refilling his master's glass. His name was Job. He was a thin, somber, middle-aged man, graying around the temples; and he was, of course, a slave. It was customary for Southern officers to bring their slaves to war with them and in addition to Job, Morgan had dragged his valet, driver, groom, and several others along on this raid without the slightest thought that they might not wish to accompany him. Now as I watched Job pour his master's whiskey, I began to understand what I had to do.

I can admire Morgan's bravery, I thought, but I can never love him or be loyal to him. He may have treated me as a younger brother, given me privileges and a rank far beyond the one I deserve, and personally concerned himself with my welfare; yet he will never be capable of seeing men and women with black skin as fellow human beings, much less understand their courage, determination, and desire for freedom at any price. That is the great flaw of the Southern cause, and I pray that in the end it will help defeat not only Morgan but the entire Confederacy.

Even as I thought such things, I did not stop loving John, nor did I consider leaving the Raiders. But that was the moment I understood why God had placed me between North and South. Somehow during the course of the next few weeks, if Morgan's slaves were willing, I would help them escape. But that was not all. When John returned, Morgan would probably put me under his protection. Besides the obvious advantages such an arrangement would offer John and me, it would mean that I would be riding with the scouts in advance of the main army.

On many occasions, I might be able to warn people that the Raiders were coming, giving them time to hide their valuables and conceal their horses. Abolitionists and free blacks would be in the greatest danger since Morgan had threatened to burn the houses of the former and send the latter south in chains.

Back in Cambridge, when I was playing the role of hostess at Henry's parties, Mr. Henry Longfellow had often been our guest for dinner. He was recently widowed and glad of the company, and on one memorable evening had graciously entertained us by reading from a yet-unpublished poem. The poem had been a brilliant success, much acclaimed at the time. Now, as I lay at Morgan's feet, secretly plotting the frustration of his plans, I silently recited the first two lines.

> Listen my children and you shall hear
> Of the midnight ride of . . .

Of Claire Winston! I thought, and for the first time since Tom Morgan died I found myself smiling.

Chapter Eighteen

CLAIRE has come down to the Brandenburg docks with Morgan hoping to hear news of John. Now she stares in dismay at a short man with a handlebar mustache and a long, crooked nose. He is Captain Hines, leader of the eighty scouts Morgan sent into Indiana, and the report he has just given is so bad that she wants to put a pistol to his head and force him to retract it. Fortunately, she doesn't have a pistol, which is probably the only thing that saves her from being court-martialed for threatening a superior officer.

"Seventy-two men lost!" Morgan says.

"Yes, sir, General," says Hines, "but me and the eight boys who made it back to Kaintuck just captured you a train loaded with enough gold to buy the army boots and bacon 'til kingdom come. It was on its way to General Rosecrans, who's gonna pitch a conniption fit when he hears who took it."

"Blast it, man! Capturing that train's a splendid coup, but the fact remains that I sent you into Indiana with eighty scouts and you bring me back eight. What happened?"

"Surely the Yankees didn't kill them all!" Claire cries. The words burst out of her and hang in the air like gunsmoke.

Morgan turns and glares at her. "Never interrupt a superior officer, Corporal," he snaps, but when he turns back to Hines, he says: "The boy's cousin rode with you. John Taylor. Is Taylor among the missing?"

"Yes, sir, General. I can't say for certain if he's dead or alive, but he's one tough son of a bitch, so my best guess is he's cooling his heels in the Corydon jail with some other scouts who rode up ahead of the main party—unless, of course, they've already been transported up to Indianapolis. No, sir, I am happy to say that, despite overwhelming odds, I'm pretty sure I only lost three of my boys to Yankee lead."

"You will write the mothers of those three men immediately and console them for their losses," Morgan says. "As for the scouts who were captured, I presume you are aware that cholera and smallpox are rampant in the Yankee prison camps. Confinement in one can be as sure a sentence of death as a bullet."

"Yes, sir, General." Hines's face does not change, but Claire can tell Morgan's reprimand wounds him.

"Now tell me precisely what happened," Morgan says. "Leave out no details."

"Well," Hines begins, "we got in easy enough disguised as Indiana Grays. In fact, we were so convincing as a bunch of Union boys that the folks in Paoli fed us supper, but before the butter melted on the biscuits, we had to make a run for it." Hines intersperses his story of the ill-fated scouting expedition with information about the disposition of Union forces and other vital facts Morgan needs to plan his invasion, but Claire is no longer listening. John is alive! He's a tough son of a bitch, a survivor who's too smart to get himself shot and wreck both their lives before she has a chance to tell him how much she loves him. Her relief is so great that it's all she can do to keep herself from clapping Hines on the back and offering to buy him a drink.

She stares toward a muddy bit of road that descends from a grove of cottonwoods on the Indiana side of the river and a new plan begins to take form in her mind, one so dangerous she wonders if she's crazy to consider it. Corydon is directly in the path of the invasion, not more than fifteen miles from where she now stands. Suppose after Morgan gets the army across the river, she deserts, gallops ahead, and warns the townspeople that he's invaded Indiana and is marching straight toward them? Surely in exchange, they will let her talk to John. If she can somehow persuade him to sign a sworn statement promising never to fight for the Confederacy again, she can probably get him released from jail. Hundreds of men on both sides are paroled in this fashion every day. Morgan himself paroled the troops he captured at Lebanon even though one of them killed his brother. Would John agree to such an arrangement?

Yes, she thinks, *because John hates slavery, does not really believe in the Confederate cause, and must be sick of fighting. Yes, because he loves me. No, because he is stubbornly wed to a medieval sense of honor and believes he owes Morgan a debt for saving his leg when he was a little boy. No, because although he loves me, he does not love me enough.*

The truth is, she will not know how John feels about her or what he will agree to until she speaks to him. Claire paces the length of the dock, turns and paces back. The river is narrow at this point. She could probably swim to the other side, but not in her boots and pants, and taking them off is not an option if she wants to continue posing as Zeke Crane. Besides, Morgan has ordered her to be at his disposal in case he wants her to carry a message, and disobeying him would attract attention. She has no choice but to remain in Kentucky as long as he does. She'll just have to wait.

Fine, then, she'll wait. The troop transport is going to last far into the night and things will no doubt be chaotic once they get to Indiana. She imagines herself marching through the darkness with several thousand Raiders, dozens of whom have been temporarily separated from their own units. If she slips away, there is a good chance no one will notice her absence until dawn. After that . . .

"Git out of the way, boy!" a voice cries. Stepping aside just in time to avoid a barrel that is being rolled toward the *Alice Dean,* Claire looks with renewed interest at the activity going on around her. The holds of the ferries have been cleared of commercial cargo, and military supplies are being carried up the gangplanks. Officers are mustering men into groups small enough to fill each boat to capacity without sinking it. To her left, a long line of mule drivers is unloading supply wagons and leading the mules back up the steep main street to bring down another load. The Raiders' horses, which are to be taken over later, are not yet in sight; but in front of the tavern two troopers are busily disassembling the general's carriage and wrapping the cushions in oilcloth.

As she stares impatiently at the carriage, the full magnitude of what she has decided to do hits her. It is all very well to tell yourself you are going to desert, spread an alarm, and free your lover from jail when you are standing safely on a dock watching men roll around barrels of salt pork, but will she really be able to ride off without being challenged? She may get lost or be captured by a Yankee patrol; and if she does manage to reach Corydon, what's to stop the Home Guard from shooting her?

The cottonwoods on the far bank shudder in a weak breeze that dies before it reaches her. Already the morning is stifling. She imagines John imprisoned in a small, hot cell, gasping for breath. One thing is certain: she cannot go on standing in the sunlight while he lies in darkness. She will simply have to trust that when the time comes, she will know what to do. Fighting down her fears, she turns and walks up to some privates who are unloading provisions from a supply wagon.

"Y'all need some help?" she asks.

"Hell, yes," one of them drawls. A few minutes later, she finds herself lumbering up the gangplank of the *Alice Dean* with a sack of cornmeal on her back. Staggering into the hold, she throws it on a pile, and goes back for more. The sacks are heavy and unwieldy, but she finds relief in the sheer mindlessness of the work. Around noon, a boy in a dirty apron appears and hands her a hunk of fried catfish. She eats it standing up, wipes her fingers on her trousers, and keeps on working. The sooner they get the wagons unloaded, the sooner they will get across.

Gradually, the weather turns sullen and fog closes over the water, giving a leaden tinge to men's faces and transforming the steamships into white apparitions. Claire works on, covered with corn grit and soaked to the skin by her own sweat. At last everything is ready. As the troopers on the wharf cheer, the *Alice Dean* and the *McCombs* cast off, turn, and chug slowly upriver, becoming even more indistinct and ghostly as they labor toward the Indiana shore. On the decks, Raiders in wide-brimmed hats hang over the rails laughing and spitting tobacco juice.

"Don't worry, Zeke! You'll be with us soon!" a private from the Second Kentucky yells. He is the trooper Claire saw wounded in Lebanon. His arm is in a sling, yet he and all the other men she fought with are going to arrive in Indiana before she does. Even Hines and his remaining spies are on the first transport, and from the look of things, it will be hours before she can join them.

Waving to Claire with his good arm, the wounded raider begins to sing:

> *Oh, I've been a moonshiner for many a year*
> *I've spent all my money on whiskey and beer . . .*

As if enchanted into flight by the sound of his voice, the fog suddenly lifts, and again Claire sees the green fringe of the Indiana shore. All at once, there is a thunderous concussion and a large section of the wharf explodes in a shower of splinters. Startled half out of her wits, she hurls herself behind a wagon as officers bellow commands and troopers run for cover.

Morgan is the sole exception. Having gone up to the bluffs and then come back down to see the first transport off, he does not seem perturbed by the attack. Turning toward the river, he removes his cigar from his mouth, blows a smoke ring, and looks at the source of the cannonball as if some god had assured him he was immortal. A second cannonade explodes out of the brush on the north bank, and still he does not move. This time, the shot strikes the Texas of the *McCombs* and sends it flying in all directions.

Morgan points to a wounded trooper. "Tend to that man at once," he orders, and puts his cigar back in his mouth. Two drummer boys dash out and drag the man to safety. Morgan continues to smoke his cigar.

"Please take cover, General!" a major pleads.

"Please, sir!" yell enlisted men and officers alike.

Morgan ignores them. He seems to be waiting for something. A few more seconds pass. As he finishes his cigar and tosses it into the river, the Confederate artillery on the bluff starts pounding the Indiana shore. A ball hits the far bank, sending up a fountain of dirt. In return, the Union soldiers fire one more shot, which goes wildly astray. Then, swarming out of the brush, they run for their lives as the Raiders on the boats take aim at them, and the artillery, finding its range, lobs shells in their direction with deadly accuracy. Later Claire learns the troops who fired on them that morning were members of the Indiana Legion: a home guard composed of old men and boys, a hundred at most bravely trying to repel an invasion of thousands.

The Parrott guns on the bluff make short work of any resistance. After sending dozens of cannonballs over to the Indiana side, they fall silent, and the troop transport resumes. For eight hours the *Alice Dean* and the *McCombs* ferry men, horses, and supplies across the Ohio, and still there seems to be no end to the army.

After the first two regiments have been taken over, Claire retreats to the comparative safety of Morgan's headquarters. There, she watches the general in action and tries to absorb everything she can about his plans. A large table has been moved from the dining room to the parlor so he can ponder his maps while keeping an eye on the river. Couriers arrive constantly with dispatches and are sent away with orders. Wood must be found to stoke the boilers of the steamships. Ammunition must be protected from water damage. Skittish horses must be blindfolded before they can be coaxed onto the boats.

To make matters even more complicated, the situation is constantly changing. When a Federal gunboat shows up and begins firing on the town, Morgan immediately issues orders for the troops on the Kentucky side to conceal themselves in the woods behind Brandenburg. That done, he walks to the edge of the bluff and waves his arms, and the Raiders on the Indiana side take cover.

Again the Parrotts thunder. The gunboat replies in kind and Union shells rain down on Brandenburg. As Claire watches from the safety of the Buckner House, trees disappear in fountains of smoke and dirt; roofs explode and vanish; horses scream in agony. Morgan damns the Yankees but never wavers in his determination to get his troops across the Ohio. At last, the Confederate artillery prevails and the gunboat retreats.

When the general's dinner is brought to him, Claire begs a chicken leg from Job and sits by one of the windows gnawing on it and watching the strange scene unfolding below her. By now the sun has set, but darkness has not arrived. All along the Kentucky bank, uncapped natural gas wells burn with an eerie golden radiance, sending up tall columns of fire to light the Raiders' crossing. Above the well fires, the moon hangs in the sky, so full and bright that she can see the red in the rebel flags that fly from jack staffs of the steamboats.

Hours pass. The moon turns small and cold and moves toward the west, and still there are more troops to be taken across. At last, a messenger arrives and salutes Morgan. The man is muddy and saddle-worn, with a clumsily patched coat and a hat so battered it appears to have been trampled.

"General," he says, "Colonel McCreary presents his compliments and says he thinks y'all should know that General Hobson's boys is on our tail like flies on shit."

"How much time does McCreary estimate we have before the Union forces overtake us?" Morgan asks.

"Not much, General. Some of our boys in the rear guard is already firing on the Yankees. Beggin' your pardon, General, but the Yanks is yellin' that they're gonna take you alive and hang you for a horse thief."

Morgan pushes back the brim of his hat and smiles. "Is that so? Well, you tell McCreary to hold Hobson's forces off as long as possible. Any delay, even if it be only in minutes, is in our favor." He pauses. "And tell McCreary's boys I'll personally see that any horses they send to Brandenburg get across the river."

Morgan does not seem in the least dismayed to learn the Yankees are so close, but Claire, who is drinking from her canteen, is so horrified that she chokes and has to hurry into the dining room so her coughing won't interrupt the rest of the conversation.

Morgan's rear guard is already skirmishing with Union troops! She did not even know the Raiders were being pursued. What will happen now? Will she get across the river before General Hobson's men attack, or will she end up stranded in Brandenburg with the remains of Morgan's army as they make some crazed, gallantly suicidal gesture designed to win them glory in the history books?

Morgan's staff must be having similar thoughts. For a quarter of an hour, they plead with the general to leave. They speak in low whispers, so Claire can only catch a word or two, but they must make a good case, because when they finish, Morgan orders Claire to roll up his maps. Stamping out his cigar, he summons his hosts, thanks them, bids them a warm farewell, and announces he is departing.

Claire gets a good look at the maps before she puts them away, and although she cannot memorize every detail, she manages to retain a general impression of the roads that lead from the river to Corydon. Shortly thereafter, she finds herself on the deck of the *Alice Dean* chugging toward the opposite shore. The trip across the stretch of swiftly flowing black water is oddly beautiful. Light from the gas wells throws lines of gold on the surface that turn and circle in endless eddies like a net of tightly strung gilt threads. There is no singing or joking as they cross; only the laboring of the engine, the sound of men coughing, and a low hum of conversation that washes up from the lower decks. Once a log floats past, rolling from black to silver in the moonlight.

As the *Alice Dean* approaches Indiana, the crew shuts down her engine and tosses lines to a welcoming committee of bare-chested Raiders who stand waist-deep in the river. Slowly, the men reel the boat to the bank, bridge the gap with a plank, and General Morgan walks dry-booted and triumphant onto Northern soil.

Claire follows him at a distance, trying to be unobtrusive; but even with Hobson on his heels and some of his troops still on the wrong side of the river, he takes time to speak to her, and tonight, as on so many nights to come, his genius for the personal touch makes it impossible for her to entirely dislike him, even though she knows she should.

"Come here, Zeke," he orders. When Claire approaches, he reaches out as if to tousle her hair, then appears to recollect that, although she may be no more than a child, she is nevertheless a corporal. "We march to Corydon tomorrow," he says. "Upon arriving, we shall engage the enemy and free your cousin and the other scouts who have fallen into Yankee clutches. I do not expect us to meet with serious resistance, but if we do, have you the stomach for the fight?"

"Yes, sir," Claire says. This is a lie. Since Lebanon, she has had no stomach for battles of any kind, and she certainly doesn't intend to wait until tomorrow to ride to Corydon. She wonders what Morgan would do if he suspected she was about to warn the local populace about the invasion and attempt to persuade one of his best scouts to desert. Shoot her, probably.

"You're a brave lad and a credit to your family," Morgan says.

A credit to my family, am I? Claire thinks. *Thank God you can't see into my heart.* She expects Morgan to get into his carriage and ride off, but instead he stands on the riverbank until the *Alice Dean* crosses back to Brandenburg and returns with the Parrott guns. As the boat docks, he stares at it thoughtfully. Then he turns his attention to the *McCombs*, which is still in midriver, coming on slowly.

"When the last of Johnson's brigade is over, burn the boats," he orders.

"Sir?" says a colonel who has come down to the landing to greet him.

"Torch the *Dean* and the *McCombs*," Morgan says. "I don't want Hobson using them to transport his troops; plus I want to impress on our boys that now that we are in Lincoln's home state it would be rude to leave before we paid a long call on his friends and neighbors."

Morgan smiles. His teeth shine in the moonlight, giving him a lean, wolfish air. Clearly Lincoln's name has conjured up something dark in him. Turning away from the river, he walks toward his waiting carriage. "There's no going back," he says softly, although whether he is speaking to the colonel or to himself, Claire cannot be certain.

As soon as his carriage is out of sight, she sets about locating her horse. She is afraid it may take half the night to track the beast down, but she finds him in a makeshift corral not a hundred yards from the river. Saddling up as quickly as possible, she double-checks to make sure the cinch is tight, mounts, and heads toward the woods, but before she can make good her escape, she is challenged.

"Halt and identify yerself," a picket commands.

Claire peers at him and recognizes a familiar face. "You know me, Eugene," she says. "We're both in the Second Kentucky and we fought together in Lebanon. Why do I need to tell you my name?"

"Orders," he says. "Nobody leaves without bein' identified and givin' the password."

"Why?"

"Yankee spies. Also, yer goin' the wrong direction." He points to the main road. "Camp's thataway."

Claire shrugs. "You don't say. Well, don't that beat all. I must have got turned around. My name, as you know, is Zeke Crane and the password for this evening is 'Glencoe,' just like the Old Man's horse."

The picket lowers his rifle. "Y'all can pass," he says. "I'm right sorry to talk to you like you was some Yankee, Zeke, but orders is orders."

"No offense taken," Claire says. She turns around and heads for the road. There is a lot of traffic, for Morgan's entire army is now heaving its way north through the mud of the recent rains. Claire positions herself behind a covered wagon crammed with ammunition boxes. From time to time, the wagon lurches to a stop and then starts up again, as if the mules pulling it have just awakened and remembered they have a job to do. It is slow going, but Claire has no desire to move faster. Somewhere up ahead, Morgan's carriage is moving through the same darkness, and she does not want to risk overtaking him.

Gradually, the road climbs out of the river bottoms and begins to follow a low ridge. When it enters a stand of trees, she moves to the shoulder where the mud is piled in a long soft heap. Moonlight barely penetrates the thick canopy of leaves. Halfway through the grove, she fords a creek, which she hears rather than sees as the hooves of the gelding strike stone and water. She still does not have a plan, but this is her best chance to leave without being noticed.

Turning into the grove, she rides up the creek making as little noise as possible. A few yards in, she halts behind some bushes. Gradually her eyes adjust, and she is able to make out the shadowy forms of men and wagons. She hears wheels creaking, soldiers talking and laughing, a metallic clank that might be cooking pots. Did anyone see her leave? Has someone noticed Corporal Crane is no longer riding behind the ammunition wagon?

Finally satisfied that she has managed to get away without being observed, she follows the creek out of the grove, cuts across a stretch of barren ground, and heads toward Corydon. According to Morgan's maps, there is an old trace that will lead her back to the main road well ahead of the place where the army is camped. Morgan has dismissed the trace from his plan of attack because it is too narrow for the supply wagons and artillery, but it will do nicely for a lone rider.

Around her, the hills of southern Indiana undulate in the moonlight like the waves of an inland sea, and one hill looks much like another. She has never been particularly good at finding her way in unfamiliar territory, but she has not come unequipped. In her pocket she carries several matches, a candle stub, and a highly polished walnut box the size of a broach case. The box contains a small brass compass, which, up until a few hours ago, belonged to Morgan.

She is about to consult it when she hears the pounding of hooves. Before she has time to take cover, four Raiders dash past. Fortunately, they do not see her. Is this one of the many Rebel raiding parties out tonight, or are they hunting for her? Claire knows she should be terrified at the thought of being tracked down and perhaps shot for desertion, but, to her surprise, she suddenly finds herself filled with the same drunken exhilaration she felt in Lebanon just before Tom Morgan caught a Yankee bullet. The terrible truth about war is that, when you are not in immediate danger, it sharpens your senses.

When she can no longer hear the sound of the Raiders' horses, she strikes the match and lights the candle. In the distance, a whip-poor-will calls and falls silent. Wind sweeps through the corn, thrashing the stalks. Suddenly, to the south, the sky flares to life and a pink tinge licks at the horizon. Morgan's orders have been carried out. The boats are burning. Snapping the compass case closed, Claire puts it back in her pocket, blows out the candle, and rides on toward Corydon.

Chapter Nineteen

I n Indianapolis, the populace is already in a panic. All day the telegraph wires have hummed ceaselessly, warning that Morgan has crossed the Ohio and is marching north with a vast army. Since noon, the citizens of the state capital have formed thirteen volunteer regiments to repel the invasion. The news has even reached the small town of Greencastle, where a druggist named Eli Lilly has offered his pharmacy as a recruiting station and personally assembled an artillery battery.

But information travels more slowly along the muddy tracks that serve for roads in the south of the state and the closer people are to Morgan's army, the less likely they are to know it is there. As Claire rides toward Corydon, she discovers that families in the outlying farms have banked their fires and gone to bed as if dawn will bring nothing more than the usual round of chores. When she was on the Kentucky side of the river, she had imagined herself galloping up to their front doors crying: "Wake up! Morgan's Raiders have crossed the Ohio! Hide your horses! Bury your money and other valuables!" But the trace is muddy, filled with stones, and it twists like a cow path, which means she cannot gallop without laming her horse; and when finally, at a sedate trot, she does encounter a darkened farmhouse, she hardly gets out the first words of warning before she is driven off.

"Who the hell are you?" demands a fierce-looking man who sticks his head out of a second-story window. "And why in tarnation are you causin' such an infernal ruckus at this hour?"

"I'm a loyal Union boy!" Claire yells. Since she has taken the precaution of removing the dead corporal's coat and stuffing it into her saddlebag, she figures this is a credible story. "I have come to warn you that the Rebels have invaded Indiana!"

"A Rebel army invadin' Indianee?" the man says. "What kinda moonshine you been swillin'? Get the hell out of here before I set the dogs on you!"

"Please, sir," Claire begs. "You don't understand. General Morgan has crossed the—" The man pulls in his head and slams the wooden shutter with a bang, cutting her off in midsentence. Inside the house, a pack of dogs barks wildly. There is a thump as one throws itself against the door. Not wanting to face its teeth, Claire gives up and rides on.

Was there anyone in that house besides the man who refused to listen to her? Children, perhaps, or old people? Should she turn around and try again? Behind her, she can hear the dogs barking like a wolf pack. *They live in the middle of nowhere*, she thinks. *Maybe they will be lucky.*

She tries to figure out how long it will take her to get to Corydon. It is already well past midnight. Since this is midsummer, the sun will soon be rising. She overheard Morgan tell Duke that he intended to attack the town this morning, but given the mud and the confusion occasioned by the crossing, it seems unlikely he can launch an assault much before noon. This means she has hours before the actual battle will begin, but not long before she will lose the advantages of darkness. Given the hostile reception she just received, should she waste time stopping at farmhouses to give warnings no one wants to hear?

This proves to be a question she is not forced to answer. Farmhouses are not common along the trace, and as she rides past the silent fields, nothing stirs. The night is warm with just a hint of rain in the offing, and the air is filled with the scent of ripening blackberries. Cows and horses sleep in wide, serene pastures. In the ditches, pale heads of Queen Anne's lace glow with an eerie blue radiance. She passes a ramshackle barn; a pond where geese and other river birds float with their heads tucked under their wings. The countryside is so peaceful, she can almost believe that she has imagined the invasion.

About half a mile before she reaches the junction between the trace and the main route to Corydon, she comes upon a small Quaker meetinghouse. Several hundred yards beyond it sits a large two-story farmhouse surrounded by various outbuildings. Claire reins in her horse and looks the place over. A farm this rich sitting undefended so close to the main road has no hope of surviving unscathed. She imagines the Raiders riding down on it with yips of triumph, taking the horses, emptying the pantry and root cellar, and robbing the family of their silver if they are prosperous enough to possess any. Should she ride up the driveway, wake these people, and warn them; or will they also sic their dogs on her?

Off to one side, she spots three quilts hanging on a line. *No woman in her right mind would leave good quilts out all night with rain threatening*, she thinks. Riding over, she inspects them and realizes she has no choice but to wake the farmer and his family and tell them to flee for their lives. The quilt patterns speak to her as clearly as if they had been ink on paper. Flying Geese, the Drunkard's Path, North Star: *Move swiftly toward Canada, following the North Star. Take an indirect route so you will not be captured and sent back into slavery.*

Riding up to the front door, she dismounts and knocks in a special staccato rhythm she has known since she was thirteen. "Wake up!" she cries. "If you are truly abolitionists, you are in grave danger!"

The door opens to reveal an old woman in a flannel nightgown.

"Does thee seek sanctuary, child?" the woman asks with that peculiar Quaker gentleness that is always so unexpected under such circumstances.

"No, madam," Claire says. "I am not in peril, but you are. I have come to warn you that Confederate General John Hunt Morgan and his Raiders have crossed the Ohio River and are marching this way." Claire points to the quilts. "These quilts tell me you are running an Underground Railroad station. If I am correct in the assumption that you hung them on the line as a signal for runaway slaves, then you must gather up all your valuables and flee at once. Morgan hates abolitionists and has threatened to hang or shoot anyone he suspects of helping runaways escape. I am not sure if he would carry out such threats against a woman, but at the very least he will burn your house around you."

The old woman's hand goes to her mouth, and from the alarm in her eyes, Claire sees that she guessed correctly. "Willie!" the old woman cries. "Abel! get up!"

Two boys in nightshirts appear, rubbing their eyes. One is ten or eleven; the other a few years older. "What's wrong, Grandmother?" the oldest asks.

"This boy has come to warn us that Morgan's Raiders are coming!" The old woman snatches a cloak from a peg beside the door and throws it on over her nightgown. "Willie, hitch up the team so we can pile our things in the wagon. Abel, round up the horses and take them into the woods where the invaders will not find them. I shall gather up foodstuffs, blankets, and other essentials. General Morgan shall not eat my blackberry preserves, nor shall he have our snap beans and okra."

She turns to Claire. "I thank thee from the bottom of my heart, son. At this very moment, I have two runaway slaves hiding in my smokehouse. Yesterday they fled from Kentucky, where, alas, human bondage is still legal. I planned to pass them on to the next stage tomorrow. Instead, I will take them with me and pray we are not stopped by Rebel patrols." Reaching out, she embraces Claire and plants a kiss on her cheek. "Bless thee. Thy mother would be proud of thee could she see what thee has done. Now go quickly and warn others."

Encouraged by this success, Claire decides to follow the old woman's advice and stop at every farmhouse no matter how long it takes. Riding back to the main road, she turns north. Soon she comes to an old-fashioned log cabin chinked with white lime. The cabin, which sits only a few yards from the road, has no porch, so she is able to ride up to the door and knock without having to dismount.

"Wake up!" she cries. "Morgan's Raiders have invaded Indiana and are marching this way!"

She waits, but there is no response. She tries again. Still no response. She has just decided that no one is home, when the front door flies open, and she finds herself confronting a middle-aged woman in a long cotton nightgown.

"Git!" says the woman, lifting a shotgun and pointing the barrel at Claire.

"Wait, madam!" Claire cries. "You do not understand. I have not come to do you harm. I have come to warn you that a Rebel army is marching this way."

"I knows it!" says the woman. "You are the third Yankee dog to come to my home this night to warn me. Well, you can keep your warning, boy. I thank God General Morgan is on the march. Let him scour the North like the wrath of Jehovah and send those blue-coated devils to hell!"

Realizing she has stumbled on a Copperhead, Claire kicks the gelding into a gallop and rides off. Behind her, she hears the sound of the shotgun going off.

"Hurrah for Jeff Davis!" yells the woman. But either her aim is off or she has only fired a warning shot, because when Claire stops to check, she finds both she and her horse have escaped unharmed.

Since others have been spreading the alarm along the main road, Claire sees no reason to duplicate their work. Returning to the trace, she again plunges into a landscape of sleeping cattle and silent fields, happy to exchange speed for safety. Sooner or later, she will get to Corydon. Meanwhile every step her horse takes brings her closer to John.

She passes a stand of sorghum, a snake rail fence, something that looks as if it might have once been a sheepcote; but if there are farmhouses connected with these things, she cannot see them. For a half hour or so, she continues to peer into the shadows, searching for signs of human habitation, but she spies nothing.

Moonlight falls on her, silvering the reins, lacquering the saddle horn, turning her fingernails into pale shells. As she rides along the silver thread of the trace, her thoughts gradually turn to John. *"You want me to give my word of honor not to fight?"* she imagines him objecting. *"Claire, I have never stopped loving you."* (She gives herself the satisfaction of that phrase, for surely he will say something tender.) *"But I cannot desert my comrades. It would be dishonorable."*

"Honor?" she will say. *"Dearest John, do not speak to me of honor. Honor is just another name men give to a desire to throw away their lives and drive those who love them mad with grief. The age of cavaliers is over. This is a new kind of war, one fought with rifled muskets, trenches, armored gunboats, and minié balls. Men no longer unsheathe shining sabers and ride forth to fight the enemy. Instead they are mowed down by the anonymous thousands until even the vultures are sickened. Do Second Manassas, Antietam, Fredericksburg, Stones River, and Chancellorsville mean nothing to you? Have you forgotten Shiloh?*

"If you love me, sign the parole and leave with me before the Raiders enter Corydon. Today, Morgan may win the battle, but the Confederacy is losing the war. It is folly to sacrifice yourself for a cause you do not believe in. We can go to a place where men are not slaughtering each other and make a life together. We can be happy, John. Are not peace and happiness worth more than war and suffering?"

After a while, the trace improves so much she is able to kick the gelding into a trot. In her head, the imaginary conversation with John continues. She passes more fences, a deserted shed, three haystacks set in a row like counters. Up ahead a patch of forest obscures the trail. As she enters the shadows, she instinctively slows down. This proves to be lucky, because seconds later she runs into a rope strung between two trees. It is a trap so simple a child could have set it, but it is extraordinarily effective. Catching her across the chest, the rope jerks her out of the saddle, and before she fully understands what is happening, she is airborne, flying backward as her horse trots on without her. *Oh!* she thinks, and then she hits the ground so hard she stops thinking.

The impact knocks the air out of her lungs. As she lies face-down, gasping for breath, she sees two pairs of stout leather boots approaching. Someone coughs and a stream of tobacco juice dimples the mud beside her cheek.

"Got one," says a male voice.

"Looks like all you got is some fool of a boy," says another.

The men's accents are not Southern or Northern, but a peculiar mixture of the two. It is a familiar accent, one Claire has heard all her life.

"Rebels . . ." she gasps. She wants to warn them that a Rebel army is riding toward the very place they are standing, but she cannot get the words out.

"So you're a Reb, are you?" A hand reaches down, clutches the back of her shirt, and jerks her to her feet, and Claire finds herself looking at two soldiers of the Indiana Legion. One is a boy of perhaps fourteen with a badly pockmarked face. The other is a heavyset middle-aged man who has an official air about him, as if he might be a judge in civilian life. Both are pointing pistols at her.

"You one of Morgan's Raiders?" the boy asks. His voice shakes and so does the hand that holds the pistol.

Somehow Claire manages to suck in enough air to speak. "No," she gasps.

"He's lying." A man of about twenty strides up to the group. "Explain this," he says and throws a wad of gray cloth in Claire's face. A brass button strikes her cheek. It is the dead corporal's jacket.

Before she can say anything in her own defense, they seize her weapons, bind her hands behind her back, order her to remain silent, commandeer her horse, and march her to Corydon at gunpoint. The walk is not long, but it changes Claire's view of things considerably.

For half a mile or so, the trace continues to wind through a countryside so peaceful the very idea of war seems unimaginable; but when they rejoin the main road, everything changes abruptly. The legion has felled dozens of trees, blocking the primary route so Morgan's supply wagons and artillery will not be able to pass unless the Raiders haul out axes and chop their way through. To her right, just above the town itself, Claire sees hastily built breastworks made of logs and fence rails, braced here and there by large rocks. Behind these makeshift barricades, a small army of men and boys is hurriedly preparing to defend the town. The news that Morgan has invaded Indiana may not have reached the outlying farms, but clearly it has reached Corydon.

They continue on past the barricades and make their way down the north side of the ridge to a small creek that is shallow enough to ford on foot. Beyond the creek lies the town. On a hot July night the citizens of Corydon would ordinarily be sleeping quietly in their own beds, lulled by the humming of crickets, but instead the entire population appears to be in motion. As Claire and her captors walk up the main street, horses gallop past, carrying ammunition and supplies to the men on the ridge. Dogs bark, babies cry, every window is lighted. Some people are busy loading their possessions into wagons while others—mostly groups of women and very old men—stand about talking in panicked voices, as if they already understand the Home Guard cannot possibly defend them against such a massive Confederate attack.

Having once been the state capital, Corydon offers a particularly attractive example of southern Indiana architecture of the sort Henry would have reveled in. Claire is hardly in a mood to appreciate the town's beauties, but she cannot help but notice that the streets are unusually wide and the central square gracefully proportioned. Set in a grove of raintrees, the courthouse is built of fieldstones that gleam mutely in the moonlight like bolts of gray silk stacked in a pile. There are a number of sturdy redbrick houses that look old enough to have been built when Indiana was still a territory, including an immense three-story mansion that features a wide porch lined with half a dozen vacant rocking chairs. A sign out front proclaims it is the Eagle Hotel, an establishment for ladies and gentlemen that offers reasonable rates.

But the building that most captures her imagination is a low wooden structure directly across from the courthouse. Since it has a barred window, it can only be the Corydon jail. As she searches the window for some sign of life, a disturbing thought comes unbidden into her mind. What if, after all this, she discovers John is indeed married and that he never really loved her? Worse yet: what if, when they are finally reunited, she discovers she never really loved him? What if her grand passion proves to be no more than a phantom she conjured up to console herself for marrying Henry? The thought is so alarming, it brings her to a full stop.

"Get on," says the boy with the pocked face. He prods her in the back with his pistol. Still looking over her shoulder at the jail, Claire moves forward and collides with a lean man in a black suit and string tie.

"Watch where yer goin'!" the man snarls. He does a double take and turns to Claire's captors. "Looks like you two done captured yourself a Rebel soldier," he says. "One of Morgan's?"

"Yep," says the boy as if that single syllable encompasses all anyone will ever need to know about Claire.

The man in the string tie steps back, inspects Claire, and spits a stream of tobacco juice in her direction. "Hang him," he advises. "He ain't in uniform, which makes him a spy. And spies get hung."

"Plenty of Rebs can't afford uniforms," objects the older man who marched Claire to town at gunpoint. "They just put on whatever."

"This one took off his damn uniform and hid his damn marks

of rank," says the young man who threw the corporal's jacket in Claire's face.

The citizen in the string tie spits more tobacco juice in Claire's general direction and glares at her. "Hang him, I say."

"He's no more than a child," says Claire's defender.

"Child, hell," the pockfaced boy chimes in. "He's a Confederate corporal."

"You boys are right fierce when you get in a hanging mood," says the older man, "but all we got ourselves here is a boy so young he probably just got weaned off his mama's tit." He turns to the man in the string tie. "You say you want me to hang him, Jack? Ain't you got a boy of your own in the Union army?"

"My Davie ain't no spy," says the string tie man and sends another stream of tobacco juice into the mud.

"Well, neither is this little shoat." And with that, Claire's defender nudges her in the back with his pistol barrel and sets her to moving again.

Claire feels as if her legs have turned to water. Her breath catches in her throat. She is dizzy and light-headed with a terror so stark it is all she can do to keep from passing out, and yet she wants to be here. Needs to be here. Would not have escaped if her captors had lowered their pistols, returned her horse, and ordered her to ride away and rejoin Morgan.

Only a few minutes ago, she was wondering if she really loved John. Now she has her answer.

Claire

After the man who wanted to hang me left, my captors forced me to stand facing a bakery with my hands raised over my head. For a long time, they lingered in the street, arguing about how best to dispose of me, and while they argued I prayed. "Dear God," I pleaded, "please let them throw me in the jail." In the end they did just that, more to protect me from being lynched, I think, than because they thought I was dangerous.

As the cell door swung shut behind me, the first person I saw was John. The sight of him hit me so hard I began to cry with relief. Ever since Hines had reassured Morgan he was alive, I had told myself he would be waiting for me in Corydon, but no matter how stubbornly I had repeated those words, I had secretly feared he was dead. The thought that I might never see him again or touch him or have a chance to clear up the misunderstandings that had separated us had tormented me. But now here he was: my love, alive and well, standing at the window with his back to me, peering through the bars, so gaunt and ragged and dirty that if I had not known every inch of his dear body, I might not have recognized him.

I suddenly became aware we were not alone. There were eight other Rebel soldiers in this cell, all crammed shoulder to shoulder, and worse yet, I knew two of them and they knew me. Eight men besides John: sixteen ears listening to every word he might say to me and I to him. Fighting back my tears, I coughed as if I had a cold, and blew my nose on my sleeve. "John," I said hoarsely. "John Taylor."

John turned and stared at me as if trying to figure out who this strange boy was who knew him by name. I was shocked to see the marks two years of war had left on him. His skin was so tanned he must not have spent a day beneath a roof since we parted. There were lines on his forehead I did not remember, more lines at the corners of his eyes that radiated out toward his temples like fine cracks in china. He was so terribly thin that I wanted to sit him down and feed him, but his eyes were still the shade of green-brown that had always reminded me of a field in early spring, and his beard and hair were still the deep red-tinged gold of ripe wheat. This was the face I had fallen in love with, the face that had filled my dreams for so many years—different yet the same—and as I gazed on it, I felt such a rush of tenderness, I could not continue speaking.

"Who the hell are you?" John demanded. He stared at the boy I had become, that Confederate corporal named Zeke Crane who wore his hair short, his shirt loose, and his pant legs cuffed up to keep from tripping over them. I saw him search my face just as I had searched his, and his eyes suddenly widened in surprise.

"Claire!" he cried. There were two long years of love and longing in his voice. I wanted to run to him and embrace him, but I could not risk it, nor could I afford to let him continue speaking. I could not even get close enough to whisper my new name because there was not enough room to move from door to window; so I was forced to yell the necessary information over the heads of the others in a casual, boylike voice, and something about having to talk to him in public this way nearly broke my heart.

"Claire is just fine, Cousin John," I said. "And she's as sweet on you as ever. She told me that if I met up with you, I should tell you that she loves you to beat the band."

There were catcalls and whistles at this pronouncement.

"Didn't know you had a thweetheart, Taylor!" cried a Raider with no front teeth. His lisping drew more laughter and a few ribald comments about "Claire" that would have never been made had the men realized the lady in question was present.

I could tell John was beginning to grasp the situation. "I'm not surprised you don't recognize me," I continued. "You got such a passel of relatives, and I've grown since last you saw me. I'm your cousin Zeke, Marna Lee Crane's boy. Re-member me?"

"Zeke Crane." *John thought the name over, and then smiled so broadly I was afraid that smile alone would betray us. He had remembered our trip down the Mississippi as Mr. and Mrs. Ezekiel Crane.* "My God, Zeke, what are you doing here?"

"I joined Morgan's Raiders just like you did," *I told him.* "Took up arms to defend the sacred soil of Kentucky from Yankee aggression." *If John realized I was quoting some of the first words I had ever heard him say, he didn't give any sign of it. Instead, he looked at me with concern.*

"Surely you have not been foolish enough to expose yourself to danger," *he said, and the cell erupted with laughter.*

"He's been eatin' Yankee lead for breakfast!" *one Rebel cried.*

"Zeke's a real hellion," *said another.*

"The boy fought with us at Lebanon."

"Fierce as a mad dog."

"Morgan's pet. Sits around eatin' chicken from the Old Man's plate."

"Y'all should be proud of him, Taylor."

A Rebel with a missing ear examined me suspiciously. I did not know the man, and tales of my bravery did not seem to have impressed him. I prayed he could not see the woman beneath the boy's shirt, for the expression on his face was not in the least friendly.

"If y'all are such a pet of the general's," *he demanded,* "how'd you come to get yourself throwed in the Corydon jail? Was yuh in a patrol that got bushwacked, or did yuh just skedaddle off on your own?"

"I rode off on my own, sir," *I said, although the man was only a private and, technically, I outranked him.* "I know now that it was plain dumb to do so, but I was riled. I wanted to get to Corydon before the rest of the boys, shoot the damn Yankees who captured Cousin John, and bust him out of jail."

I suspect that in no other army could I have successfully posed as an angry relative bent on lone vengeance, but in this one a blood feud was an unanswerable excuse. The private's hostile expression softened, and instead of being upbraided for desertion, I found myself being praised.

"You got one hell of a spirit, son!" *he cried.* "I wish we had a hundred more like yuh."

"Well, durn it, Orton," another man objected, "you know good and well the South's got thousands of fire-eatin' sons of bitches, but not many this young."

The men laughed and clapped me on the shoulder. Squirming aside, they made way for me so I could join John. As I threaded past their bodies, I smelled the sour stench of sweat and confinement. When I reached the window, a summer breeze was blowing through the bars.

"Zeke," John said and clapped me on the shoulder. "Welcome. I've never been gladder to see anyone in my life." His hand remained a second longer than it should have, caressing me with a slight, invisible pressure that almost made me break down again. I could tell he longed to take me in his arms. For a moment I entertained myself by imagining how the men around us would react if he grabbed me and kissed me.

As John removed his hand from my shoulder, the other prisoners closed back around us, pushing me up against him. I was close enough to smell the familiar scent of his body and see the pulse of the blood beating in his neck. I thought of many things at that moment: our lovemaking in New Orleans, the wife and daughter he might or might not have, whether or not he had thought of me as much as I had thought of him, and whether he still felt the way he had when he wrote me all those letters. But most of all I thought about our baby and how, if the child had lived, it might have grown up to look like its father.

"So Claire is well?" John asked gravely as his eyes flickered with amusement.

"Yes," I said. I could feel my body trembling and I imagine John could feel it too. "She had a hard time after she left New Orleans," I continued. "A friend of hers wrote her letters that she did not receive. The friend—a lieutenant like you—had been gravely wounded. She would have come to him at once if she had known, but she did not find those letters until a few weeks ago."

John's eyes narrowed and the amusement went out of them. I could tell he knew who had kept those letters from me. "Tell me all the news from home, Zeke," he said. I looked at him in confusion. "How is Mother?" he prompted. I suddenly understood that he wanted me to mix ordinary events in with news of myself to further throw our audience off the track.

"Cousin Lavinia is well and thriving," I said.

"And my sisters? What of them?"

"*Cousin Emma is still at that Yankee boarding school in Michigan, but I hear she prays daily for the South to win. Cousin Agnes is in good health and sends her love. Were it not for her, I would not have known where to find you.*" I allowed my arm to brush John's again and wondered if it were possible for a person to die of desire.

"*And Lenoir? How does the town fare?*"

"*The Yankees burned the courthouse, but only a few private homes were harmed. The horses have all been commandeered—some by one side, some by the other. It was hard for folks to get their crops in this spring without mules or oxen, but since Kentucky is still in the Union, the Yankees kept everyone fed. Your mother gets pickled beef all the way from Chicago; and though it sticks in her throat to take handouts, she and your sister aren't going hungry. They are even able to buy coffee from time to time.*"

"*The only coffee we get is offa dead Yankees,*" the Rebel next to me piped up.

"*Yep,*" offered another, "*we been drinkin' chicory and ground peanuts for so long, I've plumb forgot what real coffee tastes like.*"

I was not talking to John. I was talking to John and eight men. I reminded myself of this, moved as far away from him as I could bear to, and chose my words more carefully.

"*You remember Henry Endicott?*" I asked. I used Henry's mother's maiden name since I did not dare to use Winston.

"*All too well,*" John said grimly. "*As sorry a son of a bitch as I have ever met and a sneaking coward to boot. What of him?*"

"*His wife left him a few weeks ago,*" I said. "*They say she fell in love with a handsome Rebel and ran off to join him with not much more than the clothes she stood up in.*"

"*Did she leave Henry for good?*" John asked.

"*She left him forever,*" I told him. "*She'll never go back.*" I paused and searched his face, but he was better than I was at hiding what he was feeling. I longed to ask him the question that had been tormenting me since we parted in New Orleans, but I did not know how to translate it into this code we were being forced to speak. "*Her husband lied something awful,*" I said. "*I suspect that's why she left him. He even lied about you, cousin.*"

"*Did he now?*" John's voice was even, but there was something in his eyes I wished Henry were there to see. I imagined Henry scuttling for safety at the sight of John's face. Encouraged, I continued.

"Henry told folks you were married and had a daughter," I said. I braced myself for his reply, but before John could speak, the Raider at my elbow joined our conversation.

"That is one heck of a whopper!" the man exclaimed. "Taylor ain't never been married, have you, Taylor?"

"No," John said, and with that one word, he put my greatest fear to rest.

Around us, other men picked up pieces of our conversation and, having nothing better to do to while away the boredom of imprisonment, amused themselves by providing footnotes.

"Taylor's too ugly to get hisself a wife," said one of the Rebels.

"No woman's gonna marry a fellah what's got no socks."

"Taylor, you and your cousin are jawin' away like a pair of old biddies. Shut up and let the rest of us get some sleep."

"How the hell can a man sleep standin' up?"

Darkness yielded to first light, but except that John and I fell silent, nothing changed. As we stood there, so close each could feel the heat of the other's flesh, eight men stood around us: talking, swearing, damning the Yankees, and spitting between their feet. Only twice did John reach out and touch me. Once he secretly ran his finger over my wrist so quickly it took my breath away; and later, when I began to cry silently in the darkness, he reached out and wiped away my tears.

Chapter Twenty

SHORTLY after noon, the battle of Corydon begins. For half an hour the sound of gunfire rolls down from the ridge south of town. John moves aside so Claire can look out the window, but all she can see is the street and a bit of the courthouse. Soon they hear the boom of the Parrotts.

"Looks like Morgan's brought out the fireworks," observes the Rebel at her elbow, pulling a plug of tobacco out of his pocket and biting off a hunk. There is a moment of silence as he chews. "I reckon we're whuppin' 'em."

There are murmurs of agreement from the other prisoners. They wait for more shells to explode, but after the third salvo, the Confederate artillery falls silent. After a brief interval, mounted men begin to ride past, and a confused roar of alarm fills the air. Then men on foot dash by, their faces flushed and desperate. A portly man in a checked suit stumbles onto the courthouse lawn and falls down as if stricken by apoplexy. Another sits on the curb directly in front of the jail and stays there for several minutes, fanning himself with his hat.

"Taylor, what in tarnation is goin' on out there?" asks a tall man who is wedged against the cell door.

"I can only see a patch of the street," John says, "but a whole mess of Indiana Legion boys just galloped by like the Devil himself was after them. I'd say pretty much every man in town old enough to shoot a gun has taken to his heels."

"Morgan's licked 'em!" yells the man at Claire's elbow. "It's a rout!"

"Run, Yankees, run! Yeeeehaaaa!" Picking up a tin cup, the man by the door bangs it against the bars and begins to sing "The Bonnie Blue Flag." As the chorus swells around her, Claire remembers John's brothers singing those same words. She does not like the lyrics any better than she did in the spring of '61. Suddenly her thoughts are interrupted by a small movement to her left. Taking advantage of the fact that everyone else is looking at the soldier with the cup, John has put his mouth to her ear.

"You know where the Eagle Hotel is?" he whispers. Claire nods. "When we get out of here, wait a while and then go there." Suddenly, he gives her earlobe a quick kiss, which—thank God—no one sees. The kiss is only a swift brush of the lips, but it sweeps the sadness out of her heart. John has risked a lot to kiss her and done it impulsively as if he could not help himself. Despite the two years they have been separated, he still loves her.

On every side, sweaty, unwashed Confederate prisoners of war are bumping up against her and yelling at the top of their lungs. Claire joins them in a long, high-pitched Rebel yell, and hearing the joy in her voice, John grins.

She never forgets that moment: John's face and the faces of the men; hot July sunshine flowing through the narrow bars; the shadows that stipple the whitewashed walls of the cell; the flash of the tin cup striking the bars. Long after the war is over, she only has to close her eyes to summon up the Corydon jail and feel once more that perfect happiness that lasts no longer than three seconds before it is abruptly interrupted by a distant thump followed by a high-pitched scream.

An artillery shell passes overhead wailing like an avenging angel. Striking nearby, it explodes, and the concussion shakes the floor under her feet. Plaster and dirt cascade down on her head. Startled, she coughs, instinctively moves toward John, then freezes. The other prisoners have stopped singing, and those who can manage it have turned toward the window. The inches that separate Corporal Ezekiel Crane from Lieutenant John Taylor are once again wider than the Ohio and Mississippi combined.

"That one was durn close," observes the Rebel at her elbow with a cheerfulness that, under the circumstances, seems completely insane.

"Yep," says another. "You reckon the Old Man's gonna shell the jail or does he know we're in here?"

"The general knows there are Confederate prisoners in Corydon," Claire says. "Captain Hines told him." She is surprised at the strength of her voice. Perhaps, having fought at Lebanon, she qualifies as a seasoned veteran; or perhaps she was too happy only a few seconds ago to allow herself to imagine what will happen if one of Morgan's cannonballs strikes the jail.

"Well, ain't you a useful little sprout," says the one-eared Rebel. "Taylor, I am warming to your cousin. Yessir, warming. I didn't like his looks at first, but I am warming."

John appears to be on the verge of replying when there is a second thump from the Confederate artillery and another shell comes screaming overhead.

"One, thwo, buckle my thshoe," says the raider with no front teeth. The prisoners freeze like characters in a *tableau vivant* as he counts off the seconds. Suddenly there is a deafening crash and the cell rocks as if a giant has picked it up and shaken it. More hunks of plaster rain down from the ceiling, and Claire feels something scuttle over her hand. She examines her shirtsleeve and sees a small spider running for its life. Reaching across John, she transfers the spider to the window ledge and watches enviously as it escapes through the bars.

As the seconds tick by, her courage evaporates, and panic begins to crawl up from her stomach in a long, slow sweep. Why should she be afraid now when she was so fearless when the first shell struck? Why is she spiraling into this cold, sweating, teeth-gritting terror? She closes her eyes and tries to fight the fear, but it keeps growing inside her chest, crushing her until she can hardly breathe. This has something to do with the spider, but what? She is not afraid of spiders. *I must have been trapped like this before,* she thinks.

Yes, that's it! It's not the shelling. She hates being locked in this cell, hates closed places of all kinds because she *has* been trapped before, buried half smothered and unable to cry for help. She could not have been more than five when she tried to swing on a rope without realizing it was attached to a chute. Her father heard the shelled corn fall and immediately came running to dig her out, but the seconds she spent buried alive under the corn still haunt her.

Balling her hands into fists, she forces herself to stand still. To be killed by an artillery shell in a jail cell is no worse than being killed by one on a battlefield. The result is the same. But she cannot get a grip on her panic. The cell suddenly seems as stifling as a grave. Reaching under John's arm, she touches the stones, slippery and damp, flecked with mold. The corn that covered her was slippery too, each grain sharp as a tack. She remembers what it was like to lie in darkness beneath that great, heavy pile, unable to breathe or move her limbs.

"The problem is," observes the Rebel with the missing ear, "them Parrotts is only accurate at about two miles." This is not what she needs to hear, but since the man is standing less than a foot from her, she has little choice.

"How far away are the guns?" she asks. Somehow she must again manage to keep the fear out of her voice, because he shrugs and grins at her.

"I reckon about two and a half miles, son, from the sound of 'em. Ain't nothing worse than getting blowed to bits by your own side, is there?"

Claire lowers her hand and forces herself to return his smile. "No," she says, "but instant death at Rebel hands is better than slow starvation in a Yankee prison camp." This is one of the most difficult sentences she has ever uttered, but it has a surprising effect. For some reason, speaking in a confident tone breaks the cycle and her panic starts to retreat. Unfortunately, her relief is cut short by the scream of a third artillery shell. The Rebel with the missing teeth begins to count. He does not get far before Claire hears a muffled explosion. The floor of the cell wobbles slightly, like a dancer changing direction, and a small cloud of plaster dust drifts down from the ceiling.

"Durn it," objects the man who is pressed up against Claire's left shoulder, "I think that one missed the town entirely. Them boys on the ridge needs to get their eyes checked." He seems sincerely disappointed that the center of Corydon has not been blown to bits.

Taking the shelling as a sign that they are about to be liberated, the prisoners become infected with raucous good humor. Some stamp their feet, others find objects to bang against the bars, and almost everyone takes turns pushing past John and Claire to peer out the window.

"Come and git us!" they cry.

"Hurry up, boys!"

"Unlock this durned door!"

"What's taking y'all so long?"

Again, the Confederate artillery falls silent. There is a brief pause, a distant pounding of hooves, and the first band of Raiders rides into town.

Down the main street of Corydon gallop two dozen young men on some of the finest horses Kentucky has ever produced. Their boots are muddy, their coats patched, their broad-brimmed hats misshapen and gray with dust; but the Confederate flag they carry snaps smartly in the breeze, and they have the well-satisfied look of men who have won a victory and not paid too high a price for it.

Later Claire is surprised to learn that eight of Morgan's troopers died in the battle and many more were wounded. The poorly armed citizens of Corydon defended their rail-fence barricades fiercely, fighting with a stubborn, near-suicidal bravery although they were outnumbered seven to one; but none of the price Morgan was forced to pay shows as the Raiders enter the town. In fact, if Claire did not know better, she might imagine she was watching a cavalry drill executed for the purpose of dazzling an invisible audience.

In Lebanon, snipers had been a problem, but here the Raiders meet no further resistance. For a moment they halt in front of the courthouse. Then a lean Raider in silver spurs and an embroidered vest rides up to the jail and dismounts in a motion so fluid it looks like a dance. A few moments later, they hear a key turn in the outer lock and the Raider in the vest appears, grinning broadly. Pushing back his hat and putting his hands on his hips, he examines the men in the cell.

"How y'all doing?" he asks.

"Just fine," says one of the prisoners.

"No one dead or wounded?"

"Hell no," says the man at Claire's elbow. "The Hoosiers run this jail like a first-class hotel. We been eating fried quail and apple pie and catching up on our sleep. Yankee ladies have been dropping by to mop our weary brows and bring us mint juleps, only, to tell the truth, they weren't quite ladies."

The men roar with laughter.

"Y'all are a lucky bunch of bastards," says the Raider in the vest. "They were planning to transport you up to Indianapolis today and feed you on hog slop and cockroaches." And with that, he unlocks the cell door.

As the men file out, Claire feels a great wave of relief. For a moment she remains by the window, gulping air into her lungs in long, shuddering breaths.

"Go on," John whispers, prodding her gently in the small of the back. "Walk out and don't look back, but remember: wait a while and then meet me at the Eagle Hotel."

In the front room of the jail, Claire finds the rifle her captors confiscated stacked in a pile with half a dozen others. As she retrieves it, she breathes a silent prayer of thanks. She had not been looking forward to explaining how she managed to lose three guns in less than a week. John's pearl-handled pistols sit on the sheriff's desk next to a half-filled cup of coffee. She touches the side of the cup and discovers it is still warm.

"Git the lead out of your britches, Theke," says the Rebel with two missing front teeth. "We got a thob to do."

Claire turns to face him. Behind her, she can hear John pick up his pistols, but she does not turn around.

"What kind of job?" she asks.

The Rebel gives her a smile that reminds her of a piano with missing keys. "We got to commandeer us thome fried chicken, boy. If we're lucky, maybe the ladies will even throw in bithcuts and a jar of gravy."

Claire assumes he is indulging in fantasy, but when she inquires how long he's been dreaming about fried chicken, he informs her he is not dreaming at all; he is in dead earnest. Everywhere the Raiders stop, the Yankee ladies cook for them: sometimes willingly, sometimes at gunpoint. "We git pies and cakes and all thorts of pickles," he says. And shouldering his rifle, he wanders off to find a saddlebag large enough to hold hams.

Claire crosses the street and settles down on a bench to watch the rest of the Raiders ride into Corydon. The Confederate shells seem to have done minimal damage. One building lies in ruins, but the rest appear to be intact. By day, the stones of the courthouse no longer appear gray but slightly golden. The showy yellow blossoms of the raintrees are long gone, but bunches of pink, paperlike capsules dangle from the boughs like party favors.

After a while, she rises to her feet and casually strolls toward the Eagle Hotel. As soon as she steps onto the front porch, John appears.

"Attention, Corporal," he says with a perfectly straight face. Claire snaps to attention and salutes him, and John returns her salute without so much as blinking. His acting abilities are impressive but also a bit disconcerting. Claire reminds herself that this is serious business. She cannot put Zeke Crane aside and become Claire Winston simply because she and John have been reunited. Whenever they are in public, he must not give any indication he thinks of her as anything but a younger cousin.

"Follow me," he orders and, drawing his pistols, he pushes open the front door of the hotel and strides in.

Claire follows him into a dim hallway. An elaborately carved, mirrored coatrack stands against one wall. Directly in front of them is a flight of narrow, curving stairs that leads to the upper floors of the hotel. To their right is a closed door. John knocks on it.

"Yes?" says a faint female voice.

"Ma'am," John calls through the closed door, "are you in charge of this establishment?"

"No, sir," the woman says. Her voice quavers with fear. "Mr. Kintner is the proprietor."

John gives Claire a wink and puts the pistols back in their holsters.

"Ma'am," he says, "I am Lieutenant John Taylor of the Second Kentucky Cavalry, and I have come to inform Mr. Kintner that he is about to receive a very important guest. Would you please be so good as to open this door?"

"It is not locked," the woman says in the same faint quaver.

"Oh, Permelia," says a younger, stronger female voice. "Must you always be so honest?"

John tries the handle and finds the door is indeed not locked. He opens it to reveal a formal parlor. Dark blue drapes have been pulled across the windows, throwing the room into darkness. Claire can make out a marble and wood mantel; a brass fire screen shaped like a peacock; several low, round marble-top tables; and a rug that appears to be a muddy mauve enlivened by small yellow shapes that might possibly be meant to represent flowers. Every level surface is covered with knickknacks. On the mantel sits an ancient slice of wedding cake preserved under a glass dome.

Two women are perched on a large sofa looking as if they expect to be executed on the spot. The older of the two, who appears quite frightened, is in her late thirties. She must have put on her best dress in honor of the invasion, for she is wearing a black wool gown, which makes Claire almost faint with heatstroke just to contemplate it. The younger woman, who cannot be more than twenty, wears a light summer dress of spotted muslin, and the look she gives John and Claire is defiant.

"My name is Sallie Kintner," says the younger woman as soon as they step across the threshold. "And I hope that, whatever your opinions may be on the rights of individual states to rebel against a lawfully elected government, you and the other bandits you ride with have not injured the Constitution Elm."

"Sallie!" the older woman gasps.

"Please, Permelia," says the younger woman. "Let me do the talking." She glares at John. "Well?" she demands. "Have you destroyed the elm with your shells, sir, or have you allowed it to survive?"

"I am afraid I do not understand the question, miss," John says. "What is the Constitution Elm?"

"The great tree under which the Indiana State Constitution was signed in the year 1816," Sallie Kintner snaps. "As you would know perfectly well if you were a resident of Corydon and not an invading Rebel."

Claire cannot help admiring Sallie Kintner's spirit. How many young women are prepared to face down two armed men without flinching, not to mention scold them for possibly destroying a historical landmark?

"I regret to say that I do not know if the particular tree in question survived our artillery bombardment," John says. "As soon as General Morgan arrives, you may apply to him for information on its welfare. Meanwhile, I would appreciate it if you would inform your staff that the general will be taking his breakfast in your main dining room in approximately three quarters of an hour."

"Morgan is coming here?" The older woman clutches an arm of the sofa as if she were about to swoon.

"What does the Great Horse Thief eat?" asks Sallie coolly.

John grins at her. "Ham, eggs, grits, gravy, hot biscuits, and either pound cake or apple pie, Miss Kintner; plus a substantial amount of very hot, very fresh coffee served without insults."

Sallie Kintner presses her lips together and nods. "I take it you are warning me the general is not a man to be trifled with?"

"Not even by a young lady as charming as yourself," John says. Claire feels a pang of jealousy. Sallie is very pretty, not to mention that a young woman wearing a thin muslin dress and silk ribbons in her hair will always look better than a woman wearing a baggy shirt, ill-fitting pants, and a pair of muddy boots. She begins to regret that she chopped off so much of her hair. Perhaps she could have just cut a little off and pinned the rest up. John loves her hair, or at least he used to.

"The corporal and I must now ensure that this building is free of potential assassins," John continues. "Are there any other guests in residence at present?"

"No," says the older woman. "All the guests fled as soon as they heard General Morgan had crossed the Ohio. Only members of the family, myself, and some of the kitchen staff remain."

"Thank you, madam," John says. "I am sure you would not intentionally give us misinformation, but nevertheless, the corporal and I now need to search all the bedchambers." He stretches out his hand. "The keys, please, Miss Kintner."

"The doors can only be bolted from the inside," Sallie says. "Since you have frightened off all our guests, I assume you will have no trouble entering any room you choose."

A few moments later, Claire finds herself behind John, mounting the staircase that leads to the upper stories of the hotel. When they reach the third floor, he opens the first door they come to, puts his arm around her waist, and pulls her in.

She has a brief impression of white walls, starched curtains billowing in a light breeze, and a big canopied bed covered with a white and yellow quilt, before he kicks the door shut, throws the bolt, takes her in his arms, and starts kissing her as if he never means to stop. For a moment they cling together, and in that brief space of time—which again cannot be more than a few seconds—she finds passion and tenderness, but more than anything else, she finds a sense of finally having come home.

Taking off her cap, John throws it to the floor, runs his fingers through her hair, and kisses her on the forehead, ears, and neck. His hands are rougher than she remembered, but his touch is gentle. "I have to leave you for a little while," he says.

Claire, who has been anticipating a declaration of love, is surprised. She steps back and examines his face but cannot read it. "Why?" she asks.

"I need to search for Yankee snipers. If one takes a shot at Morgan from one of these windows, both of us could end up in front of a firing squad." He gives her another quick kiss and pulls out his pistols.

"Let me go with you," Claire says.

"Better not. I can do it faster by myself, and I'll only be gone for a few minutes." Again he kisses her. "Close your eyes. I have something to keep you company while I'm away."

Claire gives in and closes her eyes. She feels him slip something over her head.

"Count to three before you open your eyes, and then bolt the door behind me."

Claire begins counting. When she gets to three, she opens her eyes to discover that she is wearing the gold watch chain she left behind in New Orleans.

Chapter Twenty-one

OUTSIDE the Eagle Hotel, the Raiders are flowing through Corydon like a cloud of locusts. Horses are commandeered and hundreds of exhausted Kentucky Thoroughbreds turned out to pasture. Housewives suddenly find themselves feeding bands of hungry men who politely tip their broad-brimmed hats before they rifle through the pantry and wander upstairs to take clothing and whatever else strikes their fancy. Fried chicken and whole pies disappear, along with hams, barrels of flour, slabs of lard, pecks of cornmeal, razors, socks, suspenders, and leather-bound volumes of romantic poetry. When some four hundred Union prisoners are herded into the square to await Morgan's arrival, so many barefoot Rebels acquire shoes that for hours the most common sight in central Corydon is a citizen volunteer sitting on the ground pulling off his boots.

On the south side of town, the Raiders transform a Presbyterian church into a hospital. Requisitioning the fans the congregation uses on hot summer Sundays, they hand them to small girls and order them to fan the flies away from men too weak to lift their arms. When the wounded discover each fan carries an advertisement for a local funeral parlor, they make grim jokes. "Fan us into our graves," they tell the girls. "The Devil can't keep Hades any hotter than Corydon."

In the churchyard, their faces covered with sheets, pillowcases, and their own bloody jackets, the recently dead rest on the graves of the long-deceased. When Morgan rides by on Glencoe, he dismounts, takes off his hat, and pauses to say a silent prayer. It is a somber moment, but by the time he has mounted up again, his hat is planted firmly back on his head and the sadness has left his face. Although this victory has come at a price greater than he intended to pay, he believes men who have just won a battle should see their general ride into town smiling and triumphant.

In the square, the Union prisoners mill around in confusion or sit on the lawn in front of the courthouse watching the enemy loot the county treasury. Many are so exhausted they can hardly lift their heads. Since Colonel Jordan surrendered, they have been marched several miles at gunpoint on a day so hot the road feels like a griddle. Thanks to the telegraph wire that brought them news even when it failed to bring them reinforcements, they know Morgan's men came close to murdering the prisoners they took in Lebanon. Have they been captured by an army or a gang of bandits? they wonder. Will Morgan parole them or shoot them?

In due time, Morgan makes his grand entrance, riding down the main street through a mob of cheering Raiders. Dismounting in front of the courthouse, he strides past the prisoners as if they present no more danger than a herd of sheep. "That one," he says, pointing to a man in a black suit. "That one." He points to another. "And that one."

He walks to the courthouse with the men he has indicated following nervously along behind him like a line of ducklings. Mounting the front steps, he turns and looks them over before he speaks. They are all prosperous citizens who probably would have had gold watches in their pockets if the Raiders had not already relieved them of such valuables.

"Good afternoon, gentlemen," he says. "I am General John Hunt Morgan." Most of the men continue to stare at him with grim fascination, but one is so startled by the conventional politeness of this introduction that he stretches out his hand and murmurs: "Pleased to meet you, General Morgan. I am Robert Smally."

Morgan shakes Smally's hand. "Mr. Smally," he asks, "what is your profession?"

Smally turns pale and hurriedly retracts his hand. "I am in the hauling business," he says. "Or I was until some of your boys stole my mules."

"You were not paid for them?"

"Yes, sir, I was paid, but in Confederate script." Smally is on the verge of complaining that a fifty-dollar Confederate bill won't buy a man a chicken, much less a new team of mules, when he sees something in Morgan's face that makes him reconsider.

"Let us move on to the problem at hand," Morgan says. "Do you know who owns the three mills near Corydon?"

"Yes, sir, I do."

"Ah." Morgan smiles a wolfish smile that makes Smally wish he had never gotten out of bed this morning. "You are just the man I am looking for. Tell me the names of the mill owners." Smally glances at his fellow citizens, several of whom shake their heads as if warning him not to reply.

"Come now," Morgan says. "I give you my word of honor I will not harm these gentlemen. Who are they?"

Reluctantly, Smally points at a man who is sitting on the ground nearby. "Harbin Applegate owns one of the mills," he says. "Robert Leffer owns another, but I don't see him here today."

"Bring Mr. Applegate over here," Morgan orders. He turns back to Smally. "And the owner of the third mill? What is his name and where is he?"

"I am right here," says a tall man who has been standing at the far end of the group. "Name's Brown."

When both millers stand in front of him, Morgan tells them

simply and without preamble that if they do not immediately pay a two-thousand-dollar ransom, he will burn their mills. The millers immediately see the futility of arguing with a Confederate general who commands an army of wild-looking raiders, but having been in business a long time, they are not accustomed to take the first offer tendered. They bargain with Morgan and convince him to drop the price.

An hour later, after some scrambling to retrieve strongboxes and open safes, Morgan is in possession of fifteen hundred dollars in gold. Satisfied, he thanks the millers for this contribution to his treasury and orders all Union prisoners paroled on the condition that they promise never again to take up arms against the Confederacy. "Good day to you, gentlemen," he says and walks to the Eagle Hotel to eat a much-delayed breakfast.

Upstairs, behind a bolted door, while stores are being looted, mills ransomed, and prisoners paroled, Claire and John lie on a big double bed in a pile of snarled sheets. They have made love three times: first urgently, then slowly, then softly and tenderly, all in absolute silence for fear of being discovered. It has been foolish to take such a terrible risk, but neither has been able to summon the sense to ask the other to stop. So, throwing aside caution, they have given in to their longing, rolled in each other's arms, kissed until their lips burned. Each time Claire climaxes, John puts his hand over her mouth so her cries will not betray them; and when it is his turn, she does the same for him.

All the while, whenever she has been able to think clearly— which has not been all that often—Claire has been torn between fear and desire. If they are surprised in bed in a state of undress . . . if John is found in the arms of a Yankee when he is supposed to be on the lookout for snipers . . . She never manages to complete her thoughts because every time she forms them, they are interrupted with more kisses followed by more lovemaking.

We should get up at once and put our clothes back on, she thinks. And then those words—all words—leave her mind. Even when they finally fall back exhausted and satisfied and lie side by side propped up against the headboard with their arms around each other, she still cannot bear to say anything that will separate them. She does not want to think about getting up and pulling on Zeke Crane's shirt and trousers. She wants to lie beside John for as long as possible and pretend there is no war going on. But as long as they are naked, they cannot risk speaking, and she has a lot to say to him and only a little time to say it.

At last, he gives her a reluctant look, shrugs, and slides out of bed. Walking to the window, he cautiously peers through the curtains. When he returns, he sits down beside her, kisses her on the forehead, and points to her clothing. Claire grabs up the bandages, he helps her bind her breasts, and a few moments later, they are both dressed, and she has made the bed. Surveying the room, she satisfies herself that no trace of their lovemaking remains before she speaks.

"I have something to tell you," she says. She has spent the better part of two years imagining how she might tell him about their baby if she ever saw him again, but now she forgets her plans and the words simply tumble out. "When we parted in New Orleans I was . . . with child. We had a baby but it didn't live. I wanted it so much, John, so very much; but I miscarried and—" All the pain of the day she lost the baby suddenly rises up to choke her. She stops speaking and looks at him, unable to continue. She thinks of those baby clothes, the ones their baby never wore, and finds herself wishing she had kept them instead of giving them away because then, at least, she would have had something to show him. The memory is too painful to bear. She breaks into tears. "No one knew except the doctor who attended me. I was so frightened and so . . . alone. . . ."

"Oh, Claire," John says, pulling her to him. "I wish I'd known. I wish I could have been with you."

"It's not your fault. At first I thought it was. I blamed you. I'm sorry, but I took it so hard, John. I know these things happen all the time, but I couldn't find peace afterward, couldn't forget our baby. I felt like I'd lost everything...." John strokes her hair and holds her closer. She thinks of what a wonderful father he would have been. The grief of their loss seems unbearable. "I'll never forgive myself," she says.

"Forgive yourself for what, darlin'?"

"For leaving you in New Orleans. I was a fool to go back to Henry. I've regretted it every day we've been apart, but he convinced me you were married and had a daughter. His lawyer showed me the license and birth certificate. Oh, why didn't you come back to the hotel sooner! Why couldn't I find you at the docks?"

"God damn Henry and his lawyer to eternal hellfire!" John cries. "I've never been married, and if I ever have a child with any woman, it will be with you. You couldn't find me at the docks because I had been knocked unconscious by a pair of thieves who stole my father's watch. I didn't tell you about it in my letters because I thought . . . never mind what I thought. I was a fool, too. Claire, darlin', don't cry, please don't cry. When this war is over, we'll have children together; I swear it by all I hold holy."

She hears a catch in his voice, and when she looks up, she sees a grief in his eyes equal to her own. "Tell me," he says softly, "was our baby a boy or a girl?"

"I don't know. It was too early. But one night—" Henry lied to her at every turn, but John has never deceived her. She can tell him anything, even the secrets of her heart. "One night," she continues, "I had a dream about a little boy. He was playing with a hoop. Chasing it through a garden filled with flowers. He had your eyes."

John is silent for a long time. When at last he speaks, his voice is choked and strange. "A boy then. Let's give him a name, Claire. Let's call him Clayton William Cyrus Taylor so his uncles will know him when he gets to heaven."

"Clayton." Claire stops crying and stands quietly for a moment considering this name. Gradually she feels some of her sadness lifting. "Yes, let's call him Clayton. We'll never forget him, will we?"

"Never."

For a while longer, they stand there holding each other. Finally the sound of horses galloping past the hotel brings them back to the danger of their situation. Claire disentangles herself from John's arms and wipes her eyes. She doesn't know what to say next. She had planned to ask him to agree to be paroled so they could go away together, but that won't work because he's no longer a prisoner.

She tries to imagine persuading him to desert. She thinks how honorable he is, how loyal, and how much she loves him for those traits. She might be able to force him to come away with her by playing on his guilt about not being with her when she lost their baby, but she too has a sense of honor. She doesn't want to manipulate him. She wants him to be who he is. She will never collect on the memory of their child as if it were a debt.

"I can't leave, darlin'," he says. "You know that."

Yes, she knows. She's not even surprised they've been thinking the same thoughts. But the disappointment is still sharp. He must see it in her face, for he takes her hand and leads her to the window. "Come over here," he says. "I need to show you something." Drawing the curtains aside, he points to the town square. "Do you see those men down there? Not the Union prisoners, but our boys?"

Still unable to trust herself to speak, Claire nods. She doesn't want to start crying again. She feels as if she has cried enough tears to last a lifetime.

John stares at the soldiers in the square for a few seconds, then lets the curtain drop and turns away from the window. When she sees the expression on his face, she is so shocked she finds her voice. "What's wrong?" she asks. "What aren't you telling me?"

"All of them are going to die," he says.

"All of who is going to die?"

"All those boys down there. Or maybe they'll be lucky; maybe only three-quarters of them will die. I'm in charge of a party of scouts. I can't abandon them—not even for you—not when the general they idolize is a hotheaded, self-appointed prophet who plans to lead them on a suicide mission."

"But I thought you said you'd follow Morgan to hell and back! I thought you admired him."

"I used to. There are many admirable things about him, but he's changed, darlin'. I've known he was blinded by his own pride since I was ten years old, but I kept silent because I felt I owed him my life. Since the war began, I've watched his blindness grow steadily worse. He's never been able to see why slavery is evil. He can't say the word 'Union' without spitting. Every day he grows more stubborn and less willing to obey orders from his superiors. Not more than five minutes after we got out of jail, I met one of Hines's boys, who told me we were headed north to take revenge on the Yankees. My guess is that if Morgan does lead us in that direction, he won't stop until Federal troops have picked off most of the army. Even at that point, he may not surrender. I can easily see him deciding this is an opportunity to even the score and win eternal fame by ordering his men to die with him. And if he asks them to die, they will. Southerners love their generals."

Claire lays her hand on his arm. "John, what if you're wrong?"

"I wish I were."

"Maybe you are. God knows I'm no general. You could put what I know about military strategy in a thimble, but only a few days ago, I heard Morgan tell his staff that if Union troops pursued him too hotly, he intended to slip back into Kentucky. He said that this time of year there are places the army can ford the river without using boats."

"He must have said that before he heard about Vicksburg and Gettysburg."

His reply confuses her. "Vicksburg? What about Vicksburg? We've had no news for days. Has the city fallen? And where is

Gettysburg? I've heard of a town in Ohio by that name and another in Pennsylvania, but surely both are far too small to be of military importance."

A strange expression comes into John's eyes—one Claire will later see in the eyes of a great many Southerners. "I thought Morgan knew," he says softly. "I thought the whole world knew." And then, in as few words as possible, he tells her about the surrender of Vicksburg and the great Southern defeat in Pennsylvania.

"I am convinced this is the turning point of the war, Claire. The Mississippi is cut in half, the Confederacy is split, and tens of thousands of our best men lie dead. The Army of Northern Virginia is in shambles. Lee may regroup, but I doubt he will ever invade the North again. In other words, the fighting may go on for months, even years, but the South has lost the war."

Claire has often prayed the Union would win some great victory, but the price of the Confederate defeat at Gettysburg makes her sick. John takes her in his arms again as if to console her, but what he says next is not comforting.

"We're going to have to part. You must go to Morgan at once and confess you're a female. He'll be angry that you deceived him—perhaps very angry—but he won't harm you. He's gallant to women on principle. Once he even entertained a pretty Union spy—fed her dinner and gave her an armed escort when she left. He may not offer you wine and fried chicken, but he won't shoot you. Do this for both of us. Then, no matter what happens, I'll at least have the comfort of knowing you're safe."

"I can't leave you."

"You have to."

"I can't."

"By God, Claire, don't argue with me about this! You're wearing a corporal's uniform. As your superior officer, I order you to commandeer a horse and leave now. This may be the most dangerous raid ever made by a Southern general. The slaughter will be terrible, and I won't be able to protect you." She starts to protest, but he puts his finger over her lips. "Now don't go telling me you don't need protection. I know how independent you are. But no matter how brave a heart you have, it can't stop a Yankee bullet."

Claire removes his finger. "You don't understand. I don't mean that I don't *want* to leave—although I certainly don't—I mean I literally *cannot*, because I have nowhere to go."

"I'm not asking you to go back to your husband. Your parents will take you in."

"If I go to my parents' home, I'll destroy them and myself with them. When I was going through Henry's things, looking for something that might give me legal grounds for divorce, I found a copy of a promissory note signed by my father. The sum is staggering. Henry could easily call in the debt."

John starts to speak, but she silences him with a gesture. "I know you are about to offer to help. Papa would not accept money from you, and even if he did, it would do no good. Henry will find me in Charlesport just like he found me in New Orleans, and once he knows where I am, nothing will stop him from dragging me back to Cambridge. Worse yet, he will have the full force of the law on his side. You see, he has been making plans for my future— plans I knew nothing about."

"What sort of plans?"

"He's had me certified as mentally incompetent."

"What!"

"I know it's hard to believe, but I found the documents. And that's not all: he's been corresponding with an alienist."

"What in blazes is an alienist?"

"A physician who specializes in mental disorders. Apparently this one runs a sanatorium in Maine. Henry was making arrangements to have me committed."

"Never! Not as long as I draw breath!"

"Nor as long as I do."

"Why, in God's name?"

"A good question. One I asked myself as I fled from his house.

Henry's afraid of scandal, so there must be something else going on that I don't know about. He's cunning. He never does anything without a reason. Obviously he believes he needs to discredit me and isolate me from my family, but why? Does he think I know some secret that will destroy him if it's made public?"

"Do you?"

"No. I had suspicions about all sorts of things, including male concubinage, but I never found a shred of evidence to support them. Does my bluntness shock you?"

"No. You've always been plain spoken. I'm just surprised that after riding with the Second Kentucky you're still using the Latin terms. As for my uncle, let's just call him a skunk and be done with it. You're right. You've got nowhere to go." He takes her hands and lifts them to his lips. "So stay with me, darlin', and we'll fight side by side; and if we die, at least we'll die together."

Claire pulls her hands out of his, places her palms on either side of his face, and draws him close. "I have no intention of dying, Lieutenant Taylor." She gives him a long, passionate kiss. "And I'm confident"—she gives him another kiss—"that sooner or later, I'll find a way to persuade you to give me those children you promised."

Claire

*A*nd so, when Morgan's men rode out of Corydon that afternoon, I rode with them disguised as Zeke Crane. But before we put the town behind us, an event happened that is forever burned in my memory. As Morgan sat in the dining room eating breakfast, Sallie Kintner appeared holding a newspaper.

At first, no one noticed her. The general had just greeted John warmly and me coldly. Clearly he did not intend to forgive me for riding to Corydon without his permission, and every look he gave—or refused to give—me told me I was no longer his pet.

"The boy is a deserter," he said, jabbing his fork in my direction. "If he weren't your cousin, Taylor, I would strip him of rank and send him back to his mother in disgrace, but I can't spare a man for nursemaid duty; so I'm putting him directly under your command. I want you to eat with him, sleep with him, and make sure the little brat doesn't run off again, do anything stupid, or get himself killed. Is that clear?"

"Yes, sir, General," John said without a trace of a smile, although he must have been considerably amused at the thought of being ordered to sleep with me every night.

Morgan took a sip of coffee and started in on a slice of fried ham. There was complete silence in the room as he chewed and swallowed. Outside, I could hear *the sound of the Raiders riding up and down the main street yipping like a pack of dogs. Behind the general, there was a large double window covered with lace curtains. Through the lace, I saw a trooper ride past dragging a bolt of red calico.*

"Excuse me, sir," Sallie Kintner said sweetly.

Morgan looked up with a scowl. When he realized who was addressing him, his face softened. "Yes, Miss Kintner," he said, "what can I do for you?"

Sallie held the newspaper out to him, folded in half so the front headline was obscured. "I thought you might like to peruse this while you enjoyed your breakfast," she said.

"Thank you." Morgan took the paper from her, placed it on the table, and went back to his ham.

"I hope you enjoy the blackberry jam," Sallie said in those same dulcet tones. "I made it with my own hands." And, turning in a swish of muslin and petticoats, she walked—no, almost ran—out of the room. As she passed, I caught a glimpse of her face. Her eyes were hard, and her mouth was twisted into a smile of hatred and triumph. I knew instantly what she had done.

I watched helplessly as Morgan put down his fork, picked up the newspaper, spread it open, read the headline, and went ashen with shock.

Vicksburg.

Gettysburg.

I was there when he found out.

Chapter Twenty-two

MAHONEY, *Pettigrew, and Campbell*. As Claire rides north with Morgan's men, the names of the three scouts sing in her head like a nursery rhyme. Lean, leather-faced, hard-riding, unwashed, unshaven, profane, and brave, they have been John's closest companions through months of war and privation. Now they become her chaperons.

The custom of soldiers sleeping in pairs dates back to the Middle Ages if not further, so no one finds it unusual for Lieutenant Taylor and his cousin to share a blanket. Each night, as Claire and John stretch out side by side, Mahoney, Pettigrew, and Campbell stretch out near them. On the first night as she lies there listening to the ragged chorus of their snoring, Claire has to seize the corner of the blanket and stuff it into her mouth to keep from laughing. *So this is the intimacy I craved!* she thinks. *I lie next to my beloved, yet we might as well be sharing a bed with three spinsters charged with preserving our chastity.*

Even so, there is something surprisingly sweet about so much unfulfilled longing. Under their blanket, she and John gradually carve out a private realm for themselves. Shutting their eyes and feigning sleep, they stroke each other, tentatively at first, then more boldly. Slowly, silently, they let the tips of their fingers drift up and down, wander beneath shirts and pants and the edges of the linen strips that bind Claire's breasts. Before the night is over, they have discovered ways to bring each other to a frenzy of desire without Mahoney, Pettigrew, or Campbell being any the wiser, but the danger of being discovered is always with them. The first time Claire climaxes, she utters a cry that brings Mahoney to his feet.

"What the hell was that?" Mahoney cries, drawing his pistols. Throwing off their blankets, Pettigrew and Campbell join him. For the space of a dozen breaths, the scouts stand in a pool of moonlight, peering into the shadows like retrievers on point.

"Go back to sleep, boys," John says. "Zeke's just having a nightmare."

Pettigrew gives Claire a sharp nudge with the toe of his boot. "Damn it, Zeke, you got to learn to keep your mouth shut!"

Claire stirs and pretends to wake. "Uh?" she mumbles.

"I said if you don't shut the hell up when yer dreamin', I'm gonna gag you with a snot rag."

"You're a fine one to talk, Horace," Mahoney says. "If we go gagging anyone, it should be you. I ain't sure you are aware of it, but you snore like a constipated bear."

Pettigrew grins and lowers his pistols. "Hell," he says, "I know I snore formidably. I do it on purpose to scare off the Yankees." Giving Claire another small kick for good measure, he throws himself back down on the ground, pulls his blanket over his head, and shoves the soles of his boots so close to her face she can see the heads of the nails.

Mahoney, Pettigrew, and Campbell: there is no way to get away from them at night, and by day the situation is even worse. They stick to John like cockleburs, ride with him, eat with him, drink with him when they can find whiskey, borrow his socks, challenge him to impromptu games of chance, and laugh at his jokes. Around this band of quadruplets, Claire circles like an orphan. Her job is to play the hotheaded young fool who needs to be watched so he doesn't get himself killed. She finds this role humiliating, but it has certain advantages, the most important of which is near-invisibility.

Although Zeke Crane is technically a corporal, no one would obey an order if he gave one, nor do the three scouts look at him long enough to notice the roundness of his hips or the slight swelling of his chest. When he goes off by himself to answer the call of nature, they chalk it up to boyish modesty; and when he burns his tongue on a hot ramrod trying to eat slosh or calls a saber a "knife," they just spit tobacco juice on the ground, shake their heads, and tell him he is dumb as a post. Yet despite their barely concealed contempt for his youth and inexperience, they never question his courage. They have heard the story of his midnight ride to Corydon to rescue John and, being Southerners, they frequently express their admiration for his suicidal willingness to expose himself to danger.

"Y'all are sumpin', boy," they tell her. "Yep, sumpin'." Although Claire is not sure what the word "sumpin'" encompasses, she glows under their praise and feels herself as complimented as a young lady who has just been assured she is a great beauty.

The truth is that although the scouts prevent her from being alone with John, she is grateful for the sense of stability they provide. Already, Morgan has revolutionized cavalry fighting by ordering his men to dismount and fight on foot instead of charging the enemy on horseback. Now, he sets about revolutionizing the entire concept of an invasion.

Keeping to main roads, he travels at the front of the column, followed by artillery, supply wagons, and wagons of wounded men, which grow more crowded by the day. Yet although the scouts report to him, they do not ride with him, nor does most of the army. Since Corydon, he has avoided pitched battles and allowed his troops to split into small bands, so that instead of flowing north in a single great river, they are everywhere at once: burning bridges, ripping up railroad tracks, destroying telegraph lines, commandeering horses, seizing food, inspiring panic in the local population, disrupting military communications, and forcing Union troops to play hide-and-seek with an enemy that attacks without warning and disappears without a trace.

This means that when Claire wakes in the morning, she never knows where she will be by the end of the day. Sometimes the scouts are commanded to find bridges so the Raiders can cross them and then burn them. Sometimes they are sent off to hunt for supplies or Yankee patrols. One afternoon, they are issued axes and told to help clear trees that have been felled across the road by a local militia. Within twenty minutes, Claire's hands are so blistered she can hardly grasp the handle. That night, she is too tired for secret lovemaking, and later she can't recall the name of the place they slept or what it looked like.

Palmyra, Salem, Vienna, Lexington. Paris Crossing, Dupont, Versailles. Osgood, Summansville. Harrison. Claire cannot put many of the towns they pass through that summer in chronological order until long after the war, when she reads Basil Duke's memoirs. Just as she has only seen small parts of battles, she now sees only small parts of the invasion, and many of the events she witnesses never make it into the history books. Was Palmyra the place where Ellsworth put a gun to the head of the telegraph operator and returned with the news that Hobson had abandoned his supply wagons and was pursuing them with all possible speed, or was that Vienna? Was the pump with the cold water near Paris Crossing or Lexington? Did they burn those corncribs outside of Dupont or closer to Versailles, where Morgan spared a Masonic lodge?

On rare occasions, she swims out of the fog of exhaustion long enough to remember some place with perfect clarity. On the second day, although its citizens have surrendered without firing a shot, the Raiders loot Salem, Indiana, throwing china into the street for the pleasure of watching it shatter, knocking rain barrels apart, dragging so much calico in the dust that the soiled bolts become the unofficial banners of the invasion.

"They're acting like wicked children," Claire whispers to John. "What has possessed them?"

"They're angry that the South is losing the war."

"Why doesn't Morgan stop them?"

"He can't."

"He must at least try!" But to Claire's surprise, Morgan does not intervene. In the past, he has spared civilians, paroled captured troops, and prevented his men from burning private homes, but now, for the first time, he seems to lose control. Perhaps he sees the destruction as fit retribution for the Confederate defeats at Gettysburg and Vicksburg. In any case, he permits the looting to go on unchecked.

At some point, she is not exactly sure when, the Raiders begin to average twenty-one hours a day in the saddle. This means that in the years to come, when she shuts her eyes and attempts to call up images of that summer, it is mostly faces that appear against the background of her fatigue, arranging themselves like blocks of a quilt that never got sewn together: Morgan's face as he sits in his carriage poring over maps. His short upper lip pulled back exposing his front teeth. His hair going lighter by the day. A face that inspires confidence but which seems to age even as Claire looks at it.

A woman in her midthirties, with dark hair and full lips, who brandishes a pitchfork and dares the scouts to touch so much as a hair on the head of her sick child. Pettigrew's bucktoothed grin as he sweeps off his hat, gives her a bow, and assures her she need not be alarmed: both her child and her home are safe.

Job's face, quietly amused, as he sneaks Claire a slice of pie and watches her wolf it down. "Eat quick, son," he says. "Growing boys needs feeding up."

Faces of Raiders of all ages, powdered with a film of pale dust that makes them look like an army of ghosts; their eyes wild and eager at first, then gradually going blank with exhaustion. Mud caked around their lips; skin burned and peeling; bodies going slack with sleep in the saddle, then jarring awake with a start.

Once when they are out on patrol, she catches sight of her own face in a scrap of mirror nailed to a tree above a washbasin. The Confederate corporal who stares back at her is so different from the elegant Mrs. Henry Winston of Cambridge, Massachusetts, that any fears she has of being recognized disappear. She is thinner by perhaps fifteen pounds, stronger, more resolute-looking. What little hair she has left protrudes from beneath the edges of her cap in damp coils like the ends of an unraveled rope. Her fine complexion, which she was rather vain about, has vanished, leaving her skin as tanned as the skin of her father's stable hands. The summer sun has bleached her hair and eyebrows to a bright copper; her lips are cracked and freckled. Only her eyes are the same, but even they seem more deeply set.

Does she look happy? Yes, Claire decides, despite all the dangers and hardships of the raid, she does. This the face of a woman who has put grief behind her, a woman who might not be doing what she planned to do with her life, but who is, all things considered, content.

But the faces Claire remembers most clearly in later years are the faces of the men who kill Mahoney. The sun is low on the horizon, and the scouts are returning to the main column, racing against the darkness. As they gallop around a blind bend in the road, they ride headlong into forty or more Union soldiers. Claire has a fleeting vision of a line of faces tilted toward her, burning with a golden radiance in the dying light of the day. She hears rifles discharging, sees smoke blossom from the barrels, watches Mahoney buck back in his saddle and tumble to the ground.

"Retreat!" John yells. Claire, Campbell, Pettigrew, and John turn and ride for cover as the soldiers continue to fire. Fortunately, the enemy is on foot, although what idiocy prompted their superior officer to send them out without horses to chase down Morgan's Raiders is a question the four survivors will often debate in the days that follow.

After dark, they return to the site of the ambush, retrieve

Mahoney's body, and bury it under an elm. As John says a short prayer over the grave, Pettigrew and Campbell cry silently. That night as she and John lie together, Claire also weeps, and John comforts her as best he can.

Two days later, Campbell goes out to take a look at some horses and never comes back. "Captured or dead," Pettigrew says gruffly, spitting into the dust. "In any case, he's gone."

Two more scouts join them: a Kentucky sharpshooter named Kilpatrick whose aim is so good he can shoot quail in the head without leaving any shot in the body; and an older man from Murfreesboro, Tennessee, named Hanson. Although their unit is now back up to full strength, Claire cannot forget Mahoney and Campbell.

As for the invasion: the situation is deteriorating by the hour, just as John predicted. Morgan has not yet been forced into a major confrontation, but scattered bands of Union forces are starting to catch up with the Raiders, capturing some and picking others off in twos and threes. By the time they reach the Indiana–Ohio border, their original force of nearly three thousand has been reduced to less than two thousand desperately exhausted men who are riding so hard they wear out as many as three horses every twenty-four hours. Food is in short supply, ammunition is running low, and stealing enough fresh horses to keep the army moving has become a major problem.

"I sure as hell am glad to get out of Indiana," Pettigrew says as they watch the last Rebel troopers cross the wooden bridge that spans the Whitewater River.

"Yep," Kilpatrick agrees, taking off his hat and fanning himself with it. "Lordy, how I have come to hate them Hoozers."

A rider from the Eighth Kentucky suddenly gallops past. "I've seen their dust!" he yells. If this is true, the enemy is now at most two hours behind them. Claire knows she should be alarmed, but she is too numb with exhaustion to feel anything but a desire to lie down on the ground and sleep.

Chapter Twenty-three

THE headache twists through John's skull like a hank of snarled wire. Beside him, her face pale with fatigue, Claire rides slumped over her saddle horn. Hanson is humming the same tune he has hummed since that picket skirmish near Fort Dennison; and Pettigrew and Kilpatrick are bringing up the rear, unless, like so many others, they have fallen asleep, pitched off their horses, and are lying in the middle of the road, waiting for the Yankees to scoop them up. John is too tired to turn around to check on them. How long have they been riding? Twenty-eight hours? Thirty? Surely a clock round at least.

He shuts his eyes. Behind his closed lids, the headache takes on a life of its own. He sees flashes of light that look like shards of stained glass, a cluster of tiny, colored dots that sweeps from left to right like a swarm of fireflies. "Cincinnati," he murmurs.

"What?" a voice asks. He opens his eyes to find Claire staring at him with concern. "What did you say?"

"I said Cincinnati." His voice is so thick with fatigue he hardly recognizes it. A shudder runs down his spine. He takes the reins more firmly in hand and smiles.

"Your good cheer amazes me," she says.

They ride on, and with each step his horse takes, John's headache grows worse. Over twenty-four hours in the saddle without rest and more to come—just to avoid Cincinnati. Morgan is leading the army around it by way of its northern suburbs, because the city is one of the most important ports on the Ohio River: populous, well-supplied, and thus heavily defended.

A few hours back, or maybe more than a few—John has lost track—they stopped to feed their horses in plain sight of Fort Dennison, where some two thousand Union troops were garrisoned. Why didn't the Yankees attack? Has Ellsworth managed to convince the Union generals that Morgan has ten thousand men, or is there unrest in Cincinnati itself? There are presently draft riots going on in New York and Boston. Maybe the South should just sit back and let the North tear itself apart.

We've been lucky so far, he thinks. *Very lucky. But one concentrated assault by a superior force . . . We've never been so vulnerable. How many of the boys are never going to see Tennessee and Kentucky again? There's no way to know until this raid is over, and it won't be over until Morgan calls it to a halt, but at least he is leading us toward the river, and . . .*

Claire coughs. John opens his eyes cautiously to make sure she is not falling behind, and the sunlight burns into his pupils like a hot poker. His horse stumbles, and he pulls her up short. As he prepares to kick her into motion again, the cold and hot sensations meet in his chest. He closes his eyes and the lights behind his lids circle in geometric patterns like the colored stones in a child's kaleidoscope. "Claire," he says.

She turns just in time to see him start to slip sideways in the saddle. "John!" she cries. "What's wrong?"

"Nothing," he assures her and, allowing the reins to fall from his hands, he tumbles to the ground.

⌒

Hours later, he wakes to find himself riding in a carriage. His headache eased off a little while he was asleep. Now it starts up again. Gritting his teeth, he stares at the black leather buttons that decorate the seat back.

"I have no idea what's wrong with him," he hears Claire say. "He just collapsed. I need to find a doctor."

John looks up and sees her sitting next to the driver. He wants to tell her he's having an attack of Roman fever, but he's shaking so hard he can't form the words.

"A doctor?" the driver says. "Son, your cousin ain't gonna get no medical attention unless he needs his leg sawed off and even then he's gonna have to hop to the front of the line."

"I'm going to find out what's wrong with him," Claire snaps. "I commandeered this carriage, Private, and you'll drive it anywhere I order you to drive it. And you'll call me 'sir,' not 'son,' or I'll have you assigned to digging latrines."

"Yes, sir, Corporal," says the driver. "Which way do you reckon I should go?"

"God in heaven! How should I know?"

"Zeke," John whispers. He does not think she can hear him, but she must, because she immediately turns around.

"You're awake," she says.

"Roman . . ." He tries to form the second word, but it gets tangled on his tongue.

She leans closer. "Are you trying to tell me you have Roman fever?" John nods. "Have you had it before?" John nods again. "How high does the fever get, darling?"

The driver swivels around and gawks at Claire. John wants to warn her to be more discreet, but his teeth are chattering so hard he can't speak.

"Qui—" he says.

"Quinine?" John nods. Claire turns back to the driver. "I need quinine." She points. "Stop there."

When the driver does not stop immediately, she takes the reins out of his hands and pulls the horse to a halt. Perhaps she gets out, or perhaps they drive on. John isn't sure because he floats back into unconsciousness and dreams of a river composed of wolves running in a great, black pack.

"Open your mouth," a voice commands. John opens his mouth and something warm and bitter flows down his throat. He spits and coughs and fights his way out of the dream to discover Claire trying to force another spoonful of the terrible stuff between his lips. Clenching his teeth, he turns away. "No," he protests.

"Open up," she commands. "This is quinine. You have to take it. You're not allowed to die. Open or I swear I'll pry your teeth apart with a knife."

John opens his mouth and she dumps another dose down his throat. Leaning over, she puts her lips to his ear. "I love you," she whispers. "If you die, I'll have to spend the rest of my life wearing black, and I'll be damned if I'll go around looking like Abigail Winston for any man." She sits up and refills the spoon. "Open," she commands. "There's more."

John swallows the bitter liquid and gags. "Horrible," he says. "Mercy."

"No mercy. Open." She shoves another dose of quinine between his lips, and for the first time he notices her cheeks are wet with tears. Sitting back, she clears her throat and drops the spoon into the cup.

"How's he doing?" the driver asks.

"I think he'll live." Claire's voice is level, but John can tell she's frightened. She pulls out her bandanna and blows her nose. "He's one tough son of a bitch."

"Ain't that the truth," the driver says.

John pulls at her sleeve. "Puke," he says.

Claire gives him a severe look. "Don't you dare."

John fights down the nausea. "Where . . . ?" he asks.

"Where did I get the quinine? I robbed a pharmacy at gunpoint. If I hadn't taken it, someone else would have. The pharmacist said eight hundred Rebels had ridden past his shop since noon. None had come in because he'd pulled down his sign. I recognized the press he uses to make pills. He was foolish enough to leave it out on the counter where I could see it from the road." She picks up the cup.

"It's just one robbery among many," she continues. "You should see Kilpatrick and Pettigrew. They broke into a millinery store a few hours ago and commandeered women's hats. Kilpatrick is wearing a blue bonnet adorned with egret feathers and a veil, which he has wrapped around his face to keep out dust. Pettigrew chose a widow's bonnet, which in my experience is far too hot for the road ahead. Hanson will have none of it. He says he'd rather fry hatless in the sun than tie ribbons under his chin."

Tilting the contents of the cup into the spoon, she forces the last of the quinine between John's lips.

The next time he wakes, he finds himself in a large four-poster bed covered with a clean sheet. Claire, Pettigrew, Hanson, and Kilpatrick stand over him.

"Y'all look like a sick dawg," Kilpatrick says.

"Hell," says Pettigrew, "if I had a hound that looked as stove up as Taylor, I'd shoot the sonabitch and put him out of his misery."

John struggles to a sitting position and leans back against the headboard. His head still aches, but his fever seems to have broken. "Where are your bonnets, boys?" he asks.

"We didn't want to get too gussied up," Pettigrew says with a slow grin. "On account of we didn't want to scare you into thinkin' y'all had died and gone to heaven."

"You was in such a bad way we had already started laying claim to your worldly possessions," Hanson says. "I was gonna get your boots; Pettigrew was gonna take your hat, since he's the only one it fits; and Kilpatrick, being the greedy sort, laid claim to your spurs and pocket knife. We had such a row about who was to git yer pearl-handled pistols that we decided to award them to Zeke to prevent bloodshed."

"I take it as a good sign that y'all are tormenting me," John says. "It means I am no longer in danger of dying."

"You ain't gonna get out of Ohio that easy," Pettigrew says. "You're gonna keep on riding through hell with the rest of us."

"You're in the private home of a Southern sympathizer, about half a mile from a town named Williamsburg, cousin," Claire says with careful emphasis on the word "cousin." "When we arrived late yesterday afternoon, the general finally called the march to a halt and ordered us to go into camp and get some rest."

"High time too," says Hanson. "We done rode ninety-five miles without stopping."

"It was record-settin'," says Kilpatrick. "My ass is so wore down that when I lower my poor, broken body into a chair, I find I am a full three inches shorter."

"Hobson's boys is still on our tail like ducks on a june bug," Pettigrew says. "We scouted him out and found his whole cavalry laid up for the night about fifteen miles from here."

"Which means we got to haul out again," Pettigrew says, "and start making for the river as fast as these sorry Yankee excuses for horses can take us. So we come to bid you farewell."

"Farewell?" John says. "I'm riding with y'all, and that's an order!" Swinging his legs over the edge of the bed, he tries to stand. The next thing he knows, he is lying facedown on the rug. Grabbing him under the arms, Kilpatrick and Pettigrew deposit him back on the bed as if he were a sack of corn.

"Lieutenant," Kilpatrick says, "y'all can issue orders until yer blue in the face, but you ain't riding nowhere." John struggles into a sitting position and starts to protest, but Claire pushes him back down.

"Cousin John," she says, "Roman fever is nothing to treat lightly. You're as weak as a newly hatched chick. If you try to mount a horse, you'll fall off and possibly break your neck. General Morgan himself has ordered that you be transported in a wagon until you regain your strength. When I told him how sick you were, he said: 'Tell John to take care. I have lost more good men to disease than to Yankee bullets.'"

"Zeke's gonna ride in that wagon with you and nurse you back to health like he was your own mama," Hanson says. "I wish I had such a saint of a cousin, but all of my aunt Fen's boys are of the lying, lazy, thievish persuasion."

The scouts crack jokes for a while longer and then leave. As soon as they are out the door, Claire throws the bolt, sits down on the bed, and takes one of John's hands in hers. Her flesh feels cool against his. "I love you," she whispers. Kissing him gently on the forehead, she pulls him to her, cradles his head in her lap, and strokes his hair until he falls asleep.

⁓

Some time later, just as the sky is beginning to lighten, he wakes to find the door open and Claire gone. Outside, he can hear the army passing by in the darkness. He is beginning to wonder if he has been forgotten, when two privates suddenly enter the room carrying a wooden window shutter that has clearly been torn off the side of a house.

"Good mornin', Lieutenant," one of the privates says, giving John a crisp salute that forms a strange contrast to his shoeless feet and patched pants. "Jeb and me come to put you in an ambulance wagon."

"Have at me, boys," John says.

Taking him at his word, the privates grab him, roll him unceremoniously onto the shutter, and carry him outside, where he finds a brightly painted peddler's wagon waiting. On the side someone has inscribed the motto PROFESSOR KRATZ'S MAGIC ELIXAR in huge red letters, without, John notes, much respect for spelling. The privates dump him in the back of the wagon onto a pile of quilts. On both sides, the army is on the move. John looks up into the faces of the passing men, none of whom he recognizes. Several nod cordially, and a fellow in a red flannel shirt tips his hat.

The privates stash the shutter somewhere out of sight and return to the wagon. "Y'all take care, Lieutenant," says the short private, bobbing up and down over the edge like a prairie dog.

"Git some sleep, sir," advises the tall one.

John takes their advice. For the next few hours, as the wagon rocks and sways over the uneven road, he sleeps. When he wakes, Claire is sitting beside him fanning him with a rolled-up newspaper.

"Hello," she says, "it's dinnertime." Tearing off a small hunk of bread, she places it on his tongue. John chews, swallows, and discovers that his appetite has returned. He eats the bread and drains a stone jug filled with cold beef broth.

"I'll be back on my feet in no time," he promises; but by nightfall, he is so sick that when Pettigrew, Hanson, and Kilpatrick ride back down the line to check on him, they have nothing humorous to say, and the sober looks on their faces alarm Claire almost as much as the fever itself.

"He's tough," she tells them. "He'll rally."

"Reckon he will, Zeke," Hanson agrees, but he doesn't meet her eyes.

"How's the quinine holding out?" Kilpatrick asks.

"There's only one dose left."

"Give it to him," Pettigrew says, "and we'll git you more."

The scouts keep their promise, reappearing at odd intervals with quinine tablets. Perhaps they beg them from Copperheads or loot pharmacies or steal them from the supply wagons. Claire does not care to inquire too closely. The important thing is, the quinine keeps coming.

This is vital because John's fever rises alarmingly, and soon she finds herself spending most of her time trying to keep blankets on him as he shakes and calls out in delirium.

"Live!" she begs him. But he does not know her, and once, when his fever is at its peak, she finds him talking to his dead brothers as if they were sitting next to him. Nearly frantic with worry, she sends Pettigrew and Hanson out to steal some whiskey so she can rub him down with it.

The whiskey rub cools him off, but she is so busy dressing and undressing him, she sees very little of the towns they pass through on their way to the river. Even after his fever finally breaks, the only place she can remember in any detail is the small town of Chester. Earlier that morning, the Raiders have been given a grim reminder that time is running out when Union troops catch up with them as they enter a narrow canyon. The fighting is so fierce Claire does not once dare to raise her head over the side of the wagon to see what is going on.

In revenge for this attack, the Raiders burn a sawmill, and in the confusion their local guide escapes. Morgan will not move without a guide, so he orders the entire army to halt in Chester as he attempts to procure a new one. In the end, this decision proves disastrous, but at one o'clock on that sunny mid-July afternoon, Chester looks like a fine place to rest. The town is only twenty-five miles from the river, and rumor has it they will be back on Southern soil by this time tomorrow.

Bored by the long delay, "Lightning" Ellsworth enters a store to help himself to some tobacco and comes out waving a copy of the *Cincinnati Enquirer.* He carries it to Morgan so fast that, as Pettigrew later puts it, "you'da thought the fellah was being stung by bees." The paper contains the best news anyone has heard in days, and Pettigrew immediately rides over to the peddler's wagon to bring John the good tidings. Finding John asleep, he tells Claire instead:

"We're gonna cross the Ohio at Buffington Island. The water's only thirty inches deep there. Thirty inches! Ain't that a piece of luck, Zeke, my boy? We ain't hardly gonna get wet! And if the Yankees got gunboats, well, they can just tie 'em up to a willow and weep. There ain't no way tinclads can maneuver in less than three feet of water."

Long after the war, on summer afternoons when some freak storm sends rain pounding down on the roof shingles, Claire will remember the Raiders riding three abreast that summer, the hooves of their horses beating out the defiant anthem of the invasion. She will imagine the regimental flags waving and the drummer boys beating their drums. Closing her eyes, she will call up the deep valleys and densely forested mountainsides of West Virginia and create a wild land on the other side of the river where an entire army can disappear without leaving a trace. But when she first hears the words "Buffington Island," they have no associations for her for good or bad. Relieved to learn that they will soon be leaving Ohio, she thanks Pettigrew and promises to tell John the good news as soon as he wakes.

Chapter Twenty-four

E VERYTHING is coated with dust: fence rails, tree trunks, corn, even the heads of Queen Anne's lace, which hang limply in the ditches like broken umbrellas. Above these traces of the passage of a great army, the stars glitter with bright indifference. John is still weak, but well enough to get back on his horse. This is the miracle of the evening and the miracle, Claire supposes, of Roman fever, which attacks and then retreats with equal suddenness as if it, too, were a raider whose best weapon is surprise.

They are traveling behind the peddler's cart now instead of in it, and John is staring fixedly at the tailgate like a man not fully awake, either too tired to speak or trying to conceal what remains of his sickness. Claire can tell he is happy to be back in the saddle, but not completely happy. He wants to be up front leading his scouts, but she has insisted they move slowly until he is stronger and, to her surprise, he has given in.

At first she chalked this up to illness, but as they draw ever nearer to the river, she has begun to suspect he agreed to stay behind to protect her. He has not warned her to be prepared for an ambush so it cannot be the danger of a sudden Union attack; but he is a scout and scouts live by their instincts.

A night bird sings three long, trilling notes that float toward them over the sound of coughing men, creaking wagons, and a hundred muted conversations. John straightens up and looks around. His eyes fix on something, and he points to a trail that leads off to Claire's right. "Ride this way with me for a moment," he says.

Turning out of the line of march, he starts down the trail and Claire follows. A few minutes later they are on the crest of the ridge, looking through a gap in the trees at a sea of pale fog that seems to stretch all the way to West Virginia. Here and there, church spires or the tops of high hills protrude from the odd, glowing whiteness; but if there are Union troops, campfires, or cannons in the valley below, they are well hidden.

John gestures at the fog. "Morgan waited too long in Chester," he says. "We won't be crossing the river tonight. It's going to be pitch dark once we get down there, which means our boys won't be able to see their hands in front of their faces. All the Yankees have to do now is close in behind us, hold the ridge, and attack at first light. We won't be able to turn around and fight our way out of the valley, and we won't be able to get across the Ohio. While I was lying there sick, we marched straight into a trap."

Claire is shocked. "But the newspaper said the river is shallow enough for us to make the crossing," she objects.

"Is it? Smell the air. Somewhere it's been raining. Not here, but somewhere; and if that somewhere is upstream in the hills of West Virginia or eastern Ohio, the river will be flowing above our wagon wheels by morning." He leans over and gives her a quick kiss. "Stick close to me, darlin', and don't do anything heroic. The Yankees are damn good shots, and I love you too much to..." He stops in midsentence.

"Dig my grave?" Claire supplies.

"If I lost you, they'd be digging mine too. Just stick close, shoot straight, ride like fury when I tell you to, and we'll live long enough to get old together."

Sobered, they turn around and rejoin the line of march. For the next hour or so, Claire tries to convince herself John is mistaken. Even after they descend into the clammy embrace of the fog, she goes on telling herself that it has not rained upstream and that the army can easily cross the river in thirty inches of water. She is just trying to fill in the details of this hopeful scenario when Kilpatrick rides back to join them.

"So, Taylor," he says, "you gonna die on us, or have you decided to live and give me a chance to win back them socks I lost to you when we raced them louses?" Louse racing is a major sport among the Raiders, and piles of Confederate dollars are wagered on the horrible little creatures every time the army stops.

"I will never return your socks, Ross," John says, "but I have been inspired to go on living so I can steal your tobacco."

"Hogwash." Kilpatrick spits over the rump of John's horse with the precise aim of a born sharpshooter. "You don't even chew."

"I am considering taking up a new vice," John says. "I had originally planned to appoint myself sole sultan of a flock of soiled doves, but the lack of females has made this sin impractical for the present."

Kilpatrick grins, spits another mouthful of tobacco juice, and grins some more. When he has appreciated John's wit fully, he points toward the valley and delivers the bad news. "Pettigrew sent me up here to tell you the army's camped in a little town called Portland right across from Buffington Island. It's so dark under that damn fog, you can't see the river; you can only hear it, and what you hear ain't good. The Ohio sounds like she's risen right smartly. Worse yet, the damn Yankees got there first and threw up earthworks. Oh, it ain't much of a fort; even in the dark you can tell that. But it commands the crossing, and we got no idea in hell how many men and guns they got."

Kilpatrick takes a twist of tobacco out of his coat pocket, bites off a fresh hunk, and begins to chew. "Is the Yankees massed in front of us? Behind us? Are they on this side of the river, the other side, or both? Has Hobson caught up, or are his boys still hauling their sorry asses over our wagon tracks? General Morgan don't know. The officers don't know. We scouts don't know. We're movin' blind, Lieutenant, and me and the boys don't like it one bit."

Claire is upset to hear John's worst fears so quickly confirmed, but she is not surprised. When the man you love is one of the best scouts in the Confederate army, you are frequently liable to know more than you care to.

They ride on as John and Kilpatrick discuss the situation. When John has learned everything Kilpatrick can tell him, he and Claire kick their horses into a trot, move to the head of the column, and follow Kilpatrick down the ridge, where they find the army strung out along the northern bank of the river.

In that narrow valley between the ridge and the water, hackney coaches, omnibuses, farm wagons, and barouches are already jammed together so closely that in some instances the hubs of the wheels touch. The wounded and sick have been laid on the ground; and as Claire guides her horse between their bodies, she feels a growing sense of impending disaster.

Just beyond the makeshift ambulances, Morgan's carriage looms up out of the fog. On its leather seats, half a dozen officers sleep, piled on each other like corpses. Claire sees a lame horse limping in a confused circle and another horse, unsaddled, its back raw with sores.

When they reach the river, they halt. Since Kilpatrick has already confirmed what John suspected, Claire expects to hear a rush of water, but what she hears is more than a rush. Tonight, the Ohio sounds like a huge beast beating its way around the island.

"How fast do you reckon she's moving?" Kilpatrick asks.

John takes a cotton kerchief out of his pocket and tosses it into the current. Claire watches in dismay as the white spot is borne away with incredible speed. "Fast," John says.

"Too damn fast," Kilpatrick agrees. "We ain't never git the artillery across. That current's gonna sweep them Parrotts clear to Cairo."

Following the river downstream, they ride into Portland where, as usual, Morgan has taken over a private home for his headquarters. Half a dozen Raiders are busy demolishing its split-rail fence to feed their cooking fires, and as Claire rides by, the flames reveal one haggard face after another. She passes three officers in battered hats who crouch over a split canteen broiling something that looks suspiciously like a cat, although perhaps it is merely a skinned rabbit. Others are cooking slosh or attempting to bake stolen bread dough on their ramrods, but most are dipping rock-hard hoecakes into that liquid mixture of ground peanuts and chicory that passes for Rebel coffee.

Over the course of the march she has become accustomed to the sight of hungry men, jaded horses, and wagons filled with wounded. Tonight, the Raiders look exhausted and discouraged, but not nearly as exhausted and, in many ways, not nearly as discouraged as they looked on the long ride around Cincinnati, when dozens tumbled off their mounts and fell asleep in the middle of the road.

The house Morgan has chosen features a front porch held up by wooden posts, which the scavengers have spared because taking them would bring down the roof. Hitching their horses to the railing, Claire and John leave Kilpatrick behind and proceed to the parlor, where they find Morgan in the process of holding a council of war. The general sits in a straight-backed chair, smoking a cigar and drinking whiskey from a china teacup. Around him stand Basil Duke, Ellsworth, the surviving Morgan brothers, and more officers than Claire has yet seen gathered in one place.

As they enter, Morgan turns and acknowledges them with a nod, and the moment Claire sees his face, she knows he has run out of luck. The knowledge grips at her heart, cutting it in two. One half falls to joy and the Union; the other to sorrow and the Confederacy.

She has always wanted the South to be defeated. Yet, if Federal troops attack tomorrow, she knows she will fight with the Raiders. *I am not particularly brave,* she thinks, *but I would crawl through a hail of Yankee gunfire to drag John or Kilpatrick or any of the boys out of danger, and I know they would do the same for me.* She is so lost in these conflicting emotions that it takes her a moment to realize someone is speaking.

"The supply wagons are cumbersome and slow us down considerably," says an older officer whose face Claire does not recognize. "If you abandon them, General, the army could move swiftly upstream to a point where the fords are passable."

"What of the artillery?" Morgan asks.

"We'd have to abandon the cannons too," Duke says. "Captain Byrne and his boys wouldn't like that, would you, Byrne?"

Another officer, presumably Byrne, frowns and shrugs. "No, Colonel, I can't say I'd like it; but we can't get the Parrotts across the river anyway, not with it flowing as fast and deep as it is." Byrne turns to Morgan.

"General, the boys in my battery love those cannons like they were their sweethearts, but they will understand the necessity of leaving them behind. I will order them to spike the barrels so the Yankees can't use them against us. Then, at the first opportunity, we will overrun a Yankee battery and steal new ones."

Morgan takes a drag on his cigar and blows out a cloud of smoke that puts Claire on the edge of a sneeze. She bites her cheeks and holds her breath. This is not a moment to make herself conspicuous. "What about the ambulance wagons?" Morgan asks.

There is an uncomfortable silence. Again Duke speaks. "We would have to leave them behind too."

The silence lengthens. Morgan takes another pull on his cigar. "We have two hundred wounded men, Basil. How do you propose we carry them?"

"We can't carry them," Duke says. "We must leave them behind."

"For the Yankees?"

"Yes, God be with them, for the Yankees. It's a painful choice, but without the wounded, the able-bodied men will be able to swim across the Ohio the way they swam the Cumberland."

Morgan turns to Colonel Johnson, who commands the Second Brigade. "What do you think of that suggestion, Colonel?"

"I agree with Colonel Duke," Johnson says. "We have two hundred wounded men and seventeen hundred able-bodied men. Not all of the able-bodied can swim and some may be captured, but under the proposed plan, the majority will make it safely to West Virginia. In short, General, I believe this is a strategy that, however painful to implement, will preserve the army as an effective fighting force."

Morgan sits silently for a moment, smoking. A faint breeze blows into the room, stirring the curtains and sending the lamplight flickering. Long, fragile shadows move across his face.

"I will never leave my wounded behind," he says quietly. "Either we all make it across the river tomorrow, or none of us do."

Now I know why his men love him, Claire thinks. *He did not say "the wounded" or even "our wounded." He said "my wounded."* She waits for the officers to insist that surely it is better to sacrifice the few to save the many, but no one speaks. There is another long silence broken only by the sound of crickets and the hoofbeats of riders passing by on the road. Finally Charlton Morgan clears his throat.

"Do you have an alternate plan, sir?" he asks with such respectful formality that a stranger would never guess he was addressing his own brother.

"I do." Morgan takes another puff on his cigar and flecks of gray ash fall on the lapels of his long linen coat. "We will begin crossing at first light, leaving behind the supply wagons and artillery, but not our horses, since to abandon them would deprive us of our greatest advantage."

Morgan rests his cigar on the saucer, picks up his teacup, and takes a swig of whiskey. "At the moment, Colonel Duke has two regiments positioned to attack the Yankee earthworks, and Captain Byrne's battery is ready to provide protective cover. Regroup your regiments, gentlemen, and issue as much food and ammunition to each man as he can reasonably carry without sinking. Destroy the rest of the supplies and set the able-bodied to building flatboats so we can float the wounded over to West Virginia. Remember, our goal is not merely to flee to safety. Our aim is to go on fighting. We will let the Yankees think they have us on the run. Then, when they least expect it, we will turn around and bite them."

Draining the cup, he puts it back on the saucer and rises to his feet. "We've licked them more times than any of us can count, and tomorrow we're going to lick them again." He states this with such confidence that it almost seems possible. "And now, gentlemen, I bid you all good night."

The message is clear: Morgan has made a decision that is not up for debate. The officers gather up their hats and other possessions and prepare to leave. Since Claire and John are standing nearest the door, they are among the first to go.

Outside, Kilpatrick is nowhere in sight. A thick blanket of fog still blots out the stars. In a few seconds, the front porch will be filled with Confederate officers, but for the moment Claire and John have it to themselves. Reaching out, she touches him lightly on the arm.

"I'll be right back," she whispers. Before he can object or ask her where she is going, she walks away. Behind the house, she finds Morgan's slaves asleep on the ground beside a wagon filled with food and cooking gear. She stands in the shadows trying to decide what to do next. A major battle is about to take place, and once again the slaves are being dragged into it against their will. Job ran away a few days ago, taking Morgan's wallet with him. If the others want to escape, this may be their last chance. She should wake them up and urge them to flee, but if she does, she is likely to attract attention. She could never explain why she was raising an alarm among Morgan's slaves, not to mention that, given the nearly obsessive fear Southerners have of slave revolts, she might get them shot instead of helping them escape.

She meant to act sooner, but she has not had a chance to get anywhere near the slaves until this evening. Is it too late? She closes her eyes and tries to think, and as she does so, her father's face rises up in front of her. *What shall I do, Papa?* she asks. Ephraim Musgrove runs his fingers through his hair and smiles. *Use the code,* he says.

The code! Of course! More than once, the runaway slaves she and her father helped to freedom spoke about a secret code they used to communicate with one another. The code, they said, was passed by word of mouth from one plantation to another, and many of its symbols—like the symbols on the Underground Railroad quilts—were drawn from the old African religions.

Claire tries to recall some of the elements: A drinking gourd left on the ground in a certain way means "Go north following the North Star." A bit of tobacco means "Be swift and invisible like smoke that rises in the air." Bones can be arranged to indicate time and direction or warn of danger. A single line drawn in the dust can indicate a road; two parallel lines, railroad tracks. Grains of corn, bits of charcoal, shells—all have meaning. She does not know much, but perhaps that little will be enough.

Silently, she steals over to the chopping block beside the back door, where—as she had hoped—she finds the remains of the chicken Morgan had for supper. Gathering up the discarded head, the bones, and a handful of feathers, she walks to the water bucket, removes the drinking gourd, brings it back to the chopping block, and places everything on the ground. Now she needs tobacco, but where is she going to get some?

She thinks longingly of the plugs the scouts carry. What a pity she does not chew. If her mother had known she was going to need tobacco in the middle of the night, perhaps she would not have raised her to be such a lady. She searches the pockets of her jacket and comes up empty-handed. Not so much as a crumb. Perhaps tobacco is not necessary; but if she could just add something to attract attention, something that would indicate the need to hurry. As best she can recall, the symbol for haste must contain an object filled with "spirit"—a firecracker, a few grains of popcorn, whiskey. Could she get hold of some of Kilpatrick's moonshine? Could she sneak back into the house and pilfer Morgan's bourbon? Could she . . .

What a fool I am! she thinks. *I don't need to go anywhere. I'm carrying the perfect thing!* Reaching for her powder flask, she uncorks it and strews some gunpowder over the chicken parts. Then for good measure, she piles more on the chopping block where no one can possibly miss it. The message now reads: *Danger! Escape north now!* or at least she hopes it does.

She feels around under her shirt and locates the gold watch chain John gave her as a sign of their engagement. Slipping it over her head, she bends down and tucks it into the bowl of the drinking gourd. It's a pity she's not carrying any of the jewels Henry gave her. The sapphire broach alone would have bought Morgan's slaves train tickets and perhaps a house to live in. Even the small aquamarine in her belt buckle would have fed them for weeks.

Having done everything she can think of to help them escape, she cautiously makes her way back to the front of the house, where she finds John sitting on the front railing. Kilpatrick has returned with Pettigrew and Hanson, and the men are involved in a discussion about what they should do next. Technically, John can make this decision since he is the officer in charge, but he rarely pulls rank. Finally, the men decide that the most sensible course of action is to get some rest.

That night Claire sleeps in a trampled cornfield next to John. At first light, the Union forces attack.

Claire

If you say you fought at Gettysburg or Antietam, Shiloh or First Manassas, Chancellorsville or even Brandy Station—where no one won and only a few hundred died—people will accord you respect. They have heard of these battles. The history books mention them. School children memorize their names. Yet if you say you fought in the Battle of Portland, more commonly known—where it is known at all—as the Battle of Buffington Island, you will receive blank stares. The people of Indiana, Kentucky, and Ohio remember what happened that July morning, as do the families of the men who died, but for the rest of America this great battle, during the course of which almost an entire Confederate army was destroyed, has disappeared so thoroughly that sometimes I wonder if I dreamed it.

It was real enough at the time. I had fought at Lebanon and considered myself a seasoned soldier, but I was mistaken. I had never been in a real battle until Buffington Island, and the events that took place on the banks of the Ohio on Sunday, July 19, 1863, are burned in my heart forever.

What do I remember?

Chaos.

We woke to the sound of Union shells whistling overhead, falling to earth, and exploding; the screams of dying men and horses; order and panic; cowardice and heroism. Before we fell asleep, John and I had tethered our horses to a fence rail, but as soon as the shelling started they broke loose. Thus, the first thing I recall is leaping to my feet out of a sound sleep and running through chest-high corn to catch a brown mare.

The shelling went on, taking out ambulance wagons, killing the wounded where they lay, even desecrating corpses, although I am sure the Union soldiers were not intentionally trying to kill the Confederate dead twice over. Later we discovered the river was not only flowing well above thirty inches; it was deep enough for Federal gunboats to maneuver; but the fog was still thick when the attack began and at first none of us could figure out where the shells were coming from.

We had left our horses saddled, so as soon as I caught my mare, I mounted her. John mounted up and rode beside me, and for a while so did Kilpatrick, Pettigrew, and Hanson. Later, John and I got separated from the others. Kilpatrick and Hanson must have had their horses shot out from under them, because when I last saw them, they were fighting on top of the Indian mound that stood at the center of the battlefield. The night before, the sight of that mound had made me shudder, for although I am not usually given to superstition, it seemed an ill omen to fight on a grave. I do not know if the scouts died there or drowned trying to cross the river. So many drowned.

In addition to ceaseless bombardment, we were exposed to gunfire from all directions. We had no idea how badly we were outnumbered, but we could tell that thousands of fresh Union troops must have joined the fray. Hanson's cavalry could never have shot so fiercely and kept it up so long. In short, the race to the river was over. We had been caught on the wrong bank and surrounded; and unless we found an escape route, we would probably all be killed or forced to surrender.

I say "we" because in those first moments I became one with the Raiders. I shot without knowing what I shot at, and I hope to this day that I did not kill anyone; but in the heat of battle, I had no time to consider the niceties of politics and patriotism. I rode beside John and tried to protect him while at the same time he tried to protect me. We shielded each other with our bodies. Each of us would have died for the other without a second thought.

How few women and men have known what it is to fight side by side. I can tell you from experience that it is terrifying and intoxicating. It makes you brave and foolish and frightened and unstoppable. Although I was more afraid than I had ever been in my life, I kept fighting because I could not bear the thought of showing cowardice in front of John or not being there when he needed me. He felt the same. He was determined to take any number of bullets to protect me, and I was just as determined not to let him.

In many ways, we were lucky. We had horses and had been sleeping close to Morgan's headquarters. As Duke's men fought a desperate rear-guard battle, Morgan led about a thousand of us down a steep ravine toward the river in perfect order. This was not only valiant, it bordered on the mythic: one thousand men, the bulk of the regiments, led coolly through such confusion that even now I can hardly describe it.

An abandoned parasol rolled across my path, but my mare was too intent on reaching the water to shy at the sight. We trampled bolts of calico, abandoned jackets, fragments of wagons. We rode across a sea of wreckage and discarded plunder, and kept on riding for fourteen miles with the Federal troops in hot pursuit.

Upstream, at the Reedsville ford, Morgan again tried to lead us across the river. It was his final magic trick, the last rabbit he pulled out of his hat, but this time his famous luck failed him. Some men abandoned their horses, pulled off their boots, threw away their guns, and plunged into the current. Others, including John and myself, tried to swim our mounts across, knowing we would need them on the other side.

Although the water was cold and swift and the current frightful in its tenacity, the Kentucky thoroughbreds the Raiders had started out with probably could have made the crossing; but many of the horses we now rode were old, swaybacked, and more exhausted than we were. They lost their footing and floundered by the dozens. Only Glencoe, Morgan's horse, swam the river as easily as if it had been a stream.

Morgan was almost across when a Federal gunboat suddenly appeared and started shelling. John and I were still on the Ohio side waiting our turn. We watched in horror as the shells struck men and horses, and then in amazement as Morgan turned around and—through fountains of falling shells, gunfire, and a river tinged with blood—swam Glencoe back to the northern bank. "Either we all make it across the river tomorrow, or none of us do," he had said, and he meant it.

He made the crossing safely and rode Glencoe up the muddy bank right past me, close enough to touch. Immediately, his men began to implore him to seek refuge in West Virginia. The Raiders shouted and begged and some even cursed, but he would have none of it.

"Save yourselves," he ordered. "I shall stay here until the last man is across." Suddenly he whirled on John and me. I was taken aback. I had not even realized he knew we were there. "That means you, Taylor, and you too, Zeke. Into the river. Now!"

You did not disobey General Morgan when he gave you a direct order. Immediately, John and I spurred our horses forward and plunged into the current. There was a lull. The Federal gunboat had stopped firing for some reason. I wondered if the Union gunners had run out of cannonballs or if the sight of so many drowned and wounded had made them pity us.

The instant the water lapped over the tops of my boots and I felt the sucking pull of the current, time seemed to come to a halt. As my horse began to swim, I looked toward the far shore and saw a strange sight. Dozens of black and brown circles were floating on the surface of the water like lily pads. Later I realized these were the hats of the men who had drowned, but at the time I did not understand what I was seeing. I watched the circles turn and gather into groups like droplets of oil thrown into a ribbon of hot candle wax.

John and I were almost across when a bullet struck my mare so hard she bucked sideways. Losing my balance, I grabbed for her mane, missed, and was thrown into the water.

I went down into muddy twilight. The river swept into me, filling my mouth and nose and lungs. I fought to rise to the surface, but I could not. I was tangled in the reins and the mare was sinking. I am drowning, I thought.

I kept fighting, kept trying to break away. Just when I had come to the end of my strength, I felt someone grab me, pull me away from the mare, and cut me free. I could not see my savior's face but I knew he was John. Yet he could have been any of a hundred men. The great secret of the Raiders was that they were willing to die for each other. That is how they lasted as long as they did.

Chapter Twenty-five

THAT morning, before the rains come to beat the dust and blood off the heads of the Queen Anne's lace, more than three hundred men cross safely to West Virginia, some pausing long enough to scoop up the hats of their drowned comrades. On the Ohio side, Morgan waits until the Federal gunboat begins shelling again. Then he lifts his hand and says: "Follow me." Breaking out of the Federal trap, he leads seven hundred Raiders north into the heart of the Union. For a full week, they continue to terrorize Ohio. By the time he is forced to surrender, he is only seventy miles from Lake Erie and only three hundred survivors remain from the army of three thousand he led up from Tennessee.

Claire and John are not with him on the day he hands his revolver to Captain Burbick, an Ohio militia officer who has so little authority that Morgan is forced to surrender again to Major Rue two hours later, and yet again to General Shackelford, who has been chasing him for a month and will not be cheated out of the glory of capturing the "Thunderbolt of the Confederacy." They do not see the look of stony pride on Morgan's face as Glencoe is led off to be given to General Winfield Scott as a trophy of war—although later Claire sometimes imagines it.

When she and John fall into the river, the current sweeps them downstream, battering them against floating lumber, wagon wheels, and uprooted trees. They cling together until it throws them onto a sandbar, and when they look up, they find themselves staring down the wrong end of a Yankee gun barrel.

"Hands up, Rebs," commands a voice so clean-voweled and clipped that the words fall on Claire like cold water. This is the accent of the North, of the Upper Peninsula of Michigan, perhaps. It has been so long since she has heard it that it almost sounds like a foreign language.

Having no alternative, they surrender, and a Union patrol marches them back to Portland, where captured Raiders are being herded together to await transportation. Claire thinks of many things during that journey: of the heat and the dust, of those who died in the river and those who lived, of Morgan's courage and stubbornness and the love he inspires in his men. She thinks of her own luck too: how, by the grace of God, she did not drown like Ned and bring her parents a second, endless grief; and how John did not drown either, and how fortunate they both are to be breathing air instead of lying beneath six feet of muddy water.

She could step out of the war now, turn her back on it and walk away. All she has to do is tell the Union soldiers she's a woman. There will be questions to be answered and a scandal to be faced, but very probably by this time tomorrow—or the day after at the latest—she could be putting on clean petticoats, trading in her boots for a pair of shoes, and combing out what is left of her hair.

For a full quarter of an hour, she allows herself to imagine a hot bath filled with lavender-scented bubbles, the luxurious feel of newly ironed sheets, the taste of baked chicken, apple pie, and hot biscuits dripping with freshly churned butter. Then she puts all of these luxuries aside: the food, the clean clothing, even the end of the war, which can come for her as soon as she is willing to say the words "Claire Winston." She chooses the hard ground instead of a soft bed, dirty trousers instead of a clean dress, fear instead of safety, not because she is afraid Henry will find her if she reveals her true identity—after what she has been through this morning, Henry's threat to put her in a sanatorium hardly seems worth worrying about—but because if she leaves Zeke Crane behind, she will also have to leave John, and she will not do that, cannot do it, not even now when he is no longer in danger of being shot, not even when it would make perfect sense to turn to the blue-uniformed men who are herding her down this road and say: *I am a woman.*

Does this decision show in her face or in the way she walks, or have she and John grown so close that he can read her thoughts? She must send out some signal, because not more than five minutes after she has decided not to leave him, he begs her to do just that.

"Tell the Yankees you're a woman," he whispers.

"No," she says.

"There's nothing to be afraid of. Now that they've captured you in battle, they can't charge you with spying."

"I'm not afraid. Or rather, I am afraid, but I'm Zeke Crane."

"Claire . . ."

"Zeke, John. Call me Zeke."

"Be reasonable, darlin'."

"I am being reasonable, and don't call me darlin'."

"But if you continue to pose as a Confederate officer, the Yankees will send you to a prison camp."

"And where will they send you?" He does not answer. "I am staying with you as long as I can," she tells him. This is the same old argument, the one they have never been able to resolve, only now Claire is the one stubbornly refusing take the easy way out. She sees disappointment in his face, but not surprise. "I will go to prison with you," she says, "and when the guards find out that I'm a woman—for sooner or later, they are bound to—I will camp in front of the gate and refuse to leave until they parole you."

Unstopping her canteen, she takes a drink of water and passes it to John. "To us," she says. "Better to have one more day together than a lifetime with anyone else."

"Sweet Jesus!" John says. "I have fallen in love with a fool! A brave, stubborn, devoted, beautiful fool. Such, I suppose, is my fate." He takes the canteen out of her hand and salutes her with it. "To Zeke Crane," he says. "I only wish that the boy was more reasonable and this water was whiskey."

They march on, past trampled cornfields and dead horses. By noon, their canteens are empty, and they have no more breath to waste in conversation. Around four o'clock, they reenter Portland. The town looks as if it has been raked by a tornado. Union shells have hit houses, blowing off the roofs. Trees are shattered and uprooted. Mud and dust are mixed together in such an infernal cauldron that it is hard to tell where one ends and the other begins.

Prodded forward by the Federal troops, Claire and John stumble through a wasteland of broken wagons, overturned carriages, dead horses, hastily covered bodies, and wounded men. Abandoned plunder is scattered everywhere, looking more like the spoils of a band of pillaging barbarians than the refuse of civilized men; but no doubt when Federal troops finally invade the South, they too will steal brass candlesticks, keepsake albums, steamer trunks, shotguns, lace petticoats, silver communion chalices, gold watches, bolts of muslin, bags of flour, and ivory-backed hairbrushes.

Along the north bank of the river, hundreds of captured Raiders sit or lie on the ground, surrounded by Union troops armed with brand-new Spencer repeating rifles. There is no better symbol of the military superiority of the North than those guns. Claire imagines factories in New England turning them out by the thousands, each placed in the hands of a soldier who wears shoes on his feet instead of rags and eats beef instead of fried cornmeal. She wonders if, after seeing such rifles, her fellow prisoners finally understand that the South cannot possibly win this war. If so, you can't tell it by looking at them. Some are sleeping, some are playing cards, and some are busy picking lice out of their shirts. At least half a dozen are actually singing "The Bonnie Blue Flag." It is odd to hear their voices, rough with fatigue, belting out the defiant chorus; odder still to hear some Union soldiers join in and then reply with a spirited rendition of "The Battle Cry of Freedom."

As John and Claire are herded in with the rest, they spot Pettigrew sitting cross-legged in the shade of an overturned wagon sewing a button on his shirt. Catching sight of them, he throws down the shirt and leaps to his feet.

"Lordy!" he yells, running up to Claire and pounding her on the back so hard he sends her into a coughing fit. "Y'all are alive!" Pettigrew stops pounding long enough to ask after Kilpatrick and Hanson, and when they tell him where they last saw the scouts, the joy goes out of his face.

"I reckon they're dead," he says somberly. He removes his hat like a man attending an impromptu funeral. "I am gonna miss 'em. They was the best poker players in the army. Kilpatrick could shoot the pinfeathers off a sparrow without so much as stopping the bird in flight, and Hanson owed me five dollars." Pettigrew sighs, claps his hat back on, and gestures to his fellow prisoners.

"We're still tryin' to sort out the livin' from them that's passed to Glory. Duke is around here somewheres. He was captured in a ravine along with most of his boys. General Morgan's brothers Richard and Charlton is also guests of the Yankees at present. I reckon, includin' y'all, the sons of bitches took at least thirty of our officers prisoner." He pauses. "That says something, don't it."

"What does it say?" Claire asks.

Pettigrew stares at her as if she is mildly feebleminded. "It says our officers don't run, son. It says they stick by us enlisted men and gets themselves catched with us."

The prisoners are forced to wait all afternoon, through the night, and most of the next morning for the steamboats that will transport them to captivity. During that time, four events occur that give Claire reason to hope the country will heal after the war is over. The first is the sound of the Raiders and guards continuing to sing together. The second occurs when the Confederate prisoners receive permission to bathe in the river and, to Claire's astonishment, a number of Federal troops join them, stripping off their uniforms and splashing and laughing with their captives like boys on a holiday. The third occurs around dinnertime, when the Union boys open their haversacks and share their food, handing out cold fried chicken, hot coffee, and even, in some instances, sips of whiskey.

But the most touching and unexpected indication that the country may someday be made whole is the way the people of Portland respond to an invading army that has fought a battle in their town, destroyed their homes, looted their stores, and left their lives in ruins. Emerging from the cellars where they have taken refuge from the shelling, women, children, and old men walk across the battlefield tending to the wounded. They carry water and food to the injured, comfort the dying, and write letters for those too weak to write themselves.

Withdrawing from the other prisoners, Claire finds a shady spot under a cottonwood that has managed to survive the battle. For several hours she watches the citizens of Portland feed their enemies, nurse them, and dress their wounds. If there is a better example of Christian charity than this, she has never seen it.

After weeks on the run, it seems strange to have nothing to do. The Rebel prisoners are well treated and, although Claire and John have no privacy, they still sleep side by side. During the day, they sit for hours talking. By necessity, their conversations are never intimate, yet Claire finds them comforting. She never tires of looking at John and hearing his voice, and once or twice, very quickly, under the cover of darkness, they are briefly able to exchange a quick kiss.

On Monday, the guards feed them hardtack and coffee and march them ten miles downriver, where half a dozen steamboats are waiting. Claire, John, and most of the other officers are loaded onto a side-wheeler, which immediately departs for Cincinnati.

"The Yankees are behaving like gentlemen," John says as they stand by the rail watching the Ohio shore slip by.

The river has dropped considerably since Saturday, so much so that if the Raiders had arrived today, they would have been able to cross with ease. Claire looks at the high-water marks on the cottonwoods, the swamped cornfields, the muddy banks already beginning to dry in the sun. She thinks about the power of water and the power of a single rainstorm to destroy an army. Two years ago, she and John stood at the rail of another boat, in love and on their way to New Orleans.

Nothing ever turns out the way you imagine it will, she thinks. Behind her, the paddle of the steamer turns like a roulette wheel, churning up muddy water, carrying her toward a future she cannot predict or even imagine.

Perhaps it is just as well her imagination fails her. The first sign of trouble comes when they dock to take on more wood. There is a crowd waiting on the landing, ordinary citizens, by the look of them, who give a roar of hatred that makes Claire shudder.

"Horse thieves!" they yell.

"Murderers!"

"Traitors!"

A woman old enough to be Claire's grandmother hurls a rotten potato that hits Charlton Morgan in the chest; a little boy who cannot be more than ten throws a rock at Claire, but fortunately his aim is off. More rocks and rotten potatoes follow. Concerned for the safety of their prisoners, the Union soldiers herd the Rebels to the far side of the boat, but although they are now out of range, they are not out of earshot. The entire time the steamer is docked, the yelling continues. Once someone even fires a gun, although he must fire it into the air since the Federal troops do not fire back.

From then on, every time the steamer draws close to shore, they are greeted with such hostility that Claire becomes convinced she was wrong: the country will never heal. Occasionally, she hears a man give a Rebel yell or a woman cry "Hurrah for Morgan's boys!" but such shouts of support are few and never repeated. She wonders what happens to the Copperheads who dare to go against public opinion. Given the temper of the crowds, she wouldn't be surprised if they were beaten or worse.

When they arrive in Cincinnati, the mobs grow larger and more violent. As soon as she steps off the boat, Claire finds herself running a gauntlet between rows of angry citizens who scream that Morgan's men should be executed on the spot without benefit of trial. Only the bayonets of the guards prevent the threat from being carried out. The Raiders walk through a tunnel of blue-coated soldiers and cold steel. A few trade insults with the crowd, but most pretend not to notice. At the end of the wharf a military band waits for them. When the first Confederate prisoner passes, the band strikes up "Yankee Doodle," clearly an insult but perhaps fortunate, since the patriotic music seems to calm the crowd.

The Raiders march through the streets toward the city prison, heads held high. Some even wink at pretty girls, all of whom appear to be eager to carve them up with kitchen knives. "Hello, miss," the Raiders call to the girls, tipping their broad-brimmed hats. In reply the girls scream insults and the band strikes up "The Star Spangled Banner" followed by "The Battle Hymn of the Republic."

Despite this hostile reception, Claire is not prepared for what happens when they reach the city prison. As soon as they arrive, the guards separate the officers from the enlisted men, and a Union captain, dressed in a brand-new uniform that might well have come from one of Henry's mills, climbs up on a wagon to address them. The private soldiers, he says, will immediately be sent to Federal prison camps, where they will be treated as prisoners of war and perhaps paroled. The Rebel officers will not be paroled under any circumstances and will not be treated as captured enemy combatants. Instead, after a short stay in the city prison, they will be transported to the state penitentiary at Columbus, where they will serve out the rest of the war as common criminals in retaliation for an Ohio officer named Colonel Streight, who has reportedly been captured by General Nathan Bedford Forrest in Georgia and sent to a Southern penitentiary.

At this, a roar of anger and disbelief goes up from the Raiders. Their officers are to be treated as common criminals! Such a course of action is unheard of! Duke objects, the Morgan brothers object, but the Union captain is deaf to their protests.

"March the prisoners into the courtyard," he commands. The next thing Claire knows, she is standing in a large interior courtyard paved with cobblestones, facing firemen who hold hoses attached to a steam-powered fire engine. A small, mousy man—the sheriff or perhaps the warden, if city prisons have wardens—strolls up to the Confederate officers and looks them over. His eyes are bright and filled with hatred. "So you are Morgan's famous Raiders," he says.

"We are Confederate officers and we demand to be treated in accord with the rules of civilized warfare," Basil Duke says.

The little man walks up to Duke and shoves his face in his.

"Who are you?"

"Colonel Basil Duke, sir. I command the First Brigade of General John Hunt Morgan's division."

"Well, Duke, my name is Habakkuk Weston, and in my prison you do not command anything. You are my prisoner, and I am going to see that you don't carry lice into the cells." Turning his back on Duke, he strides to the far side of the courtyard where the firemen are waiting. "Turn the hoses on these traitors," he commands, "and wash the rebellion out of them."

There is a huffing and churning sound, a scream of escaping steam as the pump springs to life. Before any of the Confederate officers have time to brace themselves or even fully understand what is about to happen, they are hit by powerful streams of water.

"Strip off your uniforms!" Weston cries above the din. "Strip,

I tell you, or I will have the guards fire on you. I intend to burn those rags you are wearing. You smell to high heaven, all of you!"

It is clear that this is no idle threat, even though it is being issued by a civilian. The Union soldiers who entered the prison with the captives raise their rifles and take aim. Faced with the prospect of a massacre, Morgan's officers began to remove their uniforms—all except Claire, who stands as if paralyzed.

"You, boy!" Weston points at her. "Strip, or I will have you shot as an example to the others."

"No!" Claire says. "I can't!"

Richard Morgan grabs her by the shoulder. "Damn it, Zeke," he says, "take off your trousers now, and that's an order. This is no time to act like a blushing virgin."

"No!" Claire is defiant and confused. Obviously she cannot strip because . . .

"You are refusing to take an order from *me*, Corporal?" Colonel Morgan says. "From *me*?"

"Aim the hoses at that rabid little Rebel pup!" Weston cries. Suddenly Claire is hit by streams of water that send her over backward. She hits her head hard on the cobbles, rolls over, struggles to her knees, and is knocked down again.

"I can't strip!" she yells.

"Shoot him!" Weston barks.

The guards raise their rifles again, but they are regular soldiers, not prison guards, and perhaps the sight of a wet, defenseless boy sprawled on the ground takes all the sport out of shooting an unarmed enemy, for although they aim, they do not fire.

"What are you waiting for?" Weston yells. "Shoot him!"

Claire grabs a stone hitching post and pulls herself to her feet. Despite the streams of water, which continue to batter her almost senseless, she can see John struggling toward her through the spray, fighting for purchase on the slippery cobbles, falling down and getting up again. She realizes that if the soldiers shoot, he will be killed too. Grabbing the post, she pulls herself around it so she faces Weston. "I cannot strip," she yells, "because I am a woman!"

There is a sudden silence, broken only by the pounding of the water. The soldiers lower their guns. The steam pump stops, and the water gushing out of the hoses ceases.

"I am a woman," Claire repeats, and to her eternal amazement she hears Basil Duke say:

"I always suspected you were."

Part Five

Captivity

Chapter Twenty-six

August 14, 1863

Dear Claire,

I have finally received permission to write to you. My letter can only be one page and must pass the prison censors, so I must keep to general themes, although as you may imagine, I long to speak more intimately. (Perhaps I should strike the word "intimately." Perhaps the censors will not allow even this small sign of affection to pass between us, but I cannot bear to scratch it out, so I shall let it stand and take my chances.)

I am confined in the east wing of the Ohio State Penitentiary in Columbus—the wing that would give me a view of the city if I could see out, which I cannot. All of my fellow officers occupy nearby cells, including General Morgan. When we arrived, we found him waiting for us. He looked so changed, I hardly recognized him. The first thing they do to a new prisoner is shave him and cut his hair. I am sorry to say that General Morgan's beard, like my mustache, is a thing of the past.

I have a five-foot-by-seven-foot cell to myself, as well as the use of a pull-down bed, a three-legged stool, a slop bucket, and a gas burner by which I am allowed to read after we are locked in for the night. Food is abundant, the sanitary arrangements are superior, and I suspect that my cell will be warm when winter comes, so perhaps confinement as a [censored] will prove to be a stroke of luck in disguise.

I will not sign this letter with any word of affection that might cause our communication to be suspended. Please let me know if you receive it. I have no idea where you are, so I am addressing it to your parents.

> John Taylor
> Cell Number 18
> State Penitentiary, Columbus, Ohio

P.S. When you write back, you must avoid discussing the war. We are only allowed to receive news approved by the warden.

September 26, 1863

Dear John,

I received your letter! It took a long time to reach me because it traveled from Columbus to my parents' home in Charlesport and then back to Columbus, where it languished for weeks in the post office. John, I am here, perhaps not more than forty yards from you as the crow flies, but very far when it comes to the possibility of catching sight of you.

I have rented a room in a boardinghouse that faces the penitentiary. Since you warned me that we may only speak in generalities, I shall describe my view. The penitentiary is a huge, square, C-shaped building, mostly hidden behind high stone walls to which the good citizens of Columbus sometimes affix playbills and public notices. At night, it becomes a solid block of darkness encircled by a chain of dim lights, which I presume are shining through a series of small windows. I had imagined you could look up through the bars and see the stars through one of those windows, but now I know you cannot.

The front gate is a massive grill of solid iron. From two to five in the afternoon, I stand before it like a pilgrim visiting a shrine. Even though you cannot see me, I always hope you might somehow feel my presence and know I have not abandoned you. I have been doing this every day since I arrived. I have become an object of local curiosity, but since I am clearly not attempting to communicate with the prisoners, I am allowed to remain. Sometimes women who have husbands or brothers in the penitentiary join me. Often they bring their children.

I am overjoyed to learn you are well and keeping up your spirits. If it is permitted, please write and tell me what you do with your days and let me know if there is anything I can send you. My feelings for you have never changed and never will.

Claire

P.S. You can write to me c/o general delivery. I will go to the post office every day to see if I have received a letter from you. As you sit in your cell, can you feel the seasons changing? Have you heard the wild geese calling to one another? Last night, I saw a flock flying across the moon.

September 28, 1863

Dear Claire,

You are in Columbus! I cannot tell you how happy that news makes me. What has happened to you since we parted in Cincinnati?

[Paragraph censored]

You ask how I pass my time. There is not much to tell. We while away our days playing marbles and exercising on a ladder that runs between the tiers of cells. Chess has become quite popular. In fact, if you were able to send a chess manual, you would earn the undying gratitude of your former comrades-in-arms. Some of the boys have started keepsake albums. I have signed at least a dozen with as many fancy Latin quotations as I can dredge up out of my memory. At seven each night, we are locked in our cells but are allowed to read until lights-out. On Sundays, most of us read the Bible and such newspapers as the warden permits. These include: [censored].

I do not know what your financial situation is, but if you can manage it, I would very much like some novels by Mr. Thackeray and Mr. Dickens. Also, I would like to have a Latin grammar. This period of enforced leisure has allowed me to discover how great are the gaps in my education.

One thing you are not permitted to send me is food, which is a pity since I have recently been longing for [censored]. We received so many packages of delicacies during the first few weeks that the warden has forbidden anyone to mail us so much as a [censored].

Mother has managed to provide me with some money. Knowing she is financially pressed, I have tried to refuse, but she says it is from Father's estate and that I would inherit it on her death in any case. If you need funds for the books, I can arrange for you to receive up to five dollars a week.

Your [censored],
John

October 1, 1863

Dear John,

I cannot believe the censors will not allow me to say I love you. The newspapers say it night and day. But I forget: you would not know that since you are not allowed to read news that has not been approved.

Since we parted in Cincinnati, my life has been a circus of undesired publicity. When I walked out of the city prison wearing the dress the turnkey's wife gave me (to "cover my shame," as she put it), women actually spit on me because my hair was so short. People stared at me and poked me with their umbrella tips as if I were a monkey in a cage. I have lost track of how many telegrams and letters I have received urging me to repent or asking me to lecture to women's clubs. More than once, I have been waylaid by missionaries and prayed over as if I were a combination of the Great Whore of Babylon and Benedict Arnold.

How unreal all this must seem to you. It seems unreal to me. I long only to be myself, but I often feel that self slipping through my fingers. According to public opinion, I am either a romantic heroine who has given up everything for the man she loves or an adulteress and a traitor. When I attempt to explain that, although I rode with Morgan, I am pro-Union, the journalists roll their eyes and write unpleasant stories about my mental instability. One even said, and I quote: "in her present state of hysterical neurasthenia, Mrs. Winston is more to be pitied than censored"—which I suppose is better than saying I should be hanged.

No one believes me when I say that I tried to warn the citizens of Corydon, and when I vow that I did my best to help Morgan's slaves escape, I am accounted a liar or worse. The only people who have stood by me are my parents, but they have had to do so at a distance, since poor Papa has had a minor stroke, which makes it impossible for him to travel. I am racked by guilt when I think of his condition. I suspect the news that his daughter fought in a Rebel army disguised as a man may have provoked it, but Mama, who writes almost daily, firmly denies this. She will never understand why I did what I did. How could she? But she never fails to say how much she and Papa love me.

Sometimes she sends me money, which I send back by the next post. You know how dangerously in debt she and Papa are. The idea that I could be the cause of them losing everything torments me, but so far Henry has given no sign that he intends to call in the promissory note. In fact, I have not heard a word from him, which is strange when you consider that I have been denounced from three-quarters of the pulpits in Boston. On days when I am feeling hopeful, I allow myself to imagine he is so embarrassed by the scandal that all he wants to do is get rid of me.

I long to continue writing to you, but I must stop. I fear I already have run over the one-page limit.

All my love,
Claire

October 7, 1863

Dear Claire,

Thank you for the Latin grammar, and for the chess manual and the copy of *David Copperfield*. The writing materials were also a welcome addition to our stores, as were the candles.

Unfortunately, I did not receive your letter. Instead, one of the guards handed me an empty envelope, only identifiable as coming from you by the return address. Many of my fellow officers have received such envelopes. The censors give them to us as a warning when our correspondents make the error of discussing forbidden topics. General Morgan has had three empty envelopes from his wife and two from his own mother.

Please be more careful in the future, or my permission to write to you will be suspended.

John

Clandestine Note from Claire to John

My darling, this is one letter the censors will never read so in it I can speak from my heart. Since we parted, I have thought only of you night and day. I love you so much that I would gladly sell my soul to hold you in my arms, although these days I fear the Devil has far too many more attractive offers to be interested.

Without you, I feel as if half of my own self is missing. I want to tear down the walls of that damnable penitentiary with my bare hands and set you free.

I have bribed a man to take this to you. He will only carry messages in, not out, so you cannot write back to me, but if you get this, mention the words "wild geese" in your next letter. I will never give up or rest until we are together again.

October 9, 1863

Dear Claire,

Although outwardly my life has changed very little since I last wrote, I am in better spirits. The food remains plentiful. As you know, I am particularly fond of turnips, which is fortunate since we have them mashed or baked at least twice a week. We are also given beef and bread. In short, we eat better here than we ever did in the Confederate army.

After dinner, General Morgan reads his Bible. Many of us are following his example. I find myself particularly comforted by the Psalms and by those portions of the New Testament which exhort charity, compassion, and repentance. A few weeks ago, I decided to start at the beginning and read several books each evening. Wednesday I got through Proverbs, which is not as far as I would have liked, but I was unaccountably tired. Yesterday I planned only to read to The Song of Solomon, but I felt a burst of energy and read all the way to Ezekiel 8:8. I hope I am not boring you, but at present my life is only made endurable by the message of hope contained in the Scriptures.

In your first letter, you asked if I had heard the cries of the wild geese as they migrate south. Last night for the first time, I did.

Their calls would bring joy to the heart of any man, particularly a prisoner.

John

Telegram to Miss Agnes Taylor from Mrs. Henry Winston
October 10, 1863

DOES JOHN LIKE TURNIPS STOP MUST KNOW AT ONCE STOP CLAIRE

Telegram to Mrs. Henry Winston from Miss Agnes Taylor
October 11, 1863

YOU KNOW JOHN HATES TURNIPS STOP WHY DO YOU ASK STOP AGNES

October 12, 1863

Dear John,

I am delighted to learn that you have heard the calls of the wild geese. I too am made more optimistic by the changing of the seasons. As for reading the Bible, you have set me such a good example that I have decided to peruse a fine, leather-bound copy sent to me by a minister in Boston who has often written urging me to repent. To my surprise, I discovered many things I had forgotten. As you said in your last letter, life is made more endurable by such spiritual comforts.

Today, I received a telegram from my husband's lawyer, Mr. Beech, who informs me he will be visiting Columbus in the near future, accompanied by my husband's maiden aunt, Miss Eleanor Winston, a very respectable elderly lady whom I had the pleasure to meet on several occasions when I was living in Cambridge.

Henry, it appears, will not accompany them, a fact I regret, since reading the Bible under your guidance has made me reevaluate my life.

Yours sincerely,
Claire

Clandestine Note from Claire to John

I will do it. Look for me soon. Visitors are forbidden, but somehow I will manage it.

Chapter Twenty-seven

HENRY's aunt Eleanor favors clothing that keeps others at a safe distance. This afternoon, as she sits on the faded brown sofa in the parlor of Claire's boardinghouse, the hoop under her skirt forces Mr. Beech to huddle in the farthermost corner like a man being pursued by a hot air balloon. Her hat, which is designed for repulsing unexpected attempts at intimacy, is not only twice the size of any ordinary hat, but decorated with a small flock of stuffed blackbirds whose rigidly outstretched wings could easily blind the unwary. Yet despite her somewhat bizarre notion of style, Eleanor Winston is no fool. At sixty-five she still has sharp eyes and an equally sharp tongue. She speaks her mind—a trait Claire admires—and has no inhibitions about telling anyone that, although Henry might call her his "favorite aunt," he has never been her favorite nephew.

"That distinction belonged to my sister's son, Gideon," she says, lifting her teacup to her lips.

"Gideon?" Claire never knew Henry had a cousin by that name, or, for that matter, another aunt.

"Both dead these many years," says Aunt Eleanor. She inspects

Claire over the rim of her cup. "Why do you wear that dreadful dress? You look like a burlap bag stuffed with potatoes." She turns to Beech. "Do you not agree, sir?"

Beech pushes aside the voluminous folds of black cashmere and adjusts his glasses. "I really could not venture an opinion on the subject, Miss Winston, not being an expert on ladies' fashions."

"I have very little money," Claire says.

"Harrumph," Aunt Eleanor observes, taking another sip of tea.

"Moreover, even if I had all of Henry's fortune at my disposal, I would not dress in lace and silk as long as John remains behind bars."

"My grandnephew is your lover, is he not?" Aunt Eleanor says with a bluntness that makes Beech squirm.

"Yes," Claire says with equal bluntness. "I left Henry for him."

"So this brown horror of a dress is a sign that you repent of the sin of adultery?"

"No, you mistake my meaning. I repent of nothing except marrying Henry."

"You do not even repent of putting on men's clothing, which we all know is an abomination in the eyes of God? You do not repent of casting all modesty aside and fighting in the Confederate army as a common soldier?"

"Certainly not. Besides, I was not a common soldier. I was a corporal in the Second Kentucky Cavalry, commissioned on the field by General Morgan himself."

Beech makes a strangling sound as if he has inhaled his tea the wrong way. Claire does not turn to look at him, but privately she hopes he is choking. He deceived her in New Orleans and no doubt he has traveled to Columbus in the hope of deceiving her again. *He is an evil little toad*, she thinks. She leans toward her husband's aunt and looks her straight in the eye. For a moment the women sit locked in mutual challenge like hawks about to peck each other into submission.

"Let us waste no more time in idle speculation about the extent of my supposed sins," Claire says. "Why have you come here this afternoon, and what does Henry want from me?"

"Henry wants nothing from you," Aunt Eleanor says. "He is dead."

"Dead?" Claire has been wondering why Henry did not accompany them, but she has never imagined such an explanation. She sits back abruptly. Her first reaction is one of disbelief, followed by an unexpected feeling of sadness. She had once cared about Henry and even thought she loved him enough to marry him. She had not loved him, of course. She did not really know what love was until she met John. But still, Henry had been her husband. She had been angry with him for good cause, but often, even in the midst of her anger, she had pitied him. *Poor Henry*, she thinks. *What a sad, pinched life he lived.* And then, she thinks: *I am no longer a married woman! I am free!*

She looks up to find Aunt Eleanor studying her. How does she feel about her nephew's death? Claire wonders. She is wearing black, but she always wears black, and that outrageous hat hardly looks like something you would put on to mourn a dearly departed relative.

"Henry is dead?" Claire repeats, stalling for time.

"In Istanbul," Beech says. He pushes his gold-rimmed spectacles up on his nose and shrugs. "Of typhus."

"Or at least that is what the family wishes the world to think," Aunt Eleanor says. "My nephew traveled to that sink of iniquity to photograph the young children who beg in its streets; and there, under circumstances that are still not clear, he turned up dead in a cheap hotel connected to one of the public baths. Either before or after his death, his camera was stolen, along with all his photographic plates. Given the peculiar nature of his death, we must consider the theft fortunate."

A look of alarm comes over Beech's face. "Miss Winston," he says, "please let me handle this. On the journey out, we agreed that—"

"We agreed to lie, sir," Aunt Eleanor says, "but now that I am actually in the presence of my late nephew's wife, I find I have no heart for legal prevarication. The poor girl has suffered enough." She turns to Claire. "Are you aware Henry was making plans to have you committed to a lunatic asylum?"

"Yes," Claire says.

"And are you also aware that after you left him, he revised his will?"

"His will? Frankly, I never gave a thought to Henry's will. No doubt he disinherited me. If that is what you have come all the way from Cambridge to tell me, you need not have bothered. I will not contest whatever provisions he has made. I never wanted his money."

"An unusual attitude." Aunt Eleanor gives Claire an approving look. "But when you hear the specifics, you may change your mind." She turns to Beech. "Sir, please be so good as to explain Mrs. Winston's present position to her, and if possible be brief."

"Brevity may not be possible," Beech objects, once again adjusting his spectacles.

Aunt Eleanor sighs, sits back, and loses her hands in the folds of her skirt. "You will make it labyrinthine, sir. I know you will." She gives Claire a look that might almost be interpreted as sympathetic. "Make yourself comfortable. Listening to Beech explain legal matters is rather like being forced to listen to someone reciting the whole of the Begats." Again she turns to Beech. "Get on with it, if you please."

Beech clears his throat and gives Claire a pinched but cordial smile. Behind him is a window. Through the panes, Claire can see the penitentiary. In the dying light of this late October afternoon, it looks as solid as a fort.

"I hope you are well, Mrs. Winston," Beech says.

"I am in excellent health, thank you," Claire replies with as much patience as she can muster. He has offered her this same pleasantry at least three times since he arrived.

Beech nods gravely. "I am glad to hear it."

Claire resists an urge to grab the toasting fork that sits by the fireplace and prod him into more rapid revelation. "Well?" she prompts.

Beech offers her another pinch-lipped smile, which is undoubtedly meant to be pleasant. "Miss Winston has asked me to acquaint you with some of the particulars of your situation about which you may not be aware."

"For God's sake, speak plainly," Claire says.

Beech blinks and clears his throat. Claire wonders if she has just sworn. She has been removed from refined society for so long she can no longer recall what a lady is and is not permitted to say. She thinks of the eloquent string of obscenities Pettigrew let loose with on the afternoon a pack mule bit him on the buttocks. If she uttered any of those, Beech would probably have to be revived with smelling salts.

"My dear Mrs. Winston," he begins, but she cuts him off.

"I am not your 'dear' anything, sir. The last piece of information you gave me was a nightmare from which I have not yet fully recovered. In fact, I am contemplating the possibility of having you disbarred for forging a marriage certificate. You know, of course, to which certificate I refer." She has scored a direct hit. Beech turns paler than she has thought possible. Even the irises of his eyes seem to blanch.

"Yes," he says in a strangled voice.

"Good," she says. "Now that we have that settled, tell me: to whom has Henry left his fortune? A mistress perhaps? No, that, I believe we can all agree, is unlikely. Perhaps to a home for abandoned children, or perhaps"—she nods at Aunt Eleanor—"to you."

"Not to me," Aunt Eleanor says.

"Well, to whom, then?"

"He has left you five hundred dollars," Beech says.

"Indeed. That is most generous of my late husband, considering he owns property in three states and his mills have been supplying the Union army with cloth. Still, I can hardly blame him, can I? To whom did he leave the rest?"

"Harvard College," says Beech. "To be more specific, Mr. Winston's last will and testament endows the college with funds to construct a Henry Winston Museum of the Photographic Arts. Mr. Winston also set up a separate endowment to maintain the museum. He donated his own plates and photographs. To receive this bequest, all Harvard need do is keep the latter on permanent display. The college has agreed to these conditions, so from a legal standpoint, the matter is settled."

"Settled, that is, unless you decide to contest the will," Aunt Eleanor says. "As Henry's widow, you have a right to do so. Public opinion would not be on your side, but in theory you might be able to recover up to a third of my late nephew's estate. Of course, you would be fighting Harvard College, an institution whose lawyers attack in ways that make Beech look like a lapdog." Beech begins to object, but she silences him with a gesture. "In short, Beech and I have come to buy you off."

"Why bother?" Claire asks. "Since neither of you benefits from Henry's will, why do you care if I contest it?"

"Scandal." Aunt Eleanor pours herself another cup of tea. Her hands do not tremble. She is, Claire thinks, a magnificent woman. "The family fears that if you contest Henry's will, certain unsavory matters will come to light. The Winston name is old and ever so respectable." She lifts her cup to her lips and sips. "There have been Winstons in Massachusetts since shortly after the landing of the *Mayflower*. Did you know that?"

"No," Claire says.

"Ah, yes," she says with quiet pride. "During the unpleasantness at Salem, several were even burned as witches." She puts down her cup. "So tell me, what would it take to get you to sign a quit-claim promising not to contest?"

"A 'renunciation' is the proper term for such a document,"

Beech interposes, "and with all due respect, Miss Winston, I would appreciate it if you would allow me to handle this. As the legal representative of the late Mr. Winston's estate, I am bound to advise you that it is unwise for you to attempt to negotiate with his widow."

"No doubt you are doing your job, Mr. Beech," Claire says, "but you are wasting your breath. I will not speak to you. I will speak only to Aunt Eleanor."

"I warned you she would say this," Aunt Eleanor says. Is there a note of triumph in her voice? Claire cannot be sure, but in any case, it is clear that she is more than willing to take over. She turns to Claire, her eyes bright with the prospect of striking a bargain. "State your terms," she says. "If they are reasonable, I will see they are met."

"Let me think." Claire looks out the window. The sun has set and long shadows are running down the penitentiary walls. She thinks of John sitting in his cell and the probability that the war will go on for months if not years; and then she thinks of her parents sitting in this same gathering darkness. "Henry loaned Mama and Papa a great deal of money," she says. "I want the loan forgiven."

Aunt Eleanor turns to Beech. "Is that possible?"

"Yes," Beech admits with obvious reluctance.

Aunt Eleanor turns back to Claire. "Agreed," she says. "What else?"

"Henry had a gold watch that belongs to John. When I fled from Cambridge, I left it behind because I did not want to run the risk that Henry might accuse John of conspiring with me to commit theft. I want that watch back."

"Agreed. Just out of curiosity, do you intend to give it to my grandnephew?"

"Yes," Claire says, "but not until he gets out of prison. If I arrange for him to receive it while he is incarcerated, it may well be stolen a second time."

The implication of the word "stolen" is not lost on Aunt Eleanor. She nods her head gravely, sending the birds on her hat into flight. "I see," she says. "No doubt there is a story behind this watch which I will never learn. In any event, it is yours. What else?"

"When I left Henry, I took several pieces of jewelry. To be specific: I took a garnet necklace with matching earrings, a pair of pearl pendants, an emerald and diamond ring, a sapphire broach, and two gold bracelets. Although these were gifts from Henry, I believe that from a legal standpoint they remained his property since a wife, I am told, owns nothing in her own name, not even the clothes on her back. I wish this jewelry to be mine in law as well as fact."

"That seems fair," Aunt Eleanor says. "Perhaps I should remind you that the inventory of Henry's estate included a ruby necklace, a string of perfectly matched pearls, and—"

"Please, Miss Winston!" Beech exclaims.

Aunt Eleanor ignores him. "—And several other pieces of jewelry of as great or greater value than the ones you have."

"I only want the pieces I took when I left," Claire says. "As I said, they were presents, and I feel I have a right to them."

"We agree to your demands," Beech says. "You have only to sign the renunciation to come into immediate possession of all you have asked for."

Aunt Eleanor glares at Beech. "If you please, sir, I believe Mrs. Winston is not yet finished."

"I also want ten thousand dollars when Henry's estate is finally settled," Claire says and has the satisfaction of seeing Beech flinch. "I feel this is a modest sum to ask for, considering how much the estate is worth and how badly my husband treated me. I plan to start a new life and I would like to be able to buy land. And oh, yes, I almost forgot: I want the name of the best hairdresser in Columbus, Ohio."

"That last is an odd request," Aunt Eleanor says. "Are you quite certain that you want nothing more?"

"Nothing," Claire says.

Aunt Eleanor turns to Beech. "How long will it take you to draw up the necessary document?"

"I have the forms with me." Beech reaches for his portfolio. "I need only to spend a few moments filling in the details."

"Do so," Aunt Eleanor says.

"I wish to receive the five hundred dollars immediately," Claire says.

"I shall stipulate that this sum be wired to the financial institution of your choice." Beech opens his portfolio and extracts several sheets of paper covered with legal script. "I need pen and ink. My writing implements were lost in transit. The railroads have become remarkably careless with baggage."

Claire nods toward a battered writing desk that sits in the corner of the parlor. Beech stands and walks across the room with no show of haste. Only two red spots on his cheeks indicate how eager he is to bring this meeting to a conclusion.

"Is there more tea?" Aunt Eleanor asks.

"Yes," Claire says. "But I am afraid it has gone cold. Shall I go get us some hot water from the kitchen? I cannot ring for a servant. This is not the kind of establishment that provides them."

"No need." The women sit in silence, listening to Beech's pen scratch across paper. Finally Aunt Eleanor speaks. "You are obviously living in poverty. Why have you not sold the jewels you took?"

"I cannot get at them," Claire says. "They are buried in a turnip patch."

Aunt Eleanor blinks. "Ah," she says. "Did you hide them because you feared Henry would prosecute you for theft?"

"No, I hid them because I feared some Union or Confederate soldier might take them from me, and my life along with them. There is a war on, and I had to travel through unsettled areas."

"That makes sense. In your situation, I would have done the

same. I shall not ask you where this turnip patch is. I do not wish
to know. But I am curious about the rest of your demands. Why, if
you do not mind me asking, do you require the name of a hairdresser?"

"Because I need to get my hair done, and I cannot ask for a reference. No decent woman will speak to me."

"Present company excepted, I presume," says Aunt Eleanor. A
smile plays at the corners of her mouth.

"Present company excepted. I hope this visit will not tarnish
your reputation."

"I doubt it will. I am too old and far too rich."

"I have a question for you," Claire says, "one you may decline
to answer if you wish." She studies Aunt Eleanor for a moment,
thinking of all the family secrets she must harbor. "Why did
Henry marry me? Clearly he did not love me. If he only wanted a
model for his photographs, he could have found many women
more beautiful than I am. So why did he not remain a bachelor?"

"I will tell you after you have signed the renunciation," Aunt
Eleanor says.

"Perhaps I will not sign if you do not tell me beforehand."

Aunt Eleanor shrugs. "Very well. So far you have proved reasonable, so I shall chance it." She pauses. "You never met my sister-
in-law, did you?"

"No, although I have seen a portrait of her."

"I doubt any portrait could convey her true nature. Abigail was
admirably moral, but not—how shall I put it?—a warmhearted
woman. To my knowledge, none of her children ever received an
embrace from her, although they did receive a great deal of advice,
most of it unwanted. In any event, before she married, her father
had an agreement drawn up that protected her personal fortune,
which was quite substantial. When she died, my sister-in-law stip-
ulated in her will that Henry was only to inherit this money if he
were in possession of a wife on his thirty-sixth birthday. Thirty-six,

you see, was the age my brother was when he married her, and apparently having found domestic bliss with Henry's father, Abigail wanted to ensure that her son would be equally happy."

Claire does not know whether to laugh or cry at this revelation. No wonder Henry could afford to collect Etruscan bronzes. Marrying her had made him a wealthy man! She looks at the stuffed birds on Aunt Eleanor's hat, rigid in death as they had never been in life, then at Aunt Eleanor's face, which from certain angles looks so much like Henry's. "Henry turned thirty-six only a few weeks before he left for London," she says. "I ordered a cake baked for him, gave him a present, wished him a happy—" Her voice breaks, and she finds she cannot continue.

Aunt Eleanor opens her reticule, pulls out a handkerchief, and hands it to Claire. "I have always believed you should know this," she says briskly, "but until now I did not feel I had the right to tell you. I heartily disliked my sister-in-law, and she disliked me. I have no children, but if God had blessed me with any, I would not have attempted to control them like puppets.

"Abigail had no such scruples. She felt all was not well with Henry—that when it came to women her son was, as she once put it, 'disinclined to seek a wife'; so she made sure he would not only marry but stay married. A portion of his inheritance was to be paid to him on the first day of each year over a twenty-year period. If he divorced, the remainder was to go to charity."

Disinclined! Is that the word one uses to describe a man who has no more ability than a marble statue to make love to a woman? Claire imagines Abigail Winston crouched at the center of her gloomy house like a great, black spider. She can almost find it in her heart to feel sorry for Henry, but not quite.

"The renunciation is ready," Beech says. Claire turns to find him at her elbow, inkwell and pen in hand. "Please sign here." He points. "And initial paragraphs 5a, 7b, and 13c."

Claire reads the agreement and finds she has been granted

everything she asked for. Taking the pen from Beech, she dips the tip into the ink and signs away all rights to the estate of Henry Endicott Winston, a husband who never loved her and whom, to be honest, she never really loved.

Chapter Twenty-eight

O
N a blustery day in early November, a smart carriage draws up to the entrance of the Ohio State Penitentiary. Soon after, the warden's secretary, Mr. Kiply, knocks on the door of the warden's office. Filled with comfortable furniture and heated by a coal fire, the office is carpeted with a heavy wool rug. The stone walls have been concealed with cream-colored stucco and decorated with scenes of boating parties and sleigh rides. If it were not for the portraits of President Lincoln and Governor Tod behind the warden's desk and the incessant clanging of iron doors, you might almost imagine yourself in the parlor of a private home.

As Mr. Kiply enters, the warden does not look up. In front of him lies a complaint concerning the status of the Confederate prisoners. He has never approved of the housing of prisoners of war in his penitentiary, but he is not the governor of Ohio nor the state legislature. Criminals are easy to deal with, at least on paper. Prisoners of war, particularly famous ones like General Morgan, are endless trouble.

"What is it?" he asks.

"Patience is gone," Kiply says.

The warden puts down his pen. "Patience?"

"That's the nickname the guards have given to the woman in the brown dress who stands in front of the penitentiary gate every afternoon."

"Her name is not Patience," says the warden. "As you—and as I am sure the guards—know, she is the infamous Mrs. Winston, who fought with Morgan's Raiders and whose paramour is presently in our custody. I take it she has caused no trouble, attempted to contact none of the inmates, or done anything else I need concern myself with?"

"No, sir. She has merely vanished. For over a week, the guards have not seen her."

"Perhaps she has fallen ill or finally come to her senses. Is that all? I am unusually busy right now."

"No, sir. A lady is requesting an audience with you." Kiply pauses. "She has a strong Southern accent."

The warden resists an urge to blaspheme. "Not another female relative of those Rebel officers! Their sisters and wives plague me like horseflies. Tell the lady no visitors are allowed. Tell her I have turned away General Morgan's own mother."

"With all due respect, Warden, I think you will want to see her. I believe her presence may explain why Mrs. Winston has disappeared from her post. The lady handed me a calling card that claims she is Mrs. John Taylor. Mrs. Taylor is in a state of great agitation, and—well, sir, she's quite a looker. It has been a long time since I have seen such a well-turned ankle."

The warden makes a show of frowning. A discussion of ladies' ankles is not something he likes to encourage in his subordinates. He contemplates the possibility of speaking to Mrs. Taylor and decides it might not be such a bad idea. He is happily married, but his marriage is of long enough duration that he is not adverse to having a conversation with a pretty woman. *So the infamous Rebel John Taylor is married*, he thinks. *This is a prime bit of scandal. No wonder when the wife appeared, the mistress took flight.*

"Very well," he says. "Send the lady in. I suppose it can do no harm to speak to her, and I could use some diversion."

Mrs. Taylor must have been waiting directly outside the door, because as soon as Kiply opens it, she enters. She is tall and so slim as to look fragile. Her eyes are grave, but everything else about her suggests feminine warmth. Her blond tresses are piled on her head in an intricate pattern that emphasizes the pale oval of her face. She wears a blue dress made of silk that changes color in subtle ways as she moves. There is a spray of lace at her throat and gold pendants in her ears. The warden notes that her hands are admirably small, as is her waist. As for her ankles, he cannot see them, but she is wearing a hoop beneath her skirt and hoops have a habit of swaying.

He rises. "Good afternoon, madam," he says. "What can I do for you?" The question is a mere formality. He intends to do nothing except admire her. Kiply's description was inadequate. Mrs. Taylor is not merely pretty; she is a beauty.

"My husband is a prisoner here," she says in a voice honeyed with Southern vowels. "I need—" Her voice wavers. Tears brim up in her eyes, hang on her lashes, overflow, and run down her cheeks. "Oh, dear," she says. "I am so sorry. I—"

"Pray sit down, Mrs. Taylor." The warden is used to watching women cry. They often believe tears will get them what they want. In this, they are mistaken. Mrs. Taylor sinks into a chair, extracts a handkerchief from her reticule, and dabs at her eyes. The scent of tuberoses fills the office.

"I promised myself I would not cry," she says, and promptly breaks her promise by crying as if her heart would break. The warden is not a hard man, but he has no time for such melodramas.

"Pray compose yourself, madam," he says, "and state your business." His words are cold and businesslike, but his tone is not unfriendly. The lady gives a start. Drying her eyes, she stuffs her kerchief into her sleeve and stares at the warden with eyes full of desperation. He sees nothing but sincerity in her gaze.

"You are right to reprimand me," she says. "This is no time for a public display of feelings. I apologize. I know you are a busy man, so allow me to get directly to the point. I assume you are aware of my situation regarding that"—she pauses—"that *woman.*"

"Frankly, Mrs. Taylor," the warden says, "until five minutes ago, I did not know you existed; but now knowing, I believe I understand how you must feel about Mrs. Winston."

She flinches at the name. "Yes," she says weakly. "Well, then perhaps you can understand why I urgently need to speak to my husband in private for a few moments. I have something to tell him that I cannot put into a letter."

"That is quite impossible," the warden says.

She gives a small gasp, and despite his long-standing vow not to be taken in by feminine wiles, he feels as if he has been a brute. He tries to soften the blow, or rather to delay it. "In the first place, I have no proof you are who you say you are."

She brightens a little at this. Opening her reticule again, she extracts two documents. "Here is the certificate of my marriage," she says. "I am the former Miss Lucretia Conway. As you can see, John and I have legally been husband and wife for the past seven years." She offers him the second document. "This is the birth certificate of our daughter, Marie. Marie needs her father, sir."

"Many of the inmates in this penitentiary have children who need their fathers. You do realize, don't you, Mrs. Taylor, that you will not be able to talk me into granting a dangerous Rebel officer his freedom?" He gestures to the portraits that hang behind his desk. "If you seek clemency, you would have better luck applying to Governor Tod or President Lincoln."

"I do not want my husband released," Mrs. Taylor says. "On the contrary, I want you to keep him here as long as possible."

The warden is taken by surprise. He has never had a wife ask him to prolong her husband's sentence. "I do not take your meaning," he says. Mrs. Taylor leans forward with a look in her eyes that is at once so intimate and pleading that, despite himself, he is moved.

"I can only be sure my husband will not run off with that woman again if he is incarcerated. I am an abandoned wife, sir. I wish to speak to John and persuade him to cut off all contact with . . ." She still cannot bear to say the name. Again her voice grows tremulous. "I want to plead with him to repent and return to his family."

The warden realizes the time has come to make it clear that what she is asking is impossible. "No," he says.

She obviously has not expected such an abrupt answer. Again she starts as if struck. "No?" she repeats weakly.

"No. I am sorry, but I can make no exceptions. How can I permit you to talk to one of my Rebel prisoners when I have turned away General Morgan's own mother? You may write to your husband three times a week like every other relative, but you may not speak to him in person."

He expects objections, tears, anger. Instead, Mrs. Taylor falls silent and rises unsteadily to her feet. When she looks at him again, there is no longer hope in her eyes. Yet perhaps there is hope elsewhere, for she says: "I have something to tell my husband that I cannot put into a letter. Something very intimate." And then, without warning, she crumples to the floor like a great, wilting, blue silk flower. For a moment, the warden stands behind his desk admiring her ankles, which are now fully on display. Then he rings for his secretary.

"Kiply," he says, "Mrs. Taylor has fainted. Summon one of the matrons from the women's wing. Mrs. Auerbach would be a good choice. I believe she knows how to bring females to their senses."

As it turns out, there is no need to revive Mrs. Taylor. She revives herself, so that by the time Mrs. Auerbach appears, dressed in an ugly black prison employee's uniform that makes her look like a plump crow, the lady is seated and has resumed dabbing at her eyes with a square of lace the size of a postage stamp.

The matron inspects the warden's visitor. "Is there a problem, sir?" she asks. She is a burly, no-nonsense German with no patience for pretty women, each of whom in her opinion causes more trouble than ten homely ones.

The warden clears his throat. A conversation has occurred between himself and Mrs. Taylor since the lady rose from his carpet. It has not been the sort designed to put a man's mind at rest.

"This is Mrs. Taylor. She claims there is something important she must tell me, but she cannot bring herself to say what it is. Or rather, she cannot bring herself to say it to a gentleman. She insists on confiding the information to another female."

Mrs. Auerbach looks the visitor over and sees at once what the problem is. She is struck, not for the first time, by the blindness of men. "What do you wish me to do, sir?"

The warden gestures to a small door. "Take her into my sitting room, listen to her, and come back and tell me what she says. Remember the lady is not a prisoner, but a visitor. In other words, treat her with the utmost courtesy."

"Should I search her?"

Mrs. Taylor utters a small cry of alarm.

"Certainly not," the warden says. "Just listen to her."

Mrs. Auerbach takes Mrs. Taylor into the warden's sitting room. A few minutes later she reappears. "The lady claims she is with child. She had so much trouble admitting her condition, you would have thought she was confessing to a murder."

The warden is taken aback. "With child? She does not look it."

"It is common practice for women to raise their hoops to conceal their condition. She could be lying, but the only way to be certain is to have her examined by a midwife or a physician."

"Good Lord, no!" the warden says. "That is out of the question." He does some quick calculations and realizes Taylor must have impregnated his wife shortly before he abandoned her. He is not ordinarily a sentimental man, but infants die at an alarming rate. He and his wife have buried two children and may perhaps bury their one-year-old daughter before spring. He thinks of pretty Mrs. Taylor crying and distraught; of Mrs. Winston waiting outside the gates of the prison, ready to snatch up Taylor the moment he is free. He thinks of the sanctity of the home in general and his love for his own wife in particular. *This is an extraordinary circumstance*, he thinks, *and as such, it requires extraordinary measures.*

"Mrs. Auerbach, I may grant Mrs. Taylor's request to speak to her husband. If I do, have you any advice to offer?"

"Strip her and search her before you let her anywhere near him," Mrs. Auerbach says.

The warden is aware that women prisoners are regularly stripped naked and searched, but he cannot envision modest Mrs. Taylor, already upset and in a delicate condition, surviving such an ordeal. "Such a thorough search of her person will not be necessary," he says. "Simply do whatever it is you do when you admit female visitors."

"I will need to look under her hoop, sir. She could be smuggling contraband. Women do that all the time. Also, I will have to pat down her stays and bodice and run a knitting needle through her hair."

"Very well," the warden says. "I believe even in her present state of agitation, she can survive such a search without injury to the child she is carrying."

Mrs. Auerbach goes back into the warden's sitting room, and the warden goes back to the complaint on his desk. For the next ten minutes, he attempts to read it and make notes so he can respond, but he cannot concentrate. He listens for sounds, but hears nothing except the usual beehivelike murmur of the prison.

When Mrs. Auerbach returns, the news she brings is encouraging. Mrs. Taylor does not appear to be smuggling contraband. Her hair is partially fake—"a ratt" is the term Mrs. Auerbach uses—but the false hair hides nothing except the lady's own hair, clipped so short it barely covers her ears.

"She claims her mother cut her hair when she contracted scarlatina," Mrs. Auerbach says.

This last detail convinces the warden to show mercy. Summoning Mrs. Taylor into his office, he informs her she may have ten minutes alone with her husband.

———

The prison reception room has a high, barred window that shows only a small patch of lowering gray sky. Except for two straight-backed chairs with rush seats, there is no furniture. It is the sort of place where one might imagine many things happening, most of them unpleasant.

Mrs. Taylor is already seated on one of the chairs when the prisoner is brought in by two guards. At the sight of him, she rises to her feet. For a moment, she and her husband stare at each other as Mrs. Auerbach looks on disapprovingly. The matron notes that the man still wears the gray trousers and high black boots of a Rebel cavalry officer, a fact that offends her sense of order. Inmates should be clad in prison uniforms or civilian clothing. Those are the rules, or at least they were before the state decided to turn the east wing into a prisoner-of-war camp.

"So, Mrs. Taylor," the prisoner says, "we meet again." He is clean-shaven, pale, and gaunt, with that slightly glassy-eyed look inmates get after they have suffered bouts of fever or dysentery; but despite such obvious signs of ill-health and long imprisonment, a smile spreads across his face, so warm and welcoming that Mrs. Auerbach is taken by surprise. She expected him to react with cold indifference, but here he is, greeting the wife he abandoned as if he has never stopped loving her.

"The warden has instructed me to leave you alone with Mrs. Taylor for exactly ten minutes," she says. "I will be outside the door with two guards. If Mrs. Taylor makes any attempt to help you escape, she will be subject to criminal charges; you will be shot and possibly killed. Is that clear?"

"Yes," the prisoner says absently. He is still staring at his wife with a look on his face that Mrs. Auerbach has never seen on the face of her own husband. She leaves, banging the door behind her. She does not like to be ignored, and, to tell the truth, she is somewhat jealous.

"Claire," John says as soon as the matron is gone, for it is of course Claire who stands before him dressed in blue silk. He starts forward to embrace her, but before he can reach her, they hear a clanging sound. There is a small, rectangular window in the door. The metal cover has just been drawn back, and two eyes are pressed to the glass.

"Damn." Claire bites her tongue to keep from doing an imitation of Pettigrew being bitten by a pack mule. Despite those prying eyes, nothing matters: not the stone walls, not the bars on the window, nothing. John stands in front of her, alive and close enough to touch, even though she can't touch him. She wants to laugh and cry and hug him senseless, but she's supposed to be the wife he left, not the woman he loves. She darts a quick glance at the spy hole. "That 'damn' was from Zeke Crane," she says. "How is it you and I always end up in prison together?"

"Pure luck." John's smile grows broader. "I liked you as Zeke, Claire, I really did; but I had almost forgotten how unbelievably beautiful you are in skirts."

"I am playing the lady this afternoon. I got in here posing as your wife. Henry's not the only one who can forge a marriage certificate. By the way, who was Lucretia Conway? Was she real, or did Henry invent her?"

"Lucretia was a girl I tried to help. I saved her from hanging herself, and her brothers took that to mean I was the father of her child. Later she confessed who the real father was and they made him marry her. What in God's name have you done to your hair, Claire? It looks like a pudding."

Claire laughs the first real laugh she has laughed in months. "Why, Lieutenant Taylor," she says, "I do declare: your compliments overwhelm me. This blond 'pudding,' as you call it, is an expensive French wig that itches like fury. I fear lice. Seriously, John, we don't have much time and—"

"Do you have any idea how much I want to kiss you?"

"I want to do far more than kiss you, but we can't risk it. I have missed you so much, it's driven me half mad; but we must speak quickly and hope whoever is looking through that spy hole can't read lips. I got your letter, the one with the reference to Ezekiel 8:8. I thought you had chosen Ezekiel because of "Zeke Crane," but when I looked the verse up, I discovered it read: *Son of man, dig now in the wall; and when I had digged in the wall, behold a door.* You're tunneling out, aren't you?"

John switches positions with her so his back is to the door. "Yes," he whispers. "Hines discovered a ventilation space under the cells on the ground floor. We've started digging in shifts with a pair of knives we stole from the mess hall, but it's slow going."

"I've brought you two chisels. They're in my shoes. Some other time I'll tell you how I managed it, but for now . . ." She glares at the spy hole. "I can't give them to you as long as that Valkyrie is watching us. Loan me your bandanna. A lady in high dudgeon is usually irresistible." John hands her his bandanna. Striding over to the door, she pounds on it and hears the sound of the key being turned in the lock. The door swings open.

"Finished already?" asks Mrs. Auerbach, who has just taken a step backward to avoid being struck in the face.

"No, I am not finished," Claire says haughtily. "The warden promised me I could speak to my husband in *private*, and I do not consider his promise has been honored when y'all are staring at us as if we were goldfish." She waves John's bandanna in Mrs. Auerbach's face. "I am going to drape this over the window. You are not to disturb us until our ten minutes is up, or I will see that you answer to the warden."

Without waiting for a reply, Claire drapes the bandanna over the top of the door, so it covers the spy hole, and slams the door.

A few moments later, she has her shoes off and John is sitting in one of the chairs stuffing the chisels into his boots.

"Will they search you again before they take you back to your cell?" she asks.

"Probably not. Besides, it's worth the risk. Without these chisels it will take us weeks to make a tunnel large enough to crawl through."

"You look as if you've been ill."

"Roman fever again."

"Your 'wife' could send you quinine."

John grins at the word "wife." "No need. What we really want is civilian clothing. Escaped prisoners in Confederate uniforms won't be able to travel through Union territory unnoticed. As for quinine tablets, the prison doctor dispenses them to us by the gross. The problem is, they do me no good, because every time they throw me into the dungeon, I have a relapse."

"The dungeon! What in God's name is that?"

"A damp, unheated punishment cell infested with vermin. They've shut me up in there three times: twice for possessing contraband newspapers—which I do not regret because without them we would never have learned that Bragg whipped Rosecrans at Chickamauga." John finishes stuffing the chisels into his boots and pulls them on.

"And the third time? What was that for?"

"Nothing important," he says, not meeting her eyes.

"You lie badly. I suggest you never take up a career as riverboat gambler. What was your third offense?"

"One of the guards found that first note you sent me. I should have ripped it up, but I couldn't bring myself to. To tell the truth, it was worth a trip to the dungeon to have you with me even on paper." He stands up and looks at her with an indifference to his own suffering that makes her sorry she ever wrote to him.

"Oh, John," she says, biting her lips to hold back the tears. "What have they done to you?"

"Nothing that they haven't done to the rest of the boys."

"I'm not in love with the rest of the boys, I . . ." She feels like storming into the warden's office and telling him in no uncertain terms that any man who throws other human beings in a dungeon is going to have to answer to God for it someday. "I'm getting you out of here before you die of fever," she says. "I'll send you civilian clothing as soon as possible. Is there anything else you need?"

"Opium, but I can't think of any way you could get it to us."

"Opium! Are you in pain?"

"No, we need it to drug the guard dogs that are set loose in the prison yard every night. Don't fret about me, Claire."

Claire walks across the cell to a damp wall covered with mold. She stares at the stones thinking how much damper and more horrible the walls must be in the dungeon. When he rode with the scouts, John never put himself first. She knows nothing she can say now will change that. She takes a deep breath, turns around, and returns to more practical considerations.

"In your letter, you mentioned 'turnips.' I know that means you need money, but I can't get to my jewels to dig them up. However, I have recently received an unexpected windfall of five hundred dollars. I have spent fifty or so on this dress and wig and a few well-placed bribes but that still leaves quite a sum."

John is clearly surprised. When they parted in Cincinnati, she had less than three dollars to her name. "Have Confederate sympathizers been sending you money?" he asks.

"Yes, but beyond the bare necessities, I haven't been spending it. I've donated every penny I can spare to the Sanitary Commission to buy medical supplies for battlefield hospitals. The five hundred comes from Henry, who is dead. He left the money to me in his will."

"Dead? Then you're a widow?"

"Yes."

They look at each other silently for a moment, but neither says what they both are thinking. It is not decent to celebrate the death of any man with talk of marriage, not even the death of one whom neither of them has reason to mourn.

"Oddly enough," Claire continues, "the news of his death made me sad. I can remember times when he was kind to me, and he lived such an unhappy life." John says nothing. She takes his hands in hers.

"I love you," she says. "I will always love you. But I need to ask you a question: if I send you this money, I know you'll use it to help Morgan escape. If he gets out, will he raid the North again? I've struggled with my conscience. I've asked myself how I can betray the Union by setting him at liberty. Will he reassemble his army? Will there be another raid?"

John lifts her hands to his lips and kisses them. "No one can say, darlin', but my best guess is that the Raiders will never ride again."

The touch of his lips is so sweet it makes her feel as if she has taken a swig of Kilpatrick's moonshine. She remembers that afternoon in the garden when their love began. And then she remembers Morgan was at Lavinia's party too; Morgan, whose life got so entangled with theirs. "So you truly believe he's finished?"

"Darlin', he crossed the Ohio against direct orders from General Bragg. He lost almost his entire army. If he weren't such a hero in the South, he'd probably be court-martialed within weeks of returning. Thanks to his reputation, he'll probably escape punishment, but I don't believe he'll ever be given another command. He's going to wear himself out fighting the bureaucrats in Richmond. If he survives the war, I think he'll die a bitter man, but I wouldn't count on him surviving." He pauses. "I suppose all this should make me sad, but it doesn't. I've seen too many of my friends die in the name of Southern gallantry."

Claire removes her hands from his. For a moment the silence is so complete, they can hear the inmates calling to one another in the prison yard. "You've eased my conscience," she says. "The truth is: we both know Morgan will escape with or without my help. The governor of Ohio made a grave mistake when he imprisoned Confederate officers in a penitentiary. Common criminals don't work together. Soldiers do. I know how stubborn you and my former comrades are. 'Pigheaded' might be a more apt description. Your oath—which was once mine—requires you to try to escape if captured. I don't intend to risk having the man I love shot or torn apart by guard dogs. I'll send you three books. Sewn into the covers you'll find four hundred dollars."

"Two hundred would be more than enough. We can't possibly need more, and if the guards discover the money, you can try again."

"Two hundred then."

"Claire, thank you for doing this. I know what it must cost you."

"Don't thank me. Just escape. It's winter and my feet are cold." They laugh, and for a moment the prison walls seem to vanish and Claire feels as if they are back in Corydon in the Eagle Hotel, wrapped in each other's arms, the scent of coffee drifting up from the kitchen and the great raid still lying before them like an unopened book. Reluctantly, she calls herself back to the present.

"I've chosen Dickens's *Great Expectations*, Caesar's *Commentaries on the Gallic War*, and Hawthorne's *Scarlet Letter* in honor of a Boston clergyman who has been saying that I should be forced to wear a scarlet *A* on my breast. Now kiss me. Our time is almost up, and if I don't hold you in my arms, I don't think I'll be able to survive until I see you again."

John embraces her and they kiss, a long, passionate kiss that tries, and fails, to bridge nearly four months of separation. When the kiss is over, Claire puts her mouth to his ear. "I don't want you to worry about me," she whispers, "but if you don't get out of here soon, I may have to put Zeke's uniform back on and get myself arrested."

John does not reply because the key has turned in the lock, the door has opened, and Mrs. Auerbach stands on the threshold, flanked by the guards. "Time's up," she says. There is a glint of satisfaction in her eyes, as if she enjoys interrupting them.

"I must speak to my husband for a moment longer," Claire says. "Only a moment, I beg you."

"You should never have spoken to him at all. Pretty women don't impress me. If I were warden, you would have never gotten past the front gate. Come away quietly, Mrs. Taylor, or I will order the guards to remove you by force."

John steps between Claire and the matron. "If those Yankee bastards lay a finger on her," he says, "I will hunt them down after the war is over and kill them."

⁓

Do John's words earn him a night in the dungeon? After Claire leaves, do the guards search him, find the chisels, and throw him into that damp, vermin-ridden hole? Does he burn with fever, doubly sick with desperation because the Raiders' painstakingly laid plot to escape has been discovered? Or has the pretty Mrs. Taylor done too good a job of convincing the warden to banish the infamous mistress in favor of the wife?

All Claire knows is that by the time she returns to her boardinghouse, after changing her clothes in the shop of the obliging French hairdresser who has agreed to accept five dollars in gold for not asking questions, she finds a letter from the penitentiary waiting for her. Written by a clerk named Kiply and sent directly to her residence instead of to the post office, it informs Mrs. Henry Winston that she is henceforth forbidden to communicate with Confederate prisoner of war John Taylor.

On the chance that the wife is still favored with letter-writing privileges, Claire goes out, buys a secondhand suit in John's size, and mails it to him using the return address "Mrs. John Taylor, General Delivery." For two days, she suffers agonies of suspense. On the third day when she goes to the post office to inquire if there is any mail for "Mrs. Taylor," the clerk hands her back the package, which has been opened. Inside she finds a letter forbidding Mrs. Taylor to communicate with her husband.

I have ridden with Morgan's Raiders, she thinks, *gone hungry, been shot at, and watched Mahoney and Tom Morgan die. A warden sitting in an office with a hot dinner and a family to go home to is no match for me.*

That afternoon, she buys a cheap copy of Caesar's *De bello Gallico* and, slitting the end papers, she inserts sixty dollars. Then she takes the evening train to Cincinnati, pays a boy fifty cents to row her across the Ohio to the Kentucky shore, and spends the night on a park bench in Newport. When the post office opens the next morning, she presents herself to the clerk and mails the book to "Lt. Curis M. Ballard, Cell Number 19, Ohio State Penitentiary, Columbus, Ohio." Curis once shared a jar of blackberry jam with Zeke Crane some twenty miles north of Corydon. Although the cell he presently occupies is undoubtedly not number 19, the package, which contains a letter in a childish hand purporting to be from his niece Mary Eliza, will bear a Kentucky postmark.

Claire returns to Columbus, waits for a week, and again takes the train to Cincinnati and crosses to Kentucky using the same boy, who by now knows her. At the Newport post office, she finds her patience has been rewarded. A letter awaits Miss Mary Eliza Ballard. The letter, which appears to come from her uncle Curis, thanks Mary Eliza for *Caesar's Commentaries. When you are old enough,* Uncle Curis promises, *I will teach you to read Latin so you can enjoy it in the original. As for now, honey, I would like to have a copy of Dickens's* Great Expectations. *Could you please ask your mama to send me a volume of the same if she can manage it?*

Chapter Twenty-nine

CLAIRE is nearly frantic with worry, but all she can do is sit and stare at the penitentiary. For the last seven hours, she has seen nothing except the rain, which is coming down in torrents. She shivers, draws her cloak closer, and laps the hem over her shoes. The room is cold and so dark she can hardly make out the shape of the pitcher on the dresser. She would love to strike a match and kindle the logs in the fireplace, but she doesn't dare. The guards who usually stand watch have been driven into their guardhouse by the rain, but at any moment they might step out, notice the light, and wonder why someone is up at such an hour.

Get out of there! she tells John. *Escape before it's too late!* But the only thing moving on the other side of the street is the rain running down the prison walls.

Something must have gone wrong. She has not heard from Curis Ballard for over two weeks, even though she has made the trip to Newport so often Billy Hamilton now holds his rowboat for her if the train from Columbus runs late. Maybe the guards discovered the tunnel; maybe it caved in. How can she go on sitting here with her hands folded in her lap when things are so desperate? She wants to do something, but what?

She is helpless and time is running out. If John and the others don't escape tonight, they may not escape at all. This morning she learned that the Union military commander of the prison is being transferred. Tomorrow, the new commander plans to conduct a surprise inspection of the cells of the Confederate prisoners of war. She has been desperate to get this news to John, but she has not been able to bribe anyone to carry in a note, and there is not enough time to communicate by mail.

All day she has paced back and forth, praying he already knows what she cannot tell him. As if this were not bad enough, she has received a telegram from Lexington informing her that Mattie Morgan has gone into labor. General Morgan is devoted to his wife. Her pregnancy is one of the reasons he has vowed to escape. Claire does not relish telling him he is missing the birth of his child, not to mention that getting such a telegram may attract attention to her at a time when she needs to be invisible.

Another burst of rain slaps at the window. *A nasty night,* she thinks. *Perfect for scaling the walls without being seen. Is John crawling through the tunnel at this very moment or is he in the dungeon sharing his dinner with the rats?* The anxiety forms a lump in her throat that makes it hard to swallow. Picking up a cup of cold coffee, she drinks it down to the dregs.

A jangling sensation fills her head. She wants to curse, throw the cup against the wall, and watch it shatter. Why must women always sit and wait? Why are they always the ones left behind to worry? She should put her pants back on and become Zeke Crane again. At least as Zeke she could try to get into the prison. Even if the guards caught her, wouldn't it be better to do something? *No,* the more rational part of her mind warns. *No, it wouldn't. You'd only endanger them.*

She closes her eyes, takes a deep breath, and tries to calm down, but her mind keeps running on bad memories: Ned's body laid out on the kitchen table; her mother sobbing; the pain of losing the baby; the terror she felt in the Corydon jail during the artillery shelling. She imagines John trapped in a collapsed tunnel clawing at the mud. *Dear God*, she prays, *let him escape from that horrible place before sunrise. I don't care how he does it as long as he gets out alive. I love him so much. Dear God, please give him back to me.*

Perhaps her prayer is answered or perhaps it is only a coincidence that when she opens her eyes and looks toward the penitentiary, she sees something caught on the coping that runs along the top of the wall. Rising to her feet, she strides over to the window and wipes the condensation off the glass. The object is black and curved like a comma, and it is moving as if seeking purchase. Is it a shadow or a hook? She wants to believe it's a hook, but ... she can't be sure. The rain is coming down too hard. Should she go over there and stand beneath it? If she's wrong, if it's a shadow, her presence might alert the guards. She forces herself to wait, counting off the seconds: ten, twenty, thirty, and then she sees a pair of hands.

Turning away from the window, she grabs her carpetbag and bolts out of the room, driven by a hope that pools off into fear. The prison walls are slick. One false step and the fugitives will be discovered. She is too excited to plan her exit from the boarding-house in an orderly fashion, but her training as a scout serves her well. Not a board creaks as she runs down the stairs, and when she pulls the front door closed, it shuts without a sound. By the time she reaches the penitentiary, Morgan and two men she does not recognize are standing on top of the wall, cutting the cord that activates the alarm bell.

Slipping into the shadows, Claire watches as, one by one, eight Raiders silently descend a rope made of braided sheets and come to rest on the balls of their feet like cats. In one of those unexpected gestures typical of Southerners, each tips his hat to her as if escaping from a penitentiary is no excuse for a breach of good manners.

The last man down is John, who seizes her and kisses her for all the world to see, although only Morgan and his men are watching, probably with considerable interest since the last time they saw her she was a boy named Zeke. Claire hugs John so tightly she can feel his ribs pressing against her breasts. Four and a half months, eighteen weeks, 131 days apart, each one marked on her heart; and all that time all she has wanted to do is hold him the way she is holding him now. *He's thin*, she thinks, *so terribly thin*. And then she thinks that as soon as they are safe she will feed him, and that she must be out of her mind because she should not be thinking of feeding him but getting him to safety.

John puts his lips to her ear. "Which way is the train depot, darlin'?" he whispers. Reluctantly, Claire releases him and points to her left. "Can you lead us there?" She nods and gestures to everyone to follow her. As long as they are in sight of the penitentiary, they run; but as soon as they enter the side streets, they slow down as if trying to give the impression that they are eight ordinary men and one woman out for a stroll in the midst of a violent rainstorm.

Such a pretense, feeble as it is, is probably useless. All the escapees wear civilian clothing, including Hines, who has somehow managed to get hold of a black suit that makes him look like an undertaker; but the Raiders have not abandoned their knee-high boots and slouch hats pinned up with stars, crescents, and Masonic symbols; and they walk with the peculiar, rolling gate of cavalry officers who are only at home on horseback. To top things off, Morgan has commandeered a pair of green spectacles, which make him look at best eccentric, and, at worst, blind. Yet to Claire's amazement, the few people up and about at such an hour show no curiosity, perhaps because they too are half blinded by the rain.

Just before they reach the depot, the group splits into three smaller groups. After whispered farewells, vows of eternal fidelity, and promises to meet again, two men hurry off in one direction and one hurries off in another, leaving Claire with John, Morgan,

Hines, and a pair of Raiders whose names she only learns several weeks later when she reads them on a Wanted poster.

By the time the six of them reach the depot, they are drenched and shivering, but Morgan's famous luck holds. By now, Claire is so anxious she can hardly keep from grabbing John and bolting in the other direction, but the stationmaster does not inquire why they are in such a hurry to get to Cincinnati; and when Hines goes up to the ticket window to buy them seats on the night express, the clerk does not demand to know what he and his friends are doing wandering around in the rain without umbrellas.

The train arrives ten minutes late. They board without being recognized and spread out. John and Claire sit together, doing their best to impersonate a husband and wife who have been called out of town by a family emergency.

To Claire's horror, Morgan takes a seat next to a Union officer and, as the train lurches forward, begins to make conversation with him. The men share a flask of brandy. As the train passes the penitentiary, Morgan looks out the window, makes some remark, and the officer laughs. Claire follows Morgan's gaze and sees the rope still dangling over the wall. For a moment she is frozen with panic; then she realizes that the officer has seen nothing. That is when she finally realizes they are going to make it.

The ease of their escape seems incredible, yet in later years, when she turns to Basil Duke's memoirs, she finds every detail of that night recorded for posterity, right down to the fact that Hines bought them tickets at the Columbus depot and Morgan sat next to a Union officer on the train.

Reaching out, she clutches John's hand, and they ride in silence past fragments of scenery that appear and disappear in the window like magic lantern slides. She sees split-rail fences, telegraph poles, apple trees whose bare-limbed branches are so slick with rain they look like black glass, a white cow that looms up beside the tracks like a ghost.

Just before they reach Cincinnati, Morgan and Hines rise to

their feet and pull the emergency cord, and the train jerks to a stop. As ladies' hatboxes crash into the aisles and passengers are thrown forward into the seats in front of them, Claire, John, Hines, and Morgan leap off and hurry away. Behind her, Claire can hear the passengers protesting. Why does no one follow them? Is it common in Ohio for people to stop a train wherever they choose? Has Morgan's luck saved them again, or has the rain made pursuing them look too unpleasant to be worth the effort?

Despite the mud, it takes them only fifteen minutes to walk to the river, where they find Billy Hamilton and his rowboat waiting. Billy nods to Claire, whom he knows quite well by now.

"Good morning, ma'am," he says; and if he wonders who her dashing companions in the boots and broad-brimmed hats are, he does not ask.

Three dollars and half an hour later, they are in Newport, Kentucky, and Billy and his empty boat are back in midstream making for the Ohio shore. For a moment, Morgan stands on the bank, watching the river flow by. Claire wonders if he is thinking of the day he crossed over to Brandenburg in triumph or the afternoon when so many of his men died in the muddy waters above Buffington Island. But perhaps he is only thinking that he wants to roll himself a cigarette, for when he turns around, he asks Hines if he has any tobacco.

"Not a scrap, General," Hines says.

"I suppose we shall have to accustom ourselves to such privations," Morgan says. There is a long silence, broken only by the sound of the river eating away at the shore. Claire knows this is the moment when she should tell Morgan about his wife, but she cannot bring herself to do it. *He will find out soon enough,* she thinks.

She reaches into the pocket of her cloak and feels the telegram, crumpled and damp from the rain. An odd sensation passes through her, as if birth and death are meeting here beside the river. *This is Morgan's last crossing,* she thinks, and then she reminds herself that she does not believe in premonitions. Perhaps he will cross this river many times after the war is over. Will he go back to being a merchant? Sell hemp and cloth? Bargain with Yankee mill owners like Henry? She cannot imagine it.

"Mrs. Winston," Morgan says.

Claire starts. She has not expected him to address her. "Yes," she says. It is all she can do not to come to attention and salute him, but she is no longer Zeke Crane, and although he is still a general, he is no longer her general.

"I do not approve of a woman wearing trousers."

"I am sorry to hear that, sir."

"When a female dons men's clothing, she violates the laws of God and society. Moreover, I am embarrassed and not a little humiliated to discover I have had a woman fighting under my command. But for all that . . ." He pauses. "For all that, you have been a valiant soldier, and if the Confederacy gave out medals for courage as the Yankees do, I would award one to you. Instead, I am going to give you the father of your child."

Claire is so astounded, she cannot find her tongue. "How?" she stutters. "How?" Morgan ignores her and turns to John.

"Taylor," he says, "I hereby discharge you from military service."

"But General," John protests. Claire sees that John has not understood what Morgan has said, or at least not understood the most important part of it: *the father of your child.*

"That's an order, Lieutenant," Morgan says. He turns back to Claire. "You need to tell him soon, Mrs. Winston. A man should know these things. Why did you not tell him sooner?"

"I was afraid I might . . ." She suddenly realizes she cannot bear to admit she was afraid she might lose this baby too. Her voice breaks, and she begins to cry. "I was afraid John would do something rash if he knew," she says. "I was afraid he might get himself killed."

Morgan pulls out his handkerchief and offers it to her. There is something tender in his eyes she has never seen before. "Brave men, like brave women, act from their hearts," he says. "That is their strength, but, unless luck is with them, it is also the current that carries them to death. My brother Tom was brave and rash and stubborn. I would have had him less so and alive. When will the child come?"

"April."

"What child?" John asks.

"Our child," Claire says. She wipes her eyes and hands the handkerchief back to Morgan. "How did you know?" she asks.

Morgan does not answer. He motions to Hines, and as John and Claire watch, the two men walk upstream and disappear at a point where shadows, earth, and river merge.

Claire

On the fiftieth anniversary of the Great Raid, Morgan's men got together in Lexington for a reunion. John and I traveled all the way from Colorado to attend, a journey that was far easier in 1913 than it was back in 1863. I knew John's old comrades would welcome him, but I had no idea how they would receive me. I had ridden with them and fought with them, but I had also deceived them.

I need not have worried. The boys—many of whom were now in their seventies—greeted me with whoops and Rebel yells and called me Zeke. Kilpatrick, who had survived the war after all, said that of all the wives a man could choose from, John had taken the best; and Pettigrew, who was still a bachelor, informed me that meeting me back in '63 had put him off the rest of womankind forever. At least a dozen men who had been on the digging crew thanked me for the chisels, and a white-bearded Kentucky farmer named Hunter—whom I am ashamed to say I did not remember—told me he and his wife had named their first-born daughter after me: "Not 'Ezekiel,' of course," he said, "but 'Claire,' and she rides like the very devil, just like you did."

That night, while the other wives sat in the parlor of the hotel talking about their children and grandchildren, I sat around the campfire with the men trading war stories. We must have refought every battle from the crossing of the Cumberland to Morgan's surrender. When we got to Corydon, some of the boys remembered they'd been in the same cell with John and me, and we took a lot of kidding about that; but when we spoke of Lebanon and Tom Morgan's death, our voices grew sad, and those with hats took them off and left them off as we remembered our dead.

There was a lot of talk that night about General Morgan, who, as John had predicted, had not lived to see the South defeated, although he had ridden back into Kentucky for one final raid in the summer of 1864. Most agreed Morgan's crossing of the Ohio had delayed the invasion of east Tennessee by at least three months and made it possible for Bragg to win at Chickamauga; and with every story the man grew more mythic, until by the time the campfires were reduced to embers and the whiskey was running low, you would have thought Lee had never surrendered at Appomattox and the South had won the war thanks to the military genius of John Hunt Morgan.

The next morning, after we slept off the effects of too many bottles of fine Kentucky bourbon (for which, I admit, I still retain an unladylike taste), a photographer assembled us on the lawn for a group photograph. Basil Duke, who was president of the Morgan's Men Association, was not happy with the idea of having me included, since he had never fully recovered from the revelation that he had led a woman into battle, but the boys insisted. John loaned me his jacket, Curis Ballard gave me his hat, and Pettigrew clapped me on the shoulder.

"Zeke," Pettigrew said, "it's good to have you back." And then he turned to John in some confusion and said: "Taylor, I reckon we should ask yer permission to take her piccher, she being your wife and all."

John laughed and said I had never needed his permission to do anything, and that a woman who had raised three children, run a ranch, and could still look pretty when she was a grandma could do what she damn well pleased.

What I damn well pleased was to have my photo taken with Morgan's Raiders. I have a framed print of it on the wall of my parlor to remind me of the summer I learned that I was strong and brave and could do anything. When my grandchildren come to visit, I tell them that I'm the one in the white hat in the back row on the far left. The one without the beard.

Acknowledgments

A historical novel involves a great deal of research, and I am indebted to many people, including Pat Conroy, who told me years ago that I should write about the places I grew up in. I would like to thank the Virginia Center for the Creative Arts for supporting me during the initial stages of the creative process, my excellent editor, Jackie Cantor, for knowing exactly when to make a helpful suggestion, and Mary Ellen Bates, librarian extraordinaire. Sheldon Greene read every draft multiple times and his feedback and suggestions were, as always, invaluable. Attorney Jack King generously tracked down information about the laws governing married women, divorce, property rights, and inheritance. Edi Hartshorne coached me on the proper use of Quaker Plain Speech. Fifteen-year-old Max Doyle greeted me at the Cincinnati History Museum dressed as a Union soldier and gave me an impressive lecture about the daily life of a Civil War private. Ashley Ford, the museum's "steamboat captain," waxed equally eloquent. During the annual Civil War reenactment at Coshocton, Ohio, I had a long conversation with members of a "Confederate Artillery Battery," who generously shared their expertise. The wonderful librarians at the Indiana Historical Society Museum allowed me to read letters written by Union soldiers to their families and provided me with contemporary accounts of Morgan's 1863 raid.

During the summer of 2004, my husband, Angus Wright, and I retraced Morgan's route. Angus bore with good humor my determination to see everything, even though this sometimes meant fifteen-hour days during the peak of the summer heat. For this, and for his critical feedback and constant encouragement, I thank him. I also wish to thank the citizens of the towns we visited. Many went out of their way to lead us to the exact spot where some important event had taken place, while others were amazed to learn that a Confederate army had once camped in their pastures.

Finally, I want to thank my parents and grandparents. Without their stories about the Civil War in Indiana and Kentucky, this novel would never have been written. I first heard the name "Morgan" from my mother, who used to sing a song that began: "Morgan, Morgan the raider, and Morgan's terrible men / With bowie knives and pistols, are galloping up the glen." A few years ago, I discovered these were lines from the ballad "Kentucky Belle," written by Civil War–era poet Constance Fenimore Woolson. When I was older, my Indiana grandparents told me about a great-great-grandfather who had died for the Union at Shiloh, while my Kentucky grandparents spoke of another great-great-grandfather who had served as a Confederate surgeon.

Readers who would like to learn more about Morgan's Great Raid might like to consult some of the sources I used. A few of my favorites were: *A History of Morgan's Cavalry* by Basil W. Duke; *Touched by Fire: A Photographic Portrait of the Civil War* edited by William C. Davis; *The Longest Raid of the Civil War* by Lester V. Horwitz; *John H. Morgan and His Raiders* by Edison H. Thomas; *Life on the Mississippi* by Mark Twain; and *Hidden in Plain View: A Secret Story of Quilts and the Underground Railroad* by Jacqueline L. Tobin and Raymond G. Dobard.